Ellery Queen's Prime Crimes

Edited by Eleanor Sullivan

THE DIAL PRESS
Davis Publications, Inc.
380 Lexington Avenue
New York, New York 10017

FIRST PRINTING

Copyright © 1983 by Davis Publications, Inc.
All rights reserved.
Library of Congress Catalog Card Number: 59-13341
Printed in the U. S. A.

COPYRIGHT NOTICES AND ACKNOWLEDGMENTS

"Q"

CONTENTS

INTRODUCTION

This is the first of an annual series of Ellery Queen anthologies including only stories that have never before been published in the United States. Most of the stories have never previously been published anywhere.

Featured are a short novel by Patricia Moyes, called by *The New York Times* "One of the brightest contemporary practitioners of the classic puzzle-and-plot whodunit," and 15 short stories by such international favorites in the mystery genre as Christianna Brand, about whom Anthony Boucher said, "You have to reach for the greatest of Great Names to find Brand's rivals in the subtleties of the trade"; Edward D. Hoch ("Hoch has imagination and a comic bent"—*Publishers Weekly*); Seicho Matsumoto, the acknowledged most important figure on the Japanese detective-story scene today; and Joan Aiken, whose stories, wrote Carol Cleveland in *Twentieth Century Crime and Mystery Writers,* "flash with wit, and fantasy, and the peculiar wisdom of this very individual writer."

This collection leads off with a fine Sherlock Holmes pastiche and follows through with a prime mix of mystery and detection, some of it very light-hearted, some of it very dark indeed.

John H. Dirckx

The Adventure of the
Oval Window (a pastiche)

In glancing over the series of sketches in which I have recorded some of the more noteworthy investigations of my friend, Mr. Sherlock Holmes, I find that most of them refer to matters which have not otherwise come to the notice of the public. Even when he was consulted in cases which had aroused the attention of the press, Holmes' name seldom figured in the newspaper accounts. He habitually shunned popular esteem, preferring to allow the official police to take full credit for his most brilliant successes, and finding his own reward in the work itself.

Yet his powers were so remarkable, and his methods so singular and so often crowned with striking results, that they could not altogether escape the notice of the press. From his unravelling of the Jefferson Hope case in the early days of our association until his retirement, Holmes' reputation as a criminal investigator increased steadily.

During the '90's, his practice had grown so extensive that he was able to consult his own tastes in choosing which clients to serve and which inquiries to undertake. As his tastes inclined to the curious and the bizarre, the problems to which he applied his peculiar gifts became correspondingly extraordinary. My notes of the years just preceding his retirement are a veritable museum of the anomalous, the grotesque, and the macabre. Many of these cases are still of too recent date to be exposed fully to the public. Others proved to be but chimaeras, in which Holmes' special powers were summoned in vain.

I have said that Sherlock Holmes craved distraction and novelty. There was, moreover, a strong tincture of the dare-devil in his composition. Nothing engaged his interest in a case more keenly than a certain element of danger. The thrill of the chase was for him no more intense than the thrill of being chased. Other things being equal, he preferred a case fraught with hazards and pitfalls to one which could be resolved without danger or inconvenience.

It was perhaps chiefly owing to this almost morbid craving for sensation that Holmes agreed to look into the curious affair of the

Hanford heiress, of which I am about to give an account. The case came to our notice on a drowsy afternoon late in the summer of the year 1896. A day or two earlier, Holmes had successfully concluded the queer business of the Venetian goldsmiths, a case which had consumed all his energies for many weeks past. Now the period of reaction, whose symptoms I recognized only too well, had begun.

He had barely tasted his lunch. Lounging in a corner of the sofa, he was to all appearances sunk in the most profound lethargy. Yet, like the spider which rests motionless at the centre of its web, sensitive to the slightest disturbance in any quarter, Holmes remained perpetually alert. Even before the jangling of the bell announced the arrival of a visitor, his remarkably acute hearing had singled out, from the myriad other noises streaming in at the open window, the sounds of a cab stopping in the street and discharging its passenger at our doorstep. He was examining the cab round the edge of the blind when Mrs. Hudson knocked upon our sitting-room door.

"A gentleman to see you, sir," said she, handing in a card, which was followed immediately by its proprietor. With an impetuosity bordering upon rudeness, our caller thrust himself past our landlady and stood fidgeting and panting upon the mat. He was a dry, clerical-looking person, just turned forty. His flushed countenance and air of distraction bore testimony to the seriousness of his business, while his abrupt and restless demeanor suggested that it was a matter of some urgency as well.

"Pray take a seat, Mr. Ordway," said Holmes, indicating an armchair that stood full in the light from the window.

Our caller dropped into the proffered seat, threw open his coat as though oppressed with heat, and cast an enquiring glance from me to my companion.

"You may speak plainly before Dr. Watson," said Holmes. "He is a model of discretion, and is often good enough to assist me in my cases. His medical eye may perhaps detect some subtle clue to explain your recent loss of weight, though I confess I can suggest none besides the somewhat arduous physical labours which you have lately been obliged to perform. No doubt the commercial difficulties you have been experiencing—"

"But this is incredible!" cried our visitor, flinging himself upright in his chair and peering at Holmes with a look in which awe was mingled with distrust. "What can you know of my affairs, sir? I have not begun to state my business. You have seen nothing but my card, and yet you appear to know all."

"You are far too modest," said Holmes, sitting down and lighting his pipe. "Besides your card I have seen yourself. To a trained observer the human form—its physiognomy, its attitude, and its habiliments—presents an infinite number of suggestive points. You had scarcely entered the room when I perceived scratches on the backs of your hands, and calluses upon the palms. Yours are not the broad, muscular hands of one regularly employed in manual work. They are narrow, with long, tapering fingers—the hands of a man accustomed to hire others to do such work for him. As to the loss of weight, I am unprepared to believe your tailor so inept as to cut your coat and trousers two sizes too large."

"Those signs are plain enough, I suppose," agreed Ordway with a meditative nod. "But how came you to learn of my late financial embarrassments?"

"That is a mere trifle. I see by your card that you deal in diamonds. The papers have been full of the difficulties in the Transvaal. Surely it is no very daring inference that you have found your volume of trade much curtailed of late?"

"The accounts I have heard of your abilities have not been exaggerated, Mr. Holmes," said our visitor, pulling out a large silver watch and glancing rapidly at its dial. "But the affair about which I desire to consult you does not concern my own misfortunes. As I am much pressed for time, I must come to business at once."

"I am at your service. Please state your case as fully as you are able."

"You must know, Mr. Holmes, that when my elder brother died some years ago, he left his only daughter in my charge. The girl had lost her mother already, and would have been thrust alone upon the world had I not taken her into my own household. I am not a married man. My niece is all the family I have ever had, and she has become as dear to me as ever a daughter could be.

"My brother's wealth was immense, for he inherited nearly the whole of our father's fortune. You will have heard of Ordway and Parr, the great road-building firm?"

Holmes nodded and bade our client proceed.

"My niece, who is just nineteen, draws a generous but not opulent allowance from the estate. She will come into possession of the principal on her twenty-fifth birthday—sooner if she should marry, but Julia has shown no inclination that way, and indeed seems quite averse to the idea of ever marrying at all. To come straight to the heart of the matter, my niece has twice in the past month been the victim of murderous attacks. But for the intervention of a merciful Providence, she would not be alive at this moment."

"You amaze me," said Holmes. His eyes gleamed with the fervid light which I knew so well, and it was plain that his interest was keenly aroused. "I understand that your niece has no living relations besides yourself."

"That is true."

"You would gain a great fortune in the event of her death?"

Our visitor drew himself up with a haughty air, and fixed upon Holmes a look of the deepest indignation. "That is also perfectly true. But come, sir, if you mean to impugn me, to suggest—"

"I impugn no one and suggest nothing. I wish only to be in possession of all the relevant data. I take it that you yourself have no suspicion who is the author of these attacks?"

"None. We live a retired life. Our circle of friends is small. We go very little into society; indeed, hardly at all. It seems inconceivable how a young girl in my niece's position can have made a mortal enemy."

"Are there no rejected suitors?"

"There is a man formerly associated in my own firm. But neither his character nor the nature of their relations would permit me to entertain the slightest suspicion, if you understand me—"

"Perfectly. Still, it may be as well to have a note of the name."

Ordway consulted his watch again and thrust it away in his pocket with a gesture of impatience. "It is Lawrence, Mr. Theobald Lawrence, of Daulton Square, Soho. But my time grows shorter."

"Quite so. Pray continue with your narrative."

"The first of the attacks occurred upon a Sunday forenoon, about a month since, as we were returning from church. Since my unfortunate brother's death I have lived at Moorcroft, the family estate, near Hanford. Though the house is large, and stands in its own park, our domestic establishment is a modest one. We keep only two servants: my man Fetters, who has been with me for years, and his sister Elizabeth, who cooks our meals and serves as lady's maid to my niece.

"We had attended morning service together in the village, as is our custom, and were returning home in the dogcart when a large four-wheeled carriage drew up behind us at a great rate of speed and offered to overtake us. Fetters was driving, with me at his side, while Julia and her maid occupied the rear compartment. My first intimation of danger was the clatter of the horses' hooves. In the next instant there came a fearful explosion, which was followed immediately by the screams of the women. With great presence of mind, Fetters drew the dogcart off the road. The carriage roared quickly past and was out of sight before we had ascertained that my niece and her maid were unharmed.

"When they had regained their composure, they recited a horrifying tale. As the carriage drew nearly abreast of them, a man with his face muffled up in a dark-blue scarf had thrust a pistol out at the window and fired upon my niece at almost point-blank range. How he can have failed to inflict the slightest injury upon her is as great a mystery as who he is, or upon what motive he attempted to murder an innocent young lady in broad daylight on a public road."

"Could the police not trace the carriage?"

"No, sir. In our consternation, none of us observed any markings upon it, and the driver was as completely muffled as the blackguard who fired upon my niece."

Holmes laid aside his pipe and, placing his fingertips together and directing his gaze upwards to the ceiling, he pursued in silence some private train of thought while our visitor fairly writhed in impatience. "So much for the first attempt," remarked my friend at length. "And the other?"

"The other took place but three days ago. After the first attack I had been much alarmed for my niece's safety. She herself believed that the man was a lunatic, and that his choice of a victim had been dictated by chance and the whimsies of a disordered mind. After a time, I came to be of her opinion. The police suggested that the villain had fired a blank charge, for no bullet could be found. In short, we relaxed our vigilance, and on Tuesday I had so far overcome my fears that I permitted Julia to travel alone to London to visit the shops. As a safeguard, however, against her mysterious assailant, I required her to wear a hat with a heavy veil, and a plain drab gown borrowed from her maid.

"Well, Mr. Holmes, the scoundrel penetrated that disguise easily enough. He must have followed her up to London from Hanford. She was to have met me at one o'clock at my place of business. By half past the hour I had begun to grow uneasy, and it was after two before I learned the occasion of her delay. In alighting from her cab at Holborn Circus she was nearly run down by a heavy four-wheeled carriage which came dashing out of St. Andrew Street. The off horse shied at her and she was knocked aside by the traces, narrowly escaping serious injury."

"I suppose that the police failed again to learn anything of the carriage?"

"No, sir, they traced it at once. The driver who put Julia down at Holborn Circus noticed very particularly the markings and the number of the carriage. He gave the information to the police, and in less than a quarter of an hour they found the identical carriage, abandoned in an alley lying between St. Bride Street and the Farringdon Road. It belonged to a livery stable in the Poultry and had been twice hired by the same man."

"The earlier occasion being the Sunday of the first attack?"

"Exactly, sir."

"And the man?"

"He was described as a surly rogue who kept his face hidden in a scarf and provided his own driver. He gave a false name and an address which does not exist."

Holmes resumed his attitude of absorption, whereupon Ordway again gave tokens of the most acute anxiety. At length he could endure the silence no longer. "Your reputation as an unraveller of obscure puzzles is well known, Mr. Holmes," said he. "Upon learning of the second attempt I resolved to place the matter in your hands. I have been prevented from coming to you by an unfortunate turn of events, a veritable catastrophe, in fact. One of my agents on the Continent has allowed an unusually large consignment of precious stones to fall into the hands of a man who will not scruple to sell them as his own wares. All hope of recovering them will be lost unless I reach Calais tonight. My train leaves Victoria Station in less than an hour.

"Mr. Holmes, I am at my wit's end. I am half mad with fear for my niece's safety, and yet to stop at home would spell my utter ruin. Moreover, the nature of my business compels me to take Fetters with me. He is at my bankers' at this moment collecting a letter of credit. Julia refuses absolutely to accompany me. It is useless to press her, for she has her father's iron will. What am I to do, Mr. Holmes? The man who has twice attacked my niece has shown himself to be a desperate villain, who will stick at nothing. He will not fail again. To leave my niece alone is to sign her death warrant."

"She will have her maid with her."

"He will murder them both. Can you not help me, Mr. Holmes?"

"Do you wish to retain me to make inquiries, or to guard the person of your niece?"

"To do both. I shall return to England on Sunday, Monday at the latest. Can you not spend the interval at Moorcroft? Say that you will do it, Mr. Holmes! I will pay any fee which you care to name, though I should lie in debt all the rest of my days, if only you will put an end to these atrocities. It is worth all that I have, and more, to know that my niece will be safe during my absence."

"This is very short notice, Mr. Ordway. There are one or two small matters—"

"Put them aside!" cried our client, in a tone between entreaty and command. "Would you stand idly by while an innocent girl is done foully to death?"

"You are most persuasive. Let us suppose that I agree to take up the inquiry and stand guard over your niece; what are the young lady's views in the matter?"

"She knows nothing of it. She need never know. Fetters and his sister occupy the porter's lodge, which lies at some distance from the house. While Fetters and I are away, Elizabeth will stay in the house with my niece. You will find the lodge comfortable, though not luxurious."

"But," objected Holmes, "remaining at a distance from the young lady would seem to defeat the purpose of guarding her person."

"Not at all. The park is enclosed by a high wall fortified with chevaux de frise. The only entry to the grounds is through the gate and along the drive, which passes directly before the lodge. Perhaps this drawing will make the positions clear."

He drew from his breast a pocket-book and unfolded from it a plan of the estate, neatly executed upon tracing paper. Holmes took the drawing from him and smoothed it out upon the table.

"You are quite an accomplished draughtsman, sir," said he.

"That is the influence of my early training. I was employed for some years in my father's firm as a surveyor and draughtsman. Here is the lodge, built into a corner of the wall. You must not, of course, show a light in any of the windows facing the house. I have advised Elizabeth, my niece's maid, that someone will be on guard in the lodge, but Julia herself knows nothing. Fetters is a man of simple tastes, and his ideas of personal comfort run upon Spartan lines. Still, you will find in his quarters a camp-bed and a sofa, where two gentlemen may, I think, contrive to pass two or three nights in perfect ease."

"You needn't trouble yourself on that account," said Holmes. "Watson is an old campaigner, and I often spend an entire night in an arm-chair."

"Then as to meals: you will find the larder well stocked, and Elizabeth may contrive to bring you something hot in the evenings. You must make your tea with the spirit lamp, and not upon any account have a fire. Smoke rising from the chimney of the lodge is plainly visible from the house."

"The lack of a fire should prove no hardship in this season," said Holmes. "I suppose we may expect tradesmen to call at the lodge? How are we to know that they are what they say?"

"No tradesmen are expected. Whoever calls must be denied admission. I would particularly warn you against Ludwick, the land-agent in the village. He is an ingratiating but unscrupulous rogue, who covets my house. He has twice offered princely sums for it and twice been refused. At last, seeing his direct overtures fail, he had the effrontery to pay court to my niece. I have forbidden him my door."

"You do not connect him with the attempts on Miss Ordway's life?"

Our client seemed taken aback by the suggestion. "I should be surprised to learn that Ludwick is so low a dog as that," said he. "But my time is slipping away. When I think that even now— Can you go down before nightfall, Mr. Holmes? There is a train at 4.20 from Paddington Station. Here are twenty-five pounds for present expenses, the key to the lodge, and a note of my hotel in Calais."

Holmes scribbled a receipt on a page from his notebook. "You have thought of everything," said he.

"Julia is worth everything to me. I urge you to arm yourself with reliable weapons and not scruple to use them. You and your associate might take it in turns to watch through the night. A round of the park every hour or so between midnight and sunrise would be advisable. But, dear me, I have just time to catch my train."

With effusive expressions of gratitude, and repeated exhortations to caution and vigilance, our client rushed away as tempestuously as he had come.

"Well, Watson, what do you make of it?" asked Holmes, when our visitor had gone. "A curious little problem, is it not?"

"Say rather a sinister and diabolical one. I think you might have consulted me before pledging me to come down with you to Hanford to have my head blown off by a madman."

"There is no madness in this business, Watson. Our adversary may be bold and ruthless, but I should say that he is as sane as you or I. As to consulting you, I think I know my Watson well enough to see when he has fairly risen to the bait of an intriguing case. Our client was barely out of his chair before you had commenced a rapt perusal of Bradshaw's uninspired but invaluable pages. I hope that Ordway's information was correct as to the time of our train?"

"Precisely."

"Then we've just time to collect a few necessaries for our travels. You still keep your service revolver in working order, I think?"

When presently our cab left Baker Street it contained two respectable-looking gentlemen and a perfectly nefarious assortment of gear, including crepe-soled shoes, a dark lantern, and a brace of pistols. Holmes preserved a stony silence during the whole of the railway journey. Curled in his seat, with his chin sunk upon his breast, he appeared oblivious of the scenes of rural verdure that flashed constantly past the window.

At the station inn we hired a trap. I thought the driver eyed us suspiciously when he learned our destination, but perhaps it was only idle curiosity. He dropped us at the gates of Moorcroft just as the clock of some distant church was striking seven.

The Ordway estate occupied a plot of high ground in the midst of a vast marshy tract. The house, a stark, angular pile of grey stone, lay half submerged in a heavily wooded and ill-tended park. By contrast, the lodge that was to serve as our temporary diggings possessed a certain picturesque charm with its bright red shutters and neat hedges. Taking care to keep out of sight of the house, we used our key and presently found ourselves in a plain, low-ceilinged sitting-room. Fetters' sleeping chamber, which stood next to it, lay in deep shadows, for its windows, which faced the house, were tightly shuttered. Holmes unlatched one of the shutters and opened it slightly. For a long time he stood peering intently through the aperture, while the gloom of eventide deepened around him.

Suddenly he turned away from the window with a gesture of satisfaction and walked into the sitting-room. "All is well, I think," he said, seating himself and taking out his pipe. "I have seen one of the women drawing the curtains in an upper room. Her movements were serene and untroubled. It is as well to know at once that we have not arrived too late."

The sitting-room windows looked out upon the drive and gave an uninterrupted view of the gate and the road beyond. At long intervals a solitary farm cart or a tradesman's van made its way along the lonely road. "A suitable setting for murder, is it not, Watson?"

remarked my companion, amid clouds of blue smoke. "The house lies far back from the road, and the road itself is nearly deserted. The family seldom go out. They might all be massacred in their sleep, and no one the wiser."

"Have you reached any conclusions as to the attempts on the girl's life?"

"Conclusions! My dear fellow, have I never warned you against reaching conclusions without considering all the facts? It is like trying to walk to Greenwich without consulting the signposts. If you arrive there at all it will be by the merest chance, and then at the needless expense of much time and trouble."

"You seemed deeply absorbed during the journey from London."

"It was quite another matter that engaged my interests then. I was, and am, wrestling with the curious enigma of our client himself."

"You think it possible that he is the author of the attacks on his niece?"

"A pox on the attacks," replied Holmes with good-natured sarcasm. "It will be time to look into them when we have talked with Miss Ordway—not a likely eventuality until our client's return."

"Well, then, wherein lies the enigma? He seemed a decent enough chap to me, having a good deal of trouble with his business, and beside himself with worry on his niece's account."

"He did, did he? Yours is a generous and trusting nature, Watson, and your estimate of your fellow-men correspondingly favorable. You see the best in them, and I see the worst. No doubt the world is a pleasanter place by your way of viewing it, but rose-coloured spectacles are not a particularly useful piece of equipment to the criminal investigator." He finished his pipe in silence without enlarging on his views.

We dined simply on bread, cheese, and potted meat, with tea brewed with the aid of a spirit lamp. A sojourn in the country should be a soothing change after weeks of city life with its drab vistas, its grime and bustle and noise. But try as I might I could not dispel a sombre mood of gloom and foreboding, which seemed to increase as the shadows thickened and the chill of evening began to invade our fireless sitting-room.

Holmes returned to his post at the gap between the shutters, and presently reported that a light had appeared in one of the windows of the house. When the dusk was well advanced he took up his stick, a stout ash which he had chosen specially for the occasion, and slipped his revolver into his pocket. "What do you say to a moonlight excursion over the grounds?"

"I should like nothing better. The inaction of the past hour has begun to fray my nerves, and there is something hostile about an unfamiliar room without a light."

Closing the door to the bedroom, Holmes prepared the dark lantern before venturing outside. "We must keep to the shadows of the trees," said he, "for the moon is nearly full."

We began our tour of inspection with an examination of the gates. Holmes had some idea of shutting them for the night, but even without recourse to the lantern we could see that the great wrought-iron hinges had long since given way, and the gates were deeply sunken in the earth.

As we rounded the lodge and entered the grounds, the house sprang full into our view across the broad expanse of the park. The moon shed a silvery light on the high gables and threw the squat stone chimneys into jagged relief against the sable backdrop of the night. Far away to our left a round pond shone like a mirror of burnished pewter among the trees.

Keeping well in the shadow, we set our course by the simple expedient of following the wall. A high and very substantial wall it looked, and its ivied top bristled with a formidable row of iron spikes. Holmes took the lead, striding stealthily forward and looking sharply to right and left as he advanced. He made scarcely a sound as he passed over fallen boughs and a dense undergrowth of dry brushwood. Our shadows flitted and leapt grotesquely among the black trunks of the trees, but we found nothing more substantial there.

As we came nearer to the house, Holmes scanned the dark windows intently, keeping clear of the lighted ones. An inspection of the carriage house and stables showed them to be open and deserted. We had made nearly the whole circuit of the park when we arrived before a tumble-down out-building set in an angle of the wall near the pond. The shadows here lay thick as smoke. Holmes slackened his pace and signed to me to do the same. The shed possessed a single square window, nearly opaque with dirt. Opening the shade of his dark lantern, Holmes cast its beam through the glass.

"Nothing more sinister than gardener's implements and heaps of miscellaneous lumber," he observed.

We now deserted the shadows to approach the pond. Here we were in full view of the row of lighted windows on the ground floor of the house which told where the women were spending their solitary evening. Holmes' next proceeding seemed utterly without reason, for he went down upon his knees at the rocky margin of the pond and thrust his stick into the water as though to test its depth. Again and again he repeated this manoeuvre, until he had completed the circuit of the pond.

"Let us retire to that little copse," said he, shaking the water from his stick and dusting the knees of his trousers. "Our pipes won't attract any notice there, and the view of the house will be far better than from the lodge."

Selecting for our vigil a fallen tree covered with moss, we settled down for a quiet smoke. Holmes crouched motionless in the shadow, and only the rhythmic blush of the bowl of his pipe showed that he remained as watchful and alert as ever. The chime of the village church struck ten. The moon had nearly vanished behind a gable of the house, and an impalpable mist seemed to rise from the dull waters of the pond. The chill of a late summer's night had begun to seep into my marrow when I was suddenly galvanized into action by an event that was as violent as it was unexpected.

I have said that from our point of vantage we had a view of four lighted windows on the ground floor. These windows stood in a row, three of them being tall and rectangular, and the fourth small and oval. It was in this latter window that the light shone most brilliantly, and from time to time we had a glimpse of a female figure moving past the glass. On one of these occasions the figure paused in its passage as though to look out, and at that moment a deafening explosion rent the stillness of the night and sent us leaping to our feet.

Simultaneous with the shot, which seemed to issue from very near at hand, came the crash of glass and a woman's scream. The face had vanished from the window. "Quick, Watson! To the house!" cried my companion, setting off across the park at a brisk pace. He threw open the shade of his dark lantern but wasted no time in seeking the assassin. Looking towards the oval window as I ran, I saw the light from within caught and reflected by the jagged edges of the shattered panes. No human figure appeared there.

Holmes raced up the broad steps and pounced upon the bell, at which he hauled violently and repeatedly. "Did you see him, Holmes?" I asked, as I joined him in the pillared porch.

"Devil a bit of him. He must have fired from beyond the wall." His tone was one of deep chagrin, and I sensed how bitterly he regretted having to forego the pursuit of the assassin. "Pray God the lady isn't mortally wounded," he murmured, attacking the bell with renewed vigour.

The door was suddenly thrown open, and in the light of a flickering candle there appeared a young woman in a nightdress, her long hair flowing in disorder over her shoulders. "Oh, gentlemen, you must help me!" she cried, holding out her hand to us in a pathetic gesture of appeal. "My maid has been killed! Murdered!"

For an instant Holmes shone the light of his torch full in her face, and then, flinging past her without a word, he mounted a short stair that led in the direction of the apartment with the oval window. I followed more slowly, taking the candle from Miss Ordway's trembling hand and guiding her up the stair.

We found Holmes bending over the still form of the maid, who lay in a litter of broken glass. "Some brandy, Watson! She's only fainted, I think. There is no blood, and if I am not mistaken that is the ball lodged in the moulding above the door."

I snatched up a decanter and glass from the sideboard, and while Holmes and Miss Ordway chafed the maid's wrists and temples I administered a stiff dose of liquor. Presently our efforts were rewarded by the appearance of a tinge of colour in the young woman's cheeks, and a restless stirring of her limbs. We raised her gently and laid her upon the sofa.

"You are very good," said Miss Ordway. "To whom am I indebted for this kindness?"

My companion ran her over with one of his quick, all-comprehensive glances. As though aware for the first time of her deshabille, the lady retired a little into the shadows and began to adjust the disorder of her hair.

"I am Sherlock Holmes, and this is my friend and associate, Dr. Watson. We are employed by your uncle to watch the house during his absence."

"My uncle has told me nothing of this."

"It was his particular wish that we remain outside the house. You might have been spared this shocking trouble if we had been nearer."

"I spared! But it is my maid who was nearly murdered!"

"Do you not think it probable that the bullet was intended for you?"

"My uncle will have told you of the other attempts, Mr. Holmes? On the first occasion Elizabeth was seated next to me. Either of us might have been the object of the shot that was fired. When I was nearly run down in London I was wearing one of Elizabeth's gowns—an unfortunate whim of my uncle's."

"Can you suggest any reason why your maid should thrice be the victim of murderous attacks?"

"None. But neither can anyone have a reasonable motive for murdering me."

Elizabeth Fetters had by this time so far recovered herself as to sit upright upon the sofa, and now she fixed her mistress with a look of faint reproach. "You oughtn't to hide Mr. Lawrence's threats from the police, Miss, really you oughtn't, for it is all bound to come out in the end."

"Nonsense, Elizabeth. These gentlemen are not the police. Mr. Lawrence's words were spoken in the heat of anger. They came from a heart stung with disappointment, not a mind meditating revenge."

Without missing a word of this conversation, Holmes had for some moments past been examining what remained of the shattered window. The casement had been swung round on its pivots by the force of the bullet, so that it lay nearly horizontal in its frame. Of the four panes, the upper two had been broken, though the bullet had actually struck the leaden mullion between them.

"It is fortunate that the window was unlatched," observed my companion. "Otherwise we might have written a very different end to the chapter. The bullet, striking the unyielding surface of the mullion, would very likely have penetrated it instead of being deflected from its target. The police must be informed of this latest attempt, though I fear that the culprit is far away by now. Have you your revolver, Watson? Then you may stand guard while I go into the village. It cannot be half an hour's walk, and the night is fine. Bolt the door, open to no one until I return, and stay clear of the windows."

He had no sooner departed than the two women deserted me as well, retiring for the night and leaving me in possession of the sitting-room and the key to the front door. With a candle in one hand and my revolver in the other I made the the round of the dark and silent house, finding everything in order. Then I sat down upon a massive carved chair in the lower hall to await Holmes' return. The time passed slowly, and I was nearly nodding when I heard the sound of wheels in the gravelled drive.

Presently Holmes called my name from the porch, and I sprang up to unfasten the bolt. A brisk, heavy-featured young man strode into the hall at Holmes' heels and examined me narrowly by the light of his torch. "Inspector Skinner, that is my associate, Dr. Watson," explained Holmes. "He is not so vicious as he looks, and a good deal wiser."

My friend's tone of banter was lost upon the Inspector, who seemed much disappointed when he learned that the ladies had retired. "That is a pretty kettle of fish, now," said he. "Here I have got out of my bed in the middle of the night to take their depositions, and I find that they are quietly tucked up in theirs. I might as well have waited until the morning, for the bird is flown, and there is nothing to be seen here that cannot be seen better by the light of day."

"Very likely," agreed Holmes. "And yet, whoever fired the shot must have left some trace upon the ground. A light fall of rain or the passage of other feet may confuse or obliterate the marks."

"Oh, yes, you may look for marks if you like, Mr. Holmes. I know your methods very well, for we read our London papers in these parts just like the gentry in Park Lane and Piccadilly. But I have little hope of finding our men by looking at their foot-prints. If we find any foot-prints at all they will lead us very shortly to wheel-marks in the lane, and then we shall have lost them properly."

"Watson and I heard no wheels in the lane. The night is exceptionally still. The sound of hooves carries half a mile on such a night."

"Well, then, they've got away through the marsh, and left no trace at all. These are wily customers, Mr. Holmes, very much abler hands at covering their tracks than at hitting the mark. This is the third time they have failed to harm the lady."

The Inspector made a careful examination of the broken window and then climbed upon a chair and extracted the bullet from the moulding with his penknife. "Brass, by Jove," said he, bouncing the projectile on his palm. "A lucky thing for the maid that this bullet was deflected, for it would surely have been lethal if it had struck any vital part." He was plainly ready to conclude his inquiries until the morrow, when the two women would be available for questioning. Holmes, however, returned to the subject of foot-prints.

"Why, sir," objected Inspector Skinner, "you might search the whole night through and find nothing. The shot could have been fired from anywhere in the park."

"The shot was fired from nowhere in the park. Though the night was clear and the moon still shining low among the trees, we saw no one. Yet the shot was fired very near to us. It must have come from beyond the wall." Holmes stepped to the oval window and stood peering out into the darkness. After a time he closed and latched the window, and cast his eye about the room. "Here is Miss Ordway's sewing basket. I think she will forgive me for the trifling theft I am about to commit."

He selected a spool of heavy black thread from among the articles in the basket and unwound four or five yards upon the floor. Having tied one end round the mullion of the window at the level of the mark made by the bullet, he carried the rest across the room and mounted the chair upon which the Inspector had stood. Finally he drew the thread taut and fastened the other extremity to a large pin which he had thrust into the centre of the bullet hole.

"There is the path of the bullet," said he, springing down and returning to the window. "Now, Watson, take the dark lantern into the park, stand next to the pond, and direct the beam towards this window. I shall signal to you with the candle, and you must move in the direction that I indicate. If I raise the candle you are to move farther away, and so on."

I took up the lantern and walked out into the park to comply with his orders. Fixing the correct latitude was simple enough, but Holmes' candle went on moving upwards until I had stumbled through a dense mass of brush to the very foot of the old wall and, stretching my arm upwards, set the lantern upon its summit.

The candle disappeared from the oval window, and presently Holmes and Inspector Skinner joined me in the park. The Inspector stared up at the lantern on the wall and shook his head in dismay. "We've a weary walk before us, Mr. Holmes, if we are going to look at the other side of this wall tonight. I am not much of a climber in any case, and I don't like the look of those spikes."

"There is a ladder in the gardener's shed," said Holmes.

The ground below the lantern was soft, and thick with tangled vines, but a yard or two away there lay a broad flat stone, bare of foliage, upon which we contrived to erect the ladder. The Inspector mounted first and shone the beam of the lantern over to the far side of the wall. "There is a thicket here," he reported presently. "The ground falls away pretty sharply, and I see a bit of water at the bottom. It is just as I supposed—he has come and gone through the marsh."

"Are there no marks at the foot of the wall?" asked Holmes, chafing with impatience.

The Inspector moved a step higher and leaned forward over the wall, grasping one of the iron spikes to preserve his balance. "Why, to be sure there are, Mr. Holmes," he said. "They look in rather a muddled state, but perhaps you can read something there. The vines grow as thick and wild on the farther side of the wall as on this, and they have been disturbed just here, as though someone had climbed up."

"Let us take the lantern, and leave the ladder to mark the spot," said Holmes. Without another word he made off in the direction of the gate, so that the Inspector had little choice but to come down from the ladder and follow him. After a long walk among tangles of bracken and shallow, stagnant pools, we arrived on the outer side of the wall opposite the ladder. Here the Inspector assumed a skeptical and patronizing manner, retiring into the shadows and leaving Holmes to examine the ground alone.

Holmes, I knew, asked for nothing better. Going down on his knees in the mire, he passed the beam of the lantern rapidly back and forth over the trampled earth, reading upon that palimpsest signs invisible to other eyes. Suddenly he plucked up something that had been nearly buried in the soil, and examined it by the light of the lantern.

"What have you there, Mr. Holmes?"

"A nickel-plated screw with a large knurled head," said Holmes, handing the object to Inspector Skinner. "It has been trodden into the earth by a man springing down from the wall."

"They must be very light on their feet, these assassins," said the Inspector. "You seemed quite certain a while ago that no carriage passed along the lane. Yet here were these fellows climbing upon the very wall not ten yards from where you sat, and you heard nothing."

"There has been only one man here," observed Holmes, too intent upon his investigation to mark the archness of the other's tone. "His boot soles are broad and short. The toes are squared, and there are lozenge-shaped metal plates upon the heels."

"Holmes," said I with considerable excitement, stepping forward to examine the foot-marks over his shoulder. "These marks—"

"—are interesting, of course, but inconclusive. Whoever made them has approached the wall from that morass below, and gone away by the same route. The marks of his coming and going are not so clear as these at the foot of the wall, but plain enough to the practised eye. Then, as to his behaviour at the wall: he has stood, he has mounted up by these vines, he has sprung down again. Curious, but hardly incriminating."

"But these marks were surely made—"

"True, Watson, they were made after that screw was dropped upon the ground. But it is probable that the screw has been lost by some chance passer-by, and has no connexion with the crime."

"As you see, Mr. Holmes," said the Inspector, "midnight excursions for the examination of foot-marks are seldom worth the trouble." He turned up the collar of his coat and gave other tokens of a wish to return to his bed.

When he had driven off, Holmes and I returned to the sitting-room with the oval window, where I attacked him at once upon the subject of the foot-prints. "Those marks were by Ordway himself, Holmes, for I noticed the soles of his boots very particularly this afternoon, or rather yesterday afternoon."

"Excellent, Watson, excellent! You really are coming along remarkably well. There is something in what you say, though that style of boot is not such a rarity as you seem to imagine. But Ordway had set off for Calais before the shot was fired. He must have made the marks on some earlier occasion, if he made them at all. There is little point and no profit in arousing the suspicions of the police against one's client."

"Perhaps not. But we have only Ordway's word that he was bound for the Continent. He may have gone to Paddington Station instead of Victoria, and followed us down in our own train."

" 'Pon my word, Watson, you grow positively cynical in the small hours. What has become of your decent enough chap, beside himself over the threats to his niece's safety?"

"But Ordway is the only man with a motive for the crime, and the foot-prints are certainly suggestive."

"So they are. Did you observe any features of interest in those leading away from the wall and into the morass?"

"They were very obscure."

"Yet they were different from all the others. The outer sides of the soles had indented the earth much more deeply than the inner sides. I commend that point to your consideration, should you prefer meditation to sleep at this wretched time of the morning. No, take the sofa, Watson. I shall do very well upon the hearth-rug."

I awoke to find the full light of day streaming in at the windows. Holmes sat curled in an armchair, smoking absorbedly. "Good morning," said he. "Coffee and scones are to be had in the morning-room. I've brought up your gear from the lodge. It is on the window-seat."

"You have been abroad early."

"I have been as far as the village. I sent a cable to Ordway to apprise him of the latest events and to assure him of his niece's safety. I have also hired a trap, which is standing in the stable yard."

When I had completed a sketchy toilet and swallowed a bite of breakfast, we went out into the dewy morning. Holmes had secured a pair of our client's boots by one of those ingenious expedients with which his imagination so readily supplied him. It was the work of a moment to compare the boots with the marks and to note that they matched in every particular.

"You've lost your money by dispatching a cable to Calais," said I gloomily. "Ordway was on this spot at ten o'clock last night. He fired the shot which broke the window and nearly killed—"

"His niece's maid. Come, Watson, it won't do. Ordway is not likely to have a motive for murdering the maid, and he is scarcely capable of mistaking her for his niece, even at this distance from the house."

"But what possible interpretation do these foot-marks bear, if they do not show that Ordway came here by stealth, climbed upon the wall at the very spot from which the shot was fired, and then made off through the marsh?"

"I draw your attention once again to the differing character of this track leading down the slope," he said. "What does it suggest to you?"

"That he was carrying some heavy load which got between his knees and forced him to walk upon the outer edges of his feet."

"Capital. The faculty of reasoning analytically is a rare gift, Watson. Of course not all who possess it are equally endowed. These foot-marks are rather closer together than the others, which is against the supposition that the man who made them was walking with something between his knees. Not only does your explanation not deal with all of the facts, but it postulates others for which we have no evidence. What burden had he to carry down the hill, which he did not have when he came up? Whence did it come, and why has it left no mark or trace upon the wall or the ground?"

"I give it up, Holmes. If this jumble of marks tells any story but the obvious one, it escapes me."

"Yet I fancy the key to the mystery lay open to our view in Baker Street yesterday."

Upon our return to the house we discovered Inspector Skinner installed in the morning room with his notebook on his knee and a glass of cider at his elbow. He appeared to be upon the most

familiar terms with the women of the house, and gave every indication of making a long job of taking their depositions. We left them
in his charge and drove into the village. Holmes proposed that we
lunch at the inn with a view to hearing some of the local gossip.

The landlord, a great red-faced man as stout as a barrel, proved
to be as close and taciturn with strangers as he was free and jovial
with his regular customers. When he knew that it was we who had
driven to Moorcroft on the previous day in the trap belonging to the
inn, he fixed us with a sardonic and by no means pleasant smile.

"Your welcome has run out quickly enough, gentlemen," said he,
"but that is nothing remarkable. You'll hear no good of the Ordways
hereabouts."

"What have they done, then?" asked my companion.

"It's what they have not done that's got them a black name, sir.
They run up immense accounts with every tradesman in the district,
and when bills are presented Ordway has the cheek to demand more
credit. He hires labourers in the village and puts off paying their
wages from month to month until they are grown tired of asking."

"What need has he of labourers? I understood that his man, Fetters, looked after the house and grounds."

The landlord curled up his ample lip in disdain. "Not him. Mr.
Fetters is above all that, sir. Mr. Fetters is a very superior sort of
servant, indeed—what you might call a private secretary. When
there is labour to be done, Mr. Ordway casts about the village for
some poor drifter who doesn't know the sort of man he has to deal
with."

"I suppose by labour you mean gardening, and domestic chores
too heavy for the maid?"

"There you ask me more than I know. Perhaps Mr. Ludwick, the
estate-agent, can help you—the gentleman in the black gaiters, sir,
just passing the door of the tap-room. Farms are his usual stock in
trade, but I understand he has lately taken some business interest
in Moorcroft."

The estate-agent responded to Holmes' overtures with open rudeness. "If you come from Ordway, sir, you shall see nothing of me but
my back. But you may tell him for me that he is a wretch and a
scoundrel, and that I had sooner go to my grave this day than do
business with him."

"I did not say that I came from Ordway," returned Holmes, "but
only that I am staying at his house."

Mr. Ludwick indulged in a laugh of savage sarcasm. "His house, did you say? It is not his house, sir, but his niece's, as I have learned to my great cost. He is neither owner, nor proprietor, nor duly appointed steward. I will tell you what he is, sir—he is a hanger-on, a parasite, a blood-sucker, and if you are wise you will have nothing whatever to do with him." He went off in great haste as though afraid of being pursued.

"This grows tiresome," said Holmes. "At least let us hope we shall meet with more courteous treatment at the post-office."

The postal clerk presented Holmes with a reply to his cable, but it proved to be only a short note from the manager of Ordway's hotel in Calais. Ordway, who was well known to the sender of the message, was not at the hotel, nor even expected.

Holmes did not seem in the least surprised at this development. On the other hand, the cable came as a thunderbolt to Inspector Skinner. It was as well that Holmes drew him into the lower hall before showing it to him, for he broke out in a perfect fury. "It is the man himself," he cried, three or four times over. "I knew it—I suspected it from the first. And so did you, too, Mr. Holmes. Miss Ordway has told me of your researches with her uncle's boots. Those are his own foot-prints, are they not?"

"These are deep waters, Inspector," replied Holmes, shaking his head slowly and solemnly, "and very murky just at present."

"You would put me off, of course, for you are in the scoundrel's pay. But I must apply for a warrant, Mr. Holmes, and I should advise you to do nothing that might impede me in the execution of my duty."

"I am beginning to feel distinctly unwelcome in this quarter of the kingdom, Watson," remarked my friend airily. "Let us retire and lament in private the absence of our host."

We saw no more of the Inspector that day, and very little of the lady who had perforce to play hostess to us for the week-end. Holmes lay coiled in a corner of the sofa, with his arms folded and his gaze fixed upon the oval window, smoking pipe after pipe and vouchsafing no reply to any of my remarks. It was plain that he did not believe in the manifest guilt of our client, and equally plain that his skepticism arose not from any misplaced loyalty but from a conviction that the evidence bore some more favourable interpretation than the obvious one.

Accustomed though I was to his unsociable ways when his mind was occupied by some insoluble riddle, I found the time lying heavily upon my hands as the shadows crept into the room and the cooler breeze of sunset stirred the curtains round the shattered window. I had nearly finished a leisurely and half-hearted perusal of a week-old newspaper when Holmes suddenly sprang out of his seat and put his pipe down upon the mantelpiece.

"I have been blind, Watson, blind!" he cried, fairly dancing across the room and peering out into the park. The thread had been taken down earlier in the day, but as I stood at his elbow it was easy enough to follow his line of sight. By the last rays of the sinking sun the little pond shone like a pool of liquid gold. Deep shadows already lay beneath the trees, but I could clearly perceive the ladder still resting on the large flat stone at the foot of the wall, where Holmes and I had placed it.

"Look at that stone," said Holmes, pointing with his forefinger through the empty sash. "Why is it bare of foliage, in a place where even the vines are entwined by other vines, and the whole is engulfed in a sea of bindweed? Come, bring the dark lantern. And not a sound."

With furtive and stealthy tread we passed out of the house and into the park, where the gloom thickened from moment to moment. Holmes made straight for the gardener's shed and without a word handed me out a spade, taking up a pick and another spade for himself. "Now, then, Watson, set the lantern upon that stump, while I shift the ladder. Be as quiet as you can, but above all let us be quick."

"What does it all mean, then, Holmes?"

"Do not the size and shape of this stone suggest anything to you? Unless I am much mistaken it means murder, Watson—not murder contemplated, not murder attempted, but murder fully accomplished and concluded. Let us have this stone up, and put the matter beyond doubt."

"It is a very large and heavy stone, Holmes."

"Quite so. And yet one man put it there. Two, I fancy, can take it up again." We attacked the earth round the stone with our spades, and when the excavation had been carried to a sufficient depth Holmes inserted the pick under one edge and gave a powerful heave. As the stone shifted slightly I thrust the tip of my spade and added my strength to Holmes'.

At that moment some stir of movement near the house caught my eye. Even as our united efforts raised the stone from the earth like the lid of a coffin and tipped it back against the wall, I descri＜ d two figures crossing the porch, while a third paused for an instant, framed in the lighted doorway.

"Holmes, they are coming!"

"Who are coming?"

"The women—and another."

"Let them come."

"The fellow has a cudgel."

"Better and better."

"Holmes, it is Ordway himself."

"I doubt it." He took up the lantern and shone it into the cavity which had formerly been covered by the stone. One horrifying glimpse I had of blackened flesh and sodden garments, and then our visitors were upon us.

"So, gentlemen," said our client, "you have not been content with the duties for which you were hired, but must meddle with what does not concern you." He waved his cudgel in a vague gesture of menace, but his tone was less masterful than it might have been had not Holmes taken care to let him see that a revolver was in his hand.

"Murder is the concern of every citizen," said my companion coolly. "To ignore it or to conceal it is to be a party to it."

"Murder is a strong word, Mr. Holmes. By what right do you dig in my park, and make slanderous accusations to my face?"

"Come, sir, drop this pretence. I believe I have the honour to address Mr. Fetters?"

At this, the man with the cudgel seemed to wilt and shrink like a wounded animal. All the fight went out of him, and he nodded in dumb assent to Holmes' identification.

"And the man in the grave is Ordway?"

"Not a man, Mr. Holmes, but a monster," cried Fetters, flaring up with a new animation. "In that grave lies all that remains of the foulest blackguard who ever drew breath. You have got the better of me, fairly enough, but you said too much when you spoke of murder. If you will step into the house I shall make it all clear to you, and then you must do as you think best."

Fetters conducted us to the sitting-room and flung himself dejectedly down upon the sofa, where presently his sister Elizabeth joined him. Despite a certain similarity about the eyes, I thought them as unlike as any brother and sister I had ever known.

"How you have got hold of it by the right end, I can't think," said

Fetters, "for I thought I had done a proper job of kicking sand into your eyes, Mr. Holmes."

"That is what many another has thought. The impersonation was plain to me from the first, though I confess that your motive still eludes me."

"Well, then, I shall just begin at the beginning, and if there is anything that is not quite clear you must tell me so and I shall try to put you straight. You must know, sir, that my late master was a greedy, scheming villain, though I say it before Miss Ordway. She will perhaps deny it, but I know she has cursed a thousand times the black day on which she fell into her uncle's grasp.

"She alone stood between him and his father's fortune. His business was failing. He tried to mortgage the estate without Miss Ordway's knowledge, and ran afoul of the law. He sent a pawn of his, that smirking puppy Mr. Theobald Lawrence, to make up to her and propose marriage. After she laughed him out of the house Ordway kept her shut up like a novice in a nunnery lest she marry another and so cheat him of his expectations.

"I knew my employer to be none too scrupulous in his business dealings, nor too nice in his choice of associates. But as my sister was devoted to Miss Ordway, and my duties congenial and light, I stayed with him, never dreaming that he was capable of hiring an assassin to murder his own flesh and blood.

"It was after the second attempt on Miss Ordway's life that my eyes were suddenly opened. The attack occurred, as you know, in London, when Miss Ordway was wearing a gown of my sister's—a gown that Ordway himself had particularly instructed her to wear. Through Elizabeth, I tried to warn Miss Ordway of the terrible danger in which she lay, but she would not listen.

"I resolved to take steps myself to prevent any further attempts on her life. Arming myself with a pistol, I dogged Miss Ordway's footsteps, haunted the passage outside her apartment, and at the risk of being detected and turned out for my impertinence I took to passing my nights in a linen closet near to her chamber.

"On the very second night my vigilance was rewarded. I was awakened out of a sound sleep by muffled exclamations which seemed to come from Miss Ordway's bedchamber, and without pausing to inquire into the right or wrong of what I did I snatched up my pistol and rushed into the room. Imagine, Mr. Holmes, a suckling mouse in the clutches of a hawk, a hare fallen prey to a python, and you will know what I felt upon entering that room. He was strangling her, choking out her life with an energy and force which were at once savage and deliberate. Before he knew that I was in the room I had emptied two chambers of my pistol into his brain. Only then did I see that the band which he had twisted round Miss Ordway's throat was the sash of my own dressing gown, and perceive the full extent of his treacherous purpose.

"That was four nights ago. I buried him in the park, concealing the disturbance of earth with a slab of stone which was all that remained of a watering-trough in the stable yard. Those were the labours which left their marks upon my hands.

"If you will reflect upon the position in which Miss Ordway was placed by my hasty and too thorough intervention, you will see that it was a delicate one. If Ordway had much to gain by murdering his niece, she had something to gain from his death also. By the terms of her father's will she was entitled to take possession of the entire fortune if she married at any time between the ages of eighteen and twenty-five, or if during the same period her uncle died or became legally incompetent. It was the last provision that determined our course of action.

"Miss Ordway did not choose to marry. We could scarcely pretend that her uncle's death was accidental, and years might elapse before the law would permit presumption of death if he merely disappeared. We resolved accordingly to manufacture grounds upon which a court might grant a motion to declare Ordway incompetent.

"Our plan was to stage yet another attempt upon Miss Ordway's life before reliable witnesses, and to leave traces sufficient to support the view that Ordway had made the attempt in his own proper person. To this end it was necessary to bring him to life again for a time. I am not unlike him in height and build, and you had never seen either of us. I visited your rooms in a suit of my employer's clothes, even wearing a pair of his boots and making certain that you had observed the rather distinctive pattern of the soles. After I had persuaded you to come to Moorcroft to witness the charade we had planned, I went to Victoria Station and dispatched a telegram to Ordway's firm explaining that he had been called away suddenly to the Continent. I then went on to Paddington Station and returned here by a later train than yours, walking across the downs and concealing myself in a thicket on the edge of the marsh until after nightfall.

"At the concerted time I mounted the wall and fired off a blank charge into the air. I would not, of course, take the risk of actually firing a bullet into the room. The damage to the mullion had been done in advance with a round punch. My sister insisted upon performing the role of the victim. When she heard the expected report she had only to break the glass by dashing the window inwards against that candlestick."

"And the bullet in the moulding?"

"Fired the night before last, from across the room. I had determined the exact course of the projectile with a theodolite. It was almost the only piece of truth I spoke yesterday, Mr. Holmes, when I said that I was trained as a surveyor."

"Had you been trained as an artilleryman you would have placed your bullet in the middle of the ceiling. I do not propose to demonstrate the point by actual experiment, but I assure you that if a bullet had really struck the mullion as the appearances suggested, it would have been deflected sharply upwards. Yesterday I determined the apparent path of the bullet after it struck the mullion. A continuation of that line across the park passed just over the wall. Now, the wall is at least fifty yards from the window, and the window is no more than five from the place where the bullet was lodged. If we suppose that the deflected bullet rose only twelve inches out of its original path in traversing those five yards, then that original path must have passed ten feet above the wall.

"By the way, I think you will find that there is an adjusting screw missing from your instrument. I picked it up on the far side of the wall last night and gave it to Inspector Skinner."

"Yes," said Fetters. "I stuck it into the moss on the top of the wall to mark the spot where the bullet was supposed to have passed over. 'I thought I was doing a clever thing in choosing so well-known a private detective to be my dupe, but it seems that it is I who am the dupe, after all. I expected that as soon as you had given a statement of the apparent facts to the police you would return to London."

"But the apparent facts were a jumble of contradictions," said Holmes. "To mention only the most glaring, the boots which Miss Ordway so willingly proffered this morning were the identical ones which had made the foot-prints beyond the wall. They must have been brought or worn into the house after the marks were made, carefully cleaned, and put into Ordway's room."

"So they were. After firing off the shot I ran into the marsh, put on my own boots, made a wide circuit over the downs, and arrived back here near dawn. My sister admitted me to the house and I have been holed up in her chamber ever since, while she has been staying with Miss Ordway.

"Have I done wrong, Mr. Holmes? Is it murder to strike down a vile beast so as to prevent his choking the life out of an innocent girl? Is it a crime to work a harmless deception so that the ends of justice may be served in justice's own despite?"

"As to the graver charge," said Holmes, "no one, I think, will call you a murderer. The British law is not an unreasonable nor a vindictive one, but it will not be trifled with. You must repeat what you have told me to the police, and you must be prepared to stand trial. If Miss Ordway and your sister confirm your story under oath, a jury may be expected to view your actions in a favourable light."

On the next morning but one, Inspector Skinner had his hour of glory in the police magistrate's court. Holmes declined to appear except in the character of a witness, and as he kept his own counsel about the curious behaviour of the bullet, the women were not brought into the case at all.

Fetters was arraigned upon charges of unlawfully disposing of a dead body and of fabricating evidence. Having pleaded guilty to both charges, he was committed for trial to the Quarter Session and released upon his recognizance.

"Are there any points in the case which are not perfectly clear to you?" asked Holmes, as we returned to London by the afternoon train.

"I can't think how you came to suspect that a body lay beneath that stone."

"Why, I was persuaded that the corpse lay concealed somewhere on the premises. The marshes would not have been chosen as a burial ground by anyone who had lived long among them. Marshland is a treacherous ally in the business of hiding bodies. Just when the murderer thinks he has put his victim forever beyond human ken, the marsh yields up a wan and watery spectre to point an accusing finger at him. The pond was too shallow, the cellars were unlikely, and there was no freshly turned earth to be seen in the park."

"But why suspect a corpse at all? You were engaged to prevent a murder, not to bring one to light."

"Quite so. But the man who engaged me was a palpable fraud."

"Come, Holmes, how could you recognize Fetters as a fraud when you knew neither him nor the man whom he impersonated? He was just a perfectly ordinary fellow, with utterly commonplace features and qualities."

"That is not altogether true. Long slender fingers like Fetters' are commonplace enough, to be sure, and so are broad, short feet like Ordway's. But their apparent concurrence in the same person is enough of an anomaly to excite not merely attention but suspicion. And then, when a man loses flesh he does not grow taller in proportion. Our client's clothing had been made for a man both stouter and shorter than himself. He said he was Ordway; then Ordway he was not, and the question arose, where *was* Ordway?"

"You might have put the matter into the hands of the police and spared yourself a great deal of trouble."

"The police would have gone about making futile inquiries for a few days, and then thrown up the whole affair. No, Watson, it was a case which demanded patience and discretion. Above all it was necessary that our client believe he had taken us in."

"But why carry on the pretence with the niece? I feared for her safety all the more after the third attempt. In your position I should have put the whole matter frankly to her."

"Where one deception has been practised, you may expect others. You failed to appreciate the significance of the young lady's behaviour on the night of the supposed third attempt."

"I thought her remarkably composed and self-possessed, in the circumstances."

"Remarkably is the word, Watson. She was supposed not to know of our presence in the park. Yet when we rang the bell, but a few moments after a bullet had ostensibly passed through the sitting-room window and sent her maid into a dead faint, she had no hesitation about admitting us and soliciting our help."

"Fetters has little to fear, I suppose, at the Assizes?"

"I think not. I fancy that more difficult struggles await him nearer to home. If I am not mistaken, the lady is sorely smitten with her rescuer. He is scarcely the sort to set a young girl's heart a-pounding, and yet she could do worse. A stout fellow, is Fetters. Consider his injunction to us to carry firearms and not scruple to use them. It was fortunate for him that we ran to the house instead of getting upon the wall with our lantern and our revolvers. His progress must have been as slow as it was painful when he made his escape into the marsh. You recall those curious tracks? It is no simple matter to run while wearing boots which are two sizes too small."

"That was a macabre trick of his, Holmes, pretending that the shot was fired over the very place where Ordway's body lay."

"Perhaps, but I suspect that his motives were more practical than you suppose. Fetters wished to direct our attention to some spot on the other side of the wall, where we were to find a set of foot-prints made with Ordway's boots. Having selected the mullion of the oval window as one fixed point, he passed along the wall with his theodolite in search of a suitable place from which to plot the apparent course of the bullet. He might have given the game away if he had set down his apparatus on the bare earth. A tripod leaves a distinctive set of marks which would have been awkward to efface. Therefore he chose the one place along the wall where the tripod would leave no marks—the stone under which he had buried Ordway."

"You may talk of practical motives if you like, Holmes, but I cannot help seeing at least a gleam of romance in the circumstance."

"Say, rather, poetic justice," said my companion with a smile. "Truth is ever stranger than fiction, and the most improbable tale but the feeblest imitation of real life. Yet there is something in Boccaccio, is there not, that comes rather near to the present case?"

William Bankier

The Dog Who Hated Jazz

I was walking through the lobby of the Coronet Hotel when Jack Danforth, the owner, called me over to the desk. "Have you got a minute, Norman?"

My grocery shopping was finished, I was only in for a beer. "Sure thing, Mr. Danforth." Even though I was now an English teacher at Baytown High School, I had never forgotten my first summer job as a bellboy at the Coronet. If the boss asked me to get the bags from room 311, I'd be up those stairs two at a time.

I followed him through the back lounge and into his private office, where I sat in a chair he indicated. I watched him close the window to exclude the noise from the parking lot. Danforth's shape was blocky, like a fullback gone to seed, and when he turned he showed me that belligerent face framed by close-cut black hair, the lower lip drawn down by the weight of a cigar stub. He looked stubborn, possibly dangerous.

It was the green eyes that gave him away, eyes narrowed with amusement and lit up with the pleasure of running a small hotel in a quiet town with the warm, dry summer at its height.

"You're pretty close to Joe Benson, aren't you?" he asked, swinging his shiny black boots onto a corner of the littered surface of his desk.

"I see Joe almost every day."

"I wonder if you'd mind putting an idea to him. I'd call him myself only he may need persuading and that will come better from you."

"Sounds mysterious."

"Not at all. I'm thinking of converting the back lounge into a piano bar. Joe Benson playing jazz could be an attraction."

"You're right about that." I could understand the reason for Mr. Danforth's hesitation. Joe Benson accompanied the hymn singing at the United Church on Sunday mornings. He might consider it incongruous to be asked to spend Saturday nights in a smoky beer parlor playing the blues.

"Jazz is near and dear to Joe's heart," I confirmed. "I'm sure I can overcome any reluctance he may have."

The office door swung open. I recognized the lean and hungry shape of Lyndon Lee, a Torontonian who had met Jack Danforth's daughter Stella a few years ago and persuaded her to marry him. Lee was supposed to keep out of trouble by managing Jack's motel located ten miles down the highway. This was never easy for Lee—as I understood it, he managed to create several kinds of difficulty for himself most of the time. Antisocial is the nicest word we have for people like Lyndon Lee.

"Evening, Dad," he said, deliberately using that sadistic form of address. All he gave me was a nod.

Jack kicked shut the bottom drawer of his desk and kept his boot braced against it. The move was instinctive. I knew from my bellboy days that the boss liked to keep a metal box in there with a couple of hundred dollars in it.The flat-eyed Lee looked as if his tongue could snake into that drawer and snatch out tens like an armadillo sucking up ants from a hole in the ground. "What do you want, Lyndon?"

"Only to ask if you'd like a lift home. Stella's idea." It was a harmless suggestion, but as always when Lyndon Lee was in a room the air was electric with possibilities.

"I intend to stay here for a while," Danforth dismissed his son-in-law. "I'll call a cab when I'm ready to go home."

Lee went away and Jack said to me, "His latest enterprise was a poker game in one of the units at the motel."

"That's illegal, isn't it?"

"Especially the way my boy was doing it. Besides taking a percentage of every pot, he had something going with a marked deck of cards. One of the players threw a punch at him and came back later with the police."

"Nice for the motel."

"Fortunately, I'm on good terms with Chief Greb. But I had to be persuasive to cool that situation down."

I shook my head in sympathy. "When do you want to start the piano lounge?"

"Soon as possible. I see it as Fridays and Saturdays, eight till midnight. Half hour on, half hour off. If Joe is willing, he can ring me and we'll agree on money."

"I'll go and see him tomorrow," I said, looking forward to the exciting mission.

Queenie greeted me when I arrived at Joe Benson's apartment after telephoning him the following morning. Joe ordered her into the living room and she went obediently. I followed him into the room, where I took my favorite armchair and watched as he lowered himself onto the piano bench. Queenie established herself at his feet.

"What's it all about, Norman? You sounded eager on the phone." Joe sat with his head tipped back, his eyes focused somewhere beyond the ceiling, as if he was receiving messages from above. Blind from birth, Joe Benson is not disfigured in any obvious way. The only sign of his handicap I can see is a slightly off-center condition of the eyes so that his face reminds me of a slot machine with the indicators jammed. Joe is in his mid-thirties, prematurely grey, with a neatly trimmed beard and moustache. He's tall and slim and he wears black trousers, black shoes, a white shirt, never a tie—a physicist on his day off.

"Jack Danforth at the Coronet Hotel has an idea," I said and went on to explain the concept of the piano lounge and Joe's place there as resident jazzman two nights a week. When I finished, Joe grinned at the ceiling. He turned to the piano, Queenie changing her position to let his legs pass, and allowed his hands to hang above the keyboard. They shifted this way and that, as if each finger was fitting into a familiar slot in the air.

"Here's something I'm doing for the Sunday School next week," he said. "It's one of their favorite hymns, but we haven't had it for a while. A real rouser." He struck a major chord, then began to sing, accompanying himself with percussive enthusiasm.

"Though the angry surges roll
On my tempest-driven soul . . ."

Joe completed a verse and one chorus, leaving no doubt that he possessed an Anchor safe and sure that would ever more endure. During the evangelical outburst, Queenie stretched out, lowered her fine alsatian head to her forearms, and closed her eyes. Her job was to guide Joe Benson along familiar streets, to prevent him walking in front of a car, and to keep him company here at home. If it was his habit to produce these sounds from time to time, that was his business. Queenie, in fact, seemed to find the gospel music pleasant.

"That should double the collection next Sunday," I said. "But what about the piano lounge?"

"You don't see any conflict in my banging out 'Flying Home' on Saturday night and 'Harvest Home' on Sunday morning?"

"If God had meant us to create music only in church," I said with utter sincerity, "he wouldn't have given us Art Tatum and Oscar Peterson."

"I can tell you somebody who isn't going to like it," Joe said, reminding me of a phenomenon that had slipped my mind. "But the idea appeals to me so she'll just have to put up with it."

The Benson fingers searched again for the familiar grooves. Joe struck a chord as different from the gospel introduction as beer is from beef tea. Queenie's ears came up and her chin rose an inch or so from its resting place. Joe shuffled through a progression of chords that changed the atmosphere in the room, changed the light, the temperature, moved us from where we were into a reality which was slightly better than the one I knew would be waiting for me when the music stopped. He began to play "I Can't Get Started" at a rather faster tempo than the Berrigan standard, left hand pumping a rhythm that was almost stride, right hand producing a tremolo at the end of each phrase. It was unique, a version never heard before, perhaps never to be heard again. And I was there.

Queenie moaned, the only time I have heard a dog utter such a sound. She dragged herself to her feet with the disgust of an elderly sunbather when the kids invade the beach with their frisbees and left the room with her head down. Through her master's exquisite music I heard her claws clicking down the corridor linoleum to the kitchen.

When Joe finished, I said, "That was prime."

"Thanks. But Queenie took off." He swept a hand below the bench to confirm his dog's absence.

"She reminds me of my old mother, rest her soul," I said. "A cultured lady, despite her nicotine addiction and a tendency to blow her top. I grew up surrounded by good music, knowing Tagliavini was a great tenor, understanding what a Gregorian chant sounded like. Our radio was quickly switched from speech; it broadcast music only, whether it was Schubert on a Sunday afternoon or the Foden Motor Works Brass Band playing 'Sons of the Brave' as I headed off to school in the morning."

"Musical Marchpast," Joe recalled the program.

"But when I became a teenager and I used my allowance to buy records, tolerance evaporated. I brought home Charlie Barnet's 'Scotch and Soda' and never got to play it above half volume. One time I said to her,' Mom, listen, it's the Basie rhythm section—drums and bass and guitar playing like one man.' Do you know what her reaction was?"

"Same as Queenie's."

"She called it thump-thump-thump . . ."

That afternoon I wandered down to the Coronet, enjoying the sense of freedom I experienced when I passed the high school and saw the blind windows, noted the green scud of grass taking over the dirt playing field, and knew I wouldn't have to resume my slavery as slave-master at the head of Grade Eleven English for another six weeks.

As I walked into the hotel lobby, Stella Lee (the former Stella Danforth) was on her way out. I've always admired Stella's calm intelligent face, the thick sensible braid of her hair, the pool of quiet sanity that surrounds her wherever she goes. I like to brush up against that tranquil periphery, to slip inside and relax with her for a moment if I can. I think Stella's benign influence is, quite simply, what human evolution is all about. Give civilization another few thousand years and this will be the norm instead of the exception. Oh, to live in that paradise.

"Norman Craig, hello. I haven't seen you for a while. You look nice and relaxed."

"Hi, Stella. Summer vacation. I'm enjoying being a teacher." I mentioned the piano lounge and said I was going to see her father about Joe Benson's decision to take it on. "I'm glad he said yes. Dad's been talking about it for a year. I encouraged him to go ahead."

Just before we parted, I asked, "How's Lyndon?"

"Busy," she said, not in the way a nurse would have said that Doctor Schweitzer was busy. "I guess he can't help it."

"What do you mean?"

"I don't think it's the money—" she hesitated, then decided she trusted me enough to go on. "He never has enough. He takes things—and sells them. I've grown up with a copper coffee-mill my father's parents brought from Russia. It stood on the mantelpiece at home, and when I got married my father gave it to me."

"I can't believe this—"

"He did, Lyndon sold it to a dealer. When I missed it and asked him about it, he didn't even try to cover up." She shrugged philosophically. "Anyway, I made him hand over the money and I bought the coffee-mill back. Never mind."

Why Stella Danforth married Lyndon Lee is a tough question. The conclusion I have reached, the only one I ever *will* reach, is that she, too, has her imperfection, the flaw in an otherwise perfect personality. She is so good, she must tie herself up with something bad. It can't be explained any more than science can explain magnetism.

At one end you have positive, at the other, negative. Nature will not allow positive without negative. Go know.

I found Jack Danforth in the beverage room. He was enjoying himself, drawing glasses of beer. The bartender was reading a paper and Jack was running the tap, smiling to himself. The front door was open, warm fresh air drifting in from the street, and the place smelled beery and the drone of conversation around the room was like bees on a field of clover.

"Joe Benson likes the idea," I said.

Danforth pushed an overflowing glass my way. "On the house."

"Thanks. He'll call you to confirm it."

"Terrific. Perfect." My old boss looked as if he was proclaiming Christmas. "We'll start next Friday night."

I was there early that Friday to be sure of having a seat. The back lounge of the Coronet is not a large room, and preparations for the entertainment had made it smaller. A corner was cleared, an upright piano installed, and a space left open between it and the informal arrangement of upholstered chairs and small tables. I sat near the door of Danforth's private office and ordered a beer. Shortly before eight, Jack emerged, locked the office door behind him, and joined me.

"Looks like a success already," he said, surveying the crowded room. A new cigar was plugged into his face—the hotel owner was about to enjoy himself. "Is somebody bringing Benson?"

"Queenie will look after it," I said. "They've been here before."

Lyndon Lee appeared from the beverage room. He was carrying a briefcase. "Can we go over the motel receipts?" he asked.

"Not now," Danforth said, looking straight ahead. "Joe Benson is going to play."

"I'll wait in the office."

"The office is locked."

Lee looked at Danforth. He looked at the office door. He looked at me. His eyes conveyed disbelief that grown men would waste time sitting in a smoky room listening to somebody playing the piano. As Shakespeare reminds us, let no such man be trusted.

Danforth's son-in-law went away just as Joe Benson arrived with Queenie leading him on a short leash. Joe's grin was in place, his eyes following closely the invisible map on the ceiling. In black slacks and turtleneck, he was elegant as a cat burglar. Queenie spotted the piano and led her master to it, sprawling on the floor as soon as he sat on the bench.

There was applause and a few words from Jack Danforth about his experimental entertainment policy, and then Benson warmed up with a couple of arpeggios. The room fell silent. Joe's fingers sought and found their starting position, hesitated, listening for the instruction from above. There was extreme tension in the air. Then Joe's left hand began to strike a repetitive boogie beat, deep and heavy and precise as if the notes were being produced by a clockwork mechanism. After four bars, the right hand introduced a rollicking figure that bounced off the base notes and tumbled and fell and rose again. It was something in the style of Pinetop Smith and the crowd responded instantly.

So did the dog. Queenie's head was up, her eyes fixed mournfully on her master. How could he do this to her? They were not safe at home, they were in a strange place. I watched the internal struggle expressed on those noble features and knew loyalty was going to lose out to the dog's musical snobbery. A moment later, Queenie got up and shuffled away, disgust and disapproval showing in every swing of her lowered head.

The crowd got the message and had to react. Joe's sensitive hearing picked it up and he knew what was happening. He stopped playing and said, "You can never please your own family."

Queenie came to me, her only friend in the room. Danforth got up and unlocked his office door, let the dog escape into the dark and quiet, then closed the door. "She's in my office, Joe," he reassured the piano player. "Carry on."

The evening was a terrific success. The local paper even managed to include a review in their weekend edition. Not that the hotel needed the plug. Joe Benson was a musical institution in Baytown and his presence would guarantee a sell-out every time.

I returned for a second transfusion the following night. As I entered the hotel, I passed Lyndon Lee lurking by the brass-plated doors. Shirt and tie, clean-shaven face, briefcase perpetually in hand—I reflected that Stella's husband presented an appearance that could give respectability a bad name.

"Nice night, Lyndon," I said.

"Mmmmmm." He had no use at the moment for a vacationing school teacher.

"Coming in to hear the music?"

"No, I have to go." He looked at his watch but made no move to depart.

As I passed through the lobby to the lounge, I glanced back and saw Lee poised in the doorway. Later I would recall his posture and the image would fall into place—Second World War assault troops looked like that in landing craft approaching a beach.

The crowd was even larger than on opening night. This time, Queenie was led away and stowed in the back office before Joe began to play. After the first set, she was let out to mingle with the customers during the interval, trudging solemnly from table to table for the pleasant ritual of the laying on of hands. Then, as Joe returned to the piano, Danforth put the dog back in the office, closed the door, and came to sit with me.

The entire second set turned out to be a tour-de-force built around the standard, "April In Paris." Joe began sweetly, almost in a classical vein. Then the earthy roots took hold and pushed up lush shoots that penetrated the melody and wove variations through it that threatened to bury the song—but never went quite that far. Chorus after chorus, the blind pianist came bursting through to emerge with the melody triumphantly at his fingertips.

The ending lasted, by itself, almost a quarter of an hour. Joe threw in the famous Basie coda, both hands in unison thundering out the swinging variation on the theme, and the people in the room cheered as he went on playing.

There was so much sound in the room—the fortissimo music, the crowd reaction—and our attention was so centered on the performance, I doubt if we would have heard a plane crash in the parking lot. Certainly nobody heard what must have been the intense, if brief, confrontation in Jack Danforth's back office. We knew nothing of that until the set ended and Jack went to retrieve Benson's dog.

I heard the sound my former boss made and saw him frozen in the doorway where he had switched on the light. I joined him inside and saw Queenie lying on the floor, bleeding from wounds in her neck and shoulder.

The window onto the parking lot had been forced open. I didn't see then but was told later by the police that there were signs of somebody trying to open the desk. The same implement used to do this and to jimmy the window had inflicted the wounds on the dog—probably a screwdriver.

Queenie had to be taken to the vet. Joe went with her and so did I. The damage was serious but not critical. She would be sedated, shaved, and stitched, and would spend the night at the surgery. Joe could have her back tomorrow.

I saw Joe home in a cab and promised to bring Queenie to him the next day.

After doing that in the late morning—she had numerous stitches around the neck, a Frankenstein dog—I went to the hotel and asked Jack Danforth if there was any news about the attempted robbery.

"Chief Greb came over himself," Jack said. "He found another blood specimen on the floor—not from the dog, he thinks. She must have got her teeth into whoever it was."

"Good," I said fervently.

We were still talking when the telephone rang. Jack answered and said, "Hello, Chief. Did you really?" He listened. "Well, that's a bit of luck. I'm not sure whether I'll press charges or not. I'll have to think about that."

As he put down the telephone, I asked, "A breakthrough?"

"They have the man. The dog did bite him and drew blood. He went home and had to tell his wife something, so he said it was a stray on the street. She's a knowledgable and sensible girl—the first thought she had was rabies, and she took him to the doctor for a shot. I wouldn't have given Greb credit for this much foresight, but apparently he asked all the doctors in town to report any dog bites. He didn't even have to do a blood sample—the guy admitted it."

"What guy?"

"Who else? Lyndon. He was after the cash in my bottom drawer. The room was dark, he mustn't have seen the dog till she went for him when he started jimmying the desk."

I can't say what punishment was meted out to Lyndon Lee. He still manages Jack's motel, and as far as I know the marriage to Stella is intact. Danforth's hands are tied—if he presses charges, his son-in-law will go to prison and his daughter could never live with that. But this story is not really about Lee, anyway. Queenie is the heroine and she holds the spotlight right to the end.

The following Friday Joe Benson reappeared at the Coronet lounge and received an ovation from a packed house, as did his heroic guide dog. When Joe sat at the piano, Jack took hold of Queenie's leash, led her into the back office, and closed the door. The room went silent as Joe prepared to play.

That was when we heard the plaintive whining behind the office door. Joe's hands settled onto his lap. "She's too smart to stay in there again, Jack," he said.

Danforth opened the door, ready to take the dog somewhere else, but she was past him in a flash, between the tables and onto her spot beside the piano bench. There was applause and laughter. Joe stroked her head. "Lesser of two evils, love?" he said.

He began to play a slow, quiet blues with the measured pace of a man walking down a deserted street. Queenie's head went down for a moment, then it came up and her noble eyes rested on some point in space that only she could see.

Bless the dog, I said to myself as I sat back and lifted my glass of beer. She's going to try something my old mother refused to do—she's going to give jazz a chance.

Christianna Brand

Double Cross

S ir Thomas Cross, it must be admitted, had been an unaccommodating relative to his heirs—largely on the score of living too long and spending a great deal too much—and revenged himself for his murder by leaving an equally unaccommodating will. Having since boyhood preferred an expensive London flat to the gloomy glories of Halberd Hall, he exhibited towards it, nevertheless, a posthumous devotion. For some years the three cousins had lived there, camping out, more or less, in three or four of its enormous rooms: it cost them nothing and suited their bachelor lives. Now, said the will, not only might they continue to live there, but they must; failure to do so automatically excluding the absentee from further interest in the estate.

Dan and Jimmy greeted Rufus at the great front door. "Welcome, dear cousin!—to one third of the Hall, anyway."

"And to another one third. The rest is yours," said Jimmy, "and you're welcome to that, too—in the other sense."

"What a turn-up for the book, eh?" said Rufus. He shouldered past them into the house and released an armload of haversacks and paintboxes. "Come out and help me with the rest."

"You've certainly been busy during your protracted sojourn in France," said Dan, eyeing the canvases in the back of the hired car, "while we were carrying the can for you in re Uncle Tom."

"Not to mention Uncle Tom's Cabin," agreed Rufus amiably, looking up without affection at its Elizabethan frontage.

"Where the hell have you been all this time since it happened? But don't tell me, don't tell me!" said Jimmy. "Wandering lonely as a cloud from one nameless French hamlet to another, tent on back. No newspapers, the six o'clock news unavailable."

"It's what I do every year," protested Rufus. "I knew nothing till the police picked me up, which they did pretty smartly the moment I handed over my passport at Folkestone. And they didn't tell me much, just asked questions." He propped the last of the canvases against a wall and gave it a loving pat. "Let's go in and have a drink, and you can fill in the details."

The dining room was huge and dark, made no lovelier by nests of photographic equipment, a clutter of books and papers about birds, and a central table scattered with used crockery. "Still living as on safari, my ruddy millionaires?"

Jimmy rootled about for clean glasses. "We haven't sorted things out yet. Dan and I think it may be best to divide the old hulk into three separate flats, one for each of us and any family we may acquire. Meanwhile, the Midday Hags continue to come up of a morning and clear away this lot, and we start again, a la the Mad Hatter."

Rufus poured whisky. "What d'you mean, three separate flats? You're not going to stay on here, with all this wealth?"

"Haven't you heard? Good Lord, you know nothing! We've got to."

"Got to?"

"Halberd Hall is to be maintained to 'a required standard,' thus pronounceth from the grave Uncle Tom. And since none of us will inherit enough to so maintain it and live elsewhere, we are to pool our resources and stay on here."

"What, forever?"

"Or until such time as any of us acquires sufficient wealth to contribute an equal share to its maintenance on top of his private expenses."

"Well, I'm blowed! Live together, year in, year out? We don't even like one another."

This was true. "No wonder you're called the Cross cousins," Dorinda Jones used to say, "you're all so horrid to each other." And she would give one of her wicked giggles—for it must be acknowledged that Mrs. Jones was one of the reasons why two, at least, of the Messrs. Cross were on bad terms.

"Can't we upset the will?" said Rufus.

"You try it, do! Dan and I would scoop the lot."

"Well, blow me down!" said Rufus again. He got up and poured considerably larger tots into not yet emptied glasses. "Condemned to be penned up here together till death us do part!"

"Since death already hath us parted from Uncle Tom," suggested Dan, "and by the hand of one of us three present—I don't know that the term is exactly agreeable in this context."

"A sort of Tontine, you mean?—one of us slain off next, and then another, the inheritance accruing to the survivor?"

"It's a thought," said Jimmy.

"Not at all a funny one," said Dan. "Damn it all, one of us—one of *us*—really is a murderer."

"Yes, well, tell me all about it," said Rufus.

"What's there to tell? Uncle Tom went as usual down the Tube to get his train for the club, and somebody gave him a shove and he landed on the line: and that was Uncle Tom. That's all."

"Except that a man with a large red beard appears to have given him the said shove: and I am a man with a large red beard. It's a jolly happy thing for me," said Rufus into the ensuing rather chill silence, "that at that hour I happened to be on a cross-channel steamer, halfway between here and France."

"*If* you were on a cross-channel steamer, halfway between here and France."

"My dear old James," said Rufus, "that cock won't fight. You knew I was going that day, you both knew—it'd been planned for ages. I did go that day, as my passport shows, and by the grace of God and a stack of painting clobber and my large red beard, I seem to have been noticed at Folkestone and in fact even at Dieppe. Arriving there by the early boat. So whichever of you has been acting my Doppelganger again—"

Rufus had had his Doppelganger almost, one might say, from babyhood. Like many children, he had created an alter ego to be responsible for his misdeeds. "That must have been the other little boy," he would say; and, "You have a Doppelganger, my child," said his father, trampling about the corns of Messrs. Freud and Jung with large Edwardian boots. A Doppelganger, he kindly elaborated to four years old, was a sort of other "self"—vaguely evil and dangerous, he now recollected and perhaps one shouldn't have said quite so much. But too late—"Dop" was a member of the family and, though hated and feared by the smaller Rufus, came to make himself useful in later years, assisting him out of trouble at his Private, and even at his Public school. And now, it seemed, turning up and actually pushing Uncle Tom under a train: to the great pecuniary benefit of three so far indigent cousins.

"You've got Doppelgangers on the brain," said Jimmy.

"Considering that for the past year, one has been following me round London—"

"Oh, rot!"

"—and now I begin to see why. Building up to Uncle Tom's murder."

"I don't know how exactly?" asked Dan in his slow way.

"Nor do I. But the fact remains that people were accosted by someone looking like me and claiming to be me when I wasn't there at all. And what's more, making trouble for me with old Tom; that time when my 'double' went up to some club crony of his in the street and made a crack about him ... If I hadn't found out about that, I'd have been out of the will—as no doubt was intended."

"And where were you when that happened?"

"Never mind where *I* was—am I likely to have done such a thing? Where were you two? And where were you when Uncle Tom took his dive off the platform?"

"The police know all about it," said Dan. "I was here, hanging about for an agent who'd written to say he'd like to see some of my photographs. And Jimmy was bird-watching under a bush somewhere or other: which is how he invariably spends his weekends, as you very well know."

"Both presumably with—like me—large numbers of witnesses?"

"The message from the agent was a false one," said Dan, stiffly. "When I finally got hold of the man, he said he'd never written."

"Ha, ha, ha!" said Rufus. "And you, James? A little bird lured you to similar solitudes?"

"The operative phrase is 'as you well know,' " said Jimmy. "Anyone could be sure I'd be out of the way that day, and on my own."

"Including my Doppelganger?" Into a second silence, Rufus expostulated: "Is it likely that, conspicuous as I am, I would march onto a Tube station platform and, in front of a large concourse of people, push Uncle Tom under a train? Melting away in the succeeding excitement without anyone noticing me? There's only one way for a man with a large red beard to melt, my dear chums, and that is for him to remove the large red beard and look like anyone else. So far as I'm concerned, it's just a question of who to thank for my share of Uncle Tom's money, and at the same time for my share of the suspicion."

"Well, Dan and I haven't got red beards, so don't look at us."

"He's just said—one of us could have worn a false one," said Dan, reasonably, "to throw suspicion on him."

"Well, speak for yourself," said Jimmy. "I was in a hide on the lake, looking out for duck. I showed the police my thrown-away picnic bits."

"Anyone can throw away a few crusts of bread. You could have gone there any time and planted them."

"Well, thanks very much, Master Daniel! And you, I suppose, couldn't have waited till the Midday Hags went home and then got out your car, nipped up to London and done the deed, and nipped back?"

"I daresay I could," said Dan. "But I was waiting for this man."

"I don't know why the hell we don't just drop it," said Jimmy, back-pedaling. "We've got the money, the old man's dead—we didn't like him, we hardly ever saw him: who honestly cares who killed him?"

"If you enjoy living cheek by jowl with a murderer," said Dan, "and not knowing which he is—I don't. And one of you two—"

"And besides," said Rufus, "I don't care for that trick with the beard. And one of *you* two—"

"The police don't think it was necessarily one of us."

"What'll you bet? But they've got to consider every possibility," said Jimmy. "We needn't. Who else knew that every day Old Punctuality caught a train just about that minute for the club? He almost lived in the club, he had no men friends outside it—and no enemies inside it, apparently; though I find that hard to credit. There was nothing to be gained by a stranger pushing him on to the line—no picked pockets or whatnot, I mean; and no homicidal maniacs noticeably mopping and mowing on the scene. So unless you count a few old tabbies he used to play Bridge with occasionally—"

"For all you know, one of them was pulsating with illicit passions . . ."

"Oh, come off it, Rufus!"

"Yes, well, 'come off it!' But me and my beard are Suspects One and Two, and I don't care for it."

None of them cared for it; the guilty no more than the innocent. It was true that none of them liked the other. To have roughed it here together while each pursued his own interests had suited them, hard up as they all were, as a temporary measure; but a life imprisonment together would have been unthinkable at the best of times. And now . . . To prowl forever round one another like angry dogs, the innocent unable to know which of the other two to trust, the guilty uneasily aware that here, among those who knew his habits well, lay his greatest danger: danger in the smallest slip of the tongue—which yet must appear to wag freely lest its very lack of confidence give him away.

Rufus said: "What are the police doing?"

"Not much. They tested our alibis, they seem to have tested yours: what more can they do?"

"You haven't got any alibis."

"Perhaps that's why they seem to have failed to break them."

"I trust they have made the rounds of the artificial-beard merchants?"

"I daresay they have. Dan and I are not in their confidence to that extent."

"You told them about my Dop?"

"We told them what you'd alleged," said Jimmy. A pity, he added sourly, that Cousin Rufus had not been here to give his own account. "Most convenient for you."

"What could I do, for heaven's sake! I tell you, I knew nothing about any of it. And if you want to check on me, dear boy," said Rufus, "you go ahead and do just that. I got to Dieppe by the first boat—damn it all, I was *seen* on the thing!—went and had a meal and whatnot, hired a car and a tent at my usual places—go and ask them!—and started off down south. By which time, poor Tom's a-cold and lying in the mortuary."

"And you conveniently out of touch with civilization."

"But what was convenient about it? I don't get the message. Yes, sure I was out of touch. I went down to Arles, parked my stuff with the Widow Larivière—go and check if you like—and then just roamed off as usual looking for places to paint. Came back at half time and left the finished stuff and collected fresh canvases. So what? I honestly can't see that it matters one jot—Uncle Tom had gone Underground by then in more senses than one, and that was that. However, trace away if you feel it will do you any good. Thank goodness I seem to be easy to remember, the mad English painter with the big red beard, *tout à fait à la* Van Gogh. Only with both ears. So while you pursued your bird's-nesting—"

"I tell you I was down by the lake at the time he was killed—"

"Nobody else tells me so: nobody can. And nobody can tell me about Dan, either—all alone waiting for the man to come and see his feelthy peectures."

"Damn it all, I'd had this note, supposed to be from my agent."

"When the man didn't come—why not ring up and check?"

"So I did. He couldn't think who had sent the letter."

"A man with a big red beard no doubt had sent it?"

"Nobody knows anything. And of course I'd thrown it away, never thinking any more about it."

"But of course," said Rufus, sweetly.

The days passed. Dan fiddled with his photographs; Jimmy spent

long hours by the lake; Rufus prepared energetically for a show of
the new pictures and meanwhile carefully studied the newspapers.
At the end of three weeks, he found his way to Kensington and rang
a front doorbell. "Well, Mrs. Jones!"

"Good Lord, it's Rufus Cross!" said Dorinda. She backed ahead of
him into the little flat, automatically poured liqueur into a tiny
glass, and handed it to him.

"What on earth's this?" said Rufus.

"Calvados. Don't you like it? Good, that's another cheap one." She
took the glass out of his hand and poured the contents back into the
bottle.

"Isn't there any alternative?"

"No, it's Calvados or nothing. I have to save money these days."
She raised her own glass. "Well—I bows to you."

"And I likewise bows," said Rufus, doing so with a flourish.
"Meanwhile—to what do I owe the unaccustomed honor?"

"I saw in the paper that your divorce has come through."

"Don't tell me I'm to add your name to my list of suitors."

"No, I think you've got enough Crosses notched up already on
your little hatchet. I shall have to be content to cherish you as an
in-law."

"Don't you wish you may?" said Dorinda.

"What, neither of them?"

"I'm afraid not, Rufus." She looked rather sad about it.

"You astonish me. I thought it was positively going to be Dan."
He considered it. "The trouble is, Dorinda," he said, shrewdly, "that
Mrs. Daniel Cross would be one thing, but Mrs. Halberd Hall is
more than you could stomach."

"Well . . . " She lifted elegant shoulders in a rueful little shrug.
"You must say, one is *not* a girl for a life of unrelieved Tudor Gloom-
ery."

"You make me exceedingly anxious, Dorinda," said Rufus and
went away looking very thoughtful.

Another week and another week; and a morning came when Dan
said: "Jimmy never mentioned, when he went off on Saturday, that
he'd be staying away. If he doesn't show up tomorrow, I shall tell
the police."

"I'm going up to see them this afternoon," said Rufus.

They faced one another, grimly. "If anything's happened to Jimmy,
Rufus—then I know it was you."

"Spare me the act when we're alone together," said Rufus. "We both know it was you. I couldn't have killed Uncle Tom and I wouldn't have killed Jimmy. Why the hell should I want to?"

"If you had half his share, you could get away from this place. What's the use of it to you, when all you want is to paint? You can't paint at Halberd: you hate the countryside round here. You wanted Uncle Tom's money to set up as a great artist and now you want Jimmy's—and mine too, for all I know—so that you can get away from here and be a great artist. As for me," said Dan, "I don't care two hoots about getting away. I can set up a decent studio here, proper darkrooms and all the rest of it—I like the life."

"And Mrs. Jones, of course, will simply love it?"

"What do you know about that?" said Dan, going white.

"Only that Dorinda will never marry you while it means having to bury herself here. You're the one that needs money. And I'll tell you something, Dan: I saw this coming. Only I wasn't too sure it wouldn't be me."

"You seem quite settled in your mind that Jimmy's been murdered."

"What'll you bet?" said Rufus. "Only I'm taking no odds: you'd be betting on a certainty. But I'll tell you what I'll bet—that a man with a large red beard will turn out to have been involved in it somehow."

And that afternoon he went up to London to see the police. But first he dropped in again on Mrs. Dorinda Jones. "Now what?" said Dorinda.

"Now Jimmy has disappeared."

"He's got his birds mixed up at last," said Dorinda, "and gone off with one."

"You know very well there's only one bird in Jimmy's life."

"Well, anyway, this time it has nothing to do with me."

"Everything Dan and Jimmy ever do has something to do with you. You know that, Dorinda. I think they're both a bit insane where you're concerned. When did you last see him?"

"Who, Jimmy? Well, on Saturday, when I saw him coming out of the pub opposite, with you."

"You what?"

"On Saturday, when the pub closed. The Shorn Lamb."

"On Saturday when the Shorn Lamb closed, Dorinda, the Rose and Crown, opposite my art school, also closed; and I was there."

"Oh, for Pete's sake, Rufus! You were with Jimmy. I waved to you and you waved back." She got up and poured some Calvados, came across to him with the little glass, said, "Oh, no, you don't, do you?" and all in one movement turned and went back to the table with it. She said: "You're right about one thing, Rufus: Jimmy's half dotty about me. He's as jealous as all hell, and every time Dan came to the flat he used to go and hang about the Shorn Lamb opposite and watch him in and out and see how long he stayed . . ."

"Did Dan know this?"

"No, what was the point of telling him? It would only start another row. Besides it was so—well, humiliating for him, poor old Jimmy. I used to squint out and watch him establish himself in his window seat, eking out tankard after tankard; and when Dan had gone, he'd come up here, pretending he'd just arrived on the scene: and scene was the word."

"This was when he was supposed to be squatting in a hide, watching duck?"

"I'm afraid that's just what he was doing; only I was the duck."

"And last Saturday evening?"

"Well, Dan always came on a Saturday. My dear husband had a detective following me about," said Dorinda, "and Saturday seemed to be his afternoon off; I suppose they have to have them, poor pets."

"And last Saturday—day before yesterday, that is—you saw me with Jimmy? Complete, no doubt, with large red beard?"

"I don't know what you're talking about, Rufus. Last Saturday Dan came, we had our drama, Dan went away; I sat here and had a little howl and when I next looked out of the window, you and Jimmy were walking out of the pub together. I gave you a wave and you waved back. I took it you'd told Jimmy I must have been giving Dan his congé, and that's why he didn't come up afterwards to see me. I mean, after last time we talked together you pretty well knew, didn't you?"

"Yes," said Rufus. He thought it all over. "Dorinda, you say that Dan always came on a Saturday and Jimmy was always there, watching him. Our Uncle Tom was killed on a Saturday. Were they here that day?"

"Every Saturday in living memory," said Dorinda.

"So if Dan says he was hanging about waiting for an agent, and Jimmy says he was by the lake—"

"Oh, phooey!" said Dorinda. "The agent and the lake were always just other names for me."

So Rufus went to the police.

"My cousin, Jimmy Cross, has disappeared. I now find he was last seen on Saturday evening, coming out of a pub called the Shorn Lamb, in Kensington, with my well known Doppelganger. At the time, I may say, I also was in a pub; but it was the Rose and Crown, opposite the Turner School of Art where I go once a week for life classes. You can ask the landlord—he'll have seen me there."

"We have asked him," said the police.

"You know about all this?"

"Information has been laid," said the police.

"In other words, Madame Dorinda Jones has been on the blower. Well, well!" said Rufus. "And the landlord—?"

"The landlord said that half a dozen customers that evening probably had beards and several of them probably were red. The Turner School of Art, it seems, is patronized by a good many gentlemen with beards."

"It is in the nature of art schools," said Rufus.

"It's never occurred to you that one of *them* might have laid on this Doppelganger act?"

"No, it hasn't," said Rufus. "I hardly know the people at the school, I just use the life-class models at the weekend when the ordinary students don't come. No one there knows me well enough to play silly tricks." Meanwhile, he added, while they parleyed here, his cousin James was missing, believed—by him, Rufus, anyway—killed.

And not the only one, said the police. His cousin Dan was now also missing—believed fled the country.

"No!"

"His passport was stamped at Dover this morning."

"And you let him go?"

"We had no reason sufficient for holding him."

"But what about Jimmy?"

"A pity you didn't tell us about that a bit earlier."

"You realize that those two were in fact in London on the day of my uncle's murder? In time to have killed him and then gone on to Mrs. Jones' place?"

"Yes, we realize."

"You got that from Mrs. Jones, too?"

"We have our methods," said the police, twiddling their thumbs.

"He can't have got far. Can't you trace him? I mean, Interpol and all that?"

"It shouldn't be difficult. It appears," said the police, "that your cousin is wearing a large red beard." And they leaned forward and with a murmured apology gave his own beard a little tug. "Well, *that's* real enough," they said, sitting back, exchanging confirmatory nods between themselves.

There was nothing for it but to go home and get on with preparations for his show. He knew that it was going to be a success: the best work he had ever produced, bold, brilliant stuff, such as Van Gogh himself had done in the same sunny countryside. Not that he set up to be a Van Gogh, but the paintings would catch on, he knew they would. Even hung round the walls of the unused drawing-room at Halberd, when he had been working out his selection for the show, they had lighted up the darkness like Rembrandt gleams of gold.

Dorinda had said not to offer ordinary old champagne at the Private View. "Have Calvados; lots of people hate it, so it goes much further. And it'll be cuter." Dorinda herself was undeniably cute, weaving through the mob with her hand hooked possessively into his arm, chatting up prospective buyers. "Don't you think this one is gorgeous? Number 27. Provence, Late Evening . . . What, Rufus? Oh! Oh, well, he says it's Provence, Early Morning, but so what? Two for the price of one, I say—every morning you could look at it and think, What a lovely morning!—and every evening you could look at it and think, What a lovely evening!" She prattled profitably on; but by six o'clock, standing triumphantly alone together in the emptied gallery, he thought, glancing at her face, that she looked pale and very weary. "You've been wonderful, Dorinda. Even in Calvados, I raise my glass to you—and I bows."

"I likewise bows," said Dorinda, automatically. She added: "I say, Rufus, talking about glass, don't look now but someone's peering in through the window. And who do you think it is? It's your Dop."

"My what?" he said, maneuvering for a view.

"Your Doppelganger, you fool! Peering in."

His own face! His own eyes, looking back at him through the glass, staring back at him through the glass. He went a leaden grey; sweat, cold and clammy, broke out across his forehead. He stammered: "My God! It's myself. It's me."

"That's so improbable that don't you think it *must* be only Dan, in his falsie?"

"Dan?"

"Well, I know you're not alike, but you are cousins, there would be this family thing. And for good measure, he's got a policeman handcuffed to him."

"A policeman? Handcuffs?"

"Well, no: now I look again, no handcuffs. But a flattie all the same."

"Why should you think he's a policeman?"

"Oh, but it's Superintendent Brown," said Dorinda. "I know him well." She ran to the door. "Come in, come and buy some pictures! Number 27 is still unsold, I simply can't think why—two for the price of one, I call it. Late Evening or Early Morning, we're not too sure which. But we *are* sure where. You can just see a little bit of a church. The same one appears in a picture of Van Gogh's. But it isn't in Provence at all. It's up north, in Auvers."

"Yes, it's Auvers," said the Superintendent, "in the Ile de France. We've just come from there." To Rufus he said: "They remember you well." He put on an excruciating French accent. "Ze Eengleeshman wiz ze rred beard, altogezzer à la Van Gogh." Though one wouldn't say, he added—judging by the self-portraits, that Van Gogh had had a *large* red beard.

"He always looks to me," said Dorinda, "more as if he were in the process of growing one."

They invited him down to the station for questioning and he accepted without fuss. What was the use? And anyway, now that they were onto him, they would soon find Jimmy—deep in the lake at Halberd where he had sunk the body after bringing him home that evening from the Shorn Lamb . . . Bringing him back from the Shorn Lamb, boldly walking out in the part of his own Doppelganger. He had shown up first at the art school and then for a moment at the Rose and Crown opposite, to make sure there were one or two red beards there: people remembered red beards without necessarily putting a face to them, and no one would ever be certain in that Saturday crush that one had not belonged to *him*. And if he had been safely at the Rose and Crown—then the Doppelganger could only be Dan, dressed up for the part: Dan, who, in fact, would certainly, after his final dismissal by Dorinda, be driving sadly home all alone, and have no alibi.

It had been lucky that Dorinda should have seen them from the window—he had hoped for that—but even if she hadn't, it wouldn't have mattered. Someone in the Shorn Lamb would have remembered the Doppelganger coming in for Jimmy. You could always rely upon people remembering when they'd seen a man with a large red beard.

Always. On the platform in the Tube that day, for instance. You shaved off your own beard, you went there in a false one, pushed Uncle Tom under his train, and, in the ensuing pandemonium, shuffled off the beard and, clean-shaven and therefore unnoticed, slipped away. And it was the red beard they all remembered.

Again at Folkestone and Dieppe. It hadn't taken much to discover, just by listening in the Rose and Crown, which day it was that one of the art school red-beards was planning his own channel crossing, painter's clobber and all. The police find your passport has been stamped on that day, chaps mill forward in their hundreds to testify that they remember—again in the busy Saturday crowd—a painter with a large red beard. On the early boat—that's the point; on the early boat. You yourself (having disposed of Uncle Tom) travel, clean-shaven and therefore unremarked, by the later boat. Complete with what Dorinda would call your falsie, you show up at a garage in Dieppe where you're known and allow yourself to be traceable all the way down to Arles, in Provence. Leave some stuff there—and bat back north to the Ile de France. Van Gogh painted there also, and you want Van Gogh country; but now you have established yourself with him in his Provençal days, who is ever going to look for you up north? Halfway through the time, when your new beard is not too long to prevent your wearing—just for a few hours—the false one, you show yourself again at Arles; and at the end, of course, you go there again, with a real full-grown beard now. But—it had all been a bit academic really; for where you went, what you did between your arrival, fully bearded, at Arles and the time you returned there, fully bearded, to pick up your things and go home—who in fact is ever going to question that?

Answer, he thought ruefully: Mrs. Dorinda Jones, apparently, is going to question that. "Go and ask the people in the villages where he was painting," says Dorinda to Dan. "He won't say where he was," says Dan, "he had a tent and just wandered." "Take a look at his pictures, then, you dope," says Dorinda. "Van Gogh left a record of that countryside: try to spot landmarks in the pictures." So Dan gets out his wretched little camera and clicks away at the canvases hung all round the drawing-room at Halberd, and he and Dorinda pore over the results. And Dan talks round Scotland Yard and, policemen in attendance—to see that he's up to no tricks himself, perhaps, but anyway to identify places and cross-question witnesses—off they go. And there you are.

Vaguely evil and dangerous, his father had said, describing the Doppelganger to the little boy. "A Doppelganger is—well, a sort of other self. But evil and dangerous." He had summoned up his Doppelganger, thought Rufus, summoned up—if you liked to put it that way—his other self; and, evil and dangerous, that other self had beaten him, hands down.

He was not unprepared. They couldn't hang you nowadays, but for him, a painter, to spend the long years cut off from all beauty, from sunlight on corn, from great fields of cabbages, silvery blue, from white clouds boiling up against a cobalt sky—no thank you!

"Dorinda," he said, staring, braggadocio, into her strained, white face, "do keep Number 27—a wedding present from me." And for the final time he bowed to her and, under cover of the bow and the flourish, slipped the little tablet into his mouth. "You can cage up my Doppelganger," he said to the Superintendent before he died, "but not me as well. That would be a bit too much what Mrs. Jones would call two for the price of one."

Robert Twohy

Case Blue

A tall, niftily dressed older man came into Slime's office and said in a wispy voice, "I have a dagger in my back."

Slime got up from his desk and moved to where he could see a blue-plastic handle sticking out from between the man's stylish shoulderblades.

The man moved to the client's chair and perched on the edge of it. "It feels like a short blade."

"I'll call a doctor."

"No—that would mean publicity. I don't want publicity."

Slime sat down. "Tell me what happened."

"I was walking down the corridor to your office when someone jumped out of the men's room and stuck me."

"Who?"

"Who what?"

"Stuck you."

The man shrugged, then let out a small yelp of agony.

Slime said, "Better not to shrug. Let me take it out."

"No, leave it. Krull will take care of it. He's my houseboy. He used to be a beachcomber on the Louisiana bayous. He knows about things. He'll pull it out and put some special lizard sauce he has on the wound and recite some incantations—it'll heal splendidly."

Slime regarded him with his clear green eyes. "Who are you?"

"Folmer Zittworth. I'm well known in financial circles."

The detective said nothing. The stabbed man said, "I've never heard of you, either. I found your name in the yellow pages."

"Why do you fear publicity?"

"It would upset Trinket's father."

"Who's Trinket?"

"My wife."

"Who's her father?"

"My father-in-law. He's Spreek, of Raggbush and Spreek. I don't know who Raggbush is. I'm one of the vice-presidents. I got the job when I married her. He gave us a mansion on Pacific Heights I met her when I was selling self-cleaning doormats." He seemed to be vagarizing a bit. "What was I saying?"

"Who stabbed you?"

"I fell face-down. All I got was a glimpse of blue jogging shoes. I think it was Precious."

"Who's Precious?"

"The man Trinket's having an affair with. That's why I was on my way to your office—to get you to find out who he is and tell him I'll pay him to go away, so the gossip columnists won't get wind of the affair."

"How do you know there's an affair?"

"I found a love-note in her desk signed 'Precious.' It said how pretty her eyes are, which they aren't. But for a young woman less than five feet who weighs nearly two hundred, she has attractive hands."

Slime was silent for a while. Zittworth, in a fading voice, said, "I keep finding matchbooks with Tickle-and-Tease covers."

Slime knew the Tickle-and-Tease Club from ads in the papers—one of San Francisco's more sophisticated nighteries, on Pacific Avenue.

"Have you asked her about Precious?"

"No. She might complain to her father that I'm wrongly accusing her, and he'll get angry and fire me."

"What do Raggbush and Spreek do?"

"We have a building on Sansome Street. Our logo is a horse rampant, which means something, I'm sure. I go to lunch a lot and we have board meetings with frozen daiquiris."

Slime nodded. "I'll take your case."

Face contorting in new agony, the wounded man pulled out a wallet.

"My fee is $48.50 per day, plus expenses."

Slime took the bills and coins the client dropped on the desk. It was his first case in eight months. There are slack periods in the investigative trade. He was glad to be on the move again.

Zittworth said, "Find out if Precious is the man who daggered me. If he is, tell him I won't press charges if he'll end the affair with Trinket." His upper-class face suddenly fell apart.

Slime said, "I'll call the paramedics."

"No. Call Krull." He recited a phone number. "Tell him to come get me . . ." He fell out of the chair, forehead slamming on the edge of the desk, and lay with his knees tucked under him and the blue-plastic handle sticking up in a somewhat jovial way.

Slime dialed. A voice rasped, "Whadaya want?"

"Is this Krull?"

"Maybe it is, maybe it ain't."

"Zittworth is on the floor of my office with a dagger in his back. You're to come get him. The Phlemm Building, on Mission Street—room 505."

He got up, gazed down at the fallen man, apparently at peace, and thought how you never know who's going to wander in a detective's door, or in what condition.

A gaunt man with red whiskers wearing filthy white pants and bark sandals loped in, glared at the resting man, dropped on a knee beside him, and with a gnarled knuckle began gouging the small of his back, shouting, "Snap out of it! Come to!"

Slime told him in a quiet voice to stop doing it.

The man gouged harder and continued shouting.

Slime reached a magazine of true-crime cases from his desk and, rolling it quickly, cracked the beachcomber in the face.

The man from the bayous toppled, screaming, "Why'dja *do* that?"

Zittworth raised up. A red lump designated where his forehead had stroked the desk. He yawned and gazed around. "Oh. Hello, Krull."

"This guy magazine-whipped me!"

Zittworth told Slime, "I don't countenance brutality." He got up, then his legs went limp and he fell across Krull. The nomad stumbled out the door with him, cursing him. Slime watched as they weaved down the corridor toward the elevators, the cursing man staggering under the weight of the tall, distinguished-looking executive with the blue handle sticking out of his back.

Slime went back to his desk. It was after 3:00 o'clock.

He sat not moving, his green eyes steady on the tan office wall. He blinked infrequently. He had trained himself to not blink much. You can see more when you're not blinking, and in detective work you try to see as much as you can.

Two hours went by as he sat looking at the wall.

Then he got up and went to the nearest bus stop, catching a crowded bus to Pacific Avenue, where he walked a block to a place with a banner hanging on it that showed pink young women jumping out of cocktail glasses. Above them were printed the words, TICKLE-AND-TEASE CLUB.

A few persons crouched at tables, getting down early dinners. Alone at the bar was the bartender, a wiry, wrinkled man. He wore a white shirt and a neat blue bow tie and was trimming his nostril hairs with a lime-slicing knife. He had blue eyes.

Regarding him, Slime flashed on a bright-blue dagger handle, blue jogging shoes.

Zittworth was entering his sixties, the bartender looked about to leave them. Like a number of young women, Trinket could be attracted to thin older men.

Sometimes investigations entail a lot of slogging around and sometimes you come right to what you're looking for—you never know. Slime went to the bar. The wizened man slid the knife back among the limes and came wirily over. Slime noted he was conventionally shod in hush-puppies, but between the puppies and his trouser-cuffs was a provocative gleam of bright-blue socks.

Slime had the thought, *Color this case blue.*

The bartender was leaning on the bar. "You gonna order something or djyou just come in to look at me?"

"Do you know a girl named Trinket?"

"Trinket? Trinket? Why would I know a girl named Trinket?" Shiny blue eyes swiveled in various directions.

"You seem to favor blue."

"Blue? What blue? Blue whom? Who's blue?"

"If you had jogging shoes they'd probably be blue."

"Jogging shoes? Who's got jogging shoes?"

"If I looked in your locker—"

"You wouldn't find 'em 'cause I left 'em at ho—" He rubbed his mouth hectically. "Even if you did, so what? I mean, so what? Lots of people wear blue jogging shoes!"

"Yes. But only one person wearing them was in the men's room in a downtown building this afternoon, lying in wait for a man named Zittworth."

"Zittworth? Zittworth? Never heard of him—who's Folmer Zittworth?"

"This afternoon someone in blue jogging shoes stuck a blue-plastic dagger in his back."

"I wasn't anywhere near the Phlemm Building this afternoon!"

"You may have been there and not realized it. Do you even know where it is?"

"Certainly! It's on Lower Mission Street!" The bartender seized a clean glass and rubbed it frenziedly with a greasy rag. "So you see I know perfectly well where I wasn't!"

"Maybe so—but do you know the floor the men's room you weren't hiding in is on?"

"Of course I do!" The blue eyes snapped. "The fifth!"

Slime gazed in his unblinking way.

The eyes of the bartender gradually unsnapped. "Was I tricked into saying too much?" he whispered.

The detective nodded slowly. His face gave no sign of gloat. This was no new experience to him. He'd won many battles of wits before. "Tell me everything," he said.

The bartender talked. Fortunately, he had time—the throngs of sophisticates had not yet begun to pour into the Tickle-and-Tease. Some musicians were tuning up and a couple of young women were jumping up and down on the small stage. The few customers eating didn't look at them. Slime didn't look at them either—when on a case he had no time for women.

The bartender, dispiritedly greasing another glass, confirmed that he was indeed Precious, author of the love note. His legal name, he said, was Luther Lounce.

He quavered, "I love her."

"Who?"

"Trinket. Nobody ever called me Precious before. All my ex-wives called me loathsome. She's the first one saw me as I am." He sighed, and his blue eyes took on a tender light. Then he scowled. "Her husband don't love her. He just married her to get a good job from her father."

"So you followed him to the Phlemm Building this afternoon, saw him finger along the directory until he came to my name and room number, then jogged upstairs, beating the elevator to the fifth floor. You scampered down the hall and hid in the men's room until Zittworth sauntered by, then flung yourself on him with intent to kill."

"Wrong. If I'd wanted to kill him, would I have used a one-inch blade?"

Slime remembered that Zittworth had said that it felt like a short blade.

"I just wanted to scare him. I thought that now he'd listen when I went to him and warned him he'd better divorce her."

"He won't. It would mean publicity, which her father hates."

"Well, it's not right. He's mean to her."

"Does he beat her?"

"No, he ignores her. He never says nice things, never pats her and calls her attractive."

"That could make a pretty woman feel rejected."

"How d'you think it makes an ugly fat one feel?"

"Is Trinket ugly?"

"Is the Pope Polish?"

"Yes," said Slime, who was aware of many events and persons outside his professional sphere.

"Ugly can be nice, if someone's so ugly you can't believe it." Precious gazed over Slime's head, and his eyes had that light again.

Slime reflected on how many people of specialized tastes seem to find their way to San Francisco.

Precious asked, "Am I under arrest?"

"Just don't leave town," Slime said and walked out, while the musicians tuned up and the young ladies jumped up and down.

He went to the phonebooth on the corner, opened the directory, and paged through the Zittworths until he located the name Folmer, the address of whom he noted, then he wedged onto a bus and arrived at the approaches to Pacific Heights. Large mansions make up that area of wealth and prestige. The detective walked from the bus to Vallejo Street, walked further, climbed marble steps, and rang a bell.

Krull opened the door, saw who it was, and tried to mash his foot.

Slime pushed the door open. The houseboy, cringing, moaned, "You've got that loaded magazine under your jacket!"

"No."

Zittworth appeared. He wore a purple smoking jacket and a strip of gauze on the knob on his forehead—also pants, shirt, and slippers.

Slime said, "I found Precious."

Krull scuttled away.

The executive said, "Come in the living room."

Slime did. It was a room full of high-style antiques, with a vast brick fireplace, a 25-foot-high beamed ceiling, mullioned windows, and some stone dogs. Zittworth told him to take a chair. Slime took one.

Zittworth took a different one and asked, "Did he confess?"

"Yes. He's in love with your wife."

"So that's why he tried to kill me."

"No. He just wanted to scare you, so you'd think about a divorce."

"Impossible."

"Next time he may get serious." The detective stroked his lean teeth and for the next several minutes ran the problem across the rugged corrugations of his brain. "Hire *him* as a houseboy."

Zittworth looked appalled. "You mean have this squalid affair go on right under my own nose?"

"To avoid publicity."

Zittworth looked less appalled. "I see. She wouldn't have to go to the Tickle-and-Tease to meet him, where some gossip columnist is bound to spot them one day and make old Spreek furious at me. Yes. But I already have a houseboy—Krull."

Slime was quiet. Love was involved here. Precious was wizened and not of sound mind but he clearly loved Trinket, who by Zittworth's own admission had nice hands. So if Precious moved in, things might get settled. Slime felt his job would not be complete until he had done all he could to keep his client from being stabbed again in seriousness.

After an interval, he said, "Fire Krull."

"What! Fire him? After he just rubbed Louisiana insect sauce on my stab wound and said incantations over it? How could I possibly?"

"Tell him, 'You're fired.' "

Zittworth looked thoughtful, then jumped up, strode to the door, and shouted, "Krull!"

Krull appeared. "What the hell d'*you* want?"

"You're fired."

The wastrel's face became tight and vengeful as he thrust it at Slime. "This is *your* work, ain't it?"

Slime nodded slowly. He never shrank from responsibility.

"I knew you were bad news from the start." Krull whirled back to his former employer. "I've had it! Don't try to talk me out of it—I'm going back to the bayous! The crocodiles are more understanding than folks in San Francisco!" He strutted out, bark sandals flopping defiantly.

Slime stood up. He felt things were almost wrapped up. "Call Precious at Tickle-and-Tease, where he bartends, and make your arrangements. He uses the name Luther Lounce. My bill for expenses will be in the mail."

"What does it come to?"

"A dollar eighty cents."

"What for?"

"Bus fare to Pacific Avenue, to here, and back downtown."

"You must enjoy buses." He walked Slime to the front door."You've been expensive, but my attorneys will figure a way to absorb it."

Slime walked back to the bus stop and waited. When the bus came, it was totally packed. People were climbing up on each other, battling for air.

The driver shoved the passenger nearest him, a lovely old lady on a cane, so that she hurtled into the cluster in the doorway, knocking Slime off the top step. "Take the next one!" the driver shouted.

Slime, getting off the pavement, inquired, "How long will it be?"

"Who knows? We strike in eight minutes!" The door slammed and the bus lurched away.

Slime started to walk. He thought of how the day had developed. He wondered how Precious would work out in his new job. Perhaps not well—and being of unsteady temper, he might lay for Zittworth with a longer blade. Or Trinket might get her head turned by a man even older and more wizened, and skip away, leaving bad publicity for Zittworth and a broken heart for Precious. And Krull might tumble into a bayou full of crocodiles hungry to understand.

Things don't always work out—all you can do is your best.

And he would make out his expense sheet for $1.20, not $1.80—even though Zittworth and his attorneys would have no way to prove that he had walked home.

Because that was part of his code—never cheat a client.

He was Slime.

Joan Aiken

The Black Cliffs

It was cold on the crossing, but calm; a sea nip in the air. Dark had fallen already by the time the two Americans boarded the ferry, but in spite of this they stayed on deck most of the way over to Rosslare, watching while the sky merged with the sea and then, by degrees, became pounced at irregular intervals by large brilliant white stars. Irving murmured this phrase aloud.

"*Pounced?*" Charley said. "What sort of crazy word's that, Irv? *Pounced* with stars? How can the sky be pounced with stars?"

"It comes from Latin," Irving answered absently, "Meaning to punch, or pierce with claws—from which you get pounce-work, decoration by perforations; it's the same word as puncture—which used to mean a sudden swoop with intent to seize."

"Hey, Irv, what a hell of a lot you know," Charley exclaimed admiringly. "A sudden swoop with intent to seize—like this, hey?"

And he grabbed his friend with rough, jocular affection.

"Watch out—you'll have us over the rail!" Irving cast a quick glance towards the open lounge door, where half a dozen other passengers were standing with their drinks, admiring the luminosity of the sky. If those people had not been there. . . The rail was not very high. But they *were* there; and Irving said to Charley, hardly troubling to keep the acid from his voice, "You'll have to remember not to be too demonstrative on the other side. The Irish may not like it."

"Oh, rats, Irv. Why ever not?"

"And *don't* call me *Irv.*"

Irving Christopher St. John his full and distinguished name was, lately dignified by the addition of Professor. He had discovered, also, that on this side of the Atlantic the surname became even more aristocratic by being pronounced Sinjun; he had determined to adopt this usage forthwith. He did not think he would be able to bear it if Charley persisted in referring to him as "My friend Irv Saint John."

"Sorry, Bimbo," Charley said humbly. "I'll try to remember."

A flitting shaft of light from the swinging door briefly outlined Charley's hopelessly plebeian, undistinguished face, the shiny balding brow, with a straw-colored wavy cowlick hopefully and thinly spread over it, the doglike pleading eyes fixed on those of his friend, who made so little attempt, these days, to conceal irritation and boredom.

"Oh, let's go and eat before those louts mop up every crumb of food on the boat."

Two coachloads of Irish sports fans were returning homewards from an international match at Wembley. They wore colored paper caps, sang and laughed uproariously, and had queued up ten deep for Guinness the moment the bar showed signs of opening. Now some of them were singing "In Dublin's Fair City," strewn like wreckage from a storm all over the lounge, while clumps of others moved purposefully in the direction of the cafeteria, clutching two glasses of drink apiece. Nothing but fish and chips remained by the time Irving and Charley joined the line at the counter.

It was like that all the way over—vomit in the lavatories, empty beer cans rolling about the floor. When the ferry berthed and passengers went down to the enclosed car-deck to drive off, there ensued an endless, claustrophobic wait, because some drunken sportsman was lost in oblivion, curled up sleeping off the chagrin of his team's defeat, and could not be found to shift his car from the foot of the ramp. Irving, at the wheel of their rented automobile in the stuffy, clanging cave, which vibrated furiously with the sound of motors being irritably revved and was humid with exhaust fumes, could have screamed with exasperation at the delay; one more interruption to his plan, he felt, and he might lose all control, go berserk, do something crazy and irremediable.

Just let us get to the west coast, he thought.

At last they were off, proceeding fast but cautiously through the misty Irish night.

"It's so late now, what's the point of stopping at a hotel?" Irving said. "We'd only get half the night we'd paid for, it would be a waste of money. Why don't we just travel straight on, across to the other side? The middle of Ireland's a bore, anyway, might as well get through it in the dark. I don't mind driving if you want to sleep."

Charley, of course, was perfectly agreeable to this plan, but insisted that he must do a stint as well.

"Anything you say, Irv. I'll take the first spell if you like."

"No, I'll do first spell. I'm wide awake now, don't feel as if I could ever sleep again. You take a nap."

"Sure? Certain sure? Okay—if you say so, Bimbo," Charley replied biddably, wound his seat back, and wrapped himself in the blanket they had brought with them. They planned to camp if the weather proved suitable; otherwise stay at farms, hotels, bed-and-breakfast places, whatever offered. The project was to see the sights of the west coast, make leisurely search for Irving's ancestors (supposed to have originated from a small town called Lismaley in County Clare), and then return at a relaxed pace towards Dublin, where Irving was shortly to commence on a year's exchange from Chicago University, teaching American literature at Trinity College. A pleasant, peaceful program; they had two weeks of leisure.

In the first place, Irving had not intended Charley to come to Dublin.

"I really think it would be better, Charley, if you didn't. A year's not so long. And it would be good for you to be on your own. Give you time to get down to some course of study."

Charley had simply not taken him seriously.

"Oh, come on, Bimbo, you've got to be kidding! Not come to Dublin? Are you crazy? Why, I'm living for the day. Want to see the Ould Country." (Charley's ancestors had come from Sweden.) "I won't be in your hair, though, pal. Don't you worry about little old Charley."

"But what will you do with yourself?"

"Don't you fret about old Chas. I'll find myself some job—soda jerk in a drugstore or sump'n."

"Chemist," Irving said irritably.

"Chemist, okay, or a laundromat, or any old thing. I can always find a job," Charley said with simple pride, and it was true, he could; prepared to turn his hand to anything, with a nonexistent threshold to boredom, he could work on a lathe, a production belt, mind babies, deliver groceries. Tolerant, good-tempered, dull, he was happy performing any task, however menial.

At one time this had seemed an asset; he was endlessly hard-working and useful, had painted Irving's apartment, spent hours sanding down furniture or pasting up wallpaper. Now all this dumb docility and refusal to take offense merely added to the aggravation.

A misty hunter's moon rose behind them. Irving drove on and on, his lips compressed. The road held no other traffic. For miles they passed no dwelling; untidy hedges, garlanded with late hay brushed from farm wagons, reeled by endlessly on either side.

Charley slept the sleep of the innocent. Mouth open, gently snoring, he lay childishly curled under the blanket, his heavy-boned frame utterly relaxed in the security of knowing that his friend was driving.

And Irving, brows knit, drove on through Wexford and County Cork and Limerick. Long obsessive analysis of his problem had not made its solution any plainer beyond a certain vague urge; he simply told himself over and over that he had to get rid of Charley. This stultification, this prison life, could not continue. He was not going to have his new colleagues in Dublin form their first impressions of him as Charley's friend, Charley's patron. In the hugeness of Chicago, okay; the chaos of such a city made all lives anonymous and therefore free. But he had sensed instantly on his preliminary visit to Dublin that here was a small, observant, bright-eyed, talkative community, ready to pounce on anybody's foibles, discuss them at length, and pronounce on them either with prudish disapproval or ribald indulgence. Irving could not stomach the prospect of either attitude. No, there had to be a clean break, and Charley must be brought to accept this.

Morning found them well across to the west. They breakfasted in Limerick, a grey, lively town, set about with spires of churches. Charley grumbled that he could not understand a word the Irish said, but Irving was delighted by their conversation and asked frequent questions in order to elicit the absurd, poetic torrent of speech that flowed so readily on any and every topic.

"Yerrah, sir! And is it the back end of Erin ye would be visiting? And how do ye ever hope to get to a little ramscramble place like Lismaley—and that from here, might I ask? I'd say it couldn't be done! Ye'd do better to remain in Limerick—faith, for all know 'tis the finest town in the west, and let ye enjoy yourselves while ye may!"

Despite this advice, by mid-morning they were off again, skirting the northern shores of the Shannon estuary. Beneath his preoccupations, Irving found himself enjoying this peaceful small country—the hazel and fuchsia hedges, the lonely silences, the weed-wrapped rocks by the shore, swans and gulls amiably competing on the tidal waters. But Charley's presence became more than ever an irritant.

How could I have borne his conversation for so long? Irving demanded of himself, listening in disgust to the sophomoric jokes, the inane comments on roadside objects, the pointless questions.

"Why are the Irish villages so poor-looking? Why don't they ever fix up their ruined churches—that must be the sixth we passed since lunch. Why aren't there any factories in Ireland?"

Charley was a hopeless map-reader, and signposts confused him; he could never be brought to understand the principle whereby a sign coupling two places that lay in diametrically opposite directions must indicate a fork in the road ahead. "But, Irv, how can it lead to *both* Dublin and Kilkee? Dublin's way over on the east, and Kilkee ought to be ahead of us."

In consequence they were continually lost and had to keep pulling up to study the map. Oh, for a companion who would understand this journey, Irving thought ragingly, and then asked himself what kind of a companion that would be? Some quiet, undemonstrative intelligence, somebody who knew the land and could expound it, not this vacuum of ignorance and ill-considered pawky humor.

"Gee, I'm hungry, I could eat a horse, Bimbo," Charley suddenly burst out in the late afternoon. "Aren't *you* hungry, Bimbo? What say we start looking for somewhere to stay the night?"

"Why didn't you suggest that in Killane?" Irving demanded coldly.

"Oh, no, Irv. That was a dismal hole. Not a decent-looking joint in the whole dump."

Irving had been rather taken by Killane, a mysterious little port, silent as death, not a human to be seen in the whole length of its immensely wide main street leading down to a couple of apparently disused warehouses. If he had not been so anxious to press on, he would have liked to investigate it further. But, like some migrating bird, he was feverishly anxious to continue, to keep moving, not to rest for a moment on the road, to reach the point where the land came to an abrupt stop.

"Well, there's plainly not much chance of finding a bed round *here*," he said.

Charley was driving and they were in the process of traversing an immense tract of brown peat-bog, from which the top layer had been cut out at intervals in black strips and piled up in black heaps—a desolate, gloomy stretch of country.

"What do they *want* with all that peat?" Charley wondered.

Another hour's driving brought them at length to a melancholy, strung-out, scattered village called Ballybaha: slate-roofed, one-storey houses behind fuchsia hedges, at long distances apart, with an occasional view of the ocean behind tufted sand-dunes in the distance.

"Who'd want to live here?" demanded Charley in disgust. "Why aren't there any pretty villages like we saw in England? Thatch? Tudor cottages?"

"The Irish were too poor," Irving pointed out. "They were living in mud huts when the English were building those Tudor cottages—and the Irish were paying them taxes. The only peasant artifacts left over from those times—the only things that didn't get worn out with constant use—are the things that fell into bogs."

Bogs! he suddenly thought. Why didn't they occur to me? But the summer had been a cold, unusually dry one; the bogs they crossed seemed baked into a substance like dark fruitcake. Besides, a bog is too indefinite, its embrace is incomplete; what it takes it may give back again. Whereas ahead, on ahead . . .

"There's a bed-and-breakfast place!" said Charley in triumph.

"Well? Will it do for you?" Irving coldly inquired.

"Oh, sure. Anything will do for *me*, you know that, Irv." Charley's placid humor was unimpaired. He ran the car off the road onto an earth patch in front of the largish bungalow whose sign announced *Inishkeen Guesthouse. Select bed and breakfast. Holiday accommodation.*

"*Select*—whatever can they mean by that, Bimbo?"

"Suitable for distinguished strangers such as ourselves. Give us the key and I'll get out the bags."

But Charley insisted on doing that—as he always did. Watching him, stooped, red-faced, with his head under the boot lid, Irving had a wild wish to leap back into the car and drive off, leaving him stranded in Ballybaha.

The quiet, genteel, sad lady who ran the Inishkeen Guesthouse received them without comment, and promised a meal at seven. "Till then, if ye should wish for a drink, they'll be glad to accommodate ye at the Anglers' Arms."

Accordingly, since the guesthouse bedroom was tiny and the lounge dismal, the two travelers later strolled along the usual wide, empty, dusty street to a dour-looking establishment by the crossroads in the middle of the village. On their way they were startled to observe, not far from the customary grey fragment of ecclesiastical ruin, a shatteringly avant-garde contemporary structure, apparently the modern church replacing the ruin. It was hexagonal in shape, low, presumably to hug the windswept ground, but with a curiously peaked and angled roof made of pink slate. It had narrow slit windows, like those of a frontier-post, and a short prong in the middle of the roof.

Like an aerial, Irving thought, to get in touch with the upper regions.

Charley said predicatably, "Hey, man, what a crazy building! Is that a *church?* Looks like those folded paper boats we used to make as kids—know what I mean?"

Irving did know, but said, "I never played with paper boats."

"Want to go have a look-see?"

"I'd sooner have a drink. It would be too dark to see much, anyway."

"Okay, Bimbo—you're right, as usual."

At such an early hour, they were the only drinkers in the bar and had all the white-haired landlord's friendly attention. Thomas Roche, his name was, he told them, and happy he was indeed to meet travelers from the other side of the Atlantic. To be sure, his own brother was in Boston and his cousin in Cleveland but he himself hadn't crossed the water, and what could he be bringing them? Charley, only an occasional drinker—he usually stuck to Coke—chose sherry, which looked appalling. Irving had whisky. Its fine dryness put heart into him, and he politely congratulated the landlord on the remarkable modern church, so unusual for such a small community. To their surprise, Mr. Roche's face darkened.

"Well ye may say it is a remarkable building, and the heart's blood of the whole village draining away into it, year after year!"

He was evidently bursting to talk about it, and a few questions brought out the whole story: how when the old church finally collapsed in a winter gale five years ago the priest, Father Hegarty, fetched down an architect all the way of the road from Dublin to give them an estimate—the architect was a friend of his, d'ye see?—and how this fine fellow, with a tongue as long as his yard-measure, managed to throw a spell over the whole congregation so that they believed him when he said that for twenty thousand he could build them the finest church in the west of Ireland. "Twenty thousand! Long will his soul weep in purgatory for that lie! Faith, you'd think they were all bewitched that believed him!"

"How many inhabitants in the village?"

"Three hundred, if that."

"So what happened?"

"So his lordship the Bishop accepted the plan and the work went forward. A grand job they were doing! Only it took three years longer than was estimated, and cost five times as much. And the troubles that ensued in the course of the building ye'd never credit! Twice the steeple fell down, till they were under the necessity of settling for the thing you see. Three times the foundations sank under them. Glory be, and them wondering if the church would ever be finished before Judgment Day! And when at last finished it was, what do you think? They found Father Hegarty's fine friend had forgotten to install any heating, so it all had to be pulled apart again."

"Is it really finished now?" asked Irving.

" 'Tis, 'tis, for what it's worth. And it barely sufficient in size now for all the summer visitors, and in wintertime the tremendous noise of clangs and rumblings made by the costly heating-system will often be drowning out Father Hegarty's voice—and yet for all of that, more often than not you can freeze half out of your skin before Mass is finished. And as for paying off the great debt that it has incurred on the village, we shall be waiting to do that until our children's children are bringing home their wages, and isn't that an iniquitous thing? What a burden to lay on the poor people!"

Mr. Roche's eyes flashed angrily. The two Americans began to understand that if Father Hegarty constituted the chief spiritual power in the village, Mr. Roche the innkeeper was his main temporal opponent. He went on, talking faster and faster, to tell them how the money was dragged out of the villagers in dribs and drabs for the church fund, how if this one sold a load of hay, or that one got a good price for a few fish, Father Hegarty would be round in a flash to demand an extra contribution. " 'Tis an imposition, so it is, are ye not in agreement with me?" .

Irving, who had begun to be bored by the topic some time back, said smoothly that indeed it did seem a great waste, but he believed they must be going back to the guesthouse now, for Mrs. Kelleher would have their supper waiting.

"Come back after, and I'll be telling ye more."

God forbid, Irving thought. He explained that they had to make up for a sleepless night, and they escaped. Charley, surprisingly, looked a little mulish.

"You didn't *want* to stay and hear him ranting on about the wrongs of the parishioners?" Irving asked when they were out in the wide, empty road.

"It was interesting. Those conniving monsters of priests really screw the people," Charley grumbled. "They have it all their own way—"

He pursued this theme all the way back to the guesthouse. Irving, with his chin on his chest and hands thrust into his pockets, paid little heed. Soon, now, he was thinking. And his mind expanded to embrace the image of the cliffs ahead, the Cliffs of Scath, where the land comes to a sudden stop, as if sheared off by a guillotine. Nine hundred feet of vertical black rock. The Great Wall of Thomond. That is the place. Tomorrow. Enough of this.

That night he slept uneasily, tossing from side to side in the narrow chilly bed; Charley, across the room, snored peacefully on his back, clenched fists flung above his head like a baby. Such rest as Irving had was broken by dreams: he was struggling to build a great stone tower, but lumps of rock kept coming loose in the gale that was blowing and thundered down menacingly around him. Then the whole tower began to sway from side to side overhead. He managed to wake himself just in time before the unstable structure fell and crushed him. Awake, he found that a real gale had blown up. How would that affect his intentions? All to the good, he decided vaguely—nobody goes sightseeing in a gale. And he fell at last into a heavy sleep.

When he woke he found Charley already up, shaving and whistling to himself. This habit of tuneless whistling, half under his breath, usually flung Irving into a frenzy of irritation, but today he was able to bear it, thinking: the last time.

After they had breakfasted and paid their bill, Charley insisted on walking along to inspect the new church.

"What's the point of that? You *know* all about it already." Irving was in a fever of impatience to be off.

"After all he said, I'd like to *see* it, Irv. Hell, you're always saying why don't I take an interest in things?"

"Interest in things that *matter*, for pete's sake!"

"Well, this matters to me," Charley said doggedly. Reluctantly, Irving accompanied him. By now the gale had blown out. Wet leaves, fuchsia twigs, and wisps of hay littered the ground; a heavy damp mist lay in the air. We shan't be able to see the Aran Isles, Irving thought regretfully.

In front of the church, they discovered a tall, black-robed figure, sweeping up the storm's debris from the cobbled approach path. This must be the wicked Father Hegarty, Irving thought, the despoiler of the people. It will be interesting to see how Charley deals with him.

Straightening from his task, the priest gave them an assessing glance and a polite smile. He was a strongly built man—in his forties perhaps—with a bland unreadable face and a pair of shrewd grey eyes, rather small, set close to his nose. He seemed very much at ease with himself, and who'd wonder, Irving thought. Look what he has achieved. It would be interesting to know, though, what official process brought him here; he looks such a capable man, wasted in this tiny parish. Don't they send priests to such remote spots for disciplinary reasons?

"Good morning, Father," he said. "We were impressed by your church last night and thought we'd like to take a closer look in daylight."

"You are welcome, the both of you." His eye swept over them.

What did he make of two such ill-assorted friends? Fidgety under the priest's intent scrutiny, Irving was glad to move inside the church and observe its expected banalities: the mock-Byzantine mosaics, angular Stations of the Cross, gaudy abstract window-glass, the jazzy geometric chandeliers, the concrete crucifix with its caricature of a Christ. There was a shrill, self-conscious air about the whole interior, he thought, like a girl with her first lipstick and cigarette, hoping to shock her mother.

And there was something else, too. Something out of proportion. Something strange, mocking, *wrong* . . .

Charley, needless to say, seemed highly impressed by it. Prowling about, looking at everything.

"Wow!" he muttered. "They sure got their money's worth, even if they did have to pay through the nose for it."

"It's a dreary, phony mess. And worse. There's something the matter with it. Let's get out of here."

Irving strode toward the door without attempting to conceal the disgust the place aroused in him. Regrettably, at this moment, the priest came in and, after saluting the altar, asked what they thought of the building.

"Very striking," Irving said. Father Hegarty gave him a quick glance.

Charley burst out, "It's a great building, sir—I'll say that for it! Only, be honest now—was it really worth squeezing all the dough out of those poor people for? Wouldn't a plain wooden drill-hall have

done just as well, and then the kids could use it on wet days for
volleyball or something?"

Irving wished he had been close enough to give Charley a kick.
But the priest was not in the least offended. Evidently quite accustomed to this criticism, he remained perfectly amiable and bland in
the discussion that followed, while Charley became more and more
impassioned. Irving, refusing to become involved, stood aside, smiling faintly with his brows raised, while Charley, as might have been
expected, soon found himself driven into a corner by Father Hegarty's trained powers of disputation.

"After all, what else would the people be spending their money
on? Is it not best to devote your wealth to the glory of God?"

There was something ironic about his smile.

"A few comforts—diversions—in this back-of-beyond spot," Charley muttered.

"And fifty years from now, what would remain of those same
comforts and pleasures? Who will remember that Mrs. O'Brien once
had a TV set? But this church will endure from generation to generation."

Will it? Irving wondered skeptically.

"Do you not think the builders of Chartres, of Burgos, of St. Peter's,
gave up a few comforts and pleasures in their day—and were jus-
tified by the result?"

"Oh, come on, Father, you can hardly compare—" Irving unwisely
put in, and received such a razor-keen sideways glance from the
small grey eyes that he fell silent. *And what in heaven's name was
that little thing on the priest's watchchain?*

Father Hegarty said smoothly, "We can only do our best and hope
it will meet the approval of future generations. And of our Lord. But
now, tell me about yourselves. I can see at once what you are—" He
allowed a fractionary pause and added, "You have the air of aca-
demics, am I not right?"

"Oh, sure, my pal's a professor," Charley said, again eager as a
friendly dog. "He's going to teach for a year at Dublin College—"

"Is that so now? From Chicago University? And ye'll be spending
a year in Dublin? Aren't you the lucky pair? And Professor St.
John—" Father Hegarty pronounced it Sinjun "—will be searching
for records of his forebears. That's very interesting. So we may hope
to see more of you in these parts?"

"Possibly," said Irving, forming a private resolve that he personally would never again set foot in the village of Ballybaha. Some-

thing in Father Hegarty's questions made him profoundly uncomfortable: a touch of slightly patronizing amusement, as if the priest were saying, "Don't think for a moment you can fool me—I have you taped."

But I have you taped, too, Irving thought.

"And now you must sign our visitors' book."

Charley immediately wrote his name and tucked a pound into the offertory box. Irving managed to avoid doing so, as Charley remarked naïvely, "You weren't offended by the argument, sir?"

"Indeed, no! It's always a pleasure to talk to visitors—though little enough time I have for it. And where are you off to now, may I ask?"

"Oh, we're going to Lismaley," Charley said. "But first Irv here wants to take in the Cliffs of Scath. Not me! I've no head for heights."

"Is that so? Well, I hope the visibility improves for you. The cliffs can be a grand sight. Now I must be off with myself—I've twenty or more calls to make. I cover as much as fifty miles in a day—"

He had walked them to the gate and nodded a courteous goodbye as he mounted his bicycle, which had been leaning against the churchyard wall, and rode away.

"Quite an okay guy, really, wasn't he?" Charley remarked.

Irving said coldly, "It's my opinion that he's a warlock."

"Always kidding, Irv." Charley guffawed and slapped his friend's shoulder.

Driving north along the coast, as the sea-mist came and went, they began from time to time to get glimpses of their objective. From the height of a headland, the panoramic vista of the curved coast ahead was interrupted by a thick black bar across the horizon abruptly cut off in the middle, like an arm ending in a clenched fist. A black arm.

"Good grief," Charley muttered, peering ahead. "And that's a *cliff?* How far is it now?"

"Oh, twenty miles maybe."

"Do we really have to go there, Irv? I never was too keen on the Empire State Building—"

"Certainly we have to go. Those cliffs are one of the outstanding features of the whole country."

"Well, okay. Hey," Charley said, reverting to a more cheerful topic, "that priest really wasn't a bad guy, was he? He didn't get mad because I disagreed with him."

"It's his job not to. Besides, he wanted your money. It wasn't in his interest to antagonize you."

"Yeah, I guess," Charley said slowly. "To him we were rich Yanks. He seemed to know all about professors' salaries in American universities, didn't he? D'you think he really has a cousin at Chicago University?"

"Oh, very likely. Irish families are huge."

"You should have given him a donation, Irv."

"Why? I'm not obliged to subscribe to his meretricious church."

"If you think it's got merit, why not subscribe?"

"*Meretricious,* Charley, means phony."

"Oh, really?"

Irving did not trouble to voice his real feelings about the building and its use.

Road signs in Gothic now began directing them to the Cliffs of Scath.

"I wonder what Scath means?" said Charley idly.

"She was the Queen of Darkness," Irving briefly replied.

Another half hour's driving brought them to the official car-park for the cliffs. It was, as Irving had hoped, empty; the weather had turned wet, and in any case the holiday season was over. The seaward end of the car park lay quite close to the edge of the cliff. An arrow indicated the gift-shop but Irving was pleased to see a sign had been pasted over it which said, "Closed for the winter."

"What say we have lunch before we look at the cliff?" Charley said. He was sweating slightly.

He ran a hand up over his smooth shiny forehead. "You know how I feel about high drops, Bimbo—I guess I could take it better on a hard-boiled egg."

"Hell, Charley! We wasted such a lot of time already cashing checks in that wretched little bank—"

"Please, Irv."

"All right."

At least, Irving thought, it would be for the last time.

The mist was too thick, damp, and cold for lunching on the grass. They sat uncomfortably in the car, munching the hard-boiled eggs and sodabread Mrs. Kelleher had put up for them. Irving's raging impatience nearly choked him. At any minute somebody might arrive and spoil his chance. Though in this weather it was not too probable.

For dessert Charley produced a couple of chocolate bars he had bought in the village—he had a childlike fondness for sweet things. "Want a bite, Irv? No? Sure?"

He had bought a Madeira cake, too, and hacked at it with a plastic knife purloined from the ferry cafeteria, grumbling, as he had all the way across Ireland, "Why in God's name, Irv, didn't you remind me to bring my Swiss army knife? That's what we need. This thing's no damn good."

That's another thing I shan't have to hear again, Irving thought detachedly.

He glanced down at the zigzags of the empty road leading up to the car park and said, "Come on, Charley—I think the mist's lifting a bit. We'll be able to see the Aran Islands in a minute. Put that stuff in the trunk and let's go."

Charley, rather slowly, rather reluctantly, packed the remains of the meal together into the plastic bag, walked round to the rear of the car, and raised the lid of the luggage compartment.

"Stick it well in between the bags," Irving said. "I can't stand loose milk bottles rolling around in the back while I'm driving."

He judged his moment carefully, as Charley began to withdraw his head and shoulders after obeying this order, and brought the trunk lid crashing down with all his force, so that the sharp edge took Charley exactly on the dome of his head, splitting it as if it had been one of the hard-boiled eggs they had just eaten.

Irving had ready a large polythene bag. With a quick glance round—still no car in view or audible—he slipped the bag over Charley's head and then, hoisting the body with difficulty—not far to take it, thank goodness—staggered to where the cliff-edge was barricaded off by a rampart of earth, reinforced all along by massive rock paving-slabs, set upright against it. Rolling Charley over this parapet was not too hard. In one spot it was only about three feet high—he had marked the best point while they were eating lunch. From there to the real brink was only the width of a narrow sheep track.

He thrust the body over and saw it recede to what seemed an infinite depth before it passed the curve of the cliff to vanish completely. The black, silky sea, visible from moment to moment in the mist, lay so far below that no sound, no splash, came back to him—even the sound of the waves was audible up here only as the faintest sigh.

Briskly, Irving dusted his hands on a clump of sea-thrift, stepped back over the earth-and-rock rampart, and walked across to the rented car. A wipe with a tissue and the boot lid—beaded over already with raindrops—showed no trace. The tissue could be burned later. What about Charley's bag? Should that follow its owner over the cliff? No, he decided; he would think of some other way to dispose of it.

He shut down the lid and, turning, was badly discomposed to see the black-robed figure of Father Hegarty walking slowly up the last section of the hill, wheeling his bicycle.

"Quite a stiff climb, that," the priest remarked, nodding backward toward the road behind him.

"Surely your pastoral visits don't bring you up here, Father?" Irving said, unsticking his tongue from the roof of his mouth. Where the *devil* had the man sprung from, so suddenly? Had he been concealed by one of the bends in the road? And what—if anything—could he have seen?

"No. But I have a couple of parishioners living not far inland from here. Once in a way I take a notion to come by and wonder at God's handiwork in this mighty place. Your visit put it in my mind to do so. Did it ever occur to you, I wonder now, to ask yourself where the rest of the cliff went?"

Irving echoed stupidly, "The rest of the cliff?"

"We see this great broken edge—like a sliced loaf. What did God do with the other half?"

"Could the Aran Islands be the bit that fell off?" Irving suggested vaguely, glancing out to sea. But the mist had thickened again—no islands were visible.

"And—speaking of the other half—where is your young friend? Not over the cliff, I trust?" Father Hegarty said playfully.

"Oh—" Irving had had time to take breath now, and felt calmer. "We decided to go different ways. He caught a bus."

"Is that so, now?" Father Hegarty's slow words and cold glance were like a bowlful of icy sea mist between the shoulderblades. The priest added with seeming irrelevance, "Since I am so lucky as to meet you again, might I mention that, back there in the church, you perhaps forgot to give us a donation for our church fund? Your young friend was so generous that I am sure it was nothing more than forgetfulness on your part—"

"Oh, right—I believe I did forget. Sure—a couple of pounds. Naturally I'd be glad—"

Irving dug with wet, shaking hands in his back pocket.

"*Well*, now—I was thinking of something more in the nature of a regular subscription," Father Hegarty said gravely. "We won't trouble about the details at present—I'll be in touch with you later. You need not give me your Dublin address—I've a cousin in the English department at Trinity. I'll tell him to look you up. A fine young fellow he is—you'll take to him, I'm sure. Bless me! look at the time—I must be getting on with my visits."

And, throwing a leg over his bicycle, the priest rode off downhill, disappearing into the mist as silently as if he had flown away on black wings.

Stephen Wasylyk

The Exoneration of Phineas Droogan

Enjoying the sun in their deck chairs on the broad patio in front of the Golden Age Retirement Center, Inc., Morley and Bakov surveyed the lazily moving traffic—the thin Morley content after a substantial breakfast, rotund Bakov morose over the small dish of oatmeal laced with skim milk thrust upon him by the dietitian.

Morley sat upright suddenly, his wild grey hair standing out from his head as though in fright. "What can be wrong with Mr. Droogan?"

Bakov grumbled while scratching gently at his bald pate. "What can be wrong with anyone at this hour? It is the breakfast. I have said many times that breakfast is the most important—"

Morley jabbed an impatient finger. "Look, Bakov."

A blue-uniformed, barrel-chested, middle-aged man with tightly curled hair and a fiercely hooked nose was slinking along the tall wrought-iron fence that surrounded the center, his face carefully averted from passing traffic and pedestrians. At the gate, he looked around and, as though he had made a sudden decision, hurried up the driveway, spotted the pair on the patio, and cut across the lawn, casting glances over his shoulder like a man being hotly pursued.

He leaned close and in a trembling whisper, informed them, "You have to hide me! The police are after me!"

The street was calm. A police car passed slowly, its occupants obviously scanning the pedestrians. Morley took his arm. "Come."

He quickly led him through the broad doors of the center and out the back door, his loose, gaily patterned Hawaiian shirt whipped like a pennant by the speed of his passage. After a moment's hesitation, Bakov followed.

At the rear of the center, Morley found a secluded bench in the parklike rear grounds and the three settled down.

Droogan pulled out a handkerchief and dabbed at his face.

"Tell us of this terrible trouble," said Morley soothingly.

"They say I killed the manager of the apartment building."

Phineas Droogan was one of the daytime security men at a large apartment complex down the street, always willing to pass the time in idle conversation with Morley and Bakov as they passed on their daily walk. A healthy friendship had grown between the three.

Morley shook his head in disbelief. "Why do they say such a thing?"

Droogan buried his face in his hands, his voice hollow. "I was just reporting for duty, coming down the corridor to check in, when I heard what seemed to be a gunshot. I didn't know where it had come from, so I stood for a minute, trying to figure out what was going on. I heard nothing else, so I continued to the manager's office. The door was slightly open, and when I pushed it wide, I could smell gunpowder. The door to the inner office was open, too, and through it I could see the manager's feet sticking out from behind the desk. I ran in. Someone had shot him in the chest. There was a .38 by his side. Like a fool, I picked it up.

"I was just going to call the police when one of the tenants came in. She stood there in the doorway, screaming, '*He's killed him, he's killed the manager!*' I panicked. If *she* thought I'd killed him so would everyone else. I dropped the gun and ran."

"That was very foolish," said Morley. "You should have waited for the police and explained."

"Oh, sure—explained what? There I was with the gun in my hand, only seconds after the man was shot? My fingerprints on it? Try to explain that, especially since everyone knew the manager and I weren't on the best of terms and he'd chewed me out yesterday and threatened to fire me. And that woman screaming! That was enough to scramble anyone's brains. I tell you, I could see her on the witness stand swearing she saw me do it."

"It could happen to anyone," said Morley understandingly. "But now that this panic has left your brain, you must go to the police and tell them what happened."

"What *did* happen?" demanded Droogan. "What can I tell them? Can I say I saw a man running down the hall after I heard the shot? Can I give them a description of the person who really killed the manager? I can't do that. I didn't see anyone come out of that office—and if *I* didn't, neither did anyone else. Don't you understand? I was the only one there!"

"That is not true," said Morley. "The murderer was there."

"Fat lot of good that will do me. They'll ask, where did he go? He sure wasn't in the office when I got there! I tell you, the only thing I can do is hide out for a few days and then leave town!"

"Where will you go?"

"It makes no difference, as long as I don't go to jail, which is where I'll end up if the police find me."

"You will be a fugitive," said Bakov. "It is not a good thing to be a fugitive. I have seen this on television many times. Fugitives do not have a happy time."

"Neither do prisoners," said Droogan.

Morley rose and began to pace the graveled path, his hands clasped behind his back. "You cannot be a fugitive when you are not guilty. That is not right. We must find a way to convince the police that you did not do this terrible thing. If you do not wish to go to the police and explain, we will do so. We will talk to Lieutenant Hook, who is a detective person. He will listen to us."

Bakov snorted. "He has never yet listened to anything we have told him. Why should he listen now?"

"If he does not listen, then *we* will find the murderer."

Bakov sighed. "Always it is the same." He mimicked Morley's thin voice. "*We will find the murderer.* Someday the murderer will find us and there will be two vacancies at the Center."

"We are seventy-five years old, Bakov. Is it not time to live dangerously?"

"With three wives, I have already lived dangerously enough," said Bakov.

They left Droogan on the bench. In the secluded surroundings, the police would not spot him, nor would anyone bother him. New faces constantly appeared at the Center, both among residents and visitors, and if anyone should ask he was merely waiting for Morley and Bakov to return from their walk.

At the apartment house several blocks down the street, police activity was still in evidence. Several patrol cars were parked at the curb and a blue-uniformed mountain now stood with the regular guard.

Morley wasted no time. He marched up to the mountain. "We wish to see Lieutenant Hook. We have evidence of this terrible crime."

The mountain looked down at him. "You live here, Pop?"

"We live at the Golden Age Retirement Center."

"Then go back and relax. Lieutenant Hook isn't handling this. He's over with another one two blocks away. I don't think the detective in charge wants to be bothered by anyone who wasn't on the scene."

"We have evidence he would like to hear," Morley said mildly, "but of course if you do not wish to tell him this, then you can always make a living as a wrestler on the television after you are dismissed from the police force."

The policeman's eyes narrowed. "You really know something about this?"

"If we did not, we would be sitting in our chairs in the sun, waiting for the midmorning tea and little cakes," said Bakov ruefully.

"Well, Sergeant Kerry is in charge of the investigation. You'll find her down the hall at the manager's office."

Morley's eyebrows rose. "Her?"

"It is the equal rights," said Bakov. "Can a woman not be a detective person also? They are good at asking questions, especially my second wife. If that was all that was required, she would have been chief of the police."

They proceeded down a cavernous hallway to a group of men clustered before a door, some of them in uniform.

"We're looking for Sergeant Kerry," said Morley.

One of the men jerked his thumb inside.

In a small anteroom, a slight, dark-haired young woman in a severely tailored suit was talking on the phone. When she finished, she smiled at them. "Can I help you?"

"She is too pretty to be a detective person," whispered Bakov.

"We are Morley and Bakov from the Golden Age Retirement Center, Inc.," said Morley. "We have information about this terrible crime."

"What sort of information?"

"Is it true you're looking for Mr. Droogan, the security guard who always watches at the front door for evil persons?"

She blinked once. "We'd certainly like to talk to him," she said carefully. "Do you know where he is?"

"We know. Mr. Droogan has come to us to tell us he is innocent."

"Then why did he run?"

"The screaming woman upset him," said Bakov. "A screaming woman can upset anyone, even someone as fierce-looking as Mr. Droogan."

"You realize, of course, that it is your duty as citizens to tell me where I can find Mr. Droogan, otherwise you open yourself to a charge of aiding and abetting a fugitive. We want him for questioning and it would be best if he turned himself in immediately."

"He is afraid you will place him in jail," said Bakov.

"Mr. Droogan's civil rights will be protected and he will be treated fairly."

"Mr. Droogan is protecting his own civil rights," said Bakov. "He is hiding, which is often better than being in jail."

"Tell me," said Morley, "do you look only for Mr. Droogan or for someone else also?"

"Our investigation is continuing." She was becoming impatient. "Where is Mr. Droogan?"

"We cannot tell you," said Morley. "We cannot be the stool pigeons."

Red tinged her cheeks. "Don't you realize you can get into trouble withholding this information? This is very serious. *You* can go to jail."

Morley folded his arms across his chest. "If that is the way it must be, then let it. But it will not look good in the newspapers or on the television news that two old men came to tell you that a man is innocent and you have arrested them."

"Where is Mr. Droogan?"

Bakov glanced nervously at Morley. "She yells almost as loudly as Lieutenant Hook. It is obvious that to be a detective person, one must be able to yell good. Perhaps she will really arrest us."

"What does it matter?"

"They do not serve tea and little cakes in jail," said Bakov.

"You'll get bread and water!" snapped Sergeant Kerry.

Morley smiled. "That is what the dietitian person wishes Bakov to eat. When she learns of this she will be very happy."

The sergeant held her temples as though she had a sudden headache. "What will it take to get you to tell me where I can find Mr. Droogan?"

"Only that you will promise to look for the real murderer."

A man appeared in the doorway and beckoned to the sergeant. Almost gratefully, she stepped forward to talk to him, holding up a palm to Morley and Bakov. "You two stay right here until I get back."

Morley edged toward the door of the inner office. The office was somewhat larger than the one they had been in, a wide desk facing the doorway, heavy draperies covering the entire wall behind it.

"What are you doing?" whispered Bakov.

"How can we save Mr. Droogan if we do not look at the scene of the crime?"

Bakov held back. "Do you think the murderer is in there?"

"Will the clues be outside on the sidewalk?" asked Morley testily.

Bakov glanced around uneasily. "I do not like to say this, Morley, but if there is only one door and Mr. Droogan saw no one run from the office, then how could there be someone?"

"Mr. Droogan said he waited when he heard the shot. Perhaps he waited just long enough for the man to escape."

"But Mr. Droogan was in the hall. Surely he would have seen him."

"Perhaps it was not a him." Morley began to pace the office. "Perhaps it was the screaming woman, who hid and only pretended she was entering the office."

"That is a good thought, Morley, but where would she hide?"

"There!" Morley triumphantly pointed at a closed door. He swung it open. All the closet contained was stacks of stationery on shelves and several coat hooks. There was ample room for someone to hide.

"Aha," said Morley. "That is the answer. The screaming woman is the murderer."

Sergeant Kerry returned.

"We have solved the problem for you," Morley announced pompously. "Since Mr. Droogan is not the murderer, only one other can be."

"That's very interesting," she said. "Who do you have in mind?" A young man who had returned to the office with her looked at them blankly through gold rimmed spectacles.

"It was the screaming woman," said Morley. "It is obvious."

"The screaming woman?" asked the young man.

"He must be referring to Mrs. Stettler, the woman who saw Droogan with the gun in his hand and screamed," Sergeant Kerry explained.

"That is utter nonsense," said the young man.

Morley looked at him as though he had proposed cancelling Social Security. "Who are you?"

"This is Mr. Wesley, the assistant manager," said Sergeant Kerry.

"It is not nonsense, Mr. Assistant Manager," said Morley. "See for yourself how she accomplished this terrible thing. After she shot the manager in his office, she hid in the closet. Mr. Droogan came in and discovered the murder. She stepped out of the closet and began to scream, as though she had just entered. It must be this way, since Mr. Droogan saw no one but her, and if *he* did not kill the manager who else is there?"

Sergeant Kerry glanced at Wesley. "What do you know of Mrs. Stettler?"

"She is one of our most pleasant tenants," said Wesley indignantly.

"Could she possibly have had any reason to wish the manager dead?"

Wesley hesitated. "Perhaps you'd better ask her," he said slowly.

"Aha," said Morley softly.

"I will," said Sergeant Kerry. She went to the door and spoke to one of the uniformed men.

When she returned, she eyed Morley and Bakov coldly. "I still want to know where Mr. Droogan is."

"We will tell you once you have the real murderer," said Morley.

"That is true," said Bakov. "Once you have the real murderer, it will not be necessary for Mr. Droogan to be a fugitive."

A few minutes later, a middle-aged woman stepped through the door. She was tautly slim, her brassy blonde hair carefully arranged.

"She does not look like a murderer," Bakov whispered to Morley.

"Never yet has a murderer looked like a murderer," said Morley.

Mrs. Stettler glanced at them. "Who are these two old birds?"

Sergeant Kerry ignored that. "I'm sorry to bother you again, Mrs. Stettler, but I have a few more questions for you."

"Did you catch that crazy security man who shot the manager?" Mrs. Stettler asked, taking a chair.

"There seems to be some doubt that he did it."

"Of *course* he did it. I told you I saw him standing there with the gun in his hand!"

"How well did you know the manager?"

"Enough to know he was a pompous ass. I don't blame Droogan for shooting him. How anyone could stand working for him is beyond me."

"Am I to assume you didn't like him?"

"I'm only one of hundreds. He was a man who liked to throw his weight around."

"You had difficulties with him?"

She nodded. "He'd been promising to redecorate my apartment for months."

"And you were angry about that?"

"How many lies can a person take?"

"Tell me again where you were when you heard the shot."

"Getting off the elevator in the lobby."

Sergeant Kerry hesitated. "Are you sure?"

"Of course I'm sure! You can ask Mrs. Pidgen—she was with me."

"You didn't mention her before."

"I had no reason. She was in a hurry to get to work, so she continued out the front door while I came down the hall to the office."

Sergeant Kerry glanced significantly at Morley. "And you saw no one else?"

"Only crazy Droogan with the gun. I thought for a moment he'd shoot me, too, but he just ran past with a wild look on his face and went down the hall and out the door. A minute or two later, Mr. Wesley came in. He called you." Mrs. Stettler folded her arms. "Listen, what's this all about? Am I to go through life answering questions just because I happened to see a murder?"

"It's one of the penalties of modern society," murmured Sergeant Kerry. "That's all for now. But I may want to talk to you again."

"I hope not. Just catch Droogan and make him confess." Mrs. Stettler turned to Wesley. "I suppose this means another delay in getting my apartment redecorated?"

He looked uncomfortable. "That will be up to the new manager."

"I thought you'd take over."

He shook his head. "The decision is in the hands of the owner."

"Wouldn't you just know it?" Mrs. Stettler flounced out.

"Well, Mr. Morley," said Sergeant Kerry, "it's rather obvious that if she heard the shot while in the presence of a witness, she couldn't be your murderer."

"Then someone else hid in the closet," said Morley.

"And what happened to him? Mrs. Stettler was here, Mr. Wesley arrived shortly thereafter, and neither of them saw anyone. I'm afraid your effort to help Mr. Droogan, however well intentioned, has done more harm than good. It's becoming increasingly clear that only he could have been responsible, no matter what he chooses to tell you. Now, I demand to know where he is."

"We cannot tell you."

"Lieutenant Hook—" began Bakov.

"You know the lieutenant?" she asked.

"He's a good friend of ours," lied Morley.

"Then perhaps *he* can talk some sense into you," she said. "Ordinarily, I'd take you both in to see him, but since he's only a short distance away I'll send for him. You stay here. Don't leave this room or you'll be in as much trouble as your friend Droogan." She took a few steps, paused, and returned to close the door of the inner office. "And stay out of there. Do I make myself clear?"

Morley nodded. "How can anyone misunderstand?"

"And I am too hungry to go anywhere," said Bakov. "Always when I am a detective I miss the tea and little cakes at the Center in the morning. I do not know why we cannot be detectives in the afternoon."

She stationed a uniformed man at the door—a patrolman almost as huge as the one at the entrance. He grinned at them. "She's something, isn't she? Take my word for it, if she tells you to stay put, you'd better do it."

"Is she a good detective person?" asked Morley.

"She wouldn't be a sergeant if she wasn't."

"That may be so," said Morley, "but she is making a mistake. Mr. Droogan is not the murderer."

"Listen, I've been tuned in on what's going on, so let me tell you this. If I had a dime for every time I heard a guy say he's innocent and someone invisible did the killing, I'd be a rich man. Now you two sit down and take it easy. I'll be right outside in the hallway with an eye on the door, so if you have any ideas about leaving forget them."

Hands clasped behind his back, Morley began to pace the room again. "Do not stand, Bakov. One must think to solve a problem."

"How can I think when I am hungry?" demanded Bakov. "If she did not forbid us to leave, I would return to the Center."

"And can the answer be found there? Have I not told you the clues must be where the murder was committed? And where was this terrible murder committed?" He paused and pointed dramatically. "In there. So we must enter that office."

"We are not permitted," said Bakov. "You heard what the sergeant person said."

Morley waved a hand airily. "She meant only that we were not to go inside like a pair of curious people with nothing better to do. All things are permitted to investigators. How else can they investigate?"

He opened the door and stepped through, turning slowly and scanning the floor and walls as though the answer was written there.

Bakov fidgeted behind him. "I think we had better leave before she returns. We are in enough trouble."

"Do not worry, Bakov. Look and think. We must help Mr. Droogan.

Already she is sure he is the murderer. Surely he will be sent to jail because who will believe him when he tells what happened? Perhaps he was wise to run. It is as he said. One can see the screaming woman on the witness stand."

He resumed his pacing and studying. Bakov shrugged and joined him, carefully stepping around the chalked outline on the floor.

"Perhaps it would be better if we were to sit and think," he said.

"The walking keeps the blood moving and clears the brain, Bakov. All famous detectives walk when thinking."

"We are not famous detectives. A famous detective would not have thought the screaming woman was responsible."

"That was only a possibility, Bakov. One must explore all possibilities. It is not my fault that she was with the other woman who also heard the shot, although it would have been nice if she had been the evil person who shot the manager."

"But it means there remains only the unfortunate Mr. Droogan."

Morley's footsteps slowed and he stopped, his shoulders slumped. "That is true. To be honest, Bakov, I do not know what to do," he said. "If only two people were here and one is innocent, then the other must be guilty. I have examined the floors and the walls and the ceiling of this office and there are no clues here. Always before there were clues that the police did not see."

"Is it possible for Mr. Droogan to lie?"

"It is possible for anyone to lie. We have seen this many times. But I do not think Mr. Droogan would come to us if he did not tell the truth. He would simply run away and become a fugitive."

A heavy voice reverberated down the hall, curled the corner, penetrated both offices and reached their eardrums.

"Where are they?" it boomed. *"I told them last time that I'd put them both away if they interfered with the police again! This time I mean it! I don't care what the newsmen say! They get locked up!"*

Bakov's eyes rolled in panic. "It is Lieutenant Hook!"

Morley sighed and shook his head. "He is angry again. Perhaps this is not a good time to see him."

"No time is a good time to see Lieutenant Hook. If he is angry now, what will he be if he finds us in here where it is forbidden?"

"Then he will not find us. We will hide." Morley glanced around before parting the heavy draperies behind the desk. He blinked in surprise. Instead of the window he had been expecting, he was facing a pair of sliding glass doors that looked out over a brick patio with a swimming pool in the center, the wings of the apartment building looming on each side.

The voice in the outer office was loud and unbelieving. *"Where did they go?"*

"Aha," said Morley softly. He released the catch and slid a door open. "Come, Bakov."

He closed the door behind them, the latch clicking shut.

Beyond the patio and the swimming pool was a high wire fence, and on the other side of that a large paved parking lot.

"This is how the murderer escaped!" said Morley excitedly. "There remains only to see where he went!"

"Why did not the sergeant see this?"

"The sergeant looks only for Droogan. She has one murderer. Should she waste her time looking for another?" Morley shielded his eyes. "It would have been easy to go through the gate to the parking lot. Let us go ask the guard if he has seen anyone."

They quickly walked past the pool and through the gate in the fence to the small shack occuped by the parking-lot attendant, a blond young man moving to the music coming over a small radio.

"You have been here all morning?" asked Morley.

"Since seven, sir. What can I do for you?"

"Perhaps you saw a suspicious-looking man leave the apartment house and come through the gate."

"Not a single bod, sir. No one ever comes out that way unless they've been using the pool and it's too early for that. The tenants use those doors over there. One on each wing. See them?"

"Are you sure you saw no one?"

"No one."

Morley's shoulders slumped.

"The murderer has become invisible again," said Bakov.

"It is important—" Morley addressed the attendant, his voice desperate.

"I don't sleep on the job, man," said the attendant impatiently. "Someone gets through who has no business here and I'm in the unemployment line. The only people who get beyond this point without going through me are the delivery men with their trucks, and the guard at those doors takes care of them." He pointed at a side driveway that led from the parking lot to a pair of metal-sheathed doors not far from the glistening glass pair leading to the manager's office.

Slowly the slump left Morley's shoulders. His eyes gleamed as he surveyed the driveway and the blank, red-painted doors. "And is there always a guard there?"

"It's not necessary. The doors are always locked and can't be opened from the outside. The delivery men have to ring a bell. The guard comes to see what they want and stays with them until they make their delivery and go. Then he locks the door again and goes about his business."

"Aha!" said Morley loudly.

"Does this *aha* mean we are in more trouble?" asked Bakᴧv nervously.

"No, Bakov. It means we may yet save poor Mr. Droogan.

An angry shout assaulted the morning. A burly, bull-necked man, flanked by Sergeant Kerry and the assistant manager, stood on the patio.

Morley sighed. "It looks as though Lieutenant Hook has caught us, Bakov. Let us go."

They retraced their steps toward the manager's office, meeting the advancing trio by the swimming pool.

Hook shook a threatening finger. "All right. I told you. I warned you over and over, but you didn't listen. Now you're in real trouble."

"We are not in trouble," said Morley mildly. "The police are in trouble. They would have permitted a murderer to go free while trying to place poor Mr. Droogan in jail even though he is innocent."

"WHAT ARE YOU TALKING ABOUT?"

"We have come here to tell everyone Mr. Droogan did not commit this terrible crime, but no one believes us because no one saw another person. We have found the reason why no one saw that person. The murderer killed the poor manager, stepped through the drapes, and came out onto the patio. So no one saw him—not even Mr. Droogan, who was the first to arrive."

Hook's face acquired a purplish tinge as he looked at Sergeant Kerry. "Did you check that possibility?"

"I had no reason," she said quietly as Morley nudged Bakov in triumph, a pleased grin on his face. "After all, Mrs. Stettler saw Droogan with the gun and I had no cause to believe he wasn't guilty or that anyone else was involved. If Droogan had remained here and explained, I would have looked further. But if Mr. Morley is correct, the guard in the parking lot can give us a description."

"We have already asked," said Morley. "He saw no one." ·

"Then we're back to your invisible murderer," Sergeant Kerry said.

"He is invisible only because no one saw him," said Morley loftily. "That does not mean he was not here. If he did not flee through the gate of the parking lot, then he fled elsewhere."

"Where?" barked Hook.

Morley pointed at the metal-sheathed delivery doors. "There!"

"Nonsense," snapped Wesley. "Those doors can be opened from the outside only with a key."

"To you, everything I say is nonsense," said Morley quietly. "But to you I would only say who would have such a key and would wish the manager dead?"

All of them looked at Wesley.

He suddenly paled, his forehead beaded with perspiration. "I—" he began weakly, then desperately lowering his head, he charged past them, clearing all except Bakov. He collided with the heavy man, ricocheted, staggered, and fell into the pool. Bakov teetered on the edge, arms waving wildly as he attempted to regain his balance, and then, with an indignant yell, fell in after him, sending up a monstrous wave that soaked them all.

Hook slowly flicked water from his dripping clothes. "They've done it again," he said sadly.

Morley and Bakov, now thoroughly dried out, sat on their chairs on the porch at the Center, eyeing the growing volume of afternoon traffic.

"I think perhaps Lieutenant Hook was angry at Sergeant Kerry," said Bakov.

"It was not the sergeant's fault," said Morley grandly. "We had the advantage. We knew there was a third person, but she did not, so we looked for why this third person had not been seen. She had no reason to suspect anyone else, not even the assistant manager. Was he not the one who had called the police? She could not know of the bad way the manager treated him, as he treated everyone else. Or of the argument when he lost his head and killed the manager with his own gun. He knew someone would rush into the office, so he ran out the glass door to the delivery doors, which he opened with one of the keys only he and the manager were permitted. It was obvious that since the manager was dead, only he could open the door—which made him the murderer."

Bakov nodded. "Then he ran down the hall and entered the office again behind the screaming woman, thereby placing all the blame on poor Mr. Droogan. Well, at least Mr. Droogan will not now be a fugitive. He has gone back to his job with only a lecture from Lieutenant Hook for picking up the gun, which was a stupid thing to do. And it was nice for the screaming woman to apologize for thinking he was the murderer, even though now there is no one to redecorate her apartment until a new manager is hired."

A car swung into the U-shaped driveway, parked, and Sergeant Kerry emerged, now off duty and clad in a flowery dress that swirled and flowed as she walked toward them, carrying a large white box.

Morley sighed. "It is as I said. She is too pretty to be a detective person."

"Pretty or not," grumbled Bakov, "she already knows how to yell like one. Perhaps she is taking lessons from Lieutenant Hook."

The sergeant smiled at them as they rose. "You prevented me from making a serious mistake this morning, so to express my thanks I brought this for you. I had no idea what you might like until I remembered Mr. Bakov complaining that he was hungry."

She lifted the lid to reveal a large round cake covered with whipped cream and strawberries.

Bakov's eyes glistened. "Strawberry shortcake!"

"If you eat that, the dietitian will commit suicide," said Morley sternly.

Bakov hooked a generous scoop of whipped cream with a forefinger, popped it into his mouth, and sighed, his eyes closed in ecstasy.

"Then let us not wait," he said.

Percy Spurlark Parker

Lady with a Knife

Big Bull Benson, being six-six and weighing two hundred and seventy pounds, was used to chairs squeaking under his weight. The one in the small interrogation room sung its screeching song of strain as he leaned back, contemplating the questions Vern and Charlie had asked him concerning the body he found in the trunk of his car.

The police have a standard routine they use for their interrogations. The first cop that does the questioning will be hard as hell to deal with, not believing a word. The second one will be just the opposite, a candidate for the nicest guy in the world. The idea is that the person being questioned is so afraid of the first cop he's glad to tell all he knows to the second one.

Bull knew the good guy-bad guy routine, and he knew that in the case of the two black detectives in the room with him it was no act. Detective Sergeant Vernon Wonler really was a mellow dude and Detective Charlie Evans was a hard nose.

The one thing Bull had going for him during the question-and-answer session was that he and Vern had known each other for years. They had been kids together, did their fighting together and their ripping-off together. With that kind of background, he knew that what he told him, which was the truth, would be accepted as such.

Charlie was a different case. Charlie saw everything in fine lines. A dude was either for the law or against the law in Charlie's book. From the kids pitching pennies on the corner to the dude pulling a heist, they were all the same to Charlie, punks trying to make some fast bread.

"I guess that does it, Bull," Vern said. He was as tall as Bull but nearly a hundred pounds lighter. His face was long and rather thinnish, and a small stubble of a mustache underlined his flat nose. They were sitting at a metal table which served as the desk, while Charlie stood. "We'll get your statement typed and you can be on your way," Vern continued, writing in his notebook.

"Wait a damn minute," Charlie said, "don't tell me you believe all this joker's been tellin' ya?"

"Yes, I do," Vern said, looking up at him. "His story makes sense to me."

"Well, not to me it doesn't. I say he killed her and he should be locked up. The lieutenant will hear about this before ya let your buddy walk out of here."

"Yeah, go run to papa," Bull said. "Maybe he'll pat ya on the head and tell ya what a good boy you are."

Charlie's eyes narrowed and his mouth tightened. He seemed to hold the pose a long time before abruptly turning and stomping out of the room.

Bull laughed. He enjoyed bugging people who got wrapped up in their own self-importance and righteousness.

"Keep pushing him," Vern said, "and one day he's going to empty both his guns into you."

"Baby, if he even looks like he going for his guns I'll squash him." It was alley talk, he knew, a Bogart, a bluff, the type of retort that must be given to any challenge. He was too used to answering challenges for him to change, even though he was in the presence of a friend and he knew it wasn't necessary.

Vern was about to say something when the door opened and Charlie came back into the room with Lieutenant Hamilton.

"What is this Charlie's been telling me, Vern?" Hamilton asked. He was potbellied and bald except for thick grey sideburns and a few strands at the back of his head. Charlie stood behind Hamilton, a half smile on his puffy face.

"I don't believe we've got enough evidence to hold him, Lieutenant," Vern said. "There are too many things backing his story."

"Such as?"

Vern flipped back pages in his notebook. "Well, Bull claims he only saw the woman, Beth Robins, twice—first about ten last night when she was making a little commotion in his bar and he had to put her out, then this morning when he found her in the trunk of his car with the knife in her."

"Had to put her out?" Hamilton asked. "Bodily?" His white eyebrows raised somewhat.

"She was a little high and she wouldn't go nice," Bull said. "She even waved a knife at me."

"The lady had a knife?" Hamilton asked.

"It seems she was stood up," Vern said. "She'd been sitting in the bar for about two hours, knocking down the drinks pretty well. Then she started cursing and mumbling to herself about some dude not showing. Didn't mention any names. She pulled a knife and said something like if she caught up with him she'd cut him from here to next week. The bartender and a couple of other people who were in the bar at that time are down the hall giving statements.

"It figures that after Bull tossed her out, she must have met up with the boyfriend and they argued. Bloodstains were found on the pavement of the parking space behind the bar, where the murder took place. They probably stepped back there off the sidewalk so they could argue in private. Words got pretty heated, she pulled her knife, he took it and stabbed her in the heart with it. Then he hid the body in the trunk of Bull's car. Although no one who saw her knife at the bar can positively identify it as the murder weapon, no other knife was found at the scene. But there aren't any legible prints on the knife, so it's no help one way or the other."

Hamilton nodded. "How do you explain the body getting into the trunk of Mr. Benson's car?"

This, Bull knew, would be the rough part, the weakest point of the story. But he had discussed it with Vern. It was the only way it could have happened. No one had keys to the car but himself.

Vern looked at him and shrugged slightly. "It all centers around Jimmy Witken, Lieutenant. He's a kid Bull's got working for him. Bull brought some liquor in earlier last night and had Jimmy get it out of the car for him. Jimmy probably left the trunk open. He's always forgetting to close the lid tight. I've heard Bull get after him about it. He's also down the hall giving his statement."

Hamilton said nothing. His breathing was heavy, his lips pushed out. He was probably deciding if he could make a murder charge stick or if he should have Bull locked up for the hell of it anyway.

"I'll admit my supposition may be all wrong," Vern told him, "but we still have the lady's husband to contend with. Detectives Smith and Martinez checked out her apartment. They learned from the neighbors that she was married and her husband only returned from the Army a couple of weeks back. He wasn't home and no one could recall seeing him after he left the building about nine last night. Smith and Martinez are out checking out the place where she worked. Maybe they'll come up with something there."

"You just keep slipping by, don't you, Benson?" Hamilton said. "Well, it can't happen forever. Evans," he added, not looking around at Charlie, "you don't want to get something on this two-bit gambler any more than I do, but damn it, don't pull me out of my office unless you have more than this to sink him with." He paused, considering then looked at Vern. "Continue your investigation, Sergeant—keep me posted." He brushed out of the room.

Charlie stood a while, then, "I'll wait for you in the squad room," he finally told Vern, and he, too, left the room.

"Thanks," Bull said, "it's nice ta have a pal in the enemy camp."

"No thanks are needed, Bull. If that husband pops up clean, you'll still be hearing from Charlie and the lieutenant, but fast." Vern stood. "Come on, let's get your statement typed."

Jimmy Witken was coming down the hall as they left the interrogation room. Jimmy was a skinny kid of seventeen with a high natural that Bull envied. His hair just would not grow that long.

"Jimmy," he nodded. "Nice little mess we've got here, huh?"

"I'm awfully sorry, Bull," Jimmy said, wiping his face with his hand. "The whole thing was one big fouled-up accident. I'll never leave the trunk open again." He swallowed, looked down at the floor. "If I'm not fired, that is."

Bull laughed. "Naw, you're not fired, Jimmy. I always enjoy a run-in with Lieutenant Hamilton. Makes the day go faster."

Jimmy looked up. "How can I— I mean—"

"Forget it. Catch ya back at the place."

They shook hands, and Bull watched Jimmy as he walked down the hall.

"Talked him into going back to school yet?" Vern asked.

Bull nodded. "Just last week." Vern sensed a little pride in his tone as he said, "I told him he couldn't count on being lucky in life. He needs that diploma and he knows it. I'm not predicting big things for him, but he'll do better than a guy who owns a bar in a transient hotel."

It was another hour before he left the police station. Since his car had been impounded, he hailed a cab and headed for Springer's Gym. He had learned in the past that the best way to get Charlie and Hamilton off his back was to prove them wrong. He couldn't do it by going back to his lounge and playing with the cash register, he had to do it by finding the dude that killed Beth Robins. He'd found out from Vern that she worked at Springer's Gym, so that was where he was going to start looking.

He found Sid Springer on the second and top floor of the gym. He was watching a couple of young gladiators have it out in ring number four. The joint reeked with the sweat of its customers, the liniments they used, and the smoke from different tobaccos. The noises were

loud—grunts, groans, fists hitting punching bags, managers shouting to their boys. Bull had made some easy hustles in places like
this in earlier days. There had always been a game of some kind he
could get together.

"Try something good for a change," he said, offering Springer one
of his cigars.

Springer was a grey-haired little white dude who had gained some
weight around the middle since Bull had seen him last. Springer
spat out the nub of a cigar he was smoking and took the one offered.
"I sort of expected to see you after the cops came by. Damn, who
would have thought Beth would get herself killed?"

"Be's that way, Sid," he said, lighting Springer's cigar, then his
own. He looked around the place. "Business seems good."

Springer puffed on the cigar, took it out of his mouth, and rolled
it between his fingers. "I'm getting along—and from the taste of this
stogy you ain't doing too bad yourself."

"Naw, I'm barely making it, Sid. I'm still driving a two-year-old
Caddy."

They both laughed.

"Well, maybe I can say the same thing soon. That's my boy in the
light trunks. Frank Langley. That name's going to mean something
someday. He's got a lot of style and some good solid punches. Took
his two pro bouts on knockouts."

To Bull, Langley seemed too beefy to be graceful, and his movements in the ring were not the greatest. His thick eyebrows and
mustache gave him a sort of sinister appearance. Maybe he'd frightened his opponents into submission. "Let me know when his next
match is. I'd like to catch it." He took a drag on his cigar. "This
Robins doll, who was she playin' with while her old man was in the
Army?"

Springer shrugged. "Like I told the cops, I don't know. If it was
anybody around here she kept it quiet."

"Doesn't sound like the Sid I use to know."

Springer shrugged. "So I'm getting old."

"You know, they got this thing on my neck, Sid. Are you running
it down to me straight?"

"Sure I am," he said. "As far as I know, she didn't give anybody
around here a tumble." He shrugged in a cloud of cigar smoke. "You
still don't believe me? Wait a minute." He looked around the gym,
called out to someone.

The only best word to describe the stud that came over was "handsome." He was wearing boxer's trunks and a pair of light training gloves. Someone should hire him for an "after" picture in a muscle-building ad.

"Buddy Jones, Bull Benson." Springer said. "He wants to know something about Beth, who she was going around with."

Buddy smiled, and his face was enhanced by the whiteness of his teeth. "That's a hell of a question, man. I'd like ta know that one maself. I tried everything I knew and she didn't come around. I don't usually get said no to."

Bull nodded. "I can believe that."

"Believe it all, mister," Langley said. "I guess every stud in the joint made some kind of pass, and she K.O.'d us all."

The same answer, in different forms, from different people—but the same answer. If there was some man in Beth Robins' life beside her husband, no one around the gym knew who it was—or they weren't telling.

Sam Devlin was behind the bar when Bull came in. His dark skin was drawn so tight about his skull, it made his eyes seem to bulge. Sam had been working last night when Bull had thrown the Robins woman out.

"Bull," Sam said, his voice containing a permanent hoarseness, "fella waitin' fa ya." He motioned to the other end of the bar.

The stud was finishing off a glass of beer when Bull sat on the stool next to him. He was high yellow, with a hook nose and a thick, shabby mustache. "I'm Benson—you wanted ta see me?"

The man set the beer mug down, looking at him through pale-grey eyes. "I'm George Robins, Beth's husband."

Play it cool, Bull thought. He couldn't let Robins know how surprised he was to see him. In the back of his mind, Bull had been nursing the idea that Robins had killed his lady. But Robins' showing up here didn't fit in with that idea.

"What can I do for you, Mr. Robins?"

"I just had a long talk with the cops," Robins said, glanced around, then continued in a lower tone. "One of the dudes there—Evans, I think his name is—doesn't seem too sure you're innocent."

"That chump's been on my case for years. If he could get away with locking me up for breathing, he'd do it," Bull said, noticing the redness around Robins' nose and eyes. He was not sure if it was due to drink or grief for his wife.

"I'm not interested in your personal battles, Benson," Robins said.

"I'm just putting you on notice. If I learn you killed Beth, you won't have to worry about standing trial."

"Who are you trying to impress? The last time I talked to the cops, you were under suspicion yourself."

"They know where I was last night, Benson," Robins said, getting off the stool and leaving a tip on the bar. "You can't turn this thing around. Just don't forget what I said." He walked out.

Bull walked the length of the bar, studying his back.

"How'd ya read him?" Sam asked.

"Hell, I don't know. If it wasn't Robins, we have to go with the boyfriend angle, and that hasn't turned up anything so far."

"Well, there was somethin' I didn't tell the cops," Sam said trying for a whisper. "Last night weren't the first time that Robins chick was in here. And she ain't been comin' alone."

"You know the dude?"

"Sure does," Sam said with a nod. "Fighter works out of Springer's Gym on the west side. Springer got him under contract. Frank Langley's the name."

"You sure?"

"Course I is, I caught his last fight. Got a mean pair of hands, that boy. You know him?"

"Yeah, I met him today."

"Hey, ya ain't mad or nuthin'?" Sam asked. "The only reason I didn't tell the cops was 'cause I wasn't sure if'n you wanted me ta or not."

"Forget it, Sam. Maybe things'll work out better this way. Think how Hamilton will look if I bring the killer in and drop him on his desk."

The locker rooms were on the first floor of the gym. He found Langley in one of the smaller compartments at the far end, sitting on the long bench that fronted the row of lockers. He was tying his shoes, dressed except for a yellow shirt that hung on an open locker door. He was alone, and luckily so for the type of conversation Bull was planning.

"You back again?" Langley asked as he reached for his shirt.

"Yeah, this time just to see you."

Langley smiled twice. The first was a quick little excursion, as though to see if his mouth would work that way. The second was much larger and longer-lasting. "Me? What for? Say, I know. You liked the way I was in the ring today. Want to get my contract away from Sid. I wish somebody would. He's got me tied up for ten years."

"I don't think ya have ta worry about fulfilling your contract. You'll get a hell of a lot more than ten years for murder."

Langley left his shirt unbuttoned. The smile was gone. His face went mean. "What're you trying to say?"

"A couple of things. Like the cops believe whoever was supposed to meet Beth Robins at my place last night killed her. Like I know you and her were going together."

Langley's right cross knocked Bull back onto a row of lockers. It came without warning, with what seemed little effort on Langley's part. And Langley rushed in to deliver more. A left hook to Bull's middle sent waves of pain throughout his stomach, but he managed a straight left jab that backed Langley off.

Langley came back on the balls of his feet, dancing, jabbing. Bull was able to block some of the stuff Langley threw, but the ones that slipped by were solid. Bull swung back, missing a left, landing a right. Langley countered, delivering a rough jolt just under the heart. Bull tried stepping back to give himself some room and take a couple of deep breaths, but he stepped into the bench, started to fall, and Langley was right in for the kill.

He fell willingly, forcing himself back onto the lockers. Then, using the lockers as a brace, he swung out before Langley could take advantage of his awkwardness. The punch landed at the corner of Langley's mouth, and he saw Langley's eyes cross from the impact, felt him give ground under the force of it.

There was no way of timing the fight, the end seemed too long in coming. When it was over, Bull felt the sting of a cut over his right eye, both his jaws were sore, and his stomach ached. But Langley was on the floor, propped against the locker door with blood coming from his nose and mouth. Bull knelt down beside him, used the tips of his fingers to tilt Langley's head up. "Okay, talk."

Langley blinked drunkenly. "I didn't kill *nobody*."

"Why the physical bit if you're so innocent?"

"I don't know," Langley said, rubbing his chin. "First thing I thought to do. I don't know what I was trying to prove. I didn't kill her, and that's the truth. I made a date with her for last night, sure, but I couldn't keep it. My wife wanted to go to a movie and I didn't have time to call Beth and tell her."

"You're lying to me, Langley."

"Naw, I'm not. Ask my wife, she'll tell you . . ."

Bull wasn't about to ask Langley's wife, but when he got back to his office he phoned Vern and told him what had happened.

"You should have called me when you found out about him."

"I know, but I'm calling ya now."

"Okay, okay, so we won't argue about minor details. Do you believe Langley's story?"

"I don't know, Vern. He was the boyfriend, and if he didn't do it who does that leave? Her old man?"

"Scratch him. He came by the office after you left. He was working last night, first day on a new job, and he got some overtime in."

"It doesn't make me look too good, does it, Vern?"

"Relax, I'll be able to keep Hamilton and Charlie off your tail a little longer. We just got to solve this thing in the meantime. I'll let you know if I turn up anything."

It was Bull's own question that stayed with him after he put the phone down. If Langley or Robins didn't do it, who did that leave? *Someone* had killed her. She hadn't climbed into the trunk of Bull's car by herself.

He was lighting a fresh cigar when Jimmy came into the office, broom and dustpan in his hands.

"Okay if I clean up in here now?" Jimmy asked.

"Yeah, sure," Bull said, getting the cigar lit real good and expelling the smoke.

"Have you heard anything more about the murder?" Jimmy asked, starting to sweep.

"Naw, don't worry yourself about it."

Jimmy stopped sweeping. "I'm not worrying so much, Bull. It just somehow seems all my fault."

"Don't think that way. So ya left the trunk open, so ya won't do it again."

"You've been really good about everything, Bull," Jimmy said, not looking at him. "I feel I let you down. The whole thing was just a big accident, anyway."

"You keep calling it an accident, Jimmy. Just what d'ya mean?"

Jimmy got wide-eyed. "Just that—that it— Nothing, Bull—nothing."

"You ain't leveling with me, Jimmy, I think I deserve at least that." Bull stood and came around the desk to face Jimmy.

Perspiration covered Jimmy's forehead. He licked his lips, started to say something, stopped, then started again. "It wasn't me, Bull. She did it herself. I was going out back to see if I'd closed the trunk.

She was out there by your car with a knife. Hell, everybody knows that big Caddy's yours. I guess she was out there to slice your tires, to get even with you for kicking her out of the place. I tried to stop her. She came at me, tripped, and fell on the blade." Jimmy was crying now, tears flowing freely. "I knew right away she was dead. Hell, I was scared," he blubbered. "I didn't know what to do."

"So ya dumped her in my car and got rid of your headache."

"I didn't mean to cause no trouble, Bull."

"Sure, sure." Bull felt his anger build. He thought of the rough time Charlie and Hamilton had given him, of the threat George Robins had made on his life, of the fight he'd had with Langley. No trouble? Hell, he could be in jail now, or dead maybe. He leaned forward. "Thanks for a fun day," he said, and then he swung.

It wasn't much of a punch, but enough to send Jimmy sprawling to the floor. An accident. All that damn trouble over an accident! He watched Jimmy for a while, letting the anger seep out, regaining his cool. Then he reached for the phone and started dialing his lawyer's number. Jimmy was going to need someone good to represent him.

Louis Weinstein

Lasting Impression

My boss, Harry Lubin, got me into the missing-persons business through his big family. I've never taken inventory, but he must have enough cousins and in-laws to fill the *Queen Mary*, lifeboats included. He phoned me on a Saturday morning in late August at 9:30 A.M., just when I was getting the hang of sleeping late.

He apologized but explained that his cousin, Monroe Schechter, needed help with a problem that couldn't wait. Monroe's twenty-year-old daughter Naomi had disappeared from home and the girl's mother was falling apart like cheesecake in boiling water. Monroe automatically called Harry, the official family consigliore, and also my unofficial press agent, who brags to anyone who will listen how his young jeweler, Lou Mandel, has solved a few mysteries.

"As a big favor, Lou," Harry pleaded, "see what you can do. Monroe has high blood-pressure and a nervous stomach, so it's hard for me to say no to him. His wife, Ruth, is even worse. She has double high blood-pressure, and also a terrible ticker—specialists throw up their hands, can't find out what's wrong, not to mention . . ."

"Enough of the medical history," I answered. "I'll give it a try."

"Good," Harry said. "I'll drive right over to pick you up. The Schechters live in Staten Island."

Half an hour later Harry picked me up in front of the non-ritzy East Side apartment house where I live with my folks. On the drive downtown and on the ferryboat ride he filled me in.

Monroe Schechter, builder of half the new houses on Staten Island, worked hard, followed sports, played a little cards, sipped a little schnapps. But his big love was golf, which he played every chance he got. His wife was an opera buff and an all-around worrier, especially about the state of her health. For her it was a slow week when she didn't come down with symptoms of Rocky Mountain spotted fever or some obscure import like Punjab anthrax. But, Harry assured me, she was healthy as a horse. The Schechters' twenty-four-year-old son Gilbert was carried as an expediter in the family business, which managed to flourish without benefit of Gilbert's unorthodox architectural ideas, such as sticking a fireplace next to the refrigerator. Gilbert was a physical-fitness nut but got most of his roadwork chasing girls and a good time.

Naomi, an archaeology major at all-girls Pascal College, also dug the great outdoors and sports—tennis, surfing, and, above all, running. An attractive, freckle-faced redhead, but no great brain. An unkind cousin once remarked that the grey matter in her skull would fit into a wren's egg without crowding the occupant. She was used to doing as she pleased. The girl thought nothing of jogging around Silver Lake at midnight or pedaling off to Vancouver at four in the morning. Once, in a ten-mile road race, she ran the last two miles barefoot and then couldn't stand up for two weeks because of blisters.

"Let me warn you in advance," Harry finished. "Expect anything from this family. Craziness, bickering, rudeness. With them, fighting is like breathing. They can't say good morning without insults."

A long, tree-lined driveway led up to the Schechters' two-story mansion. Off to one side of the driveway was a clay tennis court. On the other side was a swimming pool big enough for a whale orphanage. Right alongside the driveway stretched a big rectangle of well manicured lawn, a driving-range backstop at one end, a putting green at the other. There, a tall, beefy man stood hunched over in classic putting stance. He wore an H.G. Wells minor-villain-type moustache and was every inch the sportsman in light-blue slacks, a grass-green sportshirt, and a white cap. He uncoiled himself and hurried over to greet us.

"Harry—" he pumped Harry's hand "—you are the jewel of the family, always johnny on the spot comes trouble." He talked in a staccato voice. The look he gave me out of his staring brown eyes, as if he was examining a sample of wallpaper for defects, went right through me.

"So he's young," Harry headed him off. "Why so surprised? I told you he was."

"This young?" Monroe shook his head. "If this pisher can handle this, I'll eat a brick."

"You better start sharpening your teeth," Harry came back. "How is a kid fresh out of high school supposed to look?"

"This wasn't my idea, Mr. Schechter," I said. "If you don't like what you see, say the word and I'll leave right now."

"Have I ever steered you wrong?" Harry asked Monroe. "This kid is a crackerjack."

"I want a crackerjack, I go to a ballgame." Monroe shrugged at me. "But you're here already, so give it a shot. Just don't schlepp it out too long. I have a very important golf match this afternoon, the club championship . . . Come inside. We'll get started."

The living room, big enough to hold a circus, was crowded with nonmatching furniture and several hundred knicknacks. A little dumpling of a woman, wrapped in a heavy robe, was perched on the edge of a leather armchair. Reddish hair stood out like feathers above a handkerchief wound across her forehead. Her arms folded across her ample chest, she was rocking from side to side and moaning,

"My poor little Naomi, something terrible has happened to her. My maidele, my innocent little girl. Bandits have got her—kidnapers, like before."

"Stop the geshraying. You sound like a chicken laying an egg too big for the machinery. Lou Mandel is here, like the cavalry to the rescue. Lou comes highly recommended by Harry," Monroe said.

She gave me one quick look out of her pale-blue eyes and shifted her moaning into high gear,

"Look what they send me, a boychick, looks like out of the sixth grade. Now we'll never get her back. Any minute will come the ransom note."

Monroe aimed a healthy shout toward the back of the house. "Gilbert! Finish already the damned breakfast and come in here! We got serious business!"

A tall, muscular young guy slouched in. He wore faded, beltless blue jeans, a hairy chest, and no shoes. He had long dark wavy hair, brown eyes, and a sturdy but straight nose. He was working on a leaky fried-egg sandwich.

"Lou Mandel is here about Naomi," Monroe announced.

"What am I supposed to do? Applaud?" Gilbert said, licking butter and ketchup off his fingers.

"Naomi's missing and all this loafer who calls himself my son can think of is feeding his face. At his own funeral he'll stop for lunch."

"If I starve to death, will that get her home any faster?" Gilbert said. "What's all the excitement about? The cuckoo is probably off with that Hummer or some other nudnick, having a good time."

Gilbert, too, was a wallpaper inspector but by now I expected that. They all thought I was too young to be taken seriously. I'd made a mistake not growing a beard on the ferry ride.

"When does the children's hour begin?" Gilbert said.

"Right now," I said. "When was the last time any of you saw Naomi?"

"Tuesday," Ruth piped up. "In the middle of lunch she got a phone call. Ten minutes later she came flying down the stairs and ran out, saying she didn't know when she'd be back. But running is her middle name and usually she calls inside two days."

"Inside two days she can be in fifty places," Gilbert told me. "She flits around like Madame Butterfly. Take my word for it, nothing is happening to her that hasn't already happened a hundred times."

"Who wants to take your word?" Ruth said indignantly. "Your word is worth that." She snapped her fingers, a not very loud snap. "If you were her mother, you'd worry. If you were any kind of decent brother, you'd worry."

"Just mark my words," Gilbert said. "She'll be back in plenty of time to fly back to college with that Goldberg girl from Great Kills early Monday morning."

"The Goldberg girl from Great Kills?" Monroe said sarcastically. "Since when is Millie Goldberg the Goldberg girl from Great Kills, like you met her once on a street corner three years ago? You saw her last night, and the night before that, and you've got a tennis date this afternoon. Now all of a sudden Millie is that Goldberg girl from Great Kills."

"Has this girl heard from Naomi?" I asked.

"What a silly question," Ruth said. "If we heard from Millie about Naomi, would you be here?"

"That Goldberg girl has other things on her mind, like getting her hooks into Gilbert," Monroe said.

"Gilbert's such a prize?" Ruth went on. "Something's happened. A mother's heart knows." A few tears started to spill.

"You want a towel?" Monroe said. "That handkerchief's not big enough for the river you're crying."

"Get one, wrap it around your neck—a little bit tight," Ruth said.

"Is her car around?" I tried to get the conversation back on an even keel.

"In the shop, getting fixed. Transmission trouble," Monroe said.

"Maybe she took it out. Did you check with the garage?"

"You got hardness of hearing?" Monroe answered. "I told you—it's in the service station. They're waiting for a special part, won't get it for at least another week. Don't ask about her bike. That's here."

"What about money?" I asked.

"Enough to take her to Singapore and back. Credit cards galore.

She has plenty of money of her own, left her by my sister. And don't think she doesn't get a good allowance. Her mother can't refuse her anything."

"Listen to who's talking," Ruth said. "Mr. Mean in person, or maybe Slippery Sam, always slipping her extra money on the sly."

"I've got. Why shouldn't she have?" Monroe said.

"Mr. Schechter, could I have a look at her room?" I interrupted Round Three.

"If it'll make you happy," Monroe said. "But we looked, she didn't leave a note. Are your eyes better than mine? You think old people can't see? Ruth, stay here, try to get hold of yourself. Gilbert, you may as well go finish breakfast, that's all you're good for."

The bedroom, upstairs, was a big, bright room, windows on three sides. Not dirty, but messy. Bed rumpled. Clothes, shoes, books, magazines strewn around. A big blue pennant, the letter P in gold, hanging on one wall. Trophies and photos resting on an antique white dresser. Among the photos, her mother, father, and brother, and her with five or six different guys. Naomi was good-looking in a cute outdoors way. In one picture she was almost wearing a swim suit and was laughing up at a bruiser tall enough to be a Big Ten basketball center. In another she was in a tennis outfit and flashing teeth at another big brute modeling a sweater having a red letter P on it.

"You can see she has boy friends by the platoon, and without lifting a finger." Monroe sounded proud. "And why not? She has looks, a not bad personality, and, let's face it, a rich old man. She changes boy friends every few weeks, like socks."

"Anyone special right now? Special enough to elope with?"

"Naomi elope?" Monroe laughed. "Mandel, these are modern times. Since fifteen years old, she's independent as a cat. She wants to go off with a fellow, who's to stop her? But elope? Absolutely, positively, not a chance. First she wants to finish school, bum around some more, find a handy desert, dig up some skulls. Then she'll settle down, who knows with what kind of schmo, maybe a hurdler or flute player."

I picked up two valises. They were heavy. I asked, "How many suitcases does she take to school with her?"

"Two, like you see. She's all ready. For all I know, she never unpacked all summer."

I looked around. Skis, surfboard, tennis rackets piled in one corner.

Night table holding phone, white scratch pad, looseleaf phonebook. I nosed around the cluttered rolltop desk. In the center, airline schedules for the Boston area; books and notebooks stacked in one corner; an accumulation of mail, much of it unopened—bank and credit-card statements, bills from places like Saks and Bonwit Teller, a thick unopened envelope from an outfit called ELD, another thick envelope, opened, holding registration forms for the Pascal fall semester, postcards and letters, some unopened, almost all from boys. An international roster—along with the Willies, Rebels, Chucks, and Toms were the likes of Franz, Roberto, Bjorn, Pietro, even an Ivan. Flyers and catalogues from swank mail-order firms. Notices of this race and that event. Appeals from worthy causes, everything except the Save the Gnats Society. I sifted through the wastepaper basket. Junk mail only, no letters. In the drawers stuff like stamps, envelopes, paper clips, and pens, but nothing helpful.

I checked the backs of the photos for dates, places, or other identification.

"What can you tell me about this fellow?" I handed Monroe the shot of the varsity P guy. The back of this one had a recent date, July 14.

"Him?" Monroe's lips curled in disgust. "Saul Hummer? A good-for-nothing bummika, Naomi's house guest earlier this month. Hung around a week, playing tennis, swimming, fressing out of the refrigerator day and night, acting like he owned the place, was already a member of the family. I couldn't stand him. The nerve of him, saying tennis is a real game and golf is for old men. Buttering the girl up with sweet talk and her following him around like a puppy dog, just like she does with all the prizes she drags home. And you couldn't insult him. A very fresh guy, with big ideas, a gigolo looking to fall in soft. Who wouldn't jump at the chance to marry into the Schechter family?"

I kept my ideas about that to myself and asked, "What does the P stand for?"

"Paulson—ten miles from Pascal, near Boston."

"Has Hummer phoned here much lately?"

"How should I know? I'm not Naomi's social secretary. She has her own phone. Once in a blue moon someone who can't get Naomi at her number calls our number to ask where she is. I hope you're not thinking she really goes for Hummer. He's just another bum she met on the tennis court. She has a new boy friend every muntik and dunneshtick."

"So you think it's not possible Naomi found the one big love of her life and ran off and got married?"

"Young man," Monroe lectured me sternly, "open both your ears, listen to me carefully, I don't like to waste breath repeating. Get it through your thick skull: with my Naomi is no such creature as the one big love of her life."

"You ought to know," I said, but I wasn't really convinced. She hadn't taken her luggage with her, or her registration papers, so Pascal was out. If this Saul Hummer's clever tongue had turned the girl's head, why couldn't she have rushed off to join him somewhere, on an informal elopement, as Monroe himself suggested? She had to be with someone, and Hummer was the logical candidate.

Gilbert, looking worried, came hurrying in and said to his father, "You better go down to ma. She's carrying on something terrible, she thinks she's having an asthma attack. Maybe we ought to call Dr. Roth, he can give her something to make her feel better—like a big bill."

"I better go talk to her," Monroe said. "Asthma, that's a new one."

"Do you mind if I stay here and look around a little more?" I said.

"What's the matter, the boy genius hasn't figured it out yet?" Gilbert gave me a dig.

"Why not? Am I charging you rent?" Monroe answered me, then said to Gilbert, "Why can't you be a little nice? After all, Lou is trying. Not getting anywhere, but trying. You got nothing good to say, shut up."

"Okay," Gilbert said. "Mr. Mandel, please get a move on with your detectiving before the whole day is shot."

After they left I said to Harry, "I think I should have stood in bed."

I went to the night table and leafed through the phonebook. Hundreds of names, but not Saul Hummer's. I examined the plain white scratch pad, maybe eight-by-six inches. The bottom half of the top sheet had been torn off. There was no writing visible—another helping of nothing. The clothes closet revealed Naomi's sentimental side: letters, neatly filed in shoeboxes, and three big photo albums, heavy on photos of her with young lions. But the letters and photos pointed to no one particular guy. On Saul Hummer, I drew a blank.

"There's got to be something around here to tip us off to where that fruitcake went," Harry said.

"I agree. But what? Harry, you shouldn't have built me up to these people. I can do without their insults."

"It's embarrassing to me, too," Harry said. "They shouldn't expect instant miracles."

I had a thought. I went back to the scratch pad, held it up to the light, ran my fingers over it. All was not lost. I could feel indentations on the bottom half of the second sheet. Evidently she'd jotted something down with a ballpoint pen and torn off the bottom half of the top sheet. The missing piece was nowhere around, which probably meant she'd taken it with her. Some kind of information—a name, address, phone number, directions.

I took the pad to the desk and with my pocket knife shaved lead from a pencil point. I sprinkled a thin layer of the fine black dust over the bottom of the second sheet and rubbed the dust lightly across the marks left by the pen. The paper blackened glossily, except for the impressions, which remained white and were clearly legible.

I read the numbers, in large handwriting spread over two lines, aloud.

"74384498916

"3366175551735.

"Got any ideas what they mean?"

"A social-security number, the first line?" Harry, standing beside me, suggested hopefully. "A driver's license?"

I shook my head. I was copying the numbers on a clean sheet. Maybe studying them later, at home, I'd hit on the right interpretation.

"A phone number, the numbers all run together?"

"With so many digits, taking two lines?"

"An Army serial number? Auto-engine number? Bank-account number? Credit-card number? A model number of some kind? A code for something she ordered over the phone?"

"Don't beat your brains out, Harry," I said. "It's none of those things—and who says it would help find her if we could dope out what it is. We're licked. The girl could have been murdered, or killed in an accident, the body not found yet. The smart thing to do is notify the police or call in a big private-detective agency. Let's join the party downstairs, go face the music."

Downstairs, Ruth was now stretched out on a sofa, holding a handkerchief to her face and gasping between sobs. Monroe was hovering over her, a sour expression on his face. Gilbert had migrated to a TV set in a corner. He was munching from a jar of peanuts balanced on his lap as he watched a horror movie. Nasty, big-jawed villains were chasing fleeing maidens around a dimly lit castle. It looked great. If I'd been home I'd have been watching it myself.

"Well?" Monroe challenged me. "Just as I thought—amateur night. You came up with nothing."

"Sorry, Mr. Schechter," I said. "I did my best."

"If this is your best, I'd hate to see your worst," Gilbert got out through a mouthful of peanuts.

Monroe attacked again, his eyes glittering. "And now that your juvenile hot-shot has gotten the gong, what brilliant suggestions do you have now, Harry?"

"I suggest you call the police," I said.

"I need you to tell me that?" Monroe said.

"Monroe, if you don't mind my saying so, you're acting like a horse's ass." Harry was steaming. "Don't count Lou out yet. He's working on an idea."

"Gilbert," Monroe said, "you got a fancy education and a ton of opinions on how to run my home and my business. Let me hear your opinion on what we should do."

"My opinion is," Gilbert said, "you're all making so damned much noise I can't hear the program. Ma, give the dying-swan act back to Pavlova. Get up and go with the golf nut to his big tourney this afternoon. Naomi's a big girl, off on a fun trip. There's nothing to worry about. Make a moratorium on the carrying on."

"Who asked you to tell us when to worry, when not to worry?" Monroe said. "Who needs your opinion?"

"Come on, let's get out of this nuthouse." I tugged at Harry's arm.

"Sorry it didn't work out," Harry said to Monroe. "I hope you're not sore."

"I'm really sorry," I said.

"Sorries I don't need," Monroe said. "I'm a man understands one thing—results. How much do I owe you for your trouble?"

"Nothing," I said. "The experience was enough."

I wasn't exaggerating. It had made a lasting impression on me.

As we drove off, I studied the paper with the numbers.

"Do you think we should go back, Lou? Make some phone calls from the girl's book? Maybe call the school?"

"The school is closed now, and calling from her book would cost a fortune and take a week."

"Schechter has enough money to start his own phone company. Besides, making as many long-distance calls as she does, I'm sure Naomi uses a service that bypasses the regular long lines. Like SPRINT or ELD."

"SPRINT I know about. What's ELD?"

"Economy Long Distance," Harry said.

"That's it!" I yelled. The numbers made sense now. "ELD, there's a bill on her desk. Pull over there." I pointed to a shopping center up ahead. "I've got to make one phone call."

Harry pulled into a parking spot. "What's this all about?"

"An ELD number, the figures all run together—that's what threw us off. The last thing she wrote on the pad, just before she left the house."

"But why write the whole ELD megillah?"

"Who the hell knows? Does anything the Schechters do make sense? Maybe she was just doodling, keeping her fingers busy while she talked on the phone. Maybe she's compulsive."

Calling from a pay phone, only the last ten numbers counted, beginning with the Boston area code which I'd recognized. I fed coins into the slot and the number to the operator, and waited.

"Hello," a man's voice came on the line. A deep masculine voice, very cultured, impressive. Like a diplomat, or maybe a used-car hustler.

"You wouldn't by any chance be Saul Hummer?" I put on my deepest voice.

"I'm Saul Hummer. Who am I talking to? What can I do for you?" He was brisk, but wary.

"Maybe you can help me. It's very important I get in touch with Naomi Schechter. My name is Lou Mandel, and I represent the family. Her mother is concerned about not hearing from her. Is Naomi there with you?"

He hesitated before answering in a normal human voice.

"Well, they're bound to find out sooner or later. I've been begging her to call home. But she's very stubborn, afraid to break the news to them. She's afraid they'll have a fit."

"Is she there with you now?"

"She's here. Let me put her on."

I could hear him telling her, no, it wasn't her father but some detective, you better talk to him, he's figured out where you are.

"Yes," she came on. "This is Naomi. What is it you want?" She had a high-pitched, little girl's voice.

"My name is Lou Mandel. You don't know me. I called to ask you to do a favor."

"Why should I do you a favor?"

There it was, the old family touch.

"Not for me. For your folks, especially your mother. She's tearing her hair out worrying, thinks you got lost in a swamp. Phone her—just let her hear your voice. If you want, tell her where you are, all the good news."

"Okay," she said. "I knew I should have called but I didn't know how to tell her."

A bashful Schechter, at a loss for words? Incredible.

"That you changed schools, enrolled at Paulson? That you got married? What's wrong with that? Tell her, get it over with. Be smart."

"I was scared because I knew they'd want a big wedding," she said. "How would it look, the Schechters' only girl running off to elope like a common person? Besides, my father hates Saul."

"He'll get over that. Now, do me a favor. Look at your watch. Wait ten minutes, then make your call. Congratulations. Lots of luck."

She agreed to do as I asked.

Not for anything would I miss being around while the whole crummy Schechter bunch ate crow.

A few minutes later Harry and I were ringing the Schechters' doorbell. Gilbert answered, dressed now in a polo shirt and tennis sneakers.

"Aha." He gave me a mocking smile. "The return of Horatio Kimono, youthful Oriental detective."

"Never mind the wisecracks," I told him. "Stick around a few minutes and see what you have to say then."

In the living room nothing had changed. Ruth had the sob faucet going full blast. Monroe was still scowling disgustedly at her.

"Why'd you come back?" he asked me. "You forget something?"

"No," I said. "I remembered something. Sit down and wait a couple of minutes. Smoke a cigar. Have a drink. You're in for a big surprise."

"A big surprise?" He guffawed. "The only surprise from you can be you located Naomi. Harry, what's this clown up to?"

"Do as he says," Harry said. "Have a drink. You're going to need it. No hysterics, Ruth. It's not that kind of bad news."

They waited quietly until the phone rang. The phone was on an end-table next to the sofa where Ruth was lying. Gilbert and Monroe both jumped for it but Ruth catapulted off the sofa and beat them to it.

"Yes?" she said. "Naomi? You're all right, bubbala? You've got news for me? You're majoring in physical-ed now, no more archaeology? At Paulson, you switched schools? So what's so terrible about that, dear? The main thing is, you're safe. —Did I hear that right? You're married? Gevalt! I'm so happy. You're married to Saul? He's such a nice boy, so polite. Poppa will take him in the business. He'll build you a nice house, close by, you shouldn't be strangers.

"Does he like opera? No? So he'll learn. Soon as we can, we'll make arrangements for a nice big ceremony, you should be married in style. To please me you'll do it? Oh, I'm so happy. You want to talk to Poppa? No, just tell him the news and not to interfere? I'll do that—Poppa will understand. Goodbye, dear. Take care."

She started crying again, tears of happiness.

Monroe was still practicing his scowl and muttering, "That pascudniak, doing this behind my back. That scheming Casanova lowlife skunk."

Then his face brightened and he said, "At least now I can go play golf. The day is not a total loss."

"First cancel the doctor," Ruth said. "Why should I pay the robber for nothing? I'm going to the opera instead." Her recovery was complete.

She began to hum "One Fine Day" from *Madame Butterfly*.

"In case you want Naomi's phone number, here it is." I handed her the sheet I'd written it on.

"Thanks," she said. "Harry, this is a smart boychick, a real jewel. Just like you said, the cavalry to the rescue."

"Mrs. Schechter," I said seriously, "do you know why the cavalry always comes to the rescue at the last minute?"

"No," she said.

"Slow horses," I deadpanned.

"I knew there was nothing to worry about," Gilbert said, already heading for the front door. "I kept telling you what was what."

"You knew what you always know—when's payday and where's the kitchen," Monroe said. "Go play tennis with the Goldberg girl. Elope with her. See if I care."

"Not a bad idea," Gilbert said on the way out. "We're planning something *like* that, so don't expect me home for dinner."

"Now, Mr. Schechter—" I gave Monroe back one of his patented glassy stares "—I want your autograph on a check, and no chiseling when you mail it because I didn't go to school with Methuselah. First-class payment for first-class results is what I expect. Don't you want to know how I found out?"

"Who cares? It's not important." Monroe shrugged. "How did you find out?"

"She left the phone number on the pad next to the phone."

"Monroe," Harry couldn't resist getting in a lick, "how do you want the brick, with mustard or ketchup?"

"Horseradish," Monroe mumbled. I think it was horseradish he said.

Seicho Matsumoto

Just Eighteen Months

First, the facts of the case.

The defendant, Sumura Satoko, twenty-nine years of age. The crime, murdering her husband.

Satoko graduated from a women's college during the war and immediately went to work in a business firm. At one period during the war, companies everywhere were short of staff, the men having been taken into the forces, and large numbers of women were taken on as substitutes.

After the end of the war, the men who had been soldiers began to come back by degrees, and gradually women substitutes became unnecessary. In two years' time, all the women who had been employed during the war had been dismissed, Satoko among them.

While she was with the firm, however, she fell in love with a fellow-employee, Sumura Yokichi, and promptly married him. Three years older than Satoko, he had studied no further than middle school under the old education system and it was a kind of attraction for her superior learning that had made him woo her. As this may suggest, the young man had a certain weakness in his character, but Satoko herself was attracted by his approach.

For the next eight years, they lived together uneventfully as husband and wife. Two children, a boy and a girl, were born to them. Not having attended university, Yokichi was an ordinary clerk with little prospect of future promotion, but he was a steady worker. His salary was small, but they managed to live, and to save a little as well.

One year in the late Forties, however, bad business drove his firm to cut its staff, and Yokichi, who was not regarded as having any particular ability, was fired along with the old and decrepit.

He went to pieces. With the help of connections, he found jobs for short periods in two or three companies, but always the work did not suit him, or the pay was too low. In the end, Satoko had to go to work, too.

At first she worked collecting money for a bank, but the work was tiring and the commission infinitesimal, and soon she became a canvasser for a life-insurance company a woman she met on her rounds had told her about.

In the beginning the work didn't pay, but gradually she began to get results. The older woman who had introduced her to the company taught her the essentials of the job. Although she wasn't particularly beautiful, she had large eyes and her smile was charming. Her education, moreover, gave her an intellectual air. Her income went up to twelve and sometimes thirteen thousand yen a month.

Almost as if by arrangement, her husband Yokichi responded by becoming completely unemployed. Unfitted to do anything, he ended up with nothing to do and was forced to rely on Satoko's income. He loafed about the house, continually apologizing to her.

But Satoko's income was, of course, not a regular salary—only a small part of it was fixed, the larger part being commission. In months when business was bad, it was still pitifully small.

There was keen rivalry among the agents of insurance companies. The muddy waters of competition swirled into the remotest corners of the wide metropolis until it seemed the possibilities of breaking new ground in the city were exhausted. Satoko began to wonder whether, since Tokyo offered so few new prospects, there might not be some other paths worth exploring.

The place she eventually fixed on was a dam-construction site. The electric-power companies were busy developing new resources, and there was something of a rush in dam construction. The work was undertaken by the large civil-engineering contractors, and thousands of men—sometimes more than ten thousand—were working at each site. All of them were exposed to the risk of death or injury in work high up on the dam or in blasting with dynamite. The sites were usually in the mountains, where communications were poor and even the smarter insurance agents had not yet thought of venturing.

Here, Satoko invited another woman agent with whom she was on good terms to accompany her, and the two of them went to a construction site in the mountains of one of the prefectures near Tokyo. They paid their fares themselves.

Passing over the laborers—who went from one site to another with no fixed address—they approached the engineers, operators, mechanics, foremen, and others employed directly by the civil-engineering contractors. The men were already insured collectively for a certain amount, but they had first-hand acquaintance with the dangers they faced, and responded readily to the idea of increasing their coverage. Results were gratifying. The premiums were made payable yearly in lump sums, because of the difficulty of collecting them.

Satoko's discovery proved a success. Her income doubled, and for months in succession it was over thirty thousand yen. But as their life began to get easier, Yokichi grew correspondingly more idle. By nature dependent, he came now to rely on Satoko's income for everything. He lost all desire to find work, and lapsed more and more into a feckless frame of mind. He began to go on drinking sprees, something he had never done before. Since she was away so often, Satoko trusted him with the household expenses. He stole the money for drink—at first only a little at a time, but gradually, as their income increased, more and more boldly.

Satoko made certain allowances for him, because of the depressing life she felt he must lead alone at home while she was out. But she hated the childish, sneaking way in which he drank, as though he was afraid of her, and sometimes when she came home she herself would even suggest that he go out for a drink. At such times he would set off happily as if a weight had been lifted from his mind.

It was at this stage that he found himself a mistress.

In the light of what happened later, it was to a certain extent Satoko's own responsibility, since it was she who in effect introduced the woman to him.

One day she met a college classmate in the street. The friend, Wakita Shizuyo, had been widowed and had started a pub in Shibuya. She gave Satoko her card. In her college days she had been pretty, but now she was thin and worn almost beyond recognition, with a face like a fox. One could well imagine, from her appearance, what style of bar she had.

"I'll come and see you one of these days," Satoko had said as they parted.

Back home, Satoko told Yokichi about it.

"I must go there for a drink. If she's a friend of yours she may give me a break on the price," he said.

"Why don't you go and see," she replied. If he was going to drink at any rate, he might as well do Shizuyo a good turn, too.

Not long after, Yokichi went to Shizuyo's place and reported back to Satoko.

"It's so small only five or six customers can squeeze in. It's shabby, but the liquor isn't at all bad. She charged me less because of you."

"Really?" Satoko said. "I'm glad."

Satoko was at the dam for almost a week out of every month. When she became known there, people began to tell her of other construction sites. She went from one dam to another, with no gaps without work; and her income remained high.

She gave all the money to Yokichi to look after the house with. In their home, the positions of husband and wife had become totally reversed.

Yokichi's idleness became progressively worse, and the guileful expression he used when he was cheating her out of money to go drinking gave way in time to brazenness. When Satoko came home after work, the two children would be hungry and crying. He would go out in the daytime and stay out until late at night, when he would come back breathing alcoholic fumes over everybody.

More and more frequently, on the occasions when Satoko could contain herself no longer and reproached him, he would turn and shout back at her. "I'm your husband, not a maid!" he would bawl. "It's normal for a man to drink—stop putting on airs just because you're earning a little money!"

At first, she almost sympathized with him, thinking his anger arose from his humiliation, but in time she began to get angry herself, with the result that arguments between them increased. Almost as if out of spite, he would grab the money and come back late at night drunk. When she came back from work, she had her hands full getting the meals and seeing to the children. When work took her to the dam, she had to ask the neighbors to look after things in her absence.

It seemed scarcely possible that such brutality should have lain concealed in such a timid man. But day after day now, he would beat and kick her. Worst of all, they were driven to poverty by his extravagance. With an income of thirty thousand yen, they sometimes found it hard to pay for their rations of rice. The P.T.A. fees at the children's school and the payment for their school lunches got into arrears, and there was no money to buy new clothes. On top of this, Yokichi developed the habit of waking up the children and beating them when he got drunk.

A sympathetic acquaintance was moved to inform Satoko privately that Yokichi had a mistress. When she learned that it was Shizuyo, she was dumbfounded and outraged. She couldn't believe it, she told the acquaintance. She knew she must look a fool, but she kept her emotions under control, since that was the intelligent thing to do. The same respect for intelligence made her refrain from rushing to the other woman's place and starting a loud quarrel that would let all the neighbors know what was happening.

When she accused Yokichi in a quiet voice, he hurled back at her, "Shizuyo's a lot better than you! I'll be leaving you soon to marry her!"

One by one, he carried off the clothes in their chest-of-drawers and pawned them. When Satoko was out, he could do as he pleased. Finally, she was left without even a change of clothing. The money Yokichi received from pawning them he devoted, every penny of it, to the woman. They were driven to this pass within six months from the time he first met Shizuyo.

Satoko would often cry, convinced she was the unhappiest creature in the world. At night, worry about the children's future frequently kept her awake. Yet when morning came, she would bathe her swollen eyelids in cold water and go about her canvassing with a forced smile on her face.

One cold February night, she was sitting weeping by the children as they slept. There had been no sign of Yokichi since she returned home from work. Father had gone out in the late afternoon, the children had told her.

It was closer to one o'clock than midnight when he came back and banged at the front door. The house had only two small rooms. The *tatami* mats were worn, and she had patched them in places with cardboard. She walked across these *tatami* now, stepped down into the hall, and opened the door.

For what happened next, let us refer to her own evidence.

"My husband was dead drunk. His eyes were staring and his face was pale. Seeing that I was weeping, he sat down by the children's bed and began to abuse me.

" 'What are you blubbering about? You're making yourself cry to spite me, I suppose, just because I'm home late.'

"I told him I didn't know how he had the face to come back drunk every night after spending more than half the income I worked so hard to earn on drink. I couldn't pay the children's school fees and had a problem even finding the money for the rice ration. We always argued like this. That night, though, he seemed further gone than usual.

"He began to bluster. 'Stop putting on airs just because you earn a bit of money! You think you can treat me like dirt because I'm out of work. I'm no hanger-on! I suppose you're jealous, eh? Your face is nothing to get jealous with, you damn fool. It makes me sick just to look at it.' And he suddenly started slapping me across the face. "I cowered away from him. Then he started laughing as though it was something funny. 'I'm through with you,' he said, 'I'm going to Shizuyo, so get that into your head!' I felt no jealousy. I know nothing about Shizuyo's character nowadays, but I could hardly believe she intended to marry such a nincompoop.

"He started shouting. 'What are you looking at me like that for! Is that the way for a wife to look at her husband?' And he began kicking me in the side. Then, when he saw I was breathless and unable to move, he flung off the children's quilt with his foot. When they woke up he seized them and started beating them. He always took it into his head to do that when he was raving drunk. The children screamed, 'Mother, mother!'

"I got up and rushed out into the hall. My head was full of the unhappy future facing the children, of my own wretchedness, and, more than anything else, of fear. I was really afraid. In my hand, I found the oak bar used to keep the door fast.

"My husband was still beating the children. The boy, who is seven, ran away howling, but his younger sister, who is only five, was shrieking herself hoarse under the onslaught, her cheeks aflame.

"I raised the bar and brought it down with all my might on my husband's head. At the first blow, he staggered and made as if to turn toward me, so in a panic I struck him again.

"At this, he crumpled and fell forward on his face. Even after he fell, I thought he was going to get up again, and so I brought the bar down on his head a third time.

"He vomited blood on the *tatami*. It all took a mere five or six seconds, but I felt as though it had been hours and sank to my knees exhausted."

These, more or less, were the facts against Satoko, on trial for the murder of her husband.

She confessed voluntarily to the police and was arrested. On the basis of her evidence, the First Criminal Investigation Department of the Metropolitan Police Board made detailed investigations, which confirmed what she had said. The cause of Sumura Yokichi's death was a fracture at the back of the skull.

From the first reports of the case in the press, public opinion was sympathetic to Mrs. Sumura, and a flood of letters of sympathy and gifts for the prisoner from strangers descended on the Metropolitan Police Board. A large number of them were from women. With the public hearing of the case, sympathy mounted to a still higher pitch. The women's magazines all carried the story, together with comments by well known columnists.

Of them all, the one who showed the most interest in the case was the journalist Takamori Takiko. She started expressing her views from the time the case was first reported in the press, and followed up with many detailed articles about it. The gist of her published views on the subject were as follows:

"Nothing serves to illustrate so well the tyranny of the husband in the Japanese home as this case. Unable to earn a living, yet without a thought for his family, this man, who took money from the house to go drinking and got himself a mistress into the bargain, gave not the slightest heed to his wife's misery or his children's future. The money, moreover, was money his wife had earned, through her own ability, to pay their living expenses.

"Middle-aged men, bored with their tired-out wives, are prone to run after other women. This is an act of immorality. It is the special position held by the husband in the Japanese family system that creates this type of egoism. The tendency to condone this objectionable custom must be eradicated.

"This is a particularly vicious case. A husband who will come back dead-drunk from his mistress's place, assault his wife—who has kept the family together entirely by her own efforts—and beat his own children is lost to all humanity.

"Admittedly, Mrs. Sumura, making the traditional mistake of the virtuous wife, was too forgiving and let her husband go too far. But I see beyond that failing and, as a woman, feel indignation and an enormous anger toward the husband. Is it not understandable that, ill-treated herself and seeing her children beaten before her very eyes, she should be seized with fear and apprehension for the future?

"I see her action, spiritually, as legitimate self-defense. Anybody, surely, can understand her state of mind at that time. I consider her not guilty."

Takiko's views won a sympathetic response. Bundles of letters giving them wholehearted support arrived at her home every day. Not a few of them asked her to appear in court as a special counsel for the defense.

Through her articulate support, Takiko won herself more renown.

She mobilized fellow writers and they presented a joint petition to the judge, asking for the case to be dismissed. She did undertake, in fact, to appear as special counsel for the defense. Petitions poured into the court from all over the country.

The verdict was three years of penal servitude with two years' stay of execution. Mrs. Sumura accepted it immediately at the first trial, without appealing.

One day some weeks later Takamori Takiko had a visit from a stranger, a man. At first she said she was too busy to see him, but when he said he wanted to ask her something about Sumura Satoko she decided to have him shown to the visitors' room and meet him. The name on his card was Okajima Hisao, but for some reason the address on the left was heavily scored out with black ink.

He was a sturdily built man of about thirty, and his face had a healthy tan. His bushy eyebrows, high-bridged nose, and full lips gave the impression of mature vitality, but his eyes were clear like a boy's—their innocence made a favorable impression on her.

"What can I do for you, then? What is it you wish to ask about Mrs. Sumura?" she asked.

He apologized for intruding on her without warning when she was no doubt busy. He had read and admired every article she had written concerning the Sumura Satoko case.

"It was wonderful, wasn't it, that she got a stay of execution," said Takiko.

"It was all your doing," he nodded.

"Not all my doing really." She wrinkled her nose in a smile. "Shall we say, social justice. Public opinion."

"But it was you who made people aware and moved things along."

Takiko smiled without contradicting him further. But what could this man want to ask her? His manner of speaking suggested he was sympathetic toward Mrs. Sumura, yet—

"I'm slightly acquainted with Mrs. Sumura," said Okajima Hisao as though reading what was in her mind. "It was she who persuaded me to take an insurance policy with that company, you see. So I didn't feel it was something happening to an utter stranger."

Takiko nodded understandingly.

"A civil, considerate, pleasant woman," he recalled. "The kind you'd hardly believe capable of killing her husband."

"That kind always does drastic things under the influence of strong emotions," Takiko said. "Don't forget, she'd been putting up with a great deal for a long time. I'm sure I'd have done the same in her place."

"You?" Okajima looked somewhat startled. His eyes were doubting, as if he wondered whether this well balanced woman could ever get worked up into a frenzy.

"Yes. When one flies into a passion there's no time for the intellect to work. Even an educated woman like Mrs. Sumura."

"About that—*attack* of hers," he said, peering at her. "Was there no question of her physical state at that particular time?"

Takiko remembered reading in the record of the court proceedings that Sumura Satoko had been in normal health on the night of the killing. "I don't recall there being a problem."

"No—" He looked rather embarrassed. "I don't mean her condition in that way. I mean, well, ordinary physical relations between her and her husband."

Takiko's smile disappeared. What could this man be asking?

"You mean, was there some physical defect on her husband's side?"

"The other way around. I wonder whether there wasn't something like that on her side?"

Takiko was silent for a moment. To fill in the gap, she took a sip of her tea, which was growing cold, then looked up at Okajima again.

"Do you have some reason for asking that?" Her manner was the one she always adopted toward an adversary in argument, dispassionately seeking proof of each fact in order to assess her opponent's weaknesses.

Finding himself fixed by Takiko's eyes, Okajima adopted a hesitant expression. "It's like this," he said. "I know a friend of the husband, who says he had been complaining for a long time—for about eighteen months, in fact—that his wife refused to be intimate with him. So I just wondered whether there was some physiological obstacle to their marital relations."

"I'm sure I don't know," said Takiko somewhat ill-humoredly. "I had to see the court records in my capacity as special counsel, and they said nothing about it. They would naturally have inquired into such things at the inquest, and since the records say nothing I don't imagine she had anything wrong with her. Surely she must have refused him because he was visiting his mistress?"

"No, it started well before he struck up with Shizuyo. That's what's strange about it." He looked thoughtful.

Takiko's eyebrows gathered in a faint wrinkle. "Strange? What do you mean?"

"Strange that she refused her husband without a physical reason," he said in a thin voice.

"Women," replied Takiko, "sometimes experience a sudden sense of revulsion in married life. Though I doubt whether men understand such delicate balances between mind and body."

"Of course." He nodded, but his face showed he did not, in fact, understand. "It seems that she experienced this revulsion about six months before her husband became friendly with Shizuyo. In other words, she refused him for about half a year before his relationship with Shizuyo started. It seems to me there's some causal relationship between the two facts."

"I expect there was," Takiko said, bringing her scanty eyebrows still closer together. "You mean he found an outlet for his frustration in Shizuyo."

"Well, yes." Okajima took out a cigarette. "Shizuyo's an old friend of Satoko's. It was Satoko who first sent him to her."

Takiko's eyes gleamed as he lit his cigarette. "Are you suggesting that Satoko deliberately arranged things between her husband and Shizuyo?"

"Oh, I wouldn't go so far as to say that. But in actual effect, she was responsible for bringing them together."

"There's no end to it if one starts arguing from effects," replied Takiko rather sharply. "Effects have a habit of being just the opposite of what one intends."

"True enough," agreed Okajima. A cloud of blue smoke emerged from his lips and spread through the sunlight falling through the window. "Sometimes, though," he added, "things come out as one wants, too."

Takiko was taken aback. There was a hard core of fact in what he was saying. "So you do mean that Satoko intended it right from the start?"

"I'm only deducing. Only she can know really."

"Then on what do you base your deductions?"

"On the fact that she gave Yokichi money to go drinking at Shizuyo's place."

"Ah, but," countered Takiko, "Satoko did that out of the kindness of her heart. Her husband was out of work and loafing about the house all day, and her work kept her out much of the time—so she did it out of thoughtfulness, thinking he'd be miserable.

"She says she sent him to Shizuyo's place because she thought they'd be sure to charge him less for his drinks. She felt, too, that if he was going to drink anyway, she might as well do a good turn for an old friend in difficulties. She never dreamed that her kindness would be thrown back in her face and lead to what it did. I don't like the way you're trying to twist things around."

"Well, then, let's agree it was all started by her generosity," Okajima went on. "And for all her kind intentions, Yokichi betrayed her and became infatuated with Shizuyo. The money Satoko earned he spent on the woman and on drink. He pawned things from their home. Their finances got into deeper waters every day, but still he continued going to the woman's place and coming back late every night.

"When he got back, in his cups, he would ill-treat his wife and children. All thanks to Satoko's generosity, their life had gone to pieces. I wonder why, then, Satoko never once went to Shizuyo to protest? One would have thought she might have gone to ask her to lay off before things got to that pass. It wasn't as if they were strangers—they were friends."

"Such cases often occur," replied Takiko quietly. "One hears of wives bursting in on their husbands' mistresses shouting and screaming. It's stupid and only hurts themselves—no cultured woman would do anything so unseemly and shameful. A husband's shame is a wife's shame. She considers her honor and responsibilities as a wife. Satoko is an intelligent woman, a college graduate, and as such it was impossible for her to do anything so uncouth."

"Of course, I'm sure you're right." Again Okajima let himself seem convinced. "But it remains," he said without altering his tone, "she went on refusing for a whole six months. Then she introduced him to Wakita Shizuyo, who was a widow and ran a drinking place. Yokichi was a drinker in a state of sexual frustration. No situation could be more dangerous to a wife. Naturally, things developed between Yokichi and Shizuyo. But to Shizuyo, Satoko made no protest at all. She might have been a disinterested spectator. Put things together like that and one begins to suspect an underlying intention running through everything."

The decor of Takiko's visitors' room was harmonious and discreet. The color of the walls, the pictures in their frames, the armchairs and sofa all bore witness to the refinement of her taste. The central figure, however—Takiko herself—had by now parted company with the atmosphere. Waves of irritability were passing over her face.

"By 'intention,' do you mean she was somehow planning that kind of thing?"

"I'm deducing. It's all deduction from these few facts and—"

"From extremely scanty facts," said Takiko promptly. "With most people, I can tell by looking at them what they're like. In the course of my connection with the case I read vast quantities of records and met Mrs. Sumura many times in my capacity as special counsel.

"Nowhere in the records is there anything to support your suspicions. And one need only meet Satoko to be struck by the intelligence of her character. The look in her eyes is innocence itself. One doesn't find such a fine, cultured woman very often."

"I agree with you, she is a very cultured woman," said Okajima. "I'm convinced of it."

"And where did you know her?"

"As I mentioned earlier, it was she who persuaded me to take out a life-insurance policy. I should have told you—I work at a dam-construction site in the mountains in the Tohoku district," Okajima said, identifying the company for which he worked.

"Our life in the mountains," he continued, "has absolutely no excitement or variety outside the work. You see, we're deep in the mountains, where it takes an hour and a half bouncing up and down in a truck to get to a town with a railway station. At night, when work's over, there's no amusement at all. One eats, and one sleeps, that's all.

"Some of the men study, of course, but gradually the general atmosphere of tedium gets them down. At night, people are fond of playing chess and Mah-Jongg for money. On the twice-monthly holidays they go to a small town in the foothills about four miles away, where there are some dubious establishments put up in a hurry because of the dam, and desperately try to divert themselves. Sometimes a man will spend a great deal of money at one time.

"Then they come trudging back to the mountains—but without feeling satisfied. We've been to school, and we chose the work ourselves, but even so, when one's shifting from mountain to mountain one begins to long for the town." Imperceptibly, his tone had become more confidential.

"Some of the men, of course, have love affairs. But the women are all peasant girls from the neighborhood. They've no intellect, no culture. The only thing to recommend them is that they're women. The men have no other choice. Their circumstances dictate it. It doesn't mean they're any less dissatisfied. They regret what they're doing, then they grow resigned."

Takiko listened in silence.

"Then Mrs. Sumura and another woman, Mrs. Fujii, arrived from Tokyo to canvass for an insurance company. Mrs. Fujii, being older, was of no great interest to the men, but Mrs. Sumura became a great favorite.

"She's not especially beautiful, but her face makes a good impression on men. Her way of speaking was intelligent, too. Not that she showed off her intelligence; it seemed, rather, to shine through from underneath. Strangely enough, it made her face look beautiful, even. No, back there in the mountains, she was a beauty, no doubt about it. What was more, her words, her movements, were those of a Tokyo woman—the first we'd met in ages. Can you wonder that she was so appealing?

"Another thing was that she was kind and considerate to everybody. Of course, it was her job to be so, but although everybody knew that, they liked it. They went out of their way to put her in touch with friends and acquaintances. I'm sure she achieved more than she expected. She came once every month or two and everybody made her feel welcome. Sometimes she'd bring candy and other presents from Tokyo to show she appreciated it. The things were trivial in themselves, but everybody was pleased. There were men who felt homesick at the mere sight of the wrapping paper from a Tokyo department store."

He paused for a moment and drank the cold remains of his tea.

"There was another reason she was such a success with everybody. She told us she was a widow, you see."

Takiko's eyelids, which had begun to droop, opened and she stared at Okajima.

"I suppose it was unavoidable. Individual appeal plays a large part in insurance canvassing, doesn't it? It's almost like the way women in bars and similar places always say they're single. 'I'm single, that's why I do this work,' she would insist with a smile. Nobody doubted what she said. As a result, before long there were some who sent her what amounted to love letters."

Okajima relit his cigarette, which had gone out, and continued.

"Of course, she didn't tell people her own address. All the letters went to the company for which she worked. Such a small deception can be excused, I expect. But the effect was that a number of men made clear-cut advances to her.

"Some of them urged her to come alone, without the other woman. There were some who forced their way into the place where she was staying—the only inn in the place, catering to people there to inspect the site—and refused to go home till late.

"But she smiled and dodged their advances. She knew how to get out of predicaments skillfully and gently, without damaging business or upsetting people. She was far from being a loose woman, that's quite certain. But—"

His tone changed slightly.

"But there were many men of finer caliber at the dam, men devoting their life-energy to the work. Men—to put it more poetically—grappling with the mighty masses of nature which have to be altered by man's strength. Really manly men.

"Every time she saw such men, she must have recalled her ninny of a husband with loathing. She must have felt the contrast more strongly every day, the one seeming more and more manly and fine, the other more and more miserable and despicable."

"I'm sorry to interrupt you," Takiko said with undisguised impatience, "but is this just supposition?"

"Yes. My own."

"Then there's no point in my listening at such length. I've work to attend to."

"I'm sorry." He bowed slightly. "I'll tell the rest as briefly as possible, then. It's not unnatural to suppose she felt favorably toward one of those men. Let us suppose that he felt something even stronger for her. That is not impossible, either—he was convinced she was a widow. And she must have seemed a woman of quite unique intelligence.

"She must have suffered. She had a husband, Yokichi. A husband, moreover, whom she detested with all her being. The more her affections inclined to the other, the more she longed to be free from her husband. Divorce was out of the question, since Yokichi would never let her go. Only her husband's death could set her free. Only her becoming, literally, a widow. Unfortunately, Yokichi was in robust health. If, then, his early death seemed too much to hope for, the only alternative was to encourage it."

Takiko sat, pale, searching for words.

"To murder one's husband, however," he went on, "is a capital offense. There was no point in killing him—it meant execution or a long prison term for herself. She was a clever woman and she thought: was there not some way of killing him yet avoiding actual punishment? There was only one way—a suspended sentence. That means one goes free as long as one doesn't commit another crime.

"But 'extenuating circumstances' are an essential condition for a suspended sentence. Yokichi wasn't earning anything at the time, but that would hardly fill the bill. The only alternative was to create the necessary conditions. Coolly and calmly, she set about creating them. After thoroughly sizing up his character, of course. All that remained was to lead him, like irrigation water, into the prepared channels. She allowed eighteen months for the job.

"For six months, she consistently refused him physically, to get him into a state of frustration. Next, she sent him to a woman who was a widow and kept a drinking place. Mrs. Sumura was sure that in his frustrated condition he would make advances to her. If *Shizuyo* was a failure, she would probably have found another woman—there are plenty of her kind. Shizuyo, however, was made to order. Yokichi's natural tendency to go to the dogs, plus his addiction to drink, gradually ruined him. In six months, he became in every respect the kind of person she had foreseen he would become—he had played straight into her hands. In other words, all the 'extenuating circumstances' were provided for perfectly. She went into action.

"There remained the trial. The verdict went exactly as she had calculated. About six months passed before it was handed down. In short, from her first preparation of the necessary conditions to the completion of the plan took eighteen months. And among her calculations was so-called public opinion."

He stopped and looked at Takiko. Her face was ashen and her lips quivered. "Are you still dealing in supposition? Or do you have some grounds for what you say?"

"It's not entirely supposition." His eyes surveyed her from his suntanned face. "When I proposed to her, you see, she asked me to wait for eighteen months."

He put his cigarette case back in his pocket and rose to leave.

"But don't worry. However many statements I might make about this," he told Takiko, "it wouldn't affect her stay of execution. A person can't be tried twice for the same offense. Once a verdict has been settled, the law doesn't allow a retrial that might be disadvantageous to the person concerned. She seems to have calculated even that. The one thing—" he turned his child-like gaze on her "—the one thing she miscalculated was that the man she kept waiting for eighteen months is running away."

Donald Olson

On Consignment

To say that Ron Chamberlin had driven up from New York in an agony of suspense would be an inaccurate description of his state of mind. In the bliss of suspense might be more nearly correct; in a mood of euphoria which had lingered for a week now but which demanded, for the sake of the gods who take pleasure in punishing the overconfidence of mortals, a kind of superstitious acknowledgment of what *could* go wrong. The old lady might have died during the week, her estate and everything it it beyond reach for months, even years. Or the daughter might have grown suspicious, or changed her mind, or mentioned the matter to someone who might have warned her against dealing with strangers.

But the only real agony Ron suffered was physical, having to drive all that distance with two cracked ribs—courtesy of Manny Adelgren's goons. Yet it was surprising how soothing an effect the prospect of being within reach of a fortune could have on even the most painful discomforts of the body.

East Rublee wasn't even on the map, yet Ron felt that instinct alone would have guided him back to that dull and unpicturesque New England village where the week before he had stopped off at something called the Rublee Flea Market in the wan hope of picking up something, anything, that might make the trip worthwhile. He had come up dry at all the usual sources, where he ordinarily found at least a dozen items that could be turned into cash at one or more of the small Manhattan shops for which he "picked."

The girl—well hardly a girl, thirty at least—had sat on a campstool on the fringe of the market, her paintings propped up against cardboard boxes. Neither the girl nor her paintings had inspired him to speak to her. She was rather lumpish, closer to plain than pretty, and had an awkward shyness of manner. The paintings were at worst inept, at best banal, the sort one thinks of as being turned out rather than created. He *had* spoken to her for the same reason he often spoke to such people, to ask if she knew of anyone in the area who might have old things for sale.

She had timidly mentioned some old pictures in the grandmother's attic.

Now, a week later, as he turned into the road on which the house stood, a solid but decaying Greek Revival farmhouse to which he had followed her the week before, he recalled the hopelessness he had felt as, flashlight in hand, he had crawled into that dark, sweltering cave beneath the eaves and pawed among five heavily gilt-framed paintings, all of uniform size, all thick with grime. He remembered the cobwebs, the sticky humid discomfort, his irritation at having dirtied his clothes. With his handkerchief, he had rubbed away the surface layers of grime. He had been about to admit it had been a stupid waste of time when his rudimentary examination of the third painting had revealed that startling glimpse of rose-pearl flesh tones, the luminous eyes, the girdle of flowers—and the signature, the all but illegible signature.

He had emerged from the attic drenched in sweat caused not so much by the stifling heat as by the raging fever of excited discovery, which he took great pains to dissemble.

The paintings were valueless, he had told her—Victorian reproductions of fourth-rate Renaissance artists. The frames were more valuable than the pictures. He might be able to pay her a hundred dollars for the five of them—provided the man he picked for was interested. He had given her a deposit and promised to return in a week. Of course, when he had called Paul at the De Quincy Gallery, invited him to lunch, and told him just enough to pique his interest, Paul had scoffed. The *Venus of the Windflowers!* Impossible. From the time the masterpiece had vanished from Maxfield Abbey outside London in the 1890s, there hadn't been so much as a rumor of its whereabouts. Still, Paul was enough of a gambler—although a more cautious one than Ron, whose passion for the ponies had lost him his job as assistant curator at the Bellinger Museum and a great deal more besides—to have loaned Ron five hundred to get him by for a few weeks.

The girl's name was Myra Lovejoy and when he arrived she was standing on the stone veranda wearing a faded cotton dress and sandals, her mane of drab-colored hair pulled back and fastened with a rubber band.

"I didn't think you'd come back," she said artlessly.

"I gave you a deposit, didn't I?"

"Oh, well—" she murmured in the tone of one who has learned to put no more trust in deposits than in promises.

The sound of clapping hands interrupted her and he heard the grandmother's high-pitched voice from within the house: "Is it him?"

Myra Lovejoy smiled. "*She* was sure you wouldn't be back. It seemed like so much money to her—for those."

"You brought them down, then?"

"They're out back." Ron followed her through the house to a shed-like addition beyond the kitchen which had evidently once been a workshop but now served as an art studio of sorts. A still-life of apples in a raffia basket was affixed to an easel. Ron gave it only a passing glance.

"It's all right, isn't it?" she inquired shyly. "That I cleaned them? I was careful not to damage the scrollwork. They were so filthy."

He stared at the frames stacked against the wall. The empty frames.

"Where are the pictures?"

"You didn't want them, did you? You said they were valueless."

With an effort he suppressed his sudden, wild agitation. "Well, yes—but you needn't have gone to the bother of removing them."

With a modest, pleased look she said: "I suppose I always hoped they might be worth something or I'd have thought of doing it before. Canvas and stretcher bars are so expensive to buy. So I cleaned the old pictures and painted a white ground on them. Now I can use them for my own work."

Ron's gaze fell sickly on the blank canvases. He cursed his own stupidity in telling her the paintings were junk. Why hadn't he at least told her they had *some* value? He knew she would have taken whatever he had offered for them. And they were all the same size. It was impossible to tell behind which one lay the Windflower Venus. His anger swelled to include her, as if she had outfoxed him by some willful deceit of her own. How could he logically express a wish to buy the canvases now?

His gaze returned to the painting on the easel as intently as if he had X-ray vision and might see behind the white ground the luminous eyes of La Divina Margherita, the master's mistress during his Roman period—the *Venus of the Windflowers*.

The penetration of his gaze seemed to disconcert Myra Lovejoy. "Please don't be too critical. I know I'm not a real artist, but it gives me such pleasure. I can't get away, you know. She's terribly old and awfully demanding. I only get away to do the shopping and go to the flea market. I do sell some of them. To people who just want a real oil painting to hang on the wall."

When she said this, Ron's first rage of frustration melted before the awareness that all was not lost. Remembering the ease with which he had deceived her about the *Venus*'s value, he took a step closer to the easel and appeared to deliberate.

"You're too modest. The truth is, Myra, you've an excellent eye. A fine sense of perspective. I like this one especially. How long does it take you to paint one?"

"About a week. She keeps me so busy waiting on her. And with the housework."

He adopted a businesslike manner. "May I buy this one? I'll give you a hundred dollars for it."

She uttered a little gasp of protest. "Oh, I never ask *that* much."

How smoothly she was playing into his hand. "Then here's an idea. Let me take it and any others you do from now on back to New York with me. I'm sure my friend can sell them in this shop. Let me take them on consignment. If he sells them, good. You can pay me a commission. Say ten percent?"

Clearly, the proposition dazzled her. "Oh, Mr. Chamberlin, that's awfully generous of you. We can certainly use the money."

"Call me Ron. Then we have a deal, okay? A firm contract. One new picture a week. But don't let me down: only if you *do* paint one new picture a week. Without fail, no matter what. I know with some of the money I'm giving you now you could buy new canvases, but I'm superstitious. Just for luck, use up these old canvases you've re-primed first, all right?"

"I know what you mean," she agreed. "If it hadn't been for them none of this would have happened. Oh, I'll feel terrible if they don't sell."

His smile oozed confidence. "Don't worry, they'll sell. I promise you."

Ron could scarcely wait until he was back in his apartment in New York before seizing a knife and painstakingly scraping away just enough of the still-life and its underlying ground to expose what lay beneath. If Lady Luck happened to be smiling on him today this might be *the* picture.

Only it wasn't, as he discovered the instant his knife revealed the tip of a cherub's wing in the top left-hand corner of the canvas. He was not unduly disappointed. He couldn't hope to hit the jackpot on the first try. It didn't matter, there were only four canvases left.

Four weekend trips to East Rublee at the most. Meanwhile, they were even safer than they would have been in that foul attic.

Feeling in the mood to celebrate, Ron changed his shirt and went out to his favorite bar on Third Avenue. He was working on his second Old-Fashioned when he felt a sudden, painful nudge in his sore rib.

"How you doin', Ron baby?"

"Hi, Jo-Jo. What's new?"

"Manny wants to see you."

"Well, tell Manny not to worry. Everything's fine. He'll have his money."

"*You* tell Manny."

Jo-Jo's shadow, the ever-smiling Benjie of the Brass Knuckles, loomed up on Ron's other side. Ron knew better than to argue.

On the way to the bookie's office, Ron contrived what he hoped would be a convincing story. How an old lady in Westchester, for whom he had appraised some antiques, owned a painting that was worth a mint—only she didn't know it. And Ron, having persuaded her it was worthless, was promised first chance to buy it when she sold her things within a month.

"You've checked me out," he told the bookie. "You know my background, my credentials as an art expert. Give me a month and you'll have the whole ten grand—with interest. What have you got to lose?"

Manny smiled. "It's what you got to lose, friend, if it turns out you're blowin' smoke. And I'm not talkin' busted ribs and broken arms. A month from today. Same hour, same minute, same second. You don't come up with the ten grand, you better have your will made out."

He forced himself to tarry, to quell the urge to pay for the picture and rush back to the city, because she so obviously wanted him to tarry. She was wearing a short-sleeved pale-yellow dress and had done something to her hair. They sat on the stone veranda where she served him coffee and some freshly baked cookies. Her air of tension had relaxed upon being told that Ron's friend had already sold her picture. Several times she had excused herself and gone inside in response to her grandmother's clapping summons.

"The hot weather is terrible on her. She has trouble breathing."

Ron gazed out over the low, wooded hills beyond the crumbled foundation of the barn. It was very peaceful here and he was in a benign mood. Something told him this would be his last visit. The painting, a view of the very scene spread out before him, was already in his station wagon.

"What will you do—when you're alone?" he asked her.

She responded with a hopeless, resigned shrug. "I'm alone now in some ways. It won't be much different. I'll have more spare time, that's all."

"You'll stay here?"

"I've noplace else to go. I've never had a real job. I'm not fit for anything. There'll be a little money. Insurance." Her sidelong glance, palely hopeful, touched him fleetingly. "I'll have my painting. I'll be able to turn out more than I do now. I'll be able to buy books and read about the great painters. I've never even been to an art museum. Ron, I owe you so much. It was so lucky for me, your showing up when you did. Taking my pictures. And if they keep selling—if you can keep helping me as you're doing—I won't mind being alone at all."

He rallied her with the same jocular tone he had found brought life to her plain features. "You could marry."

With a faint blush, looking away, she said she had had her chance, once. "Never again. I know that. I've no chance to meet anyone."

"Nonsense. You met me."

"I mean—socially. Are you married, Ron?"

"Not any more. My wife left me. We're divorced."

"But you have friends?"

"No one special."

She reached for the cookies. "Have another."

Thwarted by the second picture, Ron threw down the knife and paced angrily across the floor. How typical of Fate to treat him like a starving man at a banquet, forcing him to restrain his hunger while being passed one empty plate after another. He couldn't enjoy any of his usual diversions. The *Venus of the Windflowers* had become an obsession. He dreamed constantly of what he would do when the painting was in his hands, when it was finally sold and he could pay off his debts and buy all he had ever yearned to buy. Travel, have a fine apartment, the right sort of friends.

He worried occasionally about how he would handle the transaction itself. He felt there would have to be some way of protecting his honor. He didn't fancy the notion of confessing that he had tricked a forlorn spinster and her ailing grandmother out of a fortune. At the same time, the provenance of the painting would have to be brought up to date as far as possible. He was deeply curious as to how the picture had come to end up in that New England attic, but so far he had hesitated to express any interest. Myra Lovejoy was naïve, but no fool. It could be risky to betray any serious interest in the paintings themselves.

Incredibly, or so it seemed to Ron, the third picture he bore away from the house in East Rublee was also a dud. He had been so *sure,* so absolutely convinced that this would be the real treasure, his hand had trembled so violently while scraping away the surface paint he could scarcely control the knife.

He wished now that when he had last parted from Myra Lovejoy in such a glow of confidence that he would never set eyes on her again, he had not bade her, out of a guilty conscience, so warmly sentimental a farewell. He wished he had not kissed her. The memory of her foolish, radiant face tormented him.

On his next weekend visit, he detected a shy nervousness in Myra's attitude which caused him some degree of perturbation until, just before he rose to leave, the fourth picture clasped in his hand, she reached into her pocket and handed him a small, neatly wrapped package. She didn't say a word.

He smiled. "What's this?"

She hadn't the sort of face that one could say blushed prettily. "You've been so kind, Ron. You've made everything so different for me. I wanted to give you something to show my appreciation—the way I feel."

He opened the package and found a pair of ruby cufflinks. He was stunned—not so much by the feelings that had inspired the gift, but by the links themselves. The rubies were genuine, not glass. Where on earth had she gone to buy them, he wondered.

"If you don't like them—" she murmured timorously.

"Like them! Why, Myra, they're beautiful. I don't know what to say."

Her pleasure filled him with shame. The naked emotion in her large pale eyes forced him to look away. "They're very old," she said. "They were his, you see."

"His?"

"Great-uncle Matthew's. Grandfather's brother. The one who owned the paintings."

He saw a way to ask what had been so long on his mind. "But how did you happen to have them? The cufflinks, I mean."

"He died in Boston, a very long time ago. Gran used to talk about him. She always gave me the impression the family didn't approve of him. He deserted his wife and went abroad, took up with some English lady but never married her. When he did, he left Grandfather what he had—a little money, his house in Boston, those pictures and stuff. And the cufflinks."

"Is that all you know about him?"

"I've forgotten most of what Gran told me. You do like them? You won't be ashamed to wear them?"

"I'll be proud to wear them. They'll always remind me of you."

His tone or the words brought a swift dismay to her face, a sudden urgency. "That sounds as if you won't be around for long. As if you're going away and not coming back."

"Heavens, no. You can't imagine how I look forward to these weekly visits."

At this, she fairly beamed with pleasure. "Oh, not half so much as I do. I live for them. They mean *everything* to me."

There was no mistaking the fervor behind the outburst. Ron felt swamped by shame, despising for the first time the baseness of his duplicity. At that moment he made up his mind—his first unselfish impulse in years—that when he had the money from the *Venus* he would make it up to her. He truly would. And this decision miraculously cleansed his mind of any feelings of guilt about what he was doing.

He reached for her hand as he said goodbye beside the car. Her fingers felt moist and warm and he could feel them tremble in his palm.

"Goodbye, Myra. Thank you for the cufflinks. Thank you for everything."

When he started to withdraw his hand, she clung to it. Her face wore a look of rapturous, blatant infatuation. "Ron. Next week—could you come earlier? Could we spend the day together?"

"Why not? I'd like that. Maybe we could have a picnic in the backyard. I haven't had a picnic for years."

"Oh, yes! That would be fun."

He drove away with mixed feelings, but the absolute conviction that he would never see her again, that the *Venus of the Windflowers* was reposing in the back of the station wagon. He would write her a nice long letter telling her he had had to leave town for an indefinite period on urgent business. Then later he would send her a very generous check, a check that would leave her with nothing to worry about for the rest of her life.

Curiously enough, the disappointment did not come as nearly the crushing blow he might have anticipated. Possibly the earlier frustrations had subconsciously prepared him for the eventuality. He merely dropped the knife and uttered a long sigh, almost of relief. For now at least the suspense was ended. Now he knew. There was only one painting left.

Jo-Jo accosted him in the bar, a smirk on his broad, dead-eyed face. "So what you smilin' about, Ron baby? You know what day this is?"

"I know what day it is. There's still a week left, remember?"

"Yeah, well *you* remember, buddy. You don't come across with Manny's bucks in just seven days you and me got ourselves a date."

"Tell Manny not to worry. A week from today we'll all have something to celebrate."

She was waiting for him in the drive when he arrived and the moment he saw her standing there, dressed in black, her face urgent with the news, he guessed what had happened.

"Oh, Ron," she cried, pressing her head to his chest, "it's been so awful. On Thursday night she started breathing funny and she couldn't speak. She tried so hard but she couldn't. Then she just turned her head away and died."

"Myra, I'm sorry. I wish I'd known."

"I wanted to call you. I wanted to tell you. But it's been such a busy week. I was afraid you wouldn't get here before I had to go."

"Go?"

"To the funeral. It's this afternoon. I'm waiting for them to come for me now. They should be here any minute." She stepped back. "Please, Ron, come with me. It'll be so much easier for me if you do."

There was no reason he couldn't—he had allowed himself plenty of spare time—but he knew it was unthinkable. All he wanted was to take the picture and rush back to town. "Myra, I wish I could," he said gently, "but I can't. You'll think it's silly and weak of me, but ever since my mother died, I can't bear funerals—I really can't. Please try to understand."

Meekly she nodded her head. "Of course. I do understand."

The mortician's limousine pulled up behind Ron's station wagon. Before starting toward it, Myra seized Ron's hand. "I'll come back as soon as I decently can. Wait for me." She made a vague, delaying motion with her gloved hand to the chauffeur as he stepped out into the drive. "Ron, stay with me tonight. Please stay with me. I don't want to be here alone. Please stay with me."

She uttered the appeal so artlessly, with such a trusting plaintive air of desperation, he could only lower his eyes and stammer, "I don't know. I wish I—"

"Just tonight, Ron. There's so much I want to tell you. My cousin came from Boston. She's at the inn. She wants me to go back to Boston with her for a week. I don't want to. I tried to tell her so, but she's so determined. Oh, I mustn't keep them waiting. We'll talk when I get back."

"Myra, the picture—"

"Oh, yes. It's finished. I wrapped it up and wrote you a letter. I put them on the veranda just now in case I missed you."

He glanced up toward the house, saw the brown-paper-wrapped parcel leaning against the door. The tension drained out of his body. He put his arms around Myra and kissed her on the cheek. "Go along now. We'll talk when you come back."

"Promise you'll wait. Promise me, Ron."

"Of course I'll wait."

"I left the door unlocked. You can go in and make yourself some coffee, anything else you want."

He waited until she had climbed into the limousine and disappeared from sight before turning toward the house. It was over. The seemingly endless misery of suspense was finally over. He looked at his watch. There was no need to rush, and yet nothing could have induced him to delay a minute longer than necessary before getting away from this house. Thank God he would never have to see it again.

He snatched up the parcel and the letter beside it. Before getting into his car he paused for only a moment to look back at the empty, staring windows. "Goodbye, Myra," he murmured.

As it happened, he had been wise to leave when he did. A bad accident on the bridge into the city had created a massive traffic jam. He remained trapped in the car for nearly two hours before the bridge could be reopened.

He was in a state of nervous exhaustion by the time he finally let himself into his apartment. He was hungry and he badly needed a drink, but he could have been starving and dying of thirst and still wouldn't have wasted a second before propping the parcel against the back cushions of the sofa and rushing to the desk for scissors and his knife.

Tossing aside the attached letter, he cut the twine and ripped away the covering from the front of the picture with his fingers.

He couldn't help laughing when he saw it. Without a doubt it was the worst thing she had ever done. It had a smeary, lifeless quality that betrayed the obvious haste with which it had been painted. The poor creature had been busy, of course—it was a wonder she had found the time to paint it at all. It was evidently supposed to represent a sunset scene, but the coloring was all wrong. The blue shadows on the hills merged indistinguishably with the blue of the sky and even spilled over into the round globe of the sun itself.

Pulling the paper away from the lower right-hand corner of the painting, he began deftly to scrape away the hideous blue paint. Then he leaned forward on his knees, narrowing his eyes to a squint. The blade of the knife resumed its delicate surgery but as the paint peeled away the white ground remained impenetrable. Carefully, he exerted a more forceful pressure and then, frowning, he began rubbing at it with his finger. The ground did not come away. The textured bare canvas remained intact.

He flung the knife down, stood and ripped the brown paper free of the picture. He picked it up and turned it around, then stared dumbly at the clean bare wood of the stretcher bars, at the freshness of the canvas itself. She had tricked him! My God, she knew! She had always known!

But that was impossible. She couldn't have known. It didn't make sense.

His eye fell on her letter. He picked it up and tore it open.

"Dear Ron, In case I must leave before you get here, I will leave this and the picture on the veranda for you. Grandmother is dead. She died Thursday night. The funeral is this afternoon. Please wait for me. I may be going to Boston with my cousin Florence for a week. If I do, I wouldn't have a chance to paint my weekly picture for you, but we made an agreement and I wouldn't think of disappointing you, so I worked very hard and fast to finish two paintings this week. The one I did first is in the studio. The door is unlocked. You can go in and look at it. I'm afraid it's not very good. The second—I call it *Blue Sunset*—is better, I think. Ron, please try to stay until I get back from the funeral. All my love, Myra."

Jo-Jo looked at the car keys in Ron's hand. "Goin' somewhere?" he asked.

"Yes! Look, it's all under control. Tell Manny there's been a slight hitch. I'll see him tonight. I'll—"

"Cut the baloney, Chamberlin. Your time is up. And you won't need them keys. We'll furnish the transportation."

"No, wait! Listen!"

Jo-Jo's dead eyes circled the room, came to rest on the knife lying on the floor where Ron had flung it. "You're a messy housekeeper," he told Ron. "The knife. Go pick it up like a good boy. Pick it up and give it to me."

Tonita S. Gardner

You Could Have Done Better

I'm a mean woman. You'll have to take my word for it because the one person who always saw me at my worst is no longer here to confirm it.

"Ella," Henry would say to me, "when are you going to learn to control that temper of yours?"

But it wasn't only the temper. I was often nasty, spiteful, stubborn. And not because I didn't love Henry. Even with all his faults I did love him in my own limited fashion. That's why I married him—and stayed married to him for seventeen years, most of them unhappy. Which, I guess, is exactly what I deserved.

Not that my mother would agree. Up till the day she died Mama kept telling me, "You could have done better, Ella. You got at least half a brain in your head and your face isn't as ugly as some faces I've seen." Those were Mama's very words: "You could have done better."

Could I? I'm inclined to think that no other man would have proposed to me. Not with this mean streak I have—the kind that always makes me want to get my own way.

Kids, for instance. Henry wanted kids. I didn't. So we didn't have any. And in the long run *I'm* the loser. Now that Henry's gone I have nobody. So you see how, all along, I cut off my nose to spite my face. Kids could have brightened our lives. Even when Henry was alive, our lives were as dull as old pewter. Except for Friday nights when Henry played poker with his friends, one evening was exactly like another. He'd sit and read the sports pages, I'd sit and watch TV. Finally Henry would put his paper down, start to yawn, and say to me, "Getting tired, Ella? How 'bout us going off to bed?"

I'd be tired, but I knew what he wanted and I wasn't about to take the hint. "You go on up without me, Henry," I'd say. "I think I'll sit up and watch Johnny Carson for a while." Then, as soon as he was fast asleep and snoring, I'd totter off to bed myself.

Then there was the business about the food. Before we'd leave for work in the morning, Henry would give me money for shopping. "I feel like a nice juicy steak for dinner," he'd tell me, and his tongue would work itself around his lips as if he were tasting the meal in advance. So on the way home from work I'd go to the butcher's and buy him his nice juicy steak. Sometimes. Other times, when I was feeling mean, I'd tell the butcher, "Two slices of liver, Mr. Schantz." And when Henry came home and I served him the liver, his whole face would collapse and his voice would get scratchy. "I thought we were having steak?"

"It didn't look good to me," I'd fib. "So I bought liver instead." Then I'd watch him eat his dinner and I'd think to myself, You're not going to tell *me* what to do, Henry. And I'd tote up a big fat point for my side. I suppose I did it to keep him from taking me for granted. Because whenever you expect something and you always get it, it sets a pattern that's hard to break. That's why I liked to keep Henry guessing. Occasionally, when I pulled the liver switch, Henry would glare at me and clench his fists.

"Goddamn it, woman, I gave you money for steak and you buy me this dog meat!" But he always ate it just the same. And since there were plenty of times I'd buy steak or some other favorite food when he didn't expect it, I figured it all balanced out in the end.

Why did he stay with me? Henry liked a woman who had a mind of her own. "But for Peter's sake, Ella," he would scold, "there's a limit to how much a man can take!"

He meant what he said. But he also meant the opposite. I think our fighting added a little excitement to Henry's life, just as it did to mine. After all, when you spend most of your daytime hours running your own dry-cleaning store like he did or working as a telephone operator like I do maybe you need a little tiff in your off hours to get the knots out of your system.

Not that I limited my meanness to our off hours. Every so often—and here's where my job came in handy—I'd eavesdrop on Henry's phone conversations at the store. Once I overheard him complain about my peevishness to one of his card-playing buddies—and punished him by wrapping the garbage in the sports pages before he got to read them that night. From then on, whenever I listened in, I couldn't wait to get the goods on him. But outside of some old ladies calling to ask the cost of cleaning their fake furs or shag rugs, the only thing I ever heard was Henry placing a newspaper ad for someone with experience to help him run the store.

I couldn't fault him for that. Henry worked even harder in his job than I did in mine. I often wondered if his job made him happy. I know I didn't make him happy. He didn't make me happy, either.

But when a woman's got a mean streak like I have, good cheer is in short supply. I'm convinced that some people thrive on being miserable. It's like some plants. Leave them in a dark corner, forget to feed and water them, and they stay alive. But as soon as you give them a little sun, a dose of plant food, and a drink of water, they fade and droop and die. That's the way it was with Henry and me—both miserable, both thriving on it.

Because Henry could be mean, too. Like not letting me have a new car, though I finally learned to drive after years of busing to work every day. But even our old station wagon was a source of friction. Henry loved to dangle the keys in front of me. "You have to say pretty please," he'd make me beg.

"Pretty please," I'd tell him.

"Pretty please with what?"

"Pretty please with sugar."

A nasty smile. "You left something out, Ella."

"What?"

"If you don't know, you can't have the keys."

"Pretty please with sugar and cream?"

"Nope."

"*Whipped* cream."

"Now say the whole thing."

And we'd go through the whole silly business all over again. As you can imagine, I got tired of doing it. To break him of that annoying habit, I took the spare key from under the hood of his Chevy and had a key of my own made up. And the last time he pulled his little stunt—a week ago Sunday, the day he died—I was all set for him to start in with me.

Instead of pleading for the keys to the station wagon, I marched out of the house, leaving Henry with his nose buried in the sports section. I hied myself out to the garage and into the Chevy. When he heard the motor turn over, it must have dawned on him that I was about to use his precious car. He came running out of the house in his beatup old slippers, yelling at me to get out of his automobile.

"I'll be damned if I'll let you smash up that piece of machinery like you smashed up the station wagon!" he screamed loud enough for all the neighbors to hear. "It took me a month to fix the goddamn thing!" (Left unsaid was the fact that it took him a month because he wouldn't let anyone else fix it. Henry fancied himself an expert mechanic.)

I got furious at him for mentioning the smashup because it wasn't my fault and he knew it. He was right beside me when this drunk driver plowed into us and almost wrecked the old wagon. Actually, it was a bonanza in disguise. Henry collected for the damage even though he repaired it himself. And with the money he saved, he put a down payment on the Chevy. So what was he complaining about?

I hollered back at him that I intended to use the Chevy whether he liked it or not.

Trying to stop me, he came scooting up the driveway (it's on a steep incline) just as the car started to roll backward. I heard him yell, "Put your foot on the brake!" Which is what I started to do. But somehow—and who wouldn't get rattled at a time like that?—I pressed the accelerator instead. The next thing I felt was a terrible jolt.

Henry.

When I jumped out, he was lying beneath the rear wheel. I can't describe his condition because I couldn't bear to look at him. I was too hysterical.

I was also terrified that the police would accuse me of murder. So it took all my self-control to tell them exactly what happened: "I borrowed the car, Henry got mad at me for taking it, and came storming out. I got nervous and jammed my foot down on the gas pedal by mistake. And then—" I was shaking so hard I couldn't go on.

Three neighbors, all of whom had seen the accident and had come running over, verified that Henry had screamed at me.

"Loud enough to get any woman upset," said a lady from across the street whose husband had a violent temper.

After the neighbors had been questioned and dismissed, one of the detectives inquired, "Why'd you take *his* car and not yours?"

"The brakes on the station wagon are all worn down," I blubbered. "I was afraid I'd have an accident."

The irony of my answer jarred me into a new attack of hysterics. But when the police asked how much insurance Henry carried—implying that I'd done away with him for a widow's windfall—it sobered me at once.

"A hundred thousand," I said.

Of course, at that moment money was the last thing on my mind. More important was my anxiety about the investigation.

As it turned out, I had good reason to be anxious. Because when the police started digging further, some of the strange things they unearthed took me by surprise.

For instance, why did Henry hire a shapely little blonde to work behind the counter in his store even though she knew nothing about the dry-cleaning business? And why did he give up playing poker on Friday nights but still stay out until midnight? And why, when I never got a single rosebud, did he suddenly start running up huge florist bills?

"Can you explain it?" prompted the police.

"That's *your* job," I told them, dismayed that I'd let Henry put one over on me.

But even if Henry was having an affair, that didn't prove I killed him, did it? The police finally had to agree.

Yet it wasn't until I called our insurance agent that I learned another of Henry's secrets.

"By the way, Mrs. Busby—" the agent was discussing death benefits "—do you still want us to issue that new policy?"

"What new policy?" I asked.

"Your husband wanted to match the hundred thousand he'd already bought for himself. I guess he forgot to mention it."

"Well, it's too late now," I said. "You can't insure a dead man."

An embarrassed laugh. "I should hope not."

"You mean the policy wasn't on *his* life?"

"No," he said. "On yours."

I cut him off in a hurry and sat back to review the situation. And when I thought of Henry planning to insure me while letting my brakes get dangerously worn, I realized that his treachery had gone beyond hanky-panky.

And that's when I heard my mother's voice from out of the past. "He got what he deserved, Ella. You're better off without him."

I hate to think Mama was right, but on the other hand I wish with all my heart Henry was still alive. Maybe it's my mean streak, but now that I know he was even meaner than me, if I had the chance to kill him all over again it wouldn't be an accident.

"Q"

Jay Francis

Sniped At

66 "Albie, you ever going to take them squashes down to Rutland?" Lil asked. "They been setting in that truck for the past three days." She was right, but during harvest-time, a farmer has a lot on his mind, and on his hands, too. Since my two boys had got married and left, I'd sold my herd, but there was still a fair market for vegetables. I climbed into the truck then and there, and drove out of the yard.

The shortest way to the city is along old Route 175, one of them roads that seem to be carved between two hills, and as curvy as all get out. The Green Mountains are swarming with tourists in the summer and fall, not to mention the winter skiers. Right now, though, the fall foliage had passed its peak, and Route 175 was all but empty.

I couldn't of been more than five minutes from my own farm, driving along the highway at a good clip, when it happened. As soon as I rounded a curve, I heard the tinkle of glass, a shot, and its echo! I wasn't touched, but I was shook—a man don't get shot at every day. The truck started to swerve, but somehow I managed to keep it from going into the gully by the side of the road. My hand was trembling a little as I turned off the key.

At first, I just set there, getting madder by the minute, then I looked at the small hole in the side window. I'd say it was made by a .22. I turned and looked over my left shoulder, up at the hill where the shot come from. "Dang," I said out loud, "who could of done it? Kids, maybe?" Well, sure, we got a few wild ones in the township, same as any other place, but sniping's certainly never been one of their faults. Who, then? I couldn't think of no one I was acquainted with who'd want to take a pot shot at me—besides, who could of known I'd be on the Rutland road at that particular time? But setting and thinking wasn't getting me nowhere.

To avoid going back around that curve again, I drove straight to Earl Hathaway's place on the opposite side of the road from which the shot come. I drove right through Hathaway's barnyard out onto a rutty lane, where I bounced along a few miles till I come to my own farm. Lil was nowheres to be seen—must of been inside doing

155

something or other. I parked the truck by the edge of the lane and walked over to my shed. I took my own .22 down from the rack, nudged Old Timer, my labrador, who was laying stretched out in the sun, and the two of us got into the truck. I turned and drove back the way I'd just come.

I've heard tell that some folks say Vermonters are the most independent people in the world, but that's so much hogwash. I'm no more independent than the next man—but you can bet that no one takes a shot at me without me doing something about it. I parked the truck under a maple by the side of the road near where the shooting took place, and me and the dog trudged up the hill. It was easy to take cover, as the hill had a good sprinkling of small pine groves.

Finally, we come to the point at the top, overlooking the curve, where I'd been fired on. I could figure just about where the sniper must of stood—but I couldn't find nothing that would give a clue to the shooter. I tried to get Old Timer to pick up a scent, but that wasn't no use, so we both set down to rest—it had been a pretty good climb. Mostly, Vermont hills are more gradual-like than steep, but the dog and me ain't exactly youngsters any more, neither.

From where we was setting, I could see pretty far in all directions, but the only moving thing I seen was a farmer by the name of John Coates. He was partway down the other side of the hill and he looked like he was repairing his wall that runs along his line there. He was using a horse-drawn sledge, on which was setting a pile of boulders. Coates was a tall, husky man about my own age. He was a widower and lived alone. He was so busy with his mending that he didn't even notice me approaching. "Hello, John," I said.

His head jerked up. "Oh, it's you, Albie. What in hell you doing here? Hunting season begun already?" He bent down again to his work, but I didn't pay no heed to that—I'd of done the same thing if he'd interrupted me. Fall is a busy season for farmers—so much to do before the snow flies.

"Tell me, John. You been working here long?" I asked.

"Yep—two or three hours. Why?"

"You notice anyone—or anything—hereabouts?"

"Can't say as I have—but I been pretty occupied trying to fit in these dang bounders. You know how it is."

"Yeah," I says. "You didn't happen to hear a shot about an hour ago, did you, John?"

"A shot?" Coates stood up. "Wait a minute! Come to think of it,

I did hear a noise. Figured it to be one of them big tank trucks backfiring, on 175. Say, Albie, what you leading up to? Something wrong?"

"I'd say there's a whole lot wrong. Someone took a pot shot at me from the top of this hill."

"Took a—you don't say! But, Albie, what was you doing up here at the time?"

"I wasn't up here. I was down on 175, driving a load of hubbards to Rutland. This cuss—whoever it was—fired at me as I drove past. Shot went right through my window, but missed me." I pointed. "Sniper must of been standing or laying right up there."

Coates chuckled. "Albie, if I didn't know you was off the stuff, I'd be wanting to smell your breath! Or, maybe you're just pulling my leg?"

"I guess I'd better be pulling my own legs down to my truck— I can see you ain't going to be no help." I started to walk away, then I turned. "Listen, John. You just keep your eyes open, is all. Much as I dislike you, I wouldn't want to see you get hurt. And if anything unusual turns up around here, let me know in a hurry, will you?" I didn't really dislike John Coates. It's kind of a way us Grange members have of joshing each other. "And one more thing—if I was you, I'd bring my .22 along with me when you're working here alone."

He pointed to his sledge. "I got my .22 right there, Albie. Never can tell when you might run into some small game." He waved and went back to his work. Me and the dog made the short climb back to the top of the hill, then down the other side to the truck. I turned round and drove down to Rutland to deliver the squashes.

On the way back, I was very cautious when I come to that curve, but nothing happened. This time when I drove into the yard, Lil was hanging out a wash to dry. When I told her what took place, she was plenty scared.

"Now, listen, Albie," says she, "you take my advice and go right in and telephone Curtis Roberts." Roberts is the law in our township—he's Chief of a three-man force. He's a hard man to like. He's plumb lazy, and he does just about enough work to cover the law—so to speak. He's often said he took up policing instead of farming because it's a danged sight easier, and the way he goes at it, he's right. Anyways, I started to argue with Lil, but ended up telephoning. I suppose when a man's shot at, somebody should be informed. When I explained what happened, Roberts said he'd be right over.

When he arrived—about half an hour later—in his muddy old police cruiser, I could see he was as fat and red-faced as ever. He got out of the car and waddled over to me. "Well, Albie, it appears some chickens have come home to roost."

"Now, what are you getting at, Curtis?" I asked.

"Why, everybody around here knows how mean and tight-fisted Albie Stowell is," says he. "I suppose someone you struck a hard bargain with decided you was too mean to live."

"I didn't call to have you come down here and make jokes," I said, getting a little red in the face. "Matter of fact, I wouldn't of bothered to call you at all if it wasn't for Lil's insisting. I figured I could do a better job of catching the sniper than you can—but this is *my* busy season, and like everybody knows, *you* don't have one."

Curtis Roberts started to say something, but took out his notebook instead. He jotted down the facts about the time and place, and examined the bullet hole. He said he'd go have a look as soon as he could get hold of a jeep that would take him to the top of the hill. I told him I'd already been up there and found out nothing.

Roberts snorted. "I'd say you didn't let any grass grow under your feet! But you didn't look over the area with a trained eye, like I will. Another thing—did it occur to you that, while most of that hill is state property, John Coates' land abuts it! Perhaps he knows something—I'll talk to him as soon as I can."

"You can spare yourself that trip, Curtis," says I. "I already spoke with him. He didn't see a danged thing."

Curtis Roberts was getting annoyed. "It appears as how you've attended to everything, don't it? But the facts is, you don't know any more about it than I do! —Well, I have a few more calls to make, but I'll get onto this as soon as I can."

I knew one of his calls would be his usual morning cribbage game at the fire station, but all I said was, "You might think of blocking off that section of 175. The sniper got away with it once, he might try again."

Roberts eased himself into the cruiser. He rolled down the window. "I doubt that sniper is within fifty miles of here at this minute. He's had his fun, and he's moving on. But just the same, it's my duty to warn you to be extra careful until I can get to the bottom of this."

"Try to make it before Christmas!" I yelled as he started the car and roared out of the yard. I went back to performing my usual chores, but I must admit I kept the .22 handy.

Just like I figured, Curtis Roberts did nothing at all about the matter that day, and probably wouldn't have done nothing more if there hadn't been another shooting on the same spot two days later. This time it turned out to be a young woman nurse on her way to the hospital in the city. The left front tire of her Toyota was hit with what could of been a .22 slug. Her car went out of control, but stayed right side up till it bumped into the wall that fenced Earl Hathaway's property. She was shook up, of course, but had no broken bones or nothing, and she managed to make her way to the farmhouse, where Earl's young wife telephoned the police. This time Curtis Roberts really rushed over there. The girl's name was Helen Taylor, and her father is a state legislator.

In one sense, the news of this shooting was, of course, a relief to me and Lil—at least, no one was trying to get at me, exclusive. But I still found myself as mad as a wet hen at whoever tried to kill me for whatever reason. Meantime, Curtis and one of his men jeeped up the hill and, like he told a reporter, "thoroughly combed the area." Like me two days earlier, Curtis didn't find out nothing. Coates had finished with his mending and was nowhere around. Roberts said he was trying to locate him for "questioning."

The state police posted a few men up on the hill, in shifts, for a week, then when nothing further happened, they left. Curtis took up his crib game again and everybody seemed to have forgotten the whole danged business, except Lil and me, and, I suppose, Helen Taylor. As far as John Coates was concerned, it turned out he had left the day of the shooting to go to Brattleboro to look for a second-hand tractor he was thinking of buying.

Lil complained about me being so restless, but I've always been a curious coot, and I couldn't settle down until someone come up with some answers. Beside that, every time I drove on 175 and come to that curve, I got an empty feeling in the pit of my stomach—and that's no way for a man to have to live. Only trouble was, there wasn't a whole lot I could do.

About two weeks after the second shooting, me and Lil was going down to Rutland for a lobster dinner on our wedding anniversary. It was a little after six, and it was dark when we approached that curve on 175. When we rounded the curve, the blinking blue lights of state police cars ahead forced me to stop. Beyond, I could see the red blinkers of an ambulance and the yellow blinkers of a tow truck. I got out of the car and walked up to the first state trooper I come to. I asked him what the trouble was—as if I didn't know.

This man was new on the job and didn't recognize me. "The phantom sniper strikes again," he said. "If you're planning on going to Rutland, you'll have to turn round, take Route 8, and get there the long way."

I asked him, "How long ago did this happen?"

"Only about fifteen minutes ago," the trooper said.

"Was the sniping just like the last two times?"

The trooper shook his head. "Nope. This time our friend shot from the hill on *this* side of the road—right across from where he usually takes his rifle practice." He went on to say that the sniper's victim this time was a dairyman's son from Springfield, who was carting a truckload of milk to Rutland. Again, the sniper missed the driver, the bullet shattering the sideview mirror. The truck left the road and rammed into the gully. The driver was lucky to come out of the mess with what seemed to be a broken leg and minor injuries.

I thanked the trooper, and when I got in the car I told Lil what had happened. She was so upset she suggested we turn around and go home. She said we could postpone the lobster dinner, and she'd fix us some supper. I didn't argue the point, just turned the car and headed for home.

Every man—especially a married one—has to have a special place where he can get off to when he needs to think things through. My thinking-place was the toolshed next to the barn. While Lil was preparing the meal, I went there and lit the old kerosene lantern. Setting on an old milk-stool, I started thinking hard about the latest location of the sniper—the hill on the Hathaway side of the road. Maybe the sniper got discouraged after missing twice on the opposite hill was all. But it got me thinking about the Hathaway place and the people who lived there.

Up to a year or so ago, the farm was known as the Hopkins Place. Me and Clyde Hopkins had practically grown up together as boys, us being about the same age and our farms being only a few miles apart.

Running an average farm is never no picnic, but every once in a while there pops up what we call a "stump" farm, one that seems cursed with bad luck. Clyde Hopkins had such a place. He had soil problems over the years, he had water problems, and once his whole herd of Holsteins come down with a rare disease. On top of this, Clyde's wife died giving birth to his first and only child, a son. Thirty years later, this same son, now married and the father of a son himself, was crushed to death by an overturned tractor during spring seeding. If that wasn't enough, Clyde's little grandson was struck by a car on the highway and was killed. They buried the child in a plot near the house. I'll never forget how sad it was when they lowered that little coffin into the ground . . .

Anyways, even though it was his homestead, nobody could blame Clyde for selling his farm to the first people who come in answer to his ad of a farm for sale—the Hathaways. I remembered it was a little over a year ago we went over to bid goodbye to Hopkins and his daughter-in-law just before they moved to Rutland. "Goodbye" was about all we did say—Clyde and me had scarce spoken for a number of years. Clyde had turned into a discouraged, bitter man—who could blame him?—and he kept to himself. Everyone wondered what kind of luck the new owners, the Hathaways, would have on this stump farm.

I got up and walked out of the shed, over to the back stoop, and called out to Lil. "Lil," I said when she come to the back door, "you know the Hathaways pretty good, don't you?"

"Well, *she* sings in the choir, of course, but I really don't know them that good. They've only lived here about a year, you know."

"That should give *you* plenty of time. What have you got to report about her?"

"Albie, what is this?" Lil looked puzzled.

I chuckled. "Now, don't you worry none, Lil—you're still the light of my life. No young kid's going to take your place."

Lil rolled her eyes. "I'd hardly call Esther Hathaway a kid. She's thirty if she's a day. But she's really a very cheerful person considering—"

I picked up me ears. "Considering what?"

"Well, you've met her husband, Earl. He's at church most every Sunday, and I'm sure you've met him at the Farmers' Co-op."

"Sure. I met him and I've talked to him, too—or tried to. Quiet young fella—don't mix much. Is that what you mean by his wife being cheerful *considering?*"

Lil pursed her lips. "Yes, in a way. You see, they were married only a year when they bought the Hopkins place. And Earl had just been released from a Vietcong prison. Don't tell me you didn't know that."

Now I pursed *my* lips. "No, I never did hear tell of that."

"Oh, he's perfectly adjusted and all that, despite being in a horrible prison for so long a spell. He still has a nightmare now and then, but Esther says even they don't happen very often now . . . Say, do

I smell something burning in my kitchen?" Lil left the doorway in a hurry.

I hoped that what jumped into my mind was wrong. Hathaway was a hard worker, and he showed a lot of horse sense. Like I told Lil, I didn't really know the man, but I couldn't help but notice all the improvements he had made on that stump farm since he purchased it from Clyde Hopkins a year ago. Still, it was a possibility.

Naturally, I didn't say nothing to Curtis Roberts about this new angle, and I couldn't bring myself to mention it to the state detectives who come around to question me. They were trying to find out if me and the other two victims had anything in common. They ended up deciding the thing we had in common was we was all sniped at.

Like before, after a week with nothing new happening, the reporters drifted away, and pretty soon the state police left the area. Stakeouts cost money. Before they left, though, they had a long talk with Curtis Roberts, and they give him a direct line with state-police headquarters, twenty miles away.

The night after the police left—Lil had gone to choir practice—I decided to do a little spying on the Hathaway farm. I put Old Timer in the truck along with my .22 and drove round the long way to Route 175. I parked the same place I did the day I was sniped at, and with the help of a flashlight we slowly made our way to the ridge where the sniper had taken his first shot—at me. The moon was almost full, and when we reached the brow of the hill it come out from behind a cloud. I could see everything very clearly—that danged curve, and up from it, on the other side of the road, the Hathaway farmhouse. The house was dark. Esther must of gone to choir practice, and Earl—well, Earl could of been anywheres.

Suddenly, Old Timer started to growl, and there was a rustle behind me. I swung around, my rifle at the ready.

"Put that danged pea-shooter aside, Albie!" It was John Coates.

"What are you doing up here?" I demanded.

"I could better ask that of *you*," Coates answered. "I live just a piece down the hill there—remember? I saw your light and thought I better check it out. Seems like everyone's getting jittery now that the danged sniper is operating at night."

I pointed to his gun. "But it appears you and me is the only *real* worriers. I suppose you heard the state police has left?"

"Well, they couldn't be expected to stick around forever." He patted his .22. "As for this—this here goes with me from now on, whenever I'm alone at night, until this sniping business is settled . . . What do you say, Albie, to a mug of coffee down in my kitchen?" I thanked him but said I'd best be getting home. I wanted to be there before Lil got back. What she didn't know wouldn't hurt her.

"So long, then, Albie." Coates cradled his rifle and strolled down the hill, whistling. I stood and watched until he climbed over his stone wall and disappeared. I was beginning to feel a mite uncomfortable about John Coates—and his .22.

I was hoping to visit the opposite hill on the following night—it was closer to Hathaway's property, of course—but Lil was home,so what could I do? We set and watched the danged TV. And would you believe it? They ran an old picture about a sniper in a tower high above a college campus. He was wearing some kind of an Army jacket, but the danged commercials come along so fast and furious I never was able to figure what all the shooting was about. Before turning in, I made my usual check of the barnyard and I admit I felt relieved when I closed the door on the cold moonlight outside.

All the next day my mind was more on the sniping than my chores. Finally, I got so restless I got in the truck and drove along 175 to the Hathaway farm. I pretended I was just cutting through their barnyard like I do sometimes. I really wanted to see if anything unusual was going on there. I slowed down to a crawl to take in as much of the territory as I could. While I was rubbernecking, I saw Earl waving to me from his tractor in a field of cornstalks beyond the little cemetery next to the farmhouse. I didn't notice his wife around anywhere.

Later, at supper, Lil asked me what was wrong with my appetite. Naturally, I didn't mention my spying visit to Hathaways that afternoon, but it was the danged visit that was bothering me. I sensed I seen something strange there, but what in tarnation was it? I went over the whole trip again in my mind, while I sat in the toolshed after supper. Lil had just left to attend a quilting-bee to get ready for the parish bazaar. Suddenly, I remembered the unusual thing I'd seen, and everything jumped into place.

Lil had hardly drove the Ford out of the yard when I was running down to the parked truck. I jumped aboard and I had drove only a few minutes before I realized I'd left my rifle behind. But I couldn't afford to stop—there might be one or more lives at stake—and there was a chance I could prevent someone from committing murder!

I parked the truck behind one of Hathaway's barns. I took out my flashlight and made my way quietly up the hill to the ridge above the farm, until I could see the curve on Route 175 below. The moon was full and everything stood out clear in the clean air.

Suddenly, I saw a pair of headlights appear on the highway below, racing toward the curve just below where I was standing. At the same time, I caught a glimpse of a gun barrel being raised from a little hollow only a few feet away.

"Clyde—stop!" I shouted, running to the spot. The figure in the hollow slowly rose and turned, covering me with his rifle, a .22. Even though we'd been neighbors for nigh on fifty years or more, Hopkins didn't seem to recognize me. I cried out again, "Clyde Hopkins—it's me, your old neighbor, Albie Stowell!"

Hopkins' only reply was to draw a bead on my forehead. By the light of the moon, I could see his finger tightening on the trigger. My voice was breaking as I yelled, "It's going to be all right, Clyde—for God's sake, don't shoot!" I thought I could see his jaw set. It was the worst minute I ever spent in my life.

All of a sudden, Hopkins was flung to the ground from behind. His rifle flew into some bushes. As he was on the ground, stunned, a figure stepped into the moonlight. It was Earl Hathaway. "Hello, Mr. Stowell," he said, "it was a lucky thing I followed you up the hill after you crossed my barnyard."

"Lucky's a good word for it"—my voice was still hoarse.

"Naturally, I didn't know who it was," said Hathaway, "but I thought I better investigate." Hopkins started to stir on the ground, and Hathaway bent over him. "You okay, Mr. Hopkins?" Clyde sat up but didn't answer. Hathaway turned to me. "What was his reason, Mr. Stowell?"

"No one reason, Earl," I said. I was panting a little. "And my friends call me Albie. You saved my skin, and maybe we saved this man further grief."

Hopkins rose slowly to his feet. His eyes were staring straight ahead—at nothing. "I done my best, Bunky," he muttered, "I done my best . . ."

Hathaway had placed a firm grip on Clyde's arm. "Who's Bunky, Mr. Hopkins? He up here somewheres?"

I cut in.

"His mind's wandering, Earl. Bunky was his little grandson's nickname. He was the boy who was killed by a car a short time before you bought the farm."

Earl said, "We'd best get him down to my place and notify Chief Roberts." I found Clyde's gun, and the three of us started down the hill. Hopkins made no resistance. He moved like a man in a dream.

Curtis Roberts' first question when he heard what happened was, "Albie, how did you know it was Hopkins, and that he might try again tonight?"

"Well," I said, "I was over by Hathaway's farm this afternoon and I happened to notice a fresh bouquet of fresh strawflowers on Bunky's grave in the cemetery next to the house. It didn't strike me at the time, but later I remembered it. That led me to thinking about the child being killed on the curve at 175 about a year ago. Maybe a year to the day I was sniped at when I come speeding around that curve."

"You mean he was trying to avenge the death of his grandson?"

"Yes, I guess you could put it that way."

Roberts went on, "Then seeing the flowers tipped you off that Hopkins was around and he was probably the sniper."

Before I could answer, he says, "We'd best get the poor guy to state-police headquarters. He can sit in back with the two of you, who I now deputize."

The state police were kind to Clyde. They brought his daughter-in-law to the station and that relaxed him some. Then a mind-doctor—I forget what they call them—took him into an office and examined him. He recommended Clyde be sent to a sanatarium for treatment. Curtis got a report on the doctor's findings, and a few hours later, on the ride home, we pieced together what had happened.

After little Bunky—the apple of Hopkins' eye, and his only descendant—had been killed, Clyde was a changed man, according to his daughter-in-law. His attitude frightened her, and it was her who urged him to sell the farm. After they moved to Rutland, fifteen miles away, things went fairly smooth for almost a year, and she stopped worrying about him. She took a job waitressing and worked odd hours. She had no idea he was away from home those times.

"But what about transportation and maneuvers?" Earl wanted to know. "He was pretty spry for his age. I mean, he made three clean getaways."

Curtis Roberts was right there with the answers—now that the case was solved. "Well," he drawled, "he had that half-ton truck he drove. They're pretty common vehicles in these parts. And don't forget he knew every nook and cranny in the vicinity, having lived here, man and boy, for over a half a century—" He looked back at me. "Just about old Albie's age, and Albie done a lot of climbing and sleuthing around. Course, in Albie's case, it didn't hardly amount to a row of beans, except for tonight."

"And where would you have been," I asked him, "if it wasn't for me and Earl and the state police?" I would of said more, but just then the cruiser pulled up at my place. When I got out of the car, Roberts said, "My advice to you, young man, is, if you can't be good, be careful." I started to reply, but the cruiser had zoomed off up the road.

The next night we had the Hathaways in for supper, and Lil had almost the same advice as Roberts. "I want you two to be witnesses to what I'm about to say," she announced over the hot apple pie. "I'm telling Albie here that he'd better forget policing and take up farming again, or one of these fine days he's going to be sniped at again—with a rolling-pin."

Ron Goulart

Back on My Feet Again

Everything got somewhat distorted and exaggerated because of the stake through his heart.

That and finding him dead in the coffin led the media to disseminate all sorts of wild stuff about vampires and ritual murders and family curses. The other body stuffed behind a sofa in the cluttered old mansion didn't help rational thinking much, either. The police themselves were hinting at an occult angle and possible devil worship, which is something the Los Angeles police do now and then with a murder case. Even after the real murderer turned himself in and made a full and detailed confession, nothing much got clarified. He was pretty wacky by that time and he'd never known what was going on anyway.

Once again I seem to be about the only person extant who knows what must've taken place at that ramshackle mansion out in Altadena the other night. Were I to speak up I could straighten out a good many things, but I'd be putting myself in an unpleasant position. Much better to maintain my usual silence and wait until this is all forgotten.

Jerry Hoban first mentioned the wooden stake to me last week when I bumped into him in front of a pawnshop in the heart of downtown Los Angeles. He was standing close to the narrow dusty window, apparently watching a television set inside. He was a tall man of thirty-six, slightly pudgy, wearing a rumpled denim summer suit. This was a grey winter morning, the temperature down in the low 50s, and Jerry was hunched with his hands in his pockets.

I wasn't in a particularly chipper mood myself. My advertising agency had sent me into this rundown part of the city to see if any of the local liquor stores were displaying the point-of-sale posters we'd been distributing for our new wine account. The first three dealers professed never to have heard of Bombardier Fruit Wine, the fourth store was boarded up, and I reached the fifth just as an ambulance crew was rushing away the shot-up proprietor on a stretcher. Deciding to conclude my market survey, I was hurrying back toward the relatively safe garage where I'd left the agency car when I encountered Jerry.

He was watching some sort of game show, muttering, "Here's looking at you, sweetheart."

"Jerry?"

Straightening, he turned toward me. "I still do a good Bogart. Right?" He held out his hand.

"None better." The hand was damp and chill. "What are you doing down in this part—"

"I never miss *Rags To Riches*."

"Wouldn't it be simpler to watch it at home on your own set?"

"That is my set, there in the window." As he nodded at it, a gnarled hand appeared in the pawnshop window, jamming a gold-tinted athletic trophy down between an electric guitar and a case of straight razors. "Coming into view now will be my high school jock trophies."

"Still not working, huh?"

"Listen, I don't blame you and the agency for not hiring me to do voice-work any more." His eyes were back on the television screen. "I'm like a ball player, in a slump."

"I've tried to get them to use you again," I told him, which was true. "But that last batch of radio spots you did for us—we couldn't, it turned out, salvage even one. The cost—"

"Sure, I know." A lovely red-haired girl clad in a sequined bikini was standing beside a gleaming sportscar on a revolving stage, a fat lady was jumping up and down in ecstasy, the MC was beaming. "Gosh, but she's awful pretty," Jerry said in a perfect Jimmy Stewart.

I moved up to stare in at the set with him. "Oh, that's Frilly, isn't it? When did she—"

"Two months ago. They hired her to be the new Prize Girl. A real step up from that pantyhose commercial." He switched into James Mason. "Ironic, isn't it? Frilly Sancastle climbs to stardom whilst Jerry Hoban plummets toward oblivion."

"C'mon, you're still one of the best voice men in Hollywood. Even Mel Blanc says you—"

"I'm *the* best," he corrected. "Or at least I was. Remember when I did Marshmallow Man for your Gobful O' Cookies account? Those little twenty-second animated commercials won a stewpot of awards. I was a perfect Marshmallow Man, I really got into that marshmallow, did a multifaceted character."

"The thing is, Jerry, there wasn't one take on those Baby Bowwow spots for Jr. Pupp where you didn't spoil it by sobbing."

"You're absolutely right, it was all my fault," he admitted forlornly, watching the lovely Frilly bend low to open the hood of the prize car. "Gad, what a stupefying bit of feminine pulchritude, my lad," he drawled in a perfect W. C. Fields voice.

"You're still involved with Frilly, are you?"

"Well, we don't exactly live together any more."

"That might be for the best. You have to admit—"

"Okay, Frilly and I didn't always get along. But—"

"Didn't get along is understating it. All the fights you had, the squabbles, the public screaming matches. She'd move out, you'd move out, she'd move back, you'd move back. All that stress, you know, is what messed you up. Two years ago, before Frilly, you were making $200,000 a year doing voices for the top agencies and most of the cartoon studios in town."

"I like the way you talk straight from the shoulder, pilgrim," he said in a John Wayne voice. He was hunched again, staring in at Frilly as she cavorted among the piles of material goods *Rags To Riches* still had to shower on contestants this morning. "But actually, the situation is fairly simple. I love her and she loves me. Once I get some dough again, once I get back on my feet again, we'll— Ever hear that old blues song, 'My Shoeleather Done Wore So Thin I'm Back on My Feet Again?'"

"What about your uncle, couldn't he loan—"

"My uncle?" His eyes swung away from the image of Frilly to glare at me. "You mean Hurford Mildrew, former president of Mildrew-Askew, the biggest talent agency in tinsel town? Uncle Hurford, who is worth at least twenty-six and a half million smackers? My Uncle Hurford, who lives like a robber baron in that dippy mansion of his in Altadena surrounded by his fabled collection of motion-picture memorabilia?"

"He did help you out once, years ago, when you were just start—"

"Once is the key word." Jerry shook his head and dropped into mimicking his old uncle. "Ditch that golddigger, Jerrold, and perhaps we'll talk maybe."

"Could you go to your uncle's ex-partner, Marco Askew? Isn't he still associated with the talent outfit?"

"Nope, Marco quit a couple of years ago. Plus which he loathes and despises both Uncle Hurford and myself as far as I know." He frowned when a commercial for Bud's Frozen Salad came on the screen. "I almost got hired as the lettuce voice in this one. They're both crazy as bed bugs, Uncle Hurford and Marco. Right after my uncle started turning his halfwit mansion into a museum for old Bmovie props, Marco decided he'd be a collector, too. No two people can hate each other worse than rival collectors."

"Still, it might be—"

"For years now Marco's been after my uncle to sell him one of the famous props from *Castle of the Vampire*." Jerry shook his head sadly. "Imagine two senior citizens, both nearly worth their weight in gold, battling over the stake that was used to impale Igor Zarb when he played the good Count Dracula in that mouldy flick."

"Let me try again at the agency," I said as I started to ease away from him. "Maybe I can persuade—"

"I may not need any charity after today," he said hopefully. "I've got an interview coming up this afternoon, in a new area—something Frilly set up for me. Even though we aren't as close, at the moment, as we once were, she still thinks of me."

"Well, okay, good luck then." I started off down the cracked sidewalk.

He called Ronald Colman's guillotine speech from *A Tale of Two Cities* after me.

Even though Jerry's business meeting that afternoon was a brief one, it had a profound effect on his life.

Hugh Gonzer was the editor and publisher of the highly successful and well-thought-of weekly business newsletter called *The Gonzer Report*. His offices were high up in a glass building at the edge of Beverly Hills. The receptionist in the stark white waiting room was an absolutely beautiful Chinese girl of nineteen.

"He'll see you in eight minutes," she informed Jerry when he'd introduced himself, giving him a devastating and nearly meaningless smile.

"Thank you so much," he automatically replied, doing a near perfect Warner Oland as Charlie Chan.

She made a quick note on a memo pad, tore off the slip, and popped it into a low drawer of her metal desk.

Putting me down on the bigot list, he said to himself as he settled into one of the chrome-and-glass chairs.

All the magazines set out on the highly polished glass-and-chrome tables were devoted to skiing, flying, and other pursuits he could no longer afford. He sat with a hand resting on each knee, gazing out at the wintry splendor of Hollywood and environs.

Exactly eight minutes after he'd arrived, he was inside Gonzer's vast white office. He began, "You wanted to see me about—"

"Sit." Gonzer was fifty-one, wide and handsome, wearing a $900 suit and an even more expensive suntan. He was sitting behind a steel desk atop of which there was nothing except a lone yellow wooden pencil.

Seating himself in a white-leather chair, Jerry said, "I took a few business courses at UCLA before I switched to drama, so I really think I can—"

"The Zarb stake."

"Hum?"

"I want it."

Jerry sat up straight. "The prop stake from *Castle of the Vampire?* The one my Uncle Hurford keeps in his private horror museum?"

"None other."

"Listen, I got the impression from Frilly you were going to offer me some sort of—"

"I'll pay $150,000 for the stake." Gonzer poked the pencil so it rolled five inches to the left.

"That's a heck of a lot of—"

"You, Hoban, I'll pay $15,000 for negotiating successfully with that impossible uncle of yours."

Jerry leaned in, eyeing Gonzer. "You mean you collect that movie-nostalgia garbage, too?"

"You don't read the report." It wasn't a question. "You don't know memorabilia's going to be the best hedge. Better than gold. Ten years from now that stake'll be worth at least $300,000. But don't mention that fact to your senile old uncle, nor to his former partner who is also interested in the Zarb stake."

"Uncle Hurford is doddering, true," Jerry said to the financial wizard. "Marco Askew, on the other hand, is still a big powerful chap. He's over six feet high, has a temper like a Hussar, and he still runs in marathons. That's twenty-five miles."

"Twenty-six. Let me repeat my offer, once. When you persuade your crazy uncle to sell me the stake, you get $15,000. He gets $150,000."

$15,000 wasn't a huge sum, yet it would save Jerry a hell of a lot of trips down to Los Angeles pawnshops. "My uncle isn't enormously fond of me, yet I'm confident I—"

"You can go now. Call me at my private number when your uncle's ready to deal. Miss Sancastle has the number. Goodbye."

Jerry studied him for a few silent seconds, then rose and left the enormous office. The receptionist gave him a final dazzling smile on his way out.

You've probably seen old Hurford Mildrew's mansion written up in magazines, everyplace from *New West* to *Famous Monsters*. They even gave him six minutes on the *Odd, Isn't It?* television show a few months back. Using the fortune he'd amassed as one of Hollywood's toughest talent agents, Mildrew devoted some twenty years to putting together a private museum chock full of the props, costumes, and other paraphernalia of horror movies. He covered the entire span of film history, from silents to the present. Someplace in that cluttered, uncatalogued collection was the heavy hump Lon Chaney had donned for *The Hunchback of Notre Dame,* the cloak Bela Lugosi wrapped around his sinister form in *Dracula*, and three scrapbooks Boris Karloff had made of his press notices. There were suits of armor, mummy cases, and even a silk-lined coffin. There were rumors that old Mildrew often slept in that coffin.

Jerry was thinking of that as he climbed over the iron gate in the high wall of the estate late that afternoon. The day was a darker grey now and you could feel impending rain in the air. He traveled along the white gravel path that went twisting through the acres of tangled brush and trees to his uncle's Moroccan mansion.

As he was crossing the weedy red-tile courtyard toward the heavy oaken doors of the main house, they creaked open and an old man in a too-large pinstriped suit stepped out into the courtyard. "You couldn't announce yourself through the intercom at my gate, schlep? $450 a month that system costs me."

"If Mrs. Braff was on duty she'd never hear it, being about one step from stone deaf, Uncle Hurford," Jerry said, moving closer to him. "If you answered—well, sometimes you don't invite me in. So I crashed."

"How much are you going to hit your poor pain-wracked uncle for this time, Jerrold?"

"Retired all these years, Unk, and you still sound like a 1940s goniff agent." He edged nearer to the shrunken old man. "Listen, let me ask you a personal question."

"You ain't in my will."

"That I know already," Jerry said. "But while I was strolling up here to visit you and your dippy collection, I got to wondering if it was true you sleep in a coffin."

Mildrew made a dry cackling sound he intended as a laugh. "Why not, schmuck? I'm nearly dead anyways, I might as well get used to it."

"It's sort of morbid."

"The coffin was used in *Bride of the Zombie* in 1942. It is worth, especially to obsessive collectors like that schmo Marco Askew, in the neighborhood of $50,000. Would you like to see it?"

"Well, sure."

"Come in the side door over there and don't knock over anything." His uncle shuffled to a French window and tugged it open with both quavering hands. "I still haven't forgotten how you broke the urn from *I Married a Cadaver.*"

"I did that when I was eight years old, Unk." The room he followed the old man into was shadow-filled and smelled of dust, mildew, and abandoned food. "I think you ought to quit razzing me about—oops!"

"Once a clumsy oaf, always a clumsy oaf."

Jerry had nearly stepped on a caseless mummy that was reclining on the oriental carpet next to the upper half of a rusted suit of armor. "For a collection you're always bragging is worth millions, you sure don't keep it in any sort of—"

"I know where everything is." They had crossed the room and stepped into the enormous hallway. "You haven't come whining to me for nearly three months, dummy. What's wrong now? Did that dimbulb with the red fright-wig toss you out again?"

"Frilly's a natural redhead."

"She ain't anything natural, except a natural dimbulb." The old man was, very slowly, climbing a wide marble staircase, aided by both his cane and the bannister. "I really get a kick out of the names these bimbos tack on these days. Frilly? Sounds like the name of a soap powder. Names like Joan and Judy and Loretta, those are star names."

"There were stars in those days," Jerry said in a Gloria Swanson voice.

"Easy—to—see—why—you ain't—working much."

"What's wrong, Uncle Hurford?" Jerry doublestepped up to the old agent's side. "You're wheezing like a—"

"I'm—old. You'll—be—old too—someday—if you don't—walk in front—of—a—truck—you're—so—clumsy."

Jerry took hold of his uncle's frail arm and helped him the rest of the way upstairs. "I better call your doc—"

"Who needs that pansy?" Mildrew took a couple of shallow, rattling breaths. Then he pulled free of his nephew to go tottering to the nearest door. He swung out with his cane and opened it. "We'll take a gander at the coffin."

"You've moved your bedroom?"

"Easier than hauling the coffin up another flight."

The bedroom was dimlit and musty, but even so Jerry saw the stake. It was sitting on a marble-topped clawfooted table close to the coffin. It still looked sharp and functional. The coffin itself was resting on a tarnished metal stand and there was a dented, hand-wound alarm clock sitting on the closed lower end.

"So what do you think of the layout, schlep?" his wheezing old uncle inquired.

"Charming." Jerry wandered over to the stake and the dusty bell jar that covered it. "There's something important I want to talk to you about, Uncle Hurford," he said in his most sincere voice.

Before he phoned me later that evening, Jerry had talked with Frilly Sancastle. Actually, he'd called her new answering service first, then fretted around his small, nearly empty apartment in Westwood. Twenty-seven minutes later she'd returned the call. "Well?"

"Where the devil are you, Frilly?"

"At the Christian Science Reading Room in Santa Monica."

"I hear ice rattling in drinks."

Frilly asked, "You saw Gonzer, didn't you?"

"Sure, but that wasn't any kind of job lead. He didn't want a voice man, he—"

"Have you contacted your uncle yet?"

"Then you know all that sun-bronzed nitwit wants from me is—"

"Are you going to help him get it?"

"No, nope. I am not."

She sent a disappointed sigh through the phone. "Whyever not?"

"Because it turns out his ex-partner, Marco Askew, has been after my uncle for that selfsame stake to add to his own Igor Zarb collection for years." He was absolutely certain he could hear honky-tonk piano in the background. "Apparently Uncle Hurford is growing moderately sentimental in his declining years. Anyway, he's finally giving in to Marco's pleas and selling him the stupid thing. Tomorrow night, in fact. He wouldn't even listen to my proposal."

"Selling it for how much?"

"He didn't confide."

"Whyever do I keep lining up golden opportunities for you? You're as inept as some of those moronic contestants on *Rags To Riches* who—"

"Frilly, let's not have yet another argument," he suggested. "I'm truly sorry I can't swing this deal for Gonzer. Fifteen thousand bucks would help—"

"You'd better talk your uncle into selling the stake to Gonzer. Or you and I—well, I don't have any more time to waste talking to you when you're in one of your moronic failure-oriented moods."

When he phoned me an hour later, Jerry outlined what had been happening since our chance meeting in front of the pawnshop. "You're still relatively ethical," he said. "I'd like your opinion of a scheme I've worked out."

I listened and told him he'd most likely get caught and arrested. "The best thing to do is forget Frilly," I advised him. "Take a couple of weeks off, away from LA. Maybe when you get back I can come up with some voice-work for you here at—"

"I can't forget her," he said. "Nor am I going to toss aside the chance to make a fast fifteen thou. But, well, thanks for helping me clarify my thinking."

I suppose, given Jerry's particular talents, his plan for getting hold of the Zarb stake wasn't a bad one. He, unfortunately, over-estimated his abilities some and he had no way of knowing about the special relationship between Marco Askew and Gonzer's lovely Chinese receptionist.

What Jerry did, as far as I've been able to figure out, is this. Late on the afternoon of the following day he made four phone calls. He had to use the booth in the drugstore around the corner from his apartment, since his own phone had been disconnected that morning because of nonpayment of his bill.

He called Marco Askew first, reaching the muscular old ex-partner of his uncle at his beach house in Malibu. In a near flawless imitation of Hurford Mildrew's voice, he said, "Marco, my boy, I'm feeling very lousy." He threw in a very convincing wheeze. "We'll have to post-pone our eight o'clock appointment for tonight."

"Aha," growled Askew. "So it's true."

"What's true, schmuck? I'm merely going out of town for a few days for my health. When I get back, we'll make our deal. Trust me."

"Trust you? You dangle that stake in front of my nose and then doublecross me. For this I got to trust you?"

"Marco, you'll get the stake. A week at the most, no kidding, and it's yours. So help me."

"Argh," roared Askew, slamming down the phone.

I didn't expect him to get that upset, Jerry thought. Well, anyway, Marco Askew won't go out to the mansion tonight.

He next phoned Gonzer's office, talking first to the lovely receptionist and then to Gonzer himself.

"My uncle would prefer to have you pay me directly," he said in his own voice. "Some sort of tax dodge, I guess. So you can make the payment directly to me. $165,000 in cash. I'll be delivering the item tomorrow and—oh, yeah, my uncle would be happier if you don't talk too much about this transaction for a while."

"I understand. Ten."

"In the morning? Sure. And you'll have the money ready?"

"Obviously."

The next two calls proved to Jerry that he hadn't lost any of his skill as a voice impressionist. Both were to his ancient uncle.

"Hurf, this is Marco," he growled. "How the hell are you, you old pirate?"

"I'll outlive you, schmuck. What do you have to tell me that couldn't wait till tonight?"

"That's just it, I can't make it tonight."

"So suit yourself, pal. You're the one who's been begging on his hands and knees for me to sell you the stake."

"Something's come up, Hurf," Jerry went on in a very good Marco Askew voice. "I'll get back to you in a day, maybe two. We still got a deal, though."

"Maybe we do, maybe we don't," said Jerry's uncle. "Maybe the price'll still be $50,000 in two days, maybe it won't. You'll just have to wait and see, schlep." He broke the connection.

"$50,000?" Jerry asked the dead phone. "But it's worth—"

Leaving the booth, he wandered around the little drugstore for five minutes. He stopped at displays of products he'd once, in the days before his unhappy romance blighted his career, done commercials for.

Back in the booth, he again dialed his uncle's Altadena number. "You don't know me, Mr. Mildrew," he said in a highly convincing cheap-hood voice, "but you'll be interested in something I got maybe."

"No, that's doubtful, so—"

"It's a ring." All collectors are the same. No matter how much they have, there is always one more object they feel they need. Jerry knew what his old uncle yearned for. "This is a ruby ring with a funny-looking bat on it."

A joyful wheeze came rattling out of the phone. "The Igor Zarb vampire ring?" the old man said, incredulous. "But, my boy, it was buried with Zarb when he kicked off nine years ago."

"Things what get buried, grandpa, can get dug up again." A nice line, tough-sounding, and he'd delivered it well. "Are you interested in this dornick or should I maybe contact Marco Askew?"

After a few seconds the old man said, "I'd like to see it. Bring it around to my—"

"Nix, no way. You want the thing, you come to us."

"I'm old and ill. I don't—"

"Tonight at Fat Fury's Café in Venice. Nine o'clock."

"Young man, I don't even know where—"

"Find out and be there." He slammed the receiver into its cradle and smiled. "Oh, 'tis a wondrous gift ye have, me lad," he told himself in his best Barry Fitzgerald voice.

He knew Uncle Hurford was as goofy about that ring as Askew was over the stake. He wouldn't be able to resist the chance to get his hands on something that rare. He still drove his own car and Jerry was certain the old man would go to Venice tonight. Marco Askew, conned into thinking the meeting at the mansion was off, wouldn't be there. Mrs. Braff, the housekeeper, always turned in no later than nine.

That meant the mansion would be empty tonight.

Rain had started with nightfall and by nine it was heavy. The estate grounds and the mansion looked like a location out of one of the Universal horror movies his uncle so dearly loved.

Jerry had donned a pair of old sneakers for the job and water was leaking into them. When he'd reached the French windows off the courtyard, he tugged the shoes off. Then, very carefully, he tried the handle on the nearest window. As he'd expected, it wasn't locked.

Under his dark pullover he carried a fairly believable replica of the stake, one he'd fashioned himself from a hunk of hardware-store lumber. All he had to do was scoot up to the bedroom, pop this fake under the dusty bell glass, and swipe the authentic Zarb stake. His doddering old uncle would probably never notice the switch. And to keep the negotiations between him and Askew from starting up again, all Jerry had to do was make a few more phone calls—to Askew as his uncle and to his uncle as Askew. Some well placed insults would heat up their feud again.

Gonzer might eventually realize the stake was stolen property. But Jerry didn't think that would bother him all that much. By the time the financial expert got around to reselling the thing, in ten years or so maybe, Uncle Hurford would be long gone. Besides, Jerry'd have his $165,000 in cash tomorrow morning. If things got rough, he ought to be able to persuade Frilly to take a trip to some-place like South America.

Grinning, he slipped across the dark threshold.

"What a dumb move, schmuck." The lights blossomed and there was Uncle Hurford, hunched next to some mad-doctor lab equipment with a .32 revolver in his slightly shaking hand. "And look what a mess you're making. You almost put your gunboats on my *Curse of the Pyramids* mummy."

"Listen, Uncle Hurford, all I really want is that Zarb stake. You were going to sell it to Marco Askew for a mere $50,000, but I can get us three times that much. That's right—$150,000, at least. I tried to tell you that when I was here yesterday, but you wouldn't give me a chance. All I want on the deal is a finder's fee of only—"

"I only deal with people I trust. Not with housebreakers." He gestured with the gun toward the phone, which sat on a balsa-wood tombstone. "As for you, Mr. Crook, I'm calling the coppers—"

"What are you talking about, Unk? I'm your damn nephew, your only living—"

"Some nephew. Calls me up and pretends to be Marco and then, as if that impersonation wasn't lousy enough, calls me again and makes like Lionel Stander. Such a dumbness."

"I thought I fooled you."

"I wanted you to think that, dummy, so I could nab you red-handed." His wheeze was growing louder. "Now, as much as it pains me, I phone the law."

"You plan to turn me in?"

"You think, schmuck, I sat around in this dark house for two hours and sent Mrs. Braff to bed early just so I could make chitchat with you?"

"Well, you aren't going to." Jerry jumped at him, chopping at his gun hand with his fist.

His uncle gasped once and then made a terrible keening sound.

"You've killed me, schmuck." He folded up, bending at every joint, and dropped onto the floor next to the mummy.

"Quit this, Unk. You're always trying to make me feel guilty." Kneeling next to the old man, he took hold of his thin wrist.

There was no pulse.

After an undecided moment, Jerry straightened up and then bent again to take hold of his dead uncle by the armpits. It was unlikely that Mrs. Braff would have heard their tussle, but he still wanted to hide his uncle's body for awhile.

The stake was still upstairs. Before Jerry left, he'd prop the body in a chair. Sure! All he had to do was tell Gonzer he'd settled everything with the old gentleman and left! Sometime later, probably overexcited by the negotiations, Hurford Mildrew had gone on to glory. . .

After hiding the corpse behind a sofa that had been used in *Dracula's Lost Weekend*, Jerry hurried upstairs.

The stake was exactly where it had been yesterday. Even in the dim light seeping into the darkened room from the hallway he could see it.

He was reaching for the bell glass when he heard wood splintering down below.

"So much for your flimsy front door!" roared a familiar voice. "It can't keep Marco Askew out!"

What Jerry hadn't known, couldn't have been expected to know, was that Askew was keeping an eye on everyone who might be a competitor for the possession of the stake. One of the several people he'd bribed to inform him was Gonzer's stunning receptionist. She'd phoned him after Jerry's visit yesterday, and again this afternoon after Jerry had promised to deliver the stake.

A violent man, Askew had gone out and run on the beach after that last call from his informer. Finally, when a jog of thirteen miles had failed to calm him, Askew made up his fevered mind to come to Altadena for a showdown.

Jerry didn't know this, standing there in the shadowy bedroom, listening to heavy footfalls come pounding up the stairs that led to this very room. He forgot about the stake. If he could hide someplace, maybe there wouldn't be any trouble.

Silently he sprinted over to the coffin and climbed in. Before he could shut the upper half of the lid on himself, Askew burst into the room.

"You traitor! You Judas!" shouted the big man. "Promise me the one piece I need to make my collection complete, then sell it to that jerk Gonzer! For what? *Money.* You knew I couldn't come up with more than fifty thou just now. You doublecrosser!"

What would be the best thing to do? Shut the lid as unobtrusively as possible and wait this out, or sit up and tell the crazed Askew the truth, more or less? That, though, might lead to his being arrested for killing his uncle.

"Ah, here it is!" The bell glass went clattering to the floor as Askew apparently went for the Zarb stake.

Then Jerry realized exactly how to save himself. Because, despite what his late uncle had said, he really was a terrific voice man. And all Askew really wanted was that sharp hunk of wood.

From the coffin, in a near perfect imitation of Uncle Hurford's voice, Jerry said, "Okay, take your damn stake and go home already, schmuck. Let me get some sleep."

"So there you are, traitor!" Askew came charging over to the side of the coffin. "I always warned you you'd doublecross me once too often!"

Even in the dimness, Jerry could see what Askew was going to stab him with.

Jean Darling

A Bite of the Pie

It all began when Mike Murphy telephoned his wife, Marge, to ask for a divorce. Being well aware of how awkward she could be whenever an unpleasant subject was broached, he decided on contact from a distance as being preferable to eyeball-to-eyeball confrontation. Who could say what a jealous wife would say or do to snatch her husband from the clutches of another woman, particularly if said wife was over forty and her opposition was a nubile twenty-two. With this in mind, Mike dialed from the safety of a yellow-walled telephone kiosk on the other side of the city.

"What makes you think you have a hope in hell?" she shouted in answer to his request, startled at what seemed to be some kind of an exercise in mental telepathy. For the past week she had been mulling an excuse to phone him with the same request. "You know I don't believe in divorce!"

"Stop roaring. My ears aren't able for it," Mike interrupted. "It's not like we were married in church. A London Registry Office means nothing here in Dublin, we might just as well be living in sin—"

"Sin or not, the answer is no," Marge said, a plan forming in her mind. So what if it was a lie? She would do anything for Charlie, especially now. "Mike? Are you still there?"

"I am."

"You know that thing you were always on at me about?"

"What thing? Divorce is the only thing I want to discuss with you." Now that Marge was being reasonable, Mike grew wary.

"The fifty-thousand-pound payroll. I've figured a way we—"

"Not on the *phone*," he interrupted, crossed lines being a normal hazard of telephone communications in Ireland. There was never any telling who could be listening in.

"So come over then—we can talk."

Another exchange or two resulted in his grudging agreement to return to the flat they had once shared as man and wife. She would make tea and they would chat about what Marge had always sworn she never would be a party to: knocking off the payroll at Morrissey's Brewery, where she had been head pay mistress for fifteen years now.

Every Friday, fifty thousand pounds in bits and pieces was sealed into hundreds of little manila envelopes and arranged alphabetically in the metal wage boxes. At eleven o'clock sharp the boxes were picked up by Securegard's man, Charlie Ryan, who, along with another uniformed driver, delivered the payroll to the Northside factory in an armored car.

As a matter of fact, it had been the aura of possibly gettable money that had first attracted Mike Murphy to the shy Marge Callaghan. She was at the age when she would do anything to get a man of her own. The anything hopefully would be the payroll—ideally, without encumbering himself with strings. But when she failed to succumb to the black-Irish charm with which he was loaded, he proposed and, after two weeks in London, Miss Callaghan returned to Dublin as Mrs. Michael Joseph Murphy. Surely, he thought then, now that the virginity barrier was gone, it would be all systems go for making off with the payroll. Not so. Where she adapted readily to the role of wife, the slightest mention of a heist quivered her hackles with righteous indignation—until the telephone call from the yellow kiosk.

Funny how just that one little word "divorce" had her eating out of his hand, Mike thought, wondering why he hadn't suggested severing their partnership before. Congratulating himself on a job well done and patting his soon-to-be-full pockets as he went, Murphy zigzagged through traffic to Gleeson's Pub on the far side of the street, where his blonde-babydoll fiancee, Gloria, was waiting.

Mike's self-congratulations couldn't have been more wrong for Marge wanted a divorce every bit as much as he did—as soon as he had helped her and Charlie Ryan rob Morrissey's. As the word "rob" formed in her mind, a pang chilled the pit of her stomach and she comforted the tiny life beginning within her. God, she thought, it must work for you, little love. There was no way to take care of a child on Charlie's salary these days. With a baby, she would have to stop working. And a first birth at forty-three presented all sorts of problems. The chances of having an imperfect child were far higher at her age. And if the child was born with some problem, only money could help it. This being the case, Morrissey's payroll was the only way they could ever get enough money—plus the fact that money would help her keep Charlie Ryan from straying.

Ryan loved her at the moment, of that she was sure. And he was over the moon at the thought of being a father. But would he still love her in five or ten years? She had come into his life just after his mother had died and he needed an older woman to lean on—to spoil him the way Irish mothers always spoiled their sons. The poor darling couldn't even boil an egg or sew on a button. Marge smiled, grateful to the woman who had left Charlie so unable to cope with the everyday things of life.

"Who was that on the phone?" he asked, still wet from the shower. He had moved into Marge's flat two days after Mike had left, bag and baggage.

"You'll catch your death, love—it's not the Riviera you know." Marge tossed him a towel. "It was Mike, would you believe, and me racking my brain to think of an excuse to phone him. He wants a divorce! Wants to marry that little fluff he's been doing a line with—though what she sees in him." (Not what *I* did, Marge thought. I saw what seemed to be my only hope of ever getting married. I even imagined he loved me, not that all he wanted was to steal Morrissey's money. Her mouth tightened into a bitter line.)

"I didn't think you cared about him any more."

"Oh love, I *don't* care about him, *or* what he does—you know that."

"Well—" For a moment, Charlie seesawed the towel across his shoulders in silence, then he busied himself drying his feet with the meticulous care of one prone to the curse of athlete's foot. "But you do think he'll help."

"He will, of course, Charlie," Marge said, kissing the back of his neck. "Anyway, he's coming around for tea so you'd better clear your stuff away."

"Why not let him know about us?" Charlie asked, turning his face to her.

"*Because*," Marge said as though placating a child. For now it was better that he was ignorant of her motives. In a few months, after the money was divided, it wouldn't matter what he knew.

"Are you going to tell him about the baby?"

"Yes—but not the whole truth." She packed his toothbrush and shaving gear in the bottom of a laundry bag, which she then proceeded to fill with dirty laundry. "Why do you always use a straight razor?"

"It belonged to me da, and seeing I never met him—him dying before I was born—it's the closest I'll ever get to knowing him. —Well, if you think it's best, I'll clear my clothes out of the closet and take them over to my flat."

Charlie dressed quickly, shouldering into the uniform jacket over an unbuttoned shirt with undone tie around his neck. "Okay, pet, I'm ready now. You're sure you'll be all right alone with him?"

Marge watched from the window as he lay the clothes carefully on the back seat of his hatchback along with the laundry bag. How could a man ten years younger than she love her, she wondered. And such a man—so tall, with eyes as blue as the summer skies and a wide, soft mouth full of kisses. The strength of him, the tenderness of which he was capable, she thought, her heart already pounding at the memory of his touch. Oh, God, make it all work out, she prayed silently . . .

That afternoon she took particular care that the meal she prepared included all of Murphy's favorite dishes: oxtail soup, steak and French fries, and home-baked soda bread and butter.

He shoveled it all in as fast as the area could be cleared for the next bite.

"You see," she said, "I've been thinking. It's lack of money that broke us up—"

"I know, Marge, I know. Wasn't that what I was always telling you?"

"I suppose, but you know how everything was then."

Mike glanced up from his plate to see if she was slagging him about his casual-job/on-the-dole/pub way of life. She'd always complained of having to carry the financial burden. But there was no slyness in her expression, none of the looking-down-her-nose of their last few months together.

"We could start all over somewhere else," she suggested. "South America—Mexico—"

"We could," he said, "but I'd like to know what made you change your mind. Was it the divorce?"

"You'd have to promise never to see Gloria again," Marge said, exchanging his empty plate for one loaded with apple pie and cream.

"You make me pie, let me eat it in peace." Mike flapped a hand toward the teapot on her side of the table, a well known gesture that had always set Marge's teeth on edge. With difficulty, she bit back the waspish retort and silently refilled his cup.

Later, while he picked his teeth, she laid out the plan.

"Did you know we have a new security man, Charlie Ryan? He's been on the payroll run since Gogerty was shot in that bank raid out in Tallaght." Mike nodded. "Well, he's always fancied me, says he thinks I deserve better than you. I never pay him any mind, of course, not believing in adultery—"

"Are we discussing my relationship with Gloria or are we discussing the payroll at Morrissey's?"

"I never pay him any mind, not believing in adultery even by *implication*," she repeated, pleased at his reaction. She knew Mike well enough to know that, with his dog-in-the-manger attitude, Charlie would be at risk if Mike noticed any liking for the man in her attitude. "He always leaves his partner outside in the armored car when he picks up the payroll—hoping to make a date with me. Well, next time I'll say yes—go to a pub or a disco, maybe a picture or two. You know, ease into a friendly relationship over a couple of weeks so that when I ask him up here for a drink it will seem quite natural."

"Okay, okay, I don't care about all that. All I want to know is how we get the money. You got any beer?"

She nodded and gestured toward the refrigerator. He went into the kitchen and returned, pulling the tab off a can, and folding himself onto the couch.

Marge sat down beside him. "Next Friday I'll give Morrissey's two weeks' notice—tell them I'm pregnant and the doctor advises me to stop work until after the baby is born. They'll believe it because pregnancy is not so easy when one's—in their late thirties." Mike opened his mouth to say something unflattering, thought better of it, and filled the opening with another swig of beer.

"Maybe your admirer won't take to your being pregnant."

"Last Friday when I found out, I had to talk to someone and he was handy so—"

"You found out!" Mike leaned toward his wife, suddenly suspicious. They had been separated almost three months.

"Well, that's what I told him. That's what I told everybody. I said I'd had a test and Friday morning I checked with the doctor and got the results." Mike eased away from her, suspicions lulled. "Anyway, it was Charlie who said I'd probably have to take it easy until after the baby was born. It sounded like a good excuse. This is Wednesday, I'll give my notice next Friday. That should be plenty of time to plan—it's over two weeks. Now, if you find a flat somewhere—you know, a place where you wouldn't be noticed—"

"They're knocking down a terrace of houses near where I live in a couple of months."

"Are you still at the same place?"

"No, I moved to Rathmines. It must be over a month now." Mike neglected to mention it was Gloria's flat he had moved into. "Anyway, there's all these houses. The fronts are mostly boarded up, but it'd be easy enough to get in from the laneway at the back."

"That sounds fine. You'll need somewhere to take the cash boxes, take the money out of the wage packets, pack it up in old clothes ready for posting—"

"*Posting?*" Mike rose and stood over her in the menacing way she had grown to fear.

"Look, it's best if the money is somewhere safe for a while. So I thought if it was sent in care of my mother's maiden name, Bridie O'Donnell, to Poste Restante in Lifford, County Donegal, it would be safe as houses for at least a month. Then we could pick it up and divide it and go our separate ways."

Without a word, Mike went into the bathroom. A couple of minutes later he returned by way of the kitchen, opening a new can of beer. "Why Lifford?"

"It's just this side of the border, might be easier to get out of the Republic that way."

"Well, we won't argue about that now. Go on." He leaned against the wall, elbow on the mantel. "Charlie the fall guy?" Mike grinned, thinking what fun it would be if the cops were to set off on the trail of the pregnant peril instead.

"Hopefully, there'll be no fall guy. If we do it right, the blame will be put on the Provos or some other group. There are enough banks and payrolls being robbed, why should any of us be blamed? When Charlie Ryan comes up for a drink I'll put a couple of sleeping pills in his—"

"You mean you'll slip him a mickey, sweetheart?" Mike said in his best Bogart voice.

"Something like that. I have the sleeping pills I took when I was sick last year. When he passes out, you come in and carry him down to his car. If I help you, anyone passing will just think he's not able for the drink. Then you take him home to his place and tie him up, stay there for the rest of the night. In the morning, dress in his Securegard uniform, making sure the helmet is pulled well down over your face, and then wait for his partner, Joe McGee, to pick you up in the armored car."

"How do you know Charlie Ryan gets picked up in the morning?"

Marge gave him the how-stupid-can-you-get look he so detested. "I asked him. Now, if you can think of some excuse try and get him up to Ryan's flat. You can say you want to give him something, I don't know—then when he's inside, you knock him out and tie him up. Then when the police find them they'll think it was the robbers tied them up so as to steal their uniforms and the armored car. —Oh, yes, you'll have to take his uniform with you—and your own clothes, of course."

"So what happens when there's no driver? There are supposed to be two guards in the van."

"That's no problem. Lots of times Joe's so hung over he rides in the back sleeping it off. And with you and Charlie Ryan being about the same size, everything should go smooth as glass."

"Well, if there's any problem—Charlie's gun will solve it."

"Gun? There should be no violence—why mention his gun?"

"Squeamish?" Mike's eyes bored into her. After a moment, her eyes dropped. She shrugged, not trusting herself to speak. Violence had not entered her mind. The robbery as she imagined it would be safe. No one would be hurt except poor Joe McGee, and one headache or another would be much the same to him.

"What did you mean divide up the money?" he continued. "Isn't the whole idea that we should try going it together again?"

"It is, of course. But I think it would be safer if we each took half and met up in London or Paris. But it's up to you, whatever you think is best." She looked at him blithely, wondering how he could imagine any woman who knew him would give him a second glance.

"So when I've got the cash boxes in the armored car, I drive to the laneway in Rathmines and take them upstairs. Now I have millions of sealed wage packets, not to mention the car to get rid of."

"I know they're a pain. I'll try to do something with the packets if I can. But the car should be no bother. Just leave it in some side road in the Dublin mountains with the two uniforms inside. It's winter and no one's hiking or anything like that. If you look around up near the old Hell Fire Club, there are lots of overgrown dead-ends."

"Great. To bus it back from there will take an age, they go so slow. Unless—" Mike paused. He could borrow Gloria's moped, he thought, but didn't say.

"Well, you'll think of something," Marge said after some moments of silence, uneasy now that he seemed to accept her plan. She thought of repeating the "no violence" part, but if she did he might think there was some link between her and the security guard.

But if Murphy just did as she said, it all would be so simple—so

clean. Joe and Charlie would be found tied up and, hopefully, unconscious still. She would do nothing until it seemed safe to meet
Mike in Lifford to pick up the package at Poste Restante. How she
would be able to get her share of the money without violence was
a bridge that would have to be crossed. Then, the thought of Charlie
and the baby softened the corners of her mouth, making her look
almost pretty. Ten years didn't make all that much difference—lots
of famous women had lovers and husbands younger than their own
children. But first things first, she thought, and she repeated the
plan until Mike had the routine down cold.

The job went like clockwork. Joe McGee followed him up to Charlie's flat like a lamb and the guard at the plant never looked up from
his morning paper, let alone check the identity card Mike offered.
Then he was back in the armored car with the payroll locked in the
back beside McGee's uniform and Gloria's moped.

He put his foot down on the accelerator and the heavy car slewed
into a skid across Drumcondra Road, narrowly missing the oncoming
traffic. Better slow down, Mike cautioned himself as he joined the
solid band of cars heading for the City Centre. He turned left into
North Frederick Street, drove past the GPO and over O'Connell
Bridge. He rounded College Green and turned left again at South
Great George's Street. From there it was a straight run to Rathmines, where he cut through Mount Pleasant to the disused laneway
behind the derelict flats. Here he parked the van out of sight behind
a crumbling back garden wall.

Upstairs, he opened the wage boxes to find rows of unsealed manila envelopes. Half of them contained double the amount recorded
on the outside, the rest were empty. Pretty risky thing for her to do.
What if there had been some slip-up on his part? Murphy grinned.
But what else could he expect from anyone as stupid as she was.
The way she had flushed at every mention of Charlie Ryan. What
kind of an eejit did she take him for? Two evenings watching her
flat and he knew the score. The two were lovers—simple as that.
And he was meant to be the fall guy. Why else would they have cut
him in on it?

Well, she'd just outsmarted herself. He thought of Charlie Ryan
lying on the floor of his flat in his underwear, sightless eyes staring
at the ceiling. Beside him, Joe McGee had a neat round hole in his
head. It wasn't until both men were lying side by side that Mike
recalled something from his school days when one of the Brothers

had been trying to pound Greek and Roman mythology into the heads of a singularly unreceptive class. Ferry money. The dead were always given a coin for their passage across the River Styx.

He found two tenpence in his pocket and slipped one into each dead mouth. "That should baffle the hell out of the Garda Siochana," he said out loud, shuddering. Mike had a thing about touching the dead.

Wearing Joe McGee's hat so as to look proper driving an armored car, he headed for the Dublin mountains. Everything was ticking along fine. He patted the money-bulged airlines bag on the seat beside him. He had brought two along—one Aer Lingus, the other Pan Am—but one had been ample for the bank notes. The other, filled with change, was in the back. It contained well over a hundred pounds but who cared? It was too heavy to bother with and would take too long to count. Anyway, no legitimate purchaser of antique jewelry would be clunking around with a bagful of coins. He'd had a hundred cards embossed:

MICHAEL MURPHY & CO., LTD.
Dealers in antique jewelry
LONDON   Michael Murphy
PARIS   Managing Director

A fine black-leather attaché case housed the plastic-covered ring tray Murphy had acquired from a friend during the previous week at a stamp-and-coin fair.

After driving in and out of a number of side roads, he found himself at last headed down into what looked to be a long-disused quarry. Stopping as close to the edge as possible, Mike set the hand brake and went around back to remove the bike and helmet. For a moment he considered taking Charlie's gun with him, makeshift silencer and all. Then the possibility of being stopped by a Garda deterred him. They were always stopping bikers to check on whether tax had been paid or not. It would be stupid to chance failure when he was almost home and dry. He watched the gun clatter, along with dislodged stones, to the bottom of the great pit. Then, the brake released, the armored car slid into the abyss in the wake of the firearm.

It was after one o'clock when Murphy chained the moped to a parking meter near St. Stephen's Green, where he spent the next hour buying expensive second-hand diamond, ruby, and emerald rings, using his newly acquired business cards to get a trade discount. As each transaction was completed, the jewel was stored away in the ring tray, which, after a nerve-racking half hour, was cleared through Customs at the airport.

After all the rushing, Murphy found himself wandering around Dublin Airport with more than two hours to spare before they were due to check in for the flight to Zurich. Plenty of time to stop at the foreign exchange to convert most of the remaining cash into French and United States currency. Plenty of time for his nerves to start jumping as the minutes crawled by in slow motion.

Mike nursed a pint at the bar. He looked at souvenirs. He watched people hustling luggage by hand or trolley, all the while surrounded by the echoing noise of hellos and goodbyes, arguments, and unintelligible flight announcements blaring over the loudspeakers. From the wide windows facing the field, he watched planes take off into the early darkness of what promised to be a cold, wet night.

He moved across to the newsstand as the evening papers arrived. For a change they both headlined the same news: MURDER/ROBBERY AT MORRISSEY'S. Above Charlie Ryan's picture was the caption:

HAVE YOU SEEN THIS MAN?

A sudden rush of relief prickled his skin. For the time being he was safe, and would be even after Charlie was found with the money in his mouth. He checked his digital. There was still almost a half hour to get through before she was supposed to meet him at the information booth.

If only he had the tickets, they could have been checked in with one of the pretty green-clad girls at the weighing-in counters. But for some reason he couldn't recall right then, he had told her to get the tickets at the Aer Lingus office on O'Connell Street. The minutes dragged on. Four-thirty came and went. Four-forty. The pulses pounded in his temples and he thought of Marge—the way her eyes had circled into startled surprise as the third eye suddenly appeared in her forehead. Four-forty-one—

"I been looking all over for you! You were supposed to be at the Info over there!"

Mike swung around as Gloria touched his shoulder.

"Don't sneak up on me like that," he said. "You wanna give me a heart attack?"

"Sorry."

"You're late—we said four-thirty. Where've you been?"

"I've been waiting at Information." She set two small brown-plastic suitcases on the ground and unbuttoned her red-plaid coat.

"And why the suitcases? I thought we decided no—"

"We'd better get in line. Look, we'd look funny without *any* luggage." She moved over to the shortest line waiting to have tickets checked. "Is that it?" She touched the attaché case with a finger. Murphy nodded.

"We don't need any more luggage with that thing you cart around on your shoulder for a handbag! And where in hell did you get that coat you're wearing? You look like a bleeding three-ring circus!"

"Come on, Mike, stop complaining." Gloria took the tickets out of her purse and slid them over the counter. Mike set the suitcases on the scale. The airlines girl checked the weight of the luggage and stapled baggage checks to the folders and inserted the tickets. And then they were hurrying away from the counter with Mike shouting loud enough to attract curious glances from passersby.

"Lourdes! Are you mental or something? You were to get tickets to Zurich!"

"Shhh! Everyone is looking!" She drew him into comparative seclusion between two pillars. "Now listen to me. Nobody ever pays any attention to people going to Lourdes. I thought it was a brainwave myself." She tucked the tickets into her purse. "Can I hold the case for a minute." She took the bag from him.

"For a minute," Mike said, annoyed, distracted. "A jewelry salesman going to Lourdes—it just doesn't wash!"

"You could be taking me. I could have some terrible disease."

"Don't be ridiculous. You look as healthy as a horse!"

"So I'll just have to go to the jax and make myself look like death." As she spoke, Gloria shrugged out of the offending coat. "You wait over there by that sign and hold the coat. I'll be right back."

It wasn't until she was out of sight that Mike realized she had taken the attaché case away with her. Foreboding chilled his blood as he walked over to the place where she told him to wait, repeating over and over in his mind, She'll come back. She's got to come back—she will, of course.

As soon as Gloria was sure Mike couldn't see her any more, she cut across to the telephones, where she dialed 999. Then, she hurried through the door marked MNA, which is WOMEN in Gaelic. A few minutes later, a pretty blonde girl wearing a white Aran beret and fringed scarf hurried through the departure gate, paying no attention to the scuffle of police as they took a man carrying a red-plaid coat into custody.

Later, on the plane, when the no-smoking signal was out and the stewardesses were moving through the aisles offering beverages, Gloria twisted the rings on her fingers, watching the stones glitter and dance in the glow from the overhead lights.

That old fool Murphy, he couldn't have been more wrong imagining she'd waste time on him. When the plane landed at Heathrow, she wouldn't bother with the connecting flight. London was where it all was, and she would have a big bite of the pie now that she was wealthy. Sell a ring every so often, move in a social circle where a real man would fall in love with her. But her ideas of what the real man would look like didn't prepare her for the tall, agate-eyed specimen who slid into the empty seat next to her.

When he suggested they have a drink, Gloria told him a gin and tonic would be fine. Soon they were talking, heads together like lovers. He told her about himself, where he had grown up and where he had traveled. He told her how pretty she was and spoke of many other things as the plane winged across the Irish Sea—all the while thinking of the price he would get for her rings in the back room off Greek Street in Soho, probably within the week.

Edward D. Hoch

Five-Day Forecast

It was the sort of smoky, crowded singles bar Libby Knowles had always detested, and as she leaned back to study the man across the table she wondered what she was doing here.

"I'm frightened," the man told her. His name was Bryan Metzger and he was a meteorologist for Sunny Days, a private weather-forecasting service. "I want to hire you."

"That's what I'm for," Libby agreed readily. "My rates are by the day and expenses are extra."

"Sergeant O'Bannion recommended you," Metzger said, moistening his lips with a nervous tongue. "He said you're the best bodyguard in the business."

"Well," she replied, not knowing whether to curse or thank O'Bannion for sending her this one, "I'm the only one in town who makes a specialty of it. Detective agencies and private security firms are generally more interested in guarding property than people. And when they do take on bodyguard work, they generally send out a burly tough-guy type with a bulging shoulder holster that can be spotted a mile away. I like to think I'm a bit more subtle than that."

"You're certainly not the burly tough-guy type," he agreed.

"So what are you afraid of?" she asked.

"Being killed."

"By whom?"

It took him a long time to answer. She became aware of a couple dancing near the bar in time to a throbbing beat from a trio of amplified instruments at the far end of the room. "Me," he answered finally, in a voice she could barely hear above the music. "I'm afraid I'll kill myself."

Libby had started out as a policewoman, assigned mainly to the guarding of visiting dignitaries and their families. In an age when any famous person was fair game, it was a job that demanded instant reflexes and the wisdom to make the right snap decision. Libby had had a boy friend in those days—only two years ago but it seemed a lifetime. They'd talked of getting married. He was a vice-squad detective named Phil Proudy, and he had been caught in a messy internal investigation holding a pound of pure cocaine he'd taken off an East Side pimp. He had tried to outrun two police cruisers on the Crosstown Expressway and smashed into a bridge abutment. He died three hours later and Libby Knowles resigned from the force the next day.

O'Bannion had been one of those who urged her to stay. Nobody thought she was involved, after all, and her police career was just beginning. But for Libby the whole thing had a different point of view. If she wasn't guilty, she was dumb, and no one would ever forget that she'd been in love with a crooked cop. In a job where judgment was all-important, she'd made a bad call.

So she had taken her mother's small inheritance and rented an office in a moderately priced downtown building. The simple name *Libby Knowles Protection Service* didn't attract much business, but with some help from O'Bannion she began to get occasional assignments. Mostly it was guarding visitors—often well heeled out-of-town businessmen who liked the idea of shepherding a lovely young woman around town, especially a young woman who carried a snub-nosed Cobra revolver in her purse and knew how to use it.

During the past year she'd helped guard a man running for United States Senator, and another who was waging a proxy battle for control of a local corporation. She'd dined with a famous rock star and even flown to Miami with a television actress who was worried about traveling alone. In all that time Libby had fired her revolver just once, when a mugger armed with a knife had made the mistake of coming after an elderly black educator who was in town to accept an honorary degree at the university. Libby had shot the mugger in the leg and phoned the police.

But Bryan Metzger was something different.

She should have known that from the moment he phoned her and requested that they meet in a singles bar. Clients usually came to her office or made arrangements by long-distance phone and were met at the airport. Not in singles bars. And she'd never before been hired to protect anyone from themselves.

"I'm not sure I can keep you from committing suicide if you want to," she said. "After all, my fee doesn't include sleeping with you. I can camp by the bathroom door and make sure nobody interrupts while you're shaving, but I won't be in there with you to keep you from cutting your throat with the razor."

"I use an electric."

"You know what I mean. You need a psychiatrist, not a bodyguard. Why do you think you might try to kill yourself?"

"Because a good friend of mine did, just last week. And because I tried to do it once already."

"Tell me about the friend first."

"Horace Fox shared the office with me at Sunny Days. Last Saturday night a little before midnight, he jumped out of the window." Bryan shook his head with a look of incomprehension Libby understood. "He didn't have a reason in the world to kill himself, yet that's exactly what he did."

"Was he alone at the time?"

"All alone. I'd gone down the hall to get a cup of coffee out of the machine."

"Did you two always work that late on a Saturday night?"

"No. We were getting out the five-day forecasts for the West Coast. There are a great many businesses, especially in the California wine country, whose livelihood depends on private weather forecasts. They need something more detailed for their area than the National Weather Service can provide. Sunny Days is especially good on five-day forecasts. Our accuracy rate is a full ten percent better than the weather bureau."

"Tell me more about Mr. Fox."

"When I came back with the coffee he was gone and the window was open. He'd jumped. The office is on the seventh floor."

"And this was just before midnight?"

He nodded. "About a quarter to. We were due to knock off at twelve, but I wanted some coffee before I drove home."

"And he'd said nothing to indicate he was about to take his own life?"

"Not a word, but I'd noticed he seemed unusually somber. Generally he joked and chatted with me, but not that night. We pretty much went about our work in silence."

"No one else was in the office?"

Metzger shook his head. "Julie Wade, our secretary, went home around ten. And Chris Romeo, the chief meteorologist, hadn't been in at all."

Libby said, "Now what about you? Why do you think you might kill yourself, too?"

"Horace jumped on Saturday night. On Monday morning, when I was working the day shift, I found myself being drawn to the window behind his desk. I stared out of it, and for just an instant I thought about jumping, too."

"That's common enough," Libby tried to reassure him. "I think everyone has had those feelings in a high building or on a bridge. It doesn't make sense to hire me for something like that."

"I've got the money right here," he said, slipping the wallet from his pocket. "Look, today is Wednesday. Suppose I pay you for five days in advance, through the weekend. Maybe by that time I'll have snapped out of this."

Under any other circumstances Libby would have turned him down. But when he slid the money across the table she accepted it, hoping no one noticed it and took her for a high-class call girl. She accepted it because she knew he was lying. He wasn't afraid of suicide—he was afraid of being murdered by the same person who had murdered Horace Fox.

Libby had developed a regular routine in her job. In the case of female clients, she often shared a bedroom with them. Her male clients required techniques that were both more circumspect and more intensive. She began by checking out Bryan Metzger's apartment. It was a moderately priced third-floor walkup in a remodeled building near downtown. There was a sofa bed in the living room, and she decided at once that she'd be sleeping there.

"You mean you're actually going to spend the night?" he asked.

"You're paying for five days of protection and that's what you're going to get. I'll be sticking to you like glue, Mr. Metzger."

"In that case you'd better start calling me Bryan."

"All right, Bryan. But before you get any ideas, I never get personally involved with my clients."

"Of course not."

"Just so we understand each other."

Libby passed an uneventful night on the pullout bed, her fingers close to the Cobra pistol under her pillow. In the morning she got up early, checked her client, who was snoring on his back, and started to prepare breakfast. He joined her just as the toast popped up.

"Say, couldn't we make this a permanent arrangement?"

Libby smiled. "Not a chance. Do you like your toast buttered or plain?"

"Buttered. But let me do it. I'm used to making my own breakfast."

"Maybe that's what's driving you to suicide."

"Don't joke about it."

Libby emptied frozen orange juice into a pitcher. "If you're suicidal, I'm a monkey. You're one of the most normal guys I've ever met."

Metzger grinned. "If I was all that normal I'd have made a pass at you last night." Libby measured water into the pitcher without answering. "O'Bannion told me you were a policewoman. How come you quit the force?"

Libby set the orange juice on the table and sat down. "That's a long story for dinner some night, not now."

"You're the boss," he said, sitting across from her and taking a bite of toast.

"What time do you start work?" she asked.

"I'm working nine to five this week."

"We'd better hurry."

"You're not staying around all day, are you?"

"I'll see how it goes," Libby told him.

Sunny Days occupied several adjoining offices on the seventh floor of the Midway Bank Building. Libby rode up in the elevator with Bryan and was introduced to some of his co-workers. The chief meteorologist, Chris Romeo, was tall and dark-haired, with a special smile Libby suspected he reserved for young women. Bryan introduced her as a visiting cousin who wanted to see the office and Romeo didn't question the story.

The secretary, Julie Wade, was another matter. She was a good-natured blonde who joked with Bryan but eyed Libby with a distinctly suspicious gaze. "It's the first of May," she reminded Bryan. "You should have the thirty-day forecasts ready to go."

"Don't worry, I will. I just want to show Libby around a bit."

Libby followed him into his office, leaving Julie Wade looking unhappy. "I don't think she likes me," Libby said.

"Julie? She has her possessive moments, but I try to ignore it."

"Have you ever been married?"

He shook his head while he glanced through the mail on his desk. "I lived with a girl for three years but we broke up."

Libby looked around the large office with its weather gauges and computer terminals. There were two identical desks set before two large windows, separated from each other only by a short wood-and-glass partition. Metzger was at the right-hand desk—the top of the one at the left had been cleared. "Well, you each had a window to help you determine if it was raining out. But how do you go about the task of weather forecasting for the West Coast from here?" Libby asked.

He answered by turning to the computer by his desk and punching a series of numbers. Immediately the large video screen came to life. "It's really quite simple. You see, the Weather Bureau's radar pictures of dozens of cities around the country are available on the computer. You're looking at the San Francisco area right now. See the rain pattern moving in from the ocean? This is just one tool we use, of course, but it's an important one. It gives us an instant, constantly changing look at weather anywhere in the country. We also have a string of spotters all over the country to feed us information—"

"And people pay for this service because it's that much superior to regular weather forecasts?"

"You bet. Florida fruit growers, California vineyard owners, even long-distance truckers need to know the specifics of weather for a particular area, and that area is often far removed from the large metropolitan centers serviced by the weather bureau."

Libby ventured to the other side of the partition. "This was Horace Fox's area?"

"Yes." Metzger brooded. "When I came back with my coffee, his window was wide open. Even then I didn't realize he'd jumped until they came up from the street."

"How did they know he jumped from here?"

"This was the only office with a light on."

Libby opened the window and very carefully leaned out. "It's too bad the building doesn't have those modern windows that don't open."

She stared straight down at the striped canopy over the building's entrance, then quickly withdrew her head.

"I suppose he'd have found another way," Metzger said, "if he wanted to do it that badly."

"Look, Bryan, I want to check up on a few things. Do you think you can stay away from these windows for an hour or so until I get back?"

"I'm feeling better now. I think so. Having you around has been a big help."

"That's my specialty, providing confidence."

"My specialty is providing the weather."

Libby smiled. "I guess it's the age of the specialist . . ."

Sergeant O'Bannion was just finishing the morning lineup, shepherding a tearful rape victim away from the one-way mirror where she'd viewed a half dozen young men in jeans and T-shirts before finally identifying one of them as her assailant.

"Hi, Libby," he said when they were alone in the hallway. "How're things?"

"Thanks to you, I have a new client."

"Good. Who is it?"

"Bryan Metzger—a meteorologist at Sunny Days, the weather-forecasting service."

"Where the guy killed himself last weekend."

She nodded. "I was wondering if you could give me a little help with it, since you recommended me to him."

His big face crinkled into a familiar frown. O'Bannion liked her, Libby knew, but there were times when he tried to be overly protective, like a loving uncle. "I don't know about this bodyguard business, Libby. Why can't you open a nice dog-walking service instead?"

"Sergeant."

"Okay, okay, how can I help you?"

"Is there any chance Horace Fox was murdered?"

"There's always a chance, but there's no evidence. Why do you ask?"

"Because my client is afraid of something. He claims he's afraid he'll kill himself just like Fox did, but I think there's more to it. Maybe he fears the killer will come after him next."

"Well, if it *was* murder the killer covered his tracks pretty well. As near as we could tell, no one was in the building at the time except your client and Fox."

"What about Chris Romeo, the chief meteorologist for Sunny Days? And Julie Wade, the secretary? Metzger said she had been there earlier that evening."

"She signed out downstairs at 10:08. There's no record of Romeo having been in the building at all, though I'll admit these building security people can be easy to slip past. They go off to the john or someplace and an elephant could walk through the lobby."

"Was there anything in the dead man's pockets?"

"Nothing unusual. I'll show you if you'd like. The family hasn't claimed the stuff yet."

"What sort of family did Fox have?"

"Just an ex-wife out in Las Vegas. I understand she's a showgirl."

He led Libby up to his office and then went out to a filing cabinet in the squad room. When he returned, he had a manila envelope with Horace Fox's name on it.

"Doesn't the coroner usually keep these things?"

"Suspicious death," he muttered.

"Then there *was* something for you to investigate."

"Libby—you know the routine! Metzger insists the man had no reason to kill himself. That alone is cause for investigation."

"He didn't live to make a statement?"

"After a seven-floor fall? No way. He hit right in front, just to the left of the canopy over the entrance." O'Bannion opened the envelope as he spoke and let the contents of the dead man's pockets slide out onto his desk.

Libby saw at once that there was nothing unusual: a handkerchief, keys, a wallet containing credit cards and a few bills, some loose change, and a wristwatch. Then she noticed something. "The watch is stopped at ten minutes to one."

The sergeant shrugged. "I suppose it stopped when he hit the ground."

"But that was before midnight."

He consulted the police report. "You're right. The first call came in at 11:51. I guess his watch was wrong."

"Why?"

"Libby—" O'Bannion said impatiently.

"All right, I know. I was just asking. It seems strange."

"Libby, Metzger didn't hire you to solve a mystery. He simply wants to be protected."

"I know," she answered reluctantly.

"You're not on the force any more, Libby."

"I know that, too."

It was on Friday evening as she was preparing for her third night on the sofa bed at Bryan Metzger's apartment after they'd dined together at a French restaurant nearby that he said, "You know, I think I'm really over it, Libby. After these couple of days with you I'm not afraid any more."

"Good," Libby said.

"Are all your jobs as boring as this one?"

"You're paying me to keep it boring, if you know what I mean."

"Let's add a little excitement. Come to bed with me."

"No."

"I suppose you've got a guy."

"No, not right now, but that's not the point. I'm working."

"You asked me if I'd ever been married. How about you?"

"I was engaged to a cop once, when I was on the force. He was killed in an auto accident. Now you know my life story."

"There must be more to it than that."

"Maybe after our five days are up I'll tell you about it. Now I think I'll go to bed."

"You're a hard one to figure, Libby."

"Not so hard when you know me. Goodnight, Bryan."

She had been sleeping for a few hours when she came awake suddenly, her reflexes alert, knowing at once it wasn't any usual night noise that had awakened her. She lay perfectly still and listened until it came again.

A footstep.

Someone was moving very quietly across the floor, toward the bedroom door.

Libby gripped her revolver and tensed for a spring. Her eyes functioned well in the near-darkness and she could make out the shape of a man wearing dark pants and a dark pullover sweater. He was holding something long in his right hand, possibly a pistol with a silencer on the barrel.

She moved all at once, springing from the bed with a yell meant to startle the intruder. He whirled, and she saw the flash from the pistol in his hand. Then she was on him, pinning his arm against the wall before he could fire again and trying to stun him with a glancing blow to the temple.

Metzger was up and out of the bedroom. He turned on the overhead light. Libby relaxed her grip on the intruder for just a second and he scrambled free. She still had a grip on his gun but he abandoned it and dove for the open window by which he'd entered.

"Are you all right?" Metzger demanded as she raced to the window. She wanted to pursue the gunman, but she knew her responsibility was to her client. There may have been more than one of them and she couldn't risk leaving him alone.

"Yes, except that he got away. Did you recognize him?"

He shook his head. "I never saw him before."

"He used a silencer. That means he was probably a professional hit man. Is there any reason somebody might want you dead?"

He turned away from her. "Of course not."

"You haven't been leveling with me, Bryan. You weren't afraid of committing suicide. You were afraid of being murdered like Horace Fox."

"Who says Horace was murdered?"

"I do, and I can prove it—at least to my own satisfaction."

Metzger walked over to examine the window. "He came over the adjoining roof and used a glass-cutter. Do you think we should call the police?"

"That depends on what you're prepared to tell them."

He sighed and walked out to the kitchen. "Let's have some coffee and talk. Neither of us will be able to sleep for a while anyway."

"All right."

Boiling water for instant coffee, he asked, "What makes you think Fox was murdered?"

"I went to Headquarters and looked over his possessions. His wristwatch was stopped at ten minutes to one, an hour after the police report says he jumped. I puzzled about that for a while, until I remembered the date. Saturday was the last weekend in April—the start of Daylight Savings Time. He had moved his watch ahead an hour for the start of Daylight Savings at 2 A.M. If he'd been about to kill himself, I don't think he'd have done that."

"No, probably not," he agreed, looking thoughtful.

"So are you going to tell me about it?" Libby said, measuring the powdered coffee into two cups.

"You're quite a detective, aren't you?"

"I observe odd details, that's all."

"Have you observed anything odd at the office?"

Libby shrugged. "Julie Wade and Chris Romeo—are they an item?"

Metzger frowned. "What makes you think that?"

She laughed. "Maybe their names suggested it. Romeo and Juliet, you know? It just crossed my mind. —She was there the night Fox was killed, wasn't she?"

"She'd left earlier."

"But she could have come back. Or Romeo could have slipped past the guard downstairs."

The kettle whistled and Bryan poured boiling water into the cups. "You're full of ideas, aren't you?"

"But I don't like any of them. I want you to tell me who killed Fox, and why they want to kill you."

"Honestly, I don't know." He sat at the table with his coffee and helped himself to sugar.

Libby shook her head. "Fox had an ex-wife in Las Vegas, a showgirl who just might have mob connections. Maybe she had him killed and you saw too much, so they want you out of the way, too."

"It might explain a few things," he said thoughtfully. "But if I did see anything I'm not aware of it."

Libby started for the telephone. "We'd better call the police about tonight."

"That won't get us anywhere. The police will just drive them undercover. Maybe they'll try again soon and you'll get them next time. I can't afford your rates forever, you know."

"I know. You hired me for five days, and half that time is gone already."

"Will you stick it out?"

"Of course," she said. "Now let's finish our coffee and get some sleep."

"Won't it keep you awake?"

"It never has yet," she told him serenely.

They stuck close to the apartment all day Saturday, then toward evening she called Sergeant O'Bannion at home. Briefly she told him what had happened the previous night. Bryan was in the shower with the door closed and she could speak freely.

"You didn't report it?" O'Bannion growled into the phone. "What's the matter with you, Libby?"

"Bryan may be right that we need to lure them into trying again. But I wanted to tell you about it just in case there's a slip-up."

"A slip-up. Terrific. Meaning if we find both of you dead somewhere."

"That won't happen," she answered confidently.

"As long as you called, there's something else."

"What?"

"I shouldn't be telling you this, but it might tie in. The Coast Guard seized a big shipment of heroin off the California coast three nights ago—close to five million dollars' worth."

"What would that have to do with—?"

"On the boat they found weather reports from Sunny Days."

Libby was silent for a moment. Then she said, "Thanks, Sergeant."

"Funny thing—the most recent five-day forecast from Sunny Days was way off. It failed to mention a spring storm that came up suddenly in the Gulf of California. The storm caused the drug-runners' boat to founder on the rocks where the Coast Guard picked it up."

"That might explain a great deal," Libby said. The shower shut off behind the bathroom door. "I have to go now. I'll talk to you later."

"Be careful."

A few minutes later, Byran came out of the bathroom, a towel wrapped around his waist. "I think we should go out to dinner tonight."

"That might be tempting fate," Libby said. "We have plenty of food in. Let's wait till tomorrow."

They played cards and watched the eleven o'clock news before retiring. The night passed uneventfully, though Libby did not sleep as soundly as on past nights. She found herself prowling the living room and the kitchen, checking the windows and listening for unexpected noises. But the intruder did not return.

In the morning, as they were leaving the apartment for Sunday brunch at a nearby hotel, Chris Romeo arrived unexpectedly. "Sorry to bother you on your weekend off, Bryan, but something's come up."

"That's all right," Bryan said. "Come on in. You remember my cousin, Libby."

"Of course. Still enjoying our city?"

"Very much," Libby replied, wondering if Romeo had really bought the cousin story.

"I hope you'll excuse us for a few minutes," he apologized. "Bryan, the police have been checking into Fox's suicide, and that prompted Julie and me to do some checking of our own. We've discovered a number of secret accounts, mainly on the West Coast and in Florida. They were being serviced by Fox without our knowledge."

Bryan looked blank. "I don't understand."

"Neither do we, completely. I was hoping you could help. Did you ever hear Fox talking business to anyone you didn't know on the phone? Did you ever see him making up maps and five-day forecasts for areas in which we had no known clients?"

Bryan thought about it and shook his head. "No, I don't remember anything like that."

"This is very important, Bryan," Romeo insisted. "The police are nosing around. A scandal could put Sunny Days out of business."

Libby decided to join in. "What sort of scandal could involve a weather-forecasting firm? Using synthetic isobars instead of the real thing?"

Romeo ignored her but answered the question, addressing his

reply to Metzger. "We think he was providing weather information for all sorts of illegal activities, including drug shipments to the California and Florida coasts and night-flights across the Mexican border with both drugs and aliens."

Bryan shook his head. "It could explain a great deal, but I knew nothing of it till now."

"What could it explain?"

"Why he was killed, for one thing. Libby has just about convinced me it was murder."

"Libby?" Romeo shifted his attention back to her. "You'd be wise to stay out of this, you know."

"I'm trying to."

Romeo headed for the door. "If you think of anything that will help with this, give me a call, Bryan. I'll either be at my apartment or Julie's."

When he was gone, Metzger said, "I guess you were right about Romeo and Julie."

"I guess so," Libby agreed.

"I still can't believe it about Fox, though. I—"

The doorbell rang and Metzger went to open it. "That's probably Romeo back about something he forgot."

Libby started to warn him, but she wasn't in time. The ring was different this time, more hesitant. It wasn't Romeo again. Bryan opened the door and stepped back at once, raising his hands. There were two of them this time, the one from the other night and a partner who could have been his brother. Both had guns.

"Get her gun," the familiar one said.

Libby cursed herself for being off guard. The second man grabbed her purse and pulled the Cobra out of it.

Metzger looked sick. "Libby—"

"Don't worry, Bryan. I'll think of something."

The first man laughed. "A real liberated woman, eh? Kill him first, Joe. I want her for myself."

"No! Don't—" Libby started to fall sideways onto the still-open sofa bed where she'd spent the night.

"Get her!" the second men cried, and the other swung his gun to aim at her.

Libby hit the rumpled bedclothes and found her target, fastening on the other pistol under the pillow. She fired two shots through the blanket and the first man went down. "Drop it or you're dead!" she warned the other one.

"My God!" Metzger said. "You shot him!"

"Not fatally, I hope. Call the police and ask for Sergeant O'Bannion. He should be on duty now. Tell him to send an ambulance."

A half hour later, still at the apartment, O'Bannion told her, "That was good shooting. You got him in his gun arm and side, but he'll live. You think these are the ones who tossed Fox out the window?"

She turned to Metzger. "What do you think, Bryan?"

"I suppose it makes sense, especially after what Romeo told us. Fox was supplying weather data to organized crime. His information went wrong and they lost a ship that was running drugs. So they killed Fox, not knowing if the misinformation was intentional, and tried to kill me in case I knew something about any of it."

O'Bannion nodded. "We'll check Fox's bank accounts tomorrow. If he was getting regular payments, we should be able to trace them." He went downstairs with the stretcher, promising to return.

"I guess I did the right thing hiring you," Metzger told Libby. "You sure came through when I needed it. Where did you get the second gun?"

"Like you, they forgot I wrestled the silenced pistol away from that guy the other night. I had it in bed with me, and when they took my purse I knew I had to make a dive for it."

"You saved my life."

Libby shook her head. "No, perhaps I just prolonged it. You could get the death penalty in this state for killing Horace Fox."

"What?"

"I'm no dope, Bryan. You just mentioned the drug ship being lost because of the bad weather forecast, but that's something O'Bannion told me on the phone and I didn't repeat to you. And the ship wasn't lost until some days after Fox's death, so it couldn't have caused it. You found out about Fox's little arrangement and it seemed like a great way to make safe and easy money. So you killed him and took over the illegal side of Sunny Days' business. The only trouble was that Fox managed to get his revenge, even from the grave. A ship foundered in a storm and fell into the hands of the Coast Guard. After that, you knew they'd be coming to kill you. It wasn't the sort of story you could tell the police, so you hired me to protect you."

Bryan Metzger turned away. "You're right about me wanting to take over his business. Why should he get all that extra money for supplying forecasts to smugglers and organized crime when I could do it just as easily. He tricked me on that California one, though. He gave me the wrong information and when I sent out the five-day forecast after he was dead it caused the heroin shipment to run aground."

"Why didn't they simply hire the services of Sunny Days in the normal way?"

"That would mean pinpointing the section of coastline or western desert where the ship or plane would be landing. They couldn't risk the authorities learning that they wanted that information. It was worth what they paid to keep the whole business secret. But, Libby, just because I took advantage of Horace's death doesn't mean I killed him. He *jumped* out of that window."

Libby shook her head. "No, Bryan. The building's entrance canopy is directly below his window. If he'd jumped from it, he'd have hit that canopy and gone through it. But O'Bannion told me he hit to the left of the canopy. He went out the window by *your* desk, which is on the right-hand side facing the street—that's the left of the canopy from O'Bannion's point of view. You got him to your window on some pretext, pushed him out, closed that window, and opened his, because a suicide would more likely choose his own window to jump from."

O'Bannion was in the doorway, listening. "I hired you to protect me," Metzger pleaded, "not to try to convict me of murder!"

"And I did protect you from those hoods. I couldn't protect you from yourself."

"Then let me go," he said, and broke toward the window. It wasn't the one to the roof the gunman had used but a front one three stories up, facing the street.

"Stop him!" O'Bannion shouted from the doorway. Libby hesitated only an instant. Metzger had, after all, paid her for five days' protection, to keep him from killing himself. And the five days weren't up yet. She tackled him just as he reached the window.

"Q"

Patricia Moyes

The Holly Wreath

W ednesday, December fifteenth. A frosty night, with a bitter wind which cut through the streets of London and set swinging the gaudy artificial stars and Christmas trees that hung suspended over Regent Street. Margaret Cannington, coming out of the warm theater into the chill of Shaftesbury Avenue, was glad of the warmth of her black Persian-lamb coat and she hugged it even more closely round her as she paid off the cab which had brought her home to No. 16 Wilberforce Square.

Wilberforce Square is one of those rare and beautiful corners which still exist on the western fringes of Kensington. Its central garden is stocked with blossoming fruit trees, chestnuts and evergreens and is firmly fenced and locked against the unauthorized. The little Georgian houses, each with a small front garden, were built as modest middle-class residences and are now worth a fortune apiece.

No. 16 belonged, of course, to Stephen, and Margaret was finding it hard to face the fact that she would soon have to leave it—as soon as the divorce came through, in fact—unless Stephen proved unexpectedly generous or her lawyers uncommonly astute. She put the thought out of her mind and walked up the paved path, fumbling in her bag for her latch-key. Behind the drawn curtains, she could see lights burning in the drawing-room, giving the house a welcoming air. Tomorrow, thought Margaret, I must buy the holly wreath for the front door. Emma has been going on and on about it. And then she thought, a wreath is just about right. A holly wreath for a dead marriage.

Inside, everything was quiet. Margaret reflected how lucky she had been to find the Students' Baby-Sitting Bureau. Such pleasant, serious-minded young people they were—no question of rowdy parties breaking out as soon as one's back was turned. She had left this evening's sitter—an attractive, black-haired girl—in the drawing-room, settling down to devour a pile of books on French medieval history along with coffee and sandwiches. Probably she was still at it. Upstairs, the lights were out, and no sound came from the nursery.

Fortunately, Emma was a placid child who slept well and had no fear of strangers.

"I'm back!" Margaret called, slipping off her coat and throwing it onto a chair in the hall. Her voice seemed absorbed into the silence. From the dining-room, the little French clock struck eleven precise, silver notes. Margaret went quickly into the drawing-room. There was nobody there. The sofa cushions were dented where someone had been sitting. The log fire had burnt itself out into a pile of ashes.

Annoyed but not alarmed, Margaret looked into the dark kitchen and the cloakroom. They, too, were empty. So the wretched girl had gone home—and she had promised to stay until half past eleven, if necessary.

Lucky Emma isn't a neurotic child, thought Margaret. Even so, if she'd woken and started to cry . . . She's only four, after all. She went upstairs.

At first, Margaret could not take in the simple, self-evident fact that the nursery was empty. Everything was just as she had left it—the old teddy bear and the Dutch doll perched at the foot of the small bed, the elaborate new moon-rocket (a present from Stephen Emma had contrived to break within ten minutes) lying in pieces on the mantelpiece, the dogeared copy of *Winnie-the-Pooh* from which she had been reading to Emma still open at the drawing of Kanga and Baby Roo. Everything was the same except for one detail. The bed was empty.

No, not empty. Not quite. On the pillow, where Emma's straight brown hair should have been spread out, tousled in sleep, there was a piece of paper.

Margaret switched on the light and went over to the bed. She could not bring herself to touch the paper. She leaned over to read it, standing as far away as she could . It was a very ordinary piece of white paper torn from a scribbling pad and the words on it had been cut out individually from the newspapers and pasted onto it—a task which must have taken some time and trouble.

The little girl is safe and will come to no harm if you are sensible. If you attempt to contact the police or to disobey orders, she will suffer. Your telephone is tapped and your movements are under observation SO DON'T TRY ANY TRICKS. You will be given instructions later.

Margaret left the paper where it was and walked slowly downstairs. For several minutes she stood beside the telephone in the drawing-room, fighting against the numbness that seemed to have robbed her of all power of action. *Your telephone is tapped.* The telephone had suddenly become an enemy, a squat black traitor, a spy. Slowly Margaret pulled it toward her and began to dial the number of the luxury service-apartment in Mayfair where Stephen was now living.

"Cannington," said Stephen in his brisk, telephone voice. He was one of the people who obeyed the Postmaster General's instructions to the letter. He did not say "Hello," he announced his identity. Margaret had always found it disconcerting.

"Oh, Stephen—is that you? It's me."

"Margaret!" Stephen did not sound pleased. "What on earth do you want at this hour of night?"

"Stephen, I—I must see you."

"Are you out of your mind? You know very well that the lawyer said we shouldn't meet before the case comes up. I thought you understood that."

"But I must see you—right away, now."

"My dear Margaret," said Stephen, "I have just explained."

"This is serious, Stephen. Something has happened. . . ." Margaret found herself groping for words, as though she were trying to speak a foreign language.

"Well? What has happened?"

"It's—it's Emma."

"Emma?" Stephen was worried now. "Is she ill?"

"I—I don't know."

"What do you mean, you don't know?"

"I—she—she isn't here, you see."

"Not there? Then where is she?"

"I don't know. Oh, Stephen, I must see you!"

"You mean the child's lost?"

"I can't explain on the telephone. *Please* come here, Stephen. At once."

"Very well." Abruptly, Stephen rang off. One of the secrets of his success in business was his capacity for making quick, clean decisions.

Margaret stood beside the telephone and wished she could weep. After six years of marriage, she could recognize every inflection of Stephen's voice and she knew he was very angry—and when he heard the whole story he would be angrier still. Not that it mattered. The important thing was that he would know what to do. He would find Emma and bring her home. Afterward, of course, Margaret knew that she would have to bear the whole brunt of his fury. He would certainly try to take Emma away from her—on grounds that she had proved incompetent to look after the child—but at the moment, even that seemed unimportant. The only thing that mattered was to find Emma.

The sound of Stephen's car drawing up outside the house brought Margaret to her senses. Only then did she realize that she must have been standing perfectly still beside the telephone for at least ten minutes. She tried to remember what she had read about the effects of shock.

Then the car door banged and Margaret heard Stephen's footsteps coming up the paved path. She hurried to the front door. It seemed to her to be tremendously important to get it open before Stephen had to ring the bell, like a stranger.

He looked very tall, standing on the threshold outlined by the light of a street lamp. Beyond him was the darkness—and the unseen watcher. Surely they couldn't object to her contacting Stephen—they must know she had no money of her own. If there was to be a ransom Stephen would have to pay it.

"It was kind of you to come," she said.

"Now, what is all this, Margaret?" He walked straight past her and into the drawing-room. She followed him.

"Emma has been kidnaped," she said.

Stephen's blue eyes, so like Emma's, grew hard as diamonds.

"How could you have allowed such a thing to happen?"

"I—I don't know."

"To think that I left my child in your care!"

"She's my child, too."

"You'd better tell me about it."

Margaret sat down in a small armchair. Stephen remained standing, his back to the dead fire: between them, dividing them, the sofa with the dented cushions and the empty tray mocked them, dumbly insolent.

Margaret said, "Well, you see, I went out tonight. Because it's Wednesday."

"You go out every Wednesday evening, do you?"

"Yes, I have to. Because of this job I'm doing."

"Job?" Stephen was angry. "You had no business to take a job and neglect Emma. If you needed more money, you should have asked my lawyers."

He spoke, Margaret thought, exactly as though she were an employee in one of his factories. She longed to run to him, to bury her head in his shoulder, to be comforted—as she would have done a year ago—but it was no use. The old Stephen had gone for good and this stranger had taken his place.

"It has nothing to do with money," she said. "You've been very generous."

"Then why—?"

"I have a perfect right to take a job if I want to."

"All right. Get on with it, for heaven's sake."

"Well, after—after you left, I got rather depressed. I didn't seem able to shake myself out of it." She hesitated. Stephen made a small, impatient movement. She went on quickly. "Then about a month ago I met up with Freddy Barnstable. I don't think you ever knew him, but he used to be the editor of *Newslines* when I was their theater critic, before we were married. He's with Incorporated Newspapers now and he offered me a job in my old department. It's nothing very big—just a weekly column syndicated through a group of provincial papers. I go to one play a week and write it up. The plays don't have to be brand new because this is for out-of-town readers, not first-nighters. More a sort of guide to what to book for when the Mothers' Union hires a coach and—"

"Could we get back to Emma?"

"I'm sorry. Well, I arranged to go to the theater every Wednesday. It meant finding a baby-sitter for Emma and I fixed that through the Students' Baby-Sitting Bureau."

"I suppose you realize that you've been criminally stupid," said Stephen. "I've been paying you a great deal of money to look after Emma."

Margaret was stung into anger. "It's a pity," she said, "that you didn't simply engage a nursemaid."

Stephen suddenly smiled, became reasonable. "I'm not blaming you for wanting to take the job," he said, "but surely it wasn't necessary to go out on the same evening every week, was it? Once you establish a routine like that, you're practically hanging out a Welcome sign to criminals. I'm very surprised you haven't been *burgled* before now. After all, I left a lot of valuable stuff in this house. However, let's get on. What is this Students' Bureau, and how did you hear of it?"

"As a matter of fact," said Margaret, "it was Freddy's idea. He said it had been recommended by friends of his. It's just a small concern—a one-room office in Kensington run by a rather nice young man. Shabby, intellectual type—shirts frayed but always clean, leather patches on elbows of well cut suit—"

"Name?" asked Stephen.

"I've no idea. I never asked. He told me he had a rota of students who liked to make extra money by combining an evening of study with baby-sitting. I must say, they've all been charming young people."

"How many times have you employed these charming young people?"

"This evening was the fourth Wednesday."

"Each time a different student?"

"No. The first time it was an Irish blonde called Paddy—a medical student. The second and third time, a girl called Sheila Durrant—exceptionally pretty, with marvelous red hair. Emma adored her. She's a drama student and has a most beautiful voice, wonderful for bedtime stories. She was to have come again this evening, but at the last moment the Bureau telephoned to say that her mother was ill and she'd had to go down to the country. The young man said he'd send somebody else instead.

"I was very disappointed, as you can imagine—but when the new girl arrived I was very taken with her. She couldn't have been less like Sheila—she was petite, with long black hair and one of those spiky, intelligent faces, not at all beautiful but very attractive. She was wearing a pale-blue sweater and blue jeans and had a pile of history books with her."

"What was her name?"

"Grace Bridge—at least, that's what she said. She told me she was studying history at London University, and then we discovered she had a brother in the Foreign Service who had known my brother Dick in Nigeria. It all seemed too good to be true—"

"It certainly was," said Stephen drily. "Well, go on."

"I took her up to meet Emma, who was in bed and almost asleep, then I went to the theater. I got home just before eleven to find this room empty and the fire out. At first I thought the girl had simply gone home early, but when I went upstairs . . ." Margaret stood up. "You'd better come and see for yourself. I didn't touch anything." They went up to the nursery in silence.

Stephen read the note with a deepening frown. Then he said, "All that nonsense about tapping the telephone you can safely ignore. They're only trying to frighten you."

"How can you be sure?"

"Because private individuals can't tap telephones," replied Stephen, calmly omniscient. "So you found this note and you rang me. Have you been on to the police?"

"No."

He looked at her in exasperation. "Why on earth not?"

Silently, Margaret indicated the note. Stephen said nothing, but walked quickly out of the room. Margaret ran downstairs after him. When she reached the drawing-room, he had already picked up the telephone. She cried, "No! Stephen, don't! Don't!"

He paused, the receiver in his hand. "For heaven's sake, stop being hysterical."

"I'm not hysterical, I'm only thinking of Emma! Stephen, *please!*"

He replaced the telephone on its stand and said, "Margaret dear, do be rational. I'm thinking of Emma, too. If we don't—"

The ringing of the telephone cut him short in midsentence. They both looked at it as it shrilled in the silence.

"You'd better answer it," Stephen said.

Reluctantly, Margaret picked up the receiver.

"Mrs. Cannington?" It was impossible to tell whether it was a man or a woman speaking. The voice was light and nasal and disguised with a marked but unconvincing American accent.

"Yes," breathed Margaret.

"I don't need to tell you who this is. First of all, go and pull back the curtains. I want you and Mr. Cannington both to stand in the lighted window where we can see you."

Silently, Margaret obeyed, gesturing to Stephen to stand with her in the uncurtained bay window. As she picked up the phone again, the voice continued, "Good. That's very nice. You've done well up to now. It was fortunate for the little girl that you didn't try to contact anybody besides your husband."

"Where's Emma?" Margaret whispered.

"She's fine. Just fine. Still sleeping. We had to give her a little something to soothe her, you see. Now, there's no time to waste. Here are your instructions. You will go to the theater again tomorrow night. Alone. To the Majestic."

"But that's the new American musical—I'll never get a seat."

At this apparent irrelevance, Stephen took a step toward her. At once, the voice said, "Tell Mr. Cannington to keep still, please."

Stephen was by then close enough to hear the voice from the telephone and stopped dead in his tracks. The speaker went on. "Thank you, Mr. Cannington. Now, where were we? Oh, yes—Mrs. Cannington. You'll get a ticket all right. Your *friend* Mr. Barnstable will manage that for you if you ask him nicely." The voice laughed unpleasantly. "You will wear your Persian-lamb coat, but you'd better put on a warm dress under it because you won't be bringing the coat home. You will sew ten thousand pounds in used ten-pound notes between the fur and the lining and hand the coat in to the cloakroom at the theater. In the first interval, you will slip the cloakroom ticket behind the picture of Sir Henry Irving in the Stalls Bar. You will then leave the theater and go home. If you set any spies, police or otherwise, on the cloakroom the coat will not be claimed and it will be too bad for Emma. Is that clear?"

"Perfectly clear."

"Good. Leave the curtains open, please, and put the telephone down in the window where we can see it. You won't be making any more calls tonight."

There was a sharp click as the caller rang off. Margaret and Stephen looked at each other. She said, "You heard that?"

"Most of it. Quite an ingenious device. There won't be an empty seat in the house and the cloakroom will be pandemonium at the end of the performance. Nevertheless, we will inform the police."

"Stephen, we daren't. I'm not being hysterical, but we daren't. If we telephone now, they'll see us."

"My dear Margaret," said Stephen, "please use what intelligence you possess. If the telephone was really tapped, why should our anonymous friend have taken the trouble to tell you to leave the curtains undrawn? I agree that it would be foolish to ring the police from here, but as soon as I get home, I'll—"

The telephone rang again: it was as if it resented being left out of the conversation. Margaret picked it up.

"Mrs. Cannington? Sorry to bother you again. I forgot to point out that Mr. Cannington is to spend the night in your house. He is to go straight from there to his bank in the morning, to draw out the money. Just tell him that if he disobeys, he'll never see Emma again. Goodnight, Mrs. Cannington."

Margaret put down the receiver. "You heard *that?*"

Stephen looked as if he were about to explode. Dispassionately, Margaret found herself noticing that his fair-skinned, handsome face was showing a tendency to get florid when he was angry. He would soon have to start watching his weight.

"I can't possibly stay here," he said.

"It looks as though you'll have to," said Margaret. "I'll make up the bed in the spare room."

"You'll do nothing of the sort. My car is outside the door—everybody will know. I told you what the lawyer said—"

"The car *is* a bit conspicuous," Margaret said thoughtfully. Through the uncurtained windows, she could see the huge silver Rolls Royce. She could even make out the number plate— SC1. There was an SC2 as well—a dark-green Bentley. Before Stephen's departure, she herself had driven SC3, a pale-blue Alfa Romeo. She had insisted on Stephen taking it with him.

"In any case," Stephen was saying, "what about Juliette? She's—well, she's a sensitive girl, and somebody would be sure to tell her."

It's odd, thought Margaret quite calmly, Stephen goes red when he's angry. I go white. She could feel the color draining from her face.

"This is hardly the moment," she said, "to expect me to worry about your girl friend's feelings. Surprisingly enough, I'm thinking about Emma."

Stephen knew at once he had made a mistake. He sat down and smiled up at Margaret. "I'm sorry," he said. "You'd better make that bed up."

"I will," she said. She was determined not to be taken in by any sudden display of Cannington charm.

"Take a couple of aspirin and try to get some sleep," he said. "In the morning we'll make plans. Remember—they won't harm Emma as long as we are sensible and careful. Try not to worry too much."

Ten minutes later, Margaret came downstairs and into the drawing-room again. "Your bed is—" she began, and then stopped. The room was empty. She ran out into the hall and saw that the front door was standing slightly ajar. In a sort of panic, she pulled it open and stumbled out into the freezing darkness of the little garden, crying, "Stephen! Where are you?"

"It's all right." His voice came reassuringly from the road. A moment later, he came back through the gate. He said, "I was just taking a look for this mysterious Big Brother who claims to be watching us."

"Was that wise?"

"I think so. He's probably gone off duty by now. He knows very well we wouldn't risk harming Emma by disobeying him." He paused. "What interests me is: where is his vantage point?"

"It could be anywhere out there, I suppose." Margaret gestured toward the dark gardens.

"I don't think so," said Stephen. "The gardens are locked, and the fence is six feet high and has barbed wire on top of it."

"Then he must be in the street."

"I doubt it. Wilberforce Square has always been a great place for burglaries and the police keep a close eye on it. I wouldn't care to hang about here after dark unless I could give a very good account of myself. Besides, there's another thing."

Margaret shivered. "Let's go in," she said. "It's terribly cold."

"Very well."

As he shut the front door behind them, Stephen said, "Don't you want to hear the rest of my theory?"

"Yes, of course I do. It's just that—I find it hard to concentrate."

"Well, try, because it's important. Think about the telephone conversation with —let's be conventional and call him X."

"Or her."

"X will do for either. Now, there's no doubt that X, while on the telephone, could see in directly through this window. Unless—"

"Unless what?"

"Unless X was calling from a room with two telephones on separate lines, the second line connecting him with somebody who could see us. Either way, it means that the kidnapers have access to a telephone from which they can see the front of this house."

"Of course," said Margaret. "How idiotic of me not to think of that."

"X counted on his mumbo-jumbo of tapped telephones and so forth, together with your naturally confused and upset state of mind, to create the impression of a sort of superhuman surveillance of us and our movements. In fact, he could only watch us when we pulled back the curtains and stood in the window. If we eliminate the street and the gardens, that leaves—"

Incredulously, Margaret said, "One of the houses in the square?"

"Exactly. Not one directly opposite— the trees block the view. Not one on either side of us—you can't see the window from them, I've just checked. In fact, there are only four possible houses." Stephen took a pen from his pocket and made a rough sketch on the corner of a magazine. "This house, No. 16, is the center of five houses on the south side of the square. The four possible houses are Nos. 1 and 2—the nearest houses on the west side—and Nos. 12 and 13, which are the corresponding houses on the east side. From any of those four you can see diagonally across the corner and into our window."

"Then you think Emma may still be in Wilberforce Square?"

"No, of course not. X isn't as foolish as that. The worst thing we could do at the moment would be to show too much interest in those houses. Do you know who lives in them?"

Margaret considered. "No. 1 is old Lady Percival," she said. "Surely you remember her? Crippled with arthritis, ninety if she's a day—she's lived in Wilberforce Square all her life. She has a sort of lady-nursemaid-companion called Miss Taylor—one of those sad, dim creatures. I can't imagine any criminal activity there."

"And No. 2? Isn't that the young couple with the Aberdeen terrier?"

Margaret shook her head. "You're out of date, Stephen," she said. "They moved out weeks ago. As far as I know, the house is still empty."

"Is it, indeed? Should be worth investigating."

"But if the house is empty, the telephone is surely cut off?"

"We'll have to see," said Stephen. "Now—No. 12?"

"That's the Bassetts," said Margaret. "Major-General retired, plus lady wife and two poodles. I don't think. . . Oh, Stephen, I've just remembered!"

"What?"

"I met Mrs. Bassett out shopping the other day and she was telling me what a frightful noise they made."

"The poodles?"

"No, no. The people next door in No. 13. Mrs. Bassett said she was going to complain to the police. Radios playing at all hours, and so forth. Of course, the Bassetts have been spoilt. For years they had dear little Mr. Andrews living next door and he never made a sound. All the same—"

"Margaret," said Stephen, "can't you ever keep to the point?"

"I'm sorry. You see, a few weeks ago Mr. Andrews moved from No. 13 and the house was taken over."

"By whom?"

"That's just the point, Stephen. By a Students' Hostel!"

Margaret accepted the warm milk and aspirins upon which Stephen insisted and went to her room, dry-eyed and despairing, to face a long and sleepless night. In fact, as soon as she was alone and there was no longer any need to keep up a façade for Stephen's benefit, she was overcome by a fit of uncontrollable weeping. This proved extremely exhausting, as Nature had wisely intended, so that quite soon she was deeply asleep. Opening her eyes a couple of minutes later (as she thought), she saw the pale December sunlight creeping round the edge of the curtains. She leapt guiltily out of bed.

Stephen was already up, making tea in the kitchen. He looked strained and drawn, and Margaret was sure he had not slept. He looked up and smiled as she came in.

"I was about to bring you a cup of tea."

"There's no need to bother." Margaret was aware that she sounded ungracious, but she found it hard to forgive Stephen for being so kind, so tired, so patently one-up. She knew—or thought she knew—the value of that particular smile. She had seen it switched on for the benefit of business rivals just before a particularly outrageous coup, and she had watched their well founded suspicions dissolving in its deceptive warmth. She wondered what he was plotting now.

He poured a cup of tea and handed it to her. "I've been mapping out a plan of campaign," he said.

"Look, Stephen," said Margaret, "don't you think we ought to give these people a chance?"

"Give them a chance? What on earth do you mean?"

"A chance to keep their word, and return Emma. After all, ten thousand pounds is a pretty reasonable sum for somebody like you."

"Exactly." There was no trace of a smile now. "Far too reasonable. If they'd asked for fifty thousand, I might have believed they intended to give the child back. As it is—"

"But what else can we do?"

"Sit down and I'll tell you." Stephen poured himself a fresh cup of tea and they sat one on each side of the kitchen table. Margaret remembered with a sharp pang all the other mornings when they had sat just like this, breakfasting in the kitchen, in the days before Stephen's business had burgeoned into an empire and their marriage had crumbled into a mockery.

Stephen said, "It's true that you'll have to take the money to the theater tonight. I want them to think we're playing along with them. But meanwhile I intend to move over to the offensive."

"How can you? They're watching every move we make."

"Nonsense," said Stephen. "The important thing is not to be intimidated by these people. For a start, I very much doubt if there are more than two of them. One is obviously your baby-sitter—Grace Bridge, or whatever her real name is— and she'll be occupied looking after Emma. That leaves just one accomplice, probably a man, to watch this house and shadow us."

"I don't see what you're getting at," said Margaret.

"Just this. We will go together to my bank this morning, and I think we can be pretty certain that only one person will be trailing us. So if we separate—"

"He'll follow me," said Margaret promptly.

"I think not," said Stephen. "We'll go into the bank together. X won't dare follow us in. He'll wait in the street outside—in Piccadilly. What most people don't know is that the bank has a back door leading into Jermyn Street—you get to it through the manager's office. You will walk straight through the building and out the other side. There you will get into a taxi. I think we can assume that you won't be followed."

"And where am I supposed to go in this taxi?" Margaret asked. "To the police?"

"I think not. Not at this stage. Listen."

At nine o'clock, Margaret telephoned Freddy Barnstable. For some time, the bell rang unanswered. Then a sleepy voice said, " 'Lo?"

"Freddy?"

"Um. Who's this?"

"It's Maggie."

"Oh. Maggie. . . "

"Yes. Are you awake yet, or shall I call back?"

"No, no. Wide awake. What's the trouble, love?"

"No trouble, Freddy. I just want you to pull a few strings for me."

"Strings?" Freddy yawned. "Sorry. I didn't get to bed till three. What strings?"

"Can you get me a seat for *Small Green Apples* tonight?"

"*Small Green*— you mean the new musical at the Majestic? You don't want much, do you? It's booked solid until July."

"I know it is, Freddy. That's why I rang you. I thought you might have a winning way with house seats. It's terribly important."

"Well, I can try. I know the box-office manager. I'll see what I can do."

"Freddy, you're an angel. Will you call me back to confirm it?"

"O.K. Just a moment, let me write it down. Maggie Cannington, the Majestic, two seats. . . "

"One seat, Freddy."

"One? You mean you're going alone?"

"I often go to the theater alone."

"How very peculiar," said Freddy.

Half an hour later Barnstable's secretary telephoned to say that a house seat at the Majestic had been set aside for her and that Margaret should pick up her ticket at the box office before the performance.

"Good," said Stephen. "Now we can go to the bank."

Outside it was cold and sunny. In the gardens of Wilberforce Square, the trees raised their bare arms against the pale-blue of the sky. As Margaret stepped out of the gateway of No. 16, her eyes went instinctively toward the unrevealing façade of No. 13, the Students' Hostel. A girl wearing black stockings, a leather skirt, and a long striped scarf was coming out of the front door carrying an armful of books. Stephen raised his eyebrows inquiringly, but Margaret shook her head. The girl was a stranger.

Behind Margaret, a rich, crisp, aristocratic voice said, "Good morning, Mrs. Cannington."

Margaret turned around. "Good morning, Lady Percival."

Lady Percival surveyed the Rolls Royce from her wicker-work wheelchair with regal approval. She had always been a dominating woman, and in her old age she contrived to invest her invalid carriage with the dignity of a palanquin drawn by Nubian slaves. In fact, there was only one slave—the wafer-thin Miss Taylor, who now began to propel her employer along the pavement.

"Stop, Taylor! I have not yet said good morning to *Mr.* Cannington."

"Good morning," said Stephen brusquely.

"It is so *very* nice to see you back home," pursued Lady Percival relentlessly. "We quite thought we had lost you altogether from our little community. It must have been an unusually protracted business trip to keep you away for so long." Stephen opened his mouth to speak, then thought better of it. "I trust," went on the old lady, "that now you are back it will be *for good*. Your little girl has been missing you, I am sure. It is very bad for a child to be brought up without the constant influence of its father. Don't you agree, Mrs. Cannington?"

"Oh, yes—yes, of course," Margaret heard herself mumbling like an idiot.

"Well, I won't detain you any longer—but when you have the time, Mrs. Cannington, I would like a word with you about the Parish Jumble Sale. We're relying on your help, you know, and time is getting short. Very well, Taylor, I am ready to go on now. Good morning to you, Mrs. Cannington."

The wheelchair moved off with majestic slowness, and Stephen and Margaret got into the Rolls. "The old bitch," Stephen said, slamming the door. "She knows very well we've separated."

"She may not," said Margaret. "We haven't exactly announced it in the *Times*."

"Everybody knows," said Stephen. He started the car and drove off, racing the engine unnecessarily. "And now everybody knows that I came back and spent the night here. If you'd told me last night what the story was, I'd have come in a cab. Now heaven knows what the lawyers will say, let alone Juliette. It'll be all round London by lunchtime. I'd better ring her from the bank and explain before she hears it from somebody else."

Margaret said nothing. She was considering Stephen and wondering how anybody could have changed so completely in such a short time. When they'd married six years before he'd been poor and insecure and kind and funny and very sincere. He'd always been a tremendously hard worker and his fanatical determination to succeed in life had been, in Margaret's view, a defiant gesture in the face of his essential gentleness and lack of self-confidence. But now he had succeeded, and in the process Margaret had watched him turn into a different man—charming, smooth, suspicious, calculating, and ruthless. On occasion it seemed to her that he even assumed his former manner of gauche diffidence as a deliberate strategy. It seldom failed to disarm strangers.

Juliette Dean was very much a part of the new Stephen Cannington. She was ten years younger than he was, strikingly beautiful, and an accomplished and successful actress. Margaret had met Juliette several times in the brief period before Stephen's relationship with her had blazed into the love affair that administered the *coup de grace* to a dying marriage.

Trying to be fair, Margaret had to admit that Juliette had an attractive personality. Her greed and ambition were made acceptable and even endearing by the sheer zest and enthusiasm for life that went with them. It was true that she appeared to make use of other people for just as long as they happened to serve her purposes, but the people so used had nobody but themselves to blame. Juliette was not a hypocrite. When she and Stephen were photographed together—as they frequently were these days—they looked to Margaret as handsome, as brilliant, and as hard as a couple of solitaire diamonds, staring at her from the pages of some glossy magazine. And yet life with Juliette would certainly not be boring—and perhaps in Stephen Juliette had met her match at last. With sudden, painful insight, Margaret acknowledged that probably somebody like Juliette was better for Stephen at this moment than she was.

Aloud, she said, "I think you and Juliette will be very happy."

"There's no need to be bitchy," said Stephen, his eyes on the road.

"I wasn't being."

"Then you were giving a very good imitation. Now, concentrate for a moment. A small black Ford has been following us since just after we left the square. Take a good look out of the rear window and see if you can get its number, and if you know the driver."

Margaret swung round in her seat. Immediately behind the Rolls a large moving van effectively blocked the rear view. As Stephen slowed at a traffic light, the nose of a small black car came creeping round the ample posterior of the van. There was a stream of traffic coming in the opposite direction, however, and the black nose pulled in again almost at once. Margaret had only time to register that the first two letters of the registration number were AJ. Shortly afterward the van turned off to the left, leaving an uninterrupted view of the following traffic, but the black Ford had disappeared. In the miscellany of private cars, delivery vans, and taxis behind the Rolls, there was no way of telling which, if any, belonged to their personal bloodhound. Probably X had parked his car and was riding a cab.

Stephen found a parking meter at the Hyde Park Corner end of Piccadilly and he and Margaret walked together along the northern edge of Green Park in the watery sunshine. At the door of the bank, Stephen gave her arm an encouraging squeeze and said, "Now you know what to do. I'll see you at Wilberforce Square at lunchtime. Good luck."

The bank was cool, shadowy, and hushed, as became a temple of wealth. Stephen was instantly recognized and treated with deference. He had a quiet word with a cashier, and at once Margaret was ushered down the length of the polished counter with its shiny brass grilles, through the manager's office, and out of a small door at the back. A moment later, she was hailing a taxi in Jermyn Street.

The Students' Baby-Sitting Bureau shared a small, down-at-heel house in Kensington with several other enterprises. According to the plaque beside the front door, the ground floor housed Sally and Jane Handmade Lampshades and the Society for the Protection of Urban Wildlife. The Baby-Sitting Bureau was on the first floor, together with Happy Holiday Tours, while the top flat was occupied by D. Fisher. As Margaret paid the taxi, it occurred to her that it had been near to this street that she had lost sight of the small black Ford. And sure enough, there it was. At least there was an identical car parked some fifty yards up the road on the opposite side and its registration number was AJX 5067. Of course, it might be just co-incidence, but then again it might not. Margaret went into the house and climbed the stairs to the first floor.

The shabby young intellectual was sitting at an untidy desk, talking on the telephone. "Yes. . . Yes. . . Just let me write that down. Twenty-eight Penbury Gardens—Friday eighth. No, not next week, I'm afraid . . . Christmas holidays . . . " He looked up, flashed a quick smile at Margaret, put his hand over the mouthpiece of the telephone, and said, "Do sit down, Mrs. Cannington. I won't be a moment." Then, to the telephone, "Yes, I've booked that for you. Thank you so much, Lady Marston . . . Yes, yes, absolutely reliable . . . Goodbye, then." He rang off, brushed back his unruly black hair with a very white hand, and said, "Phew! Talk about busy! We never seem to stop. Now, Mrs. Cannington, what can I do for you?"

"I came about the girl you sent me last night," said Margaret.

At once the young man's face grew grave. "Oh, dear," he said. "I'm afraid I was rather expecting that. I hoped against hope that she might have behaved herself. Will you have a cigarette, Mrs. Cannington?"

"No, thank you," said Margaret. "I only wanted—"

"It's not often," said the young man, lighting a cigarette himself, "that I pick a dud. In fact, I can honestly say that this Bridge girl is the first sitter who has ever let me down. I need hardly say that I've taken her off my books." He blew out an aromatic cloud of Turkish tobacco smoke, which lingered round his head in a rich blue haze.

"Just what has she been doing?" Margaret asked.

"Skipping off duty early," said the young man. "Raiding the whisky decanter. In fact, the client has even accused her of stealing a brooch, but there's no proof of that. The woman doesn't seem to know when or where she lost the thing, so she may just be picking on this girl because she left early. All the same, it makes one think. I do hope you haven't suffered any."

"Not at all," said Margaret, trying to sound bland. "Quite the reverse, in fact. I was delighted with her."

The young man looked surprised. "You were? Well, *that's* good news. I do think, though, Mrs. Cannington, that it might be as well if you checked that nothing is missing from your house."

Margaret looked at him steadily. "Nothing is missing," she said.

"You're sure? I'm extremely glad to hear it. If only this other woman had telephoned me right away," he went on, aggrieved, "I'd never have sent Bridge to you last night. But she only got in touch this morning to complain about what happened on Monday evening."

"And you'd had no complaints about her before, Mr.—er?"

"Fisher's my name. Donald Fisher. No, as a matter of fact, Monday was her first job for me. She put her name down only last week. I accepted her in all good faith because she was a great friend of Sheila Durrant. You remember Sheila. One of my best girls. I hope her mother gets better soon."

"So do I," said Margaret. "I was going to ask you if you could give me her address in the country. I'd like to write to her."

"Of course," said Fisher. "A pleasure. I know Sheila will appreciate it."

"And I also wanted Grace Bridge's address," said Margaret.

"Whatever for?" Fisher sounded astonished.

"She left something behind last night," said Margaret. "I want to return it to her."

"Well, now." Fisher scratched his head. "Ordinarily I'd tell you to bring it here and we'd see she gets it back, but since I've just sent off a very strong letter to the girl, telling her I want no more to do with her, perhaps it *would* be less—less awkward—if you sent whatever it is to her yourself. I'll just—"

He got up and went over to a dilapidated filing cabinet, ruffled through some papers, and came up with a card. "Here we are. Sheila Durrant. Red Acre Farm, Hampton Parva, Dorset. It seems to suit her, doesn't it? Dear Sheila. Heaven knows when she'll be back. Which reminds me, Mrs. Cannington—we're closed next week for

Christmas, as you know, but I promise I'll find somebody really good for you the following Wednesday. I've a girl named—"

"As a matter of fact," Margaret said, "my plans have changed. I won't be needing a sitter every Wednesday in the future. Just odd days here and there. I'll let you know."

Donald Fisher turned and looked at her ruefully. "Oh, dear," he said. "I can see that Grace Bridge has undermined your faith in the Bureau." He smiled. "It seemed to me that if I was quite frank to you about her, and pointed out how fast I get rid of anybody unsatisfactory, you might—"

"You're quite wrong," said Margaret quickly. "I assure you I'll be in touch with you the next time I need a sitter. Now, if you'll just give me Grace Bridge's address . . ."

"Yes. Yes, of course." Fisher returned to the filing cabinet. "Balfour, Bratt, Bredon, Bridge . . . " He extracted a card and studied it. "That *is* interesting. Now I see why she was so keen to come to you."

"Was she?" Margaret asked.

"Oh, yes, indeed. She told me she'd heard all about you from Sheila, and so on. That was why I sent her to you when Sheila couldn't manage it. And now I see why."

"Why?"

"Because she lives only just across the road from you. In the new Students' Hostel at No. 13, Wilberforce Square."

It takes a thousand ten-pound notes to make up ten thousand pounds, and it takes a great deal of time and trouble to sew them, in bundles of twenty, into the interlining of a fur coat. Margaret sat in the drawing-room of the house in Wilberforce Square stitching doggedly while Stephen went to pursue enquires at No. 13.

He had arrived back soon after twelve, carring the money in a suitcase, and far from good-tempered. Juliette, it seemed, had already been informed by dear friends of his apparent defection and had slammed down the telephone at the sound of his voice. He appeared to blame Margaret entirely for this. He had then called his office, where—as far as Margaret could gather—unspecified people had made a ham-fisted hash of some delicate business negotiation.

Stephen had been unimpressed by Margaret's detective efforts, had dismissed the black Ford as unimportant, and had finally indulged in an explosion of bad temper over the amount and quality of the tinned meat and salad which was all the larder could provide for lunch. Margaret, who was not in the least hungry, remarked that she couldn't understand how Stephen could think of his stomach when Emma was probably being murdered. He retorted that some people had snored happily all night while others had sat up doing constructive planning. He failed to see, he added, how his starving to death would help Emma. He then walked out of the house, slamming the front door behind him, and leaving Margaret to face the bundles of bank notes with her needle and thread.

It was twenty minutes later that the front doorbell rang—a loud, imperious summons. Margaret went to the window and looked out. Stephen had taken the Rolls back to the garage after his trip to the bank, but now, in its place outside the front door, stood a car even more familiar to Margaret, and just as distinctive. It was the pale-blue Alfa Romeo SC3—the car which had been hers. And on the doorstep, looking dangerous, was Juliette Dean. With no enthusiasm, Margaret went to open the front door.

Juliette looked magnificent, as usual. Her dark, shining hair was swept up into a Grecian chignon, her green eyes were darkly outlined in black, and her honey-colored complection was so smoothly natural it must have taken a good hour to apply. She wore a dark-brown suit from Paris under a blond beaver coat. Margaret was bitterly aware of her own untidy brown hair and felt sure her nose was shining.

"Juliette!" she said. "What a surprise!"

"Where's Stephen?" asked Juliette abruptly.

"I really don't know," replied Margaret truthfully.

"He spent last night here, didn't he?—Well, didn't he?" Juliette's voice, which carried easily to the gallery of a large theater without the aid of a microphone, was rising ominously. At the same moment, Margaret saw on the pavement beyond the gate the wicker-work prow of Lady Percival's wheelchair advancing steadily. At Juliette's last remark, however, the chair stopped.

Margaret was in a quandary. She was reluctant to let Juliette into the house, and yet anything was better than to conduct a shouting match on the doorstep under the quick ears of Lady Percival. She said, "You'd better come in."

Juliette pushed past her and marched into the drawing-room just as Stephen had done the night before. Following her, Margaret could see her thin tall back stiffen with the intake of a deep breath—the prelude to a characteristically theatrical diatribe—but at the threshold of the room Juliette stopped. No sound came but her breath relaxed in a sigh of sheer astonishment. Margaret grinned to herself in spite of everything and wished she could see Juliette's face. Whatever the latter had expected to find at Wilberforce Square, it could hardly have been a room strewn with ten-pound notes and a dismembered fur coat. She swung round to face Margaret.

"What," she demanded, "is going on here?"

"Can't you see? I am sewing ten thousand pounds into the lining of a fur coat."

"Have you gone quite mad?" asked Juliette.

"Not quite," said Margaret. "Sit down and I'll get you a drink."

Juliette sat down, looking baffled. It was clear that the carefully rehearsed scene she had planned had taken an altogether unexpected twist and Margaret was comfortably aware that the initiative had passed to her.

"What can I get you, Juliette? Scotch, gin, sherry—?"

"I don't want a drink," said Juliette. "I want to know what the hell is going on. Is Stephen here?"

"Not at the moment."

"Where is he?"

"I've already told you. I don't know."

"Are you expecting him back?"

"Oh, yes."

"Don't laugh at me!"

Margaret looked sharply at Juliette and felt ashamed. The girl was really upset. Any satisfaction Margaret had derived from her one-up position evaporated. She said, "I'm sorry, Juliette. The truth is very simple. Emma has been kidnaped."

Juliette opened her enormous green eyes very wide. "Your little girl?"

"That's right. I was out at the theater last night, and when I got home she had gone. They—they left a note. Of course, I telephoned Stephen at once, and he came round. So you see, you can stop worrying that he's being unfaithful to you."

"And this?" Juliette gestured at the bank notes. "This is the ransom, is it?"

"Yes. And if you'll excuse me, I'd better get on with it." Margaret picked up her needle and thread and started on another envelope of bank notes.

"I think I'll have a Scotch after all," said Juliette.

"Pour it for yourself, will you? You'll find everything in the cupboard."

Juliette walked slowly over to the corner cabinet and poured herself a generous drink. Her hand was shaking so that the bottle rattled against the glass, spilling a few drops of whisky onto the carpet. She took a quick sip and then said, "Well, what's happening? What are the police doing?"

"Nothing," said Margaret. She paused to thread her needle. "They don't know."

"They don't know? Why on earth not?"

"Because we haven't told them. It's too dangerous from Emma's point of view. Stephen and I feel it's best to tackle this alone."

"I don't see how you can be so calm. I'd be round the bend."

"Don't be deceived," said Margaret. She smiled a little. "This outward stoicism is just numbness. Inside, I'm having screaming hysterics."

Juliette looked at her. She said, "I'm terribly sorry."

"Thank you."

"I mean—I came here all set to make a big scene. I'd been misinformed."

"That's quite all right," said Margaret. She knotted her thread and snapped it off. "Are you really fond of Stephen, Juliette?"

There was a short silence. "I don't think that's any of your business."

"Don't you? He *is* my husband, you know."

"Not—" began Juliette, and then stopped.

"Were you going to say 'Not any more?' " Juliette said nothing. Margaret went on, "Because if you were, it isn't true. I'm speaking purely technically. Stephen and I are still married—and will remain so until one of us takes divorce proceedings and gets a final decree."

"You don't mean you'd refuse to divorce Stephen!"

"I wouldn't refuse," said Margaret, "if I was sure he was going to be happy."

"What bloody impertinence!" said Juliette. "To think that I was beginning to feel sorry for you!"

"Please don't bother," said Margaret. "I don't need your pity."

"Of course, I'm sorry about Emma," said Juliette, "but if you're getting ideas about—" She stopped.

"About what?"

"You know very well what I mean. You're beginning to hope that this business of the child may bring you and Stephen together again."

To her fury, Margaret felt herself blushing. "What absolute non-sense," she said.

"It's not nonsense at all. Emma's the one hold you've still got over Stephen. She's the only reason he didn't leave you years ago."

"I think you'd better go now," said Margaret. She considered, as from a great distance, the possibility of attacking Juliette physically, of slashing into that perfect complection with her sharp embroidery scissors. At once, the thought frightened her—not because it seemed inherently unreasonable, but because she feared that she might be going a little mad.

Juliette laughed. "Don't play it so innocent, Margaret," she said—and Margaret realized that she wasn't being deliberately cruel, she was simply stating facts of which she thought Margaret must be well aware. "You know perfectly well that I wasn't the first of Stephen's little adventures. I just happened to be rather more tenacious than the others. And then a strange thing happened. We fell in love with each other. Even so, for a long time I thought I'd lose him. I thought he'd go back to you, as he'd always done before—because of Emma."

"I see," said Margaret. "And what made him change his mind?"

"Change his mind? Nothing. He hasn't changed his mind." Juliette stood up, draining her drink. "This may not be the ideal moment for blunt speaking, but you may as well face facts. Stephen intends to marry me *and* to keep Emma. And he'll manage it, you'll see. Once he sets his mind to a thing, he gets it. You should know that."

Margaret felt very tired. "Please go away," she said.

"Don't worry about Emma," said Juliette. Suddenly she sounded awkward, ill at ease. "She'll be all right. Stephen will cope with everything." Margaret said nothing. Juliette went to the door and let herself out.

Margaret finished sewing the money into her coat and tacked the satin lining back into place. The coat felt unnaturally heavy and crackled slightly when she picked it up. She carried it upstairs, and laid it on her bed while she bathed, dressed in a black woolen suit, and made up her face.

At seven o'clock she was ready to leave and there was still no sign of Stephen. For a moment she thought that loneliness and anguish would overcome her, that she couldn't go on alone, but the ever-present and agonizing thought of Emma obliterated all other considerations. Emma, frightened and crying—Emma, drugged and ill—Emma, so tiny and so vulnerable, fallen among thieves. Margaret pulled herself together with a great physical effort. All she could do for Emma now was to keep her head, to remain calm, to carry out her side of the bargain faithfully and without fuss. She telephoned for a taxi.

The Majestic Theater was a blaze of light. It hummed with activity, and emanated that particular, tingling sparkle which goes with success. The foyer was an excited ant-heap of theater-goers, all exhibiting the satisfaction of those who have been clever or influential enough to secure seats for the newest and most fashionable show in town. Outside, passers-by in winter coats shivered in the evening chill while on the theater steps, in the same freezing temperature, women in décolleté dresses chatted happily, warmed by their sense of occasion. Margaret dodged among them as unobtrusively as she could and made her way to the box office.

A supercilious young man in a dinner jacket eyed her coldly from behind the little glass window.

"I think," said Margaret, "that you have a ticket for me. Mrs. Cannington."

The young man smiled distantly, with no suspension of disbelief. "Mrs. Cannington? Just a moment, I will look."

He began to flip through a small box of envelopes. As he came to the last one, his smile became fixed and quite unbeatable. He was used to would-be gate-crashers. "I'm sorry, madam," he said firmly. "There is no ticket in that name."

Margaret tried not to panic. "But there is. One of the house seats—"

"I'm sorry, madam."

"But I *must*—"

"I assure you, madam," said the young man, "that if a house seat had been reserved in your name it would be here. In any case, I happen to know that the house seats are occupied tonight. There must be some mistake."

"There must indeed," said Margaret. "May I see the box-office manager?"

"I am the box-office manager."

"Oh."

"Having trouble?" Margaret swung round and almost cried with relief. Standing behind her was Freddy Barnstable, looking distinguished and slightly rakish in a well cut dinner jacket.

"Freddy! Oh, I am glad to see you! He says there's no ticket for me."

"Quite right. There isn't."

"But you promised—"

Freddy grinned. "Idiot," he said. "I've got them both here." He patted his breast pocket.

"Both?"

"Well, it seemed a bit dismal—you going to the theater all alone. Then it occurred to me that I'd like to see this show myself, and so I asked my friend in the rabbit hutch to find us a couple of stalls. I trust you don't object?"

"Oh, no—no, of course not, Freddy. It was sweet of you." Margaret did her best to keep the dismay out of her voice.

"Well, then, let's go in, shall we? Let's see . . . Stalls A to H. That'll be our entrance. I wouldn't check your coat if I were you. There's always such a scramble to get it back afterward. It's easier to put it under the seat, I always say."

"I think I will leave it all the same," said Margaret. "It's—it's rather precious, you see." She felt a hysterical desire to giggle at the understatement. "I don't want it to get crushed."

"All right, if you must. Hand it over and I'll go and deposit it."

There was nothing else she could do. Margaret took off her coat, listening anxiously for the crackle of bank notes, but it was mercifully drowned by chattering voices. She watched Freddy as he made his way to the cloakroom and stood waiting his turn in a crowd that already stood three-deep around the counter. She saw the coat disappear into the arms of one of the attendants.

Freddy came back. "I'll keep the ticket, shall I?" he said. "Then I can collect it for you at the end. You won't want to get involved in that rugger scrum."

"I—I'm sorry to be difficult, Freddy, but I'd really rather have the ticket myself."

"What on earth for, idiot girl?"

"I—" Margaret searched for an inspiration, and then began to improvise wildly. "As a matter of fact, Freddy, I haven't been very well lately and the doctor's given me some pills. It's a sort of migraine, you see, and comes on quite suddenly. The pills are in my coat pocket and I'd like to think that I could slip out and get one if—"

Freddy was looking at her curiously—a mixture of concern and disbelief on his humorous face. "I'm sorry to hear that," he said. "Of course you can have the ticket if you want it." He handed her a

square of orange paper with the figure 187 on it in bold black nu-
merals. Margaret took the ticket and put it in her handbag, wondering if he had believed her. With Freddy it was always a little
difficult to tell whether or not one was being mocked. Then the first
bell rang and they went to their seats.

Small Green Apples was the hit of the season. Critics had blown
the dust off seldom-used superlatives to describe its dancing, its
decor, the wit and pith of the book, and the no-less-witty music.
Some of them had even intimated that here, in the guise of pure
entertainment, was a piece of deep social significance—which ena-
bled intellectuals to enjoy it with no sense of guilt. All this praise
may or may not have been warranted. As far as Margaret was concerned, she might just as well have been watching a switched-off
television set. Her whole concentration was directed on her plan of
campaign.

As the curtain fell for the first interval, Freddy whispered, "Out,
quick! We'll never get a drink unless we're first in the bar."

They were well placed for a quick exit, being in aisle seats, and
were already in the aisle before the house lights went up. Margaret
was thankful that they were, at least, headed for the right bar—had
their seats been in the circle she would have had some awkward
maneuvering to do.

"What'll you have?" called Freddy over his shoulder as they entered the rapidly filling bar.

"Gin and tonic, please. I'll wait for you here." Margaret made a
bee-line for the mezzotint of Sir Henry Irving as Macbeth and sat
down on the red-plush bench beneath it. Freddy had disappeared
into the maelstrom around the counter and she had plenty of time
to extract the ticket from her bag and then, on pretext of studying
the picture, slip it behind the frame. She hoped it wouldn't fall out.
Then she leaned back against the red plush and tried to look like
a woman suffering from a severe and unexpected attack of migraine.

"Here we are then." Freddy's voice was loud and cheerful above
the chatter. "It always pays to be quick off the mark. Some of these
poor devils haven't a hope of getting served before the end of the
interval. Say when with the tonic—" He broke off and looked at
her—and about time, too, thought Margaret. She had been giving
an Oscar-winning performance of gallantly borne pain and nausea.
"I say, Maggie, are you all right?"

Margaret opened her eyes and smiled bravely. "I—I'm afraid not, Freddy. It's this beastly migraine. I'm so sorry."

"It's not your fault, old thing. Here, grab my arm and see if you can stand up. The main thing is to get you out of the crowd."

"Thank you. Yes, if I can get into the fresh air—"

Freddy put a strong arm round her shoulders and supported her out of the bar and into the comparative emptiness of the corridor.

"Now," he said, "sit down on this bench, give me your cloakroom ticket, and I'll go and get your pills for you."

"You're very sweet, Freddy, but no, it's not worth it. The sensible thing is for me to go home. I am so sorry to spoil your evening."

"I'm sorry for you, old thing," said Freddy. "It seems a shame to miss the rest of the show, but if you're sure, I'll get your coat and find a cab and take you home."

"No, you mustn't do that!" In her anxiety, Margaret spoke sharply, and realized that she must have appeared to make a sudden recovery. Quickly, she passed a limp hand over her forehead. "I'm feeling a lot better now. I can easily go home alone. I wouldn't dream of allowing you to miss the second half."

"Well—if you're quite certain."

"I am. See how much better I am already. It's just the heat and the crowd in there."

"You don't think that if you went out into the fresh air for a bit you'd feel well enough to stay for the rest of the show?"

Margaret's spirits rose. This was just what she had hoped for. "Let's give it a try," she said.

"I'll get your coat then."

"No, no—I don't need it."

"Of course you do. You'll catch a chill or something. Besides, you'd better take a pill."

There was only one thing for it. With the pettishness of an invalid, Margaret said, "Oh, Freddy, please. Don't order me about. I don't want my coat." She closed her eyes again and massaged her temples, as if to indicate that the little burst of irritation had brought on the pain again.

"Whatever you like, of course, Maggie." Poor Freddy was pathetically subdued. "I didn't mean . . . Here, take my arm. We'll go outside."

The foyer was crowded. People strolled, smoked, talked, and spilled out into the lamplit street outside the theater. Walking with becoming fragility on Freddy's arm, Margaret scanned the faces around her. But she saw only strangers.

"How do you feel now?" Freddy asked, full of solicitude.

"Much better."   .

"How long has this been going on—this migraine business?"

"Oh, not very long. Since Stephen left me, really. I suppose it's just general worry and strain. The doctor says it's not serious." Margaret hated herself, hated the fluency with which she was lying. She was immensely relieved when the bell rang.

"There's the bell, Freddy. You must go back."

"What about you, Maggie? Do you feel up to it now?"

"I'll tell you what," said Margaret, as though the idea had just occurred to her, "I'll stay out here a few minutes longer and then if I feel well enough I'll come in and join you. If I don't, I'll take a cab and go home. So don't worry about me."

"No use saying that. You know I'll worry."

"Well, you mustn't. Go in now. The second bell will be going any moment. I'll probably be with you quite soon. Better give me my ticket stub so I can get in again."

At first it looked as though Freddy was going to refuse to leave her, but by the time the third and last bell sounded he had been convinced. Margaret watched him disappear into the theater and then quickly hailed a taxi and went back to Wilberforce Square.

The lights in the house were on and it was tremendously reassuring to see through the drawing-room window that Stephen was sitting by the fire in his favorite armchair, drinking coffee. He came out into the hall when he heard her latch-key in the door.

"Well, how did it go?" He seemed in a much better mood now.

With a certain amount of satisfaction, Margaret told him about Freddy's good-hearted but misguided gesture, about the fictitious migraine and her histrionic performance, and they both laughed—for all the world as though Emma were asleep upstairs in the nursery and the Canningtons were a happily married couple. Then Stephen said, "Well, I suppose all we can do now is wait for our friend to telephone." And the nightmare closed in again.

In the drawing-room Margaret said, "How did you get on this afternoon?"

Stephen shrugged. "Badly," he said. "As expected. Grace Bridge left the hostel yesterday. Nothing unusual about that, of course—nearly all the students are away for Christmas. She left no forwarding address except London University."

"And the University?"

"Is on vacation," said Stephen. "Not a hope." He paused and took a drink of coffee. "However, I did manage to get inside the hostel and I'm pretty sure X doesn't telephone from there. There's a public phone tucked into a little booth in the hall, where there are no windows, and the principal has a private phone in her sitting-room, which is at the back of the house, upstairs. The only rooms from which you can see into this house are the Common Room on the ground floor and the dormitory above it, and neither of them has a telephone."

"It must be one of the other houses then," said Margaret.

"I had a good look at No. 2—the empty house. It seems to be bolted and barred, and I'd be surprised if it has a telephone in working order. I think we can eliminate Lady Percival. I don't see her as a kidnaper, nor do I see her letting strangers telephone from her house. That leaves the Bassetts in No. 12. Unlikely, I admit, but you never know. I had a shot at calling on them. There was no reply to the bell, but a couple of poodles had hysterics in the drawing-room. I looked in through the window and there's a beautifully placed telephone. I really don't know what to think."

"Perhaps it doesn't matter," said Margaret. "Perhaps they've got the money by now and they'll keep their word and send Emma back."

The telephone rang. Stephen jumped up and reached it in one stride. "Cannington here. Yes, this is her number. Yes, she is—who wants her? . . . Just a moment." He put down the telephone and said to Margaret, "It's your friend, Mr. Barnstable."

Margaret took the telephone. "Freddy—"

"Maggie—" Barnstable sounded thoroughly rattled "—I hope I'm not disturbing you."

"Of course you're not, Freddy."

"I thought I'd just call to find out how you are. I'd no idea you—weren't alone."

"It was sweet of you to ring, Freddy. I'm feeling a lot better, but I thought it was more sensible to come home." She paused. "Stephen has just dropped in to—to discuss a few business matters."

"Maggie—" Freddy sounded urgent and worried "—are you sure you're—all right?" There was a strange inflection in the last two words.

"Of course I am, Freddy. Perfectly all right."

"You wouldn't like me to come round?"

"Of course not."

"Well, good night then, old thing. Take care of yourself."

She put the phone down and turned round. Stephen was sitting by the fire, looking at her mockingly. "So the boy friend is suspicious of my intentions, is he?" he said.

"I don't know what you mean."

"Oh yes, you do."

"You can hardly blame Freddy for being surprised when you answered the phone."

"I don't doubt that he was surprised. He usually finds you alone, doesn't he?"

"Of course he does. Don't be childish, Stephen."

"Nag, nag, nag," said Stephen equably, pouring himself more coffee.

"I never nagged you."

"Oh, no?"

"Well, look how you bullied me."

"Bullied? Bullied, she says. My dear girl, I'd as soon try to bully the Great Pyramid."

"That's not very funny."

"It wasn't meant to be."

They glared at each other. The telephone rang again.

"I'll take it this time," said Margaret.

"Mrs. Cannington?" The voice was sickeningly familiar. "Congratulations, my dear. It all went off splendidly, didn't it?"

"I hope so," said Margaret, from a dry throat.

"We have the coat, and we have the money. All without a hitch. A real success."

"What about Emma?" said Margaret.

"Ah, yes. Emma. I was coming to that. Now, Mrs. Cannington, you've played fair with us, and you'll see that we'll play fair with you."

"You'll send her home?"

"Not too fast, now. You surely realized that this evening's little experiment was in the nature of a pilot scheme, as it were. Now that we find it works so well, we can get down to real business, can't we?"

"What do you mean?"

"Come now, Mrs. Cannington. You'll surely agree that your sweet little girl is worth more than ten thousand pounds? We don't want to be unreasonable, of course. Twenty thousand in all, that's our figure. That means another ten thousand tomorrow night."

"You devil!"

"Please don't let's get abusive, Mrs. Cannington. Everything has been so pleasant up to now. I suggest the Superdrome Cinema for tomorrow night. We don't want to bother Mr. Barnstable again, do we? You will get there in time for the last showing of the feature movie, which is at 7:45. Leave your coat and put the ticket behind the photograph of Robert Redford which is halfway up the left-hand staircase. Go to your seat and leave by a side exit after a quarter of an hour. Is that clear?"

Before Margaret could say anything, the telephone was snatched out of her hand. Stephen, standing immediately behind her, had been able to overhear the whole conversation. Now, seizing the receiver, he shouted, "No, it is not clear! You don't get another penny, do you understand?"

"Temper, temper, Mr. Cannington. Most unwise."

"I'm going straight to the police!"

"Stephen, please!" cried Margaret.

"That's right, Mrs. Cannington," said the telephone soothingly. "I'm sure I can rely on you to deal with your husband. Don't let him do anything silly, will you? Emma could so easily have a nasty accident, and we don't want that, do we?" With a gentle click, X rang off.

"Didn't I tell you this would happen?" Stephen demanded.

"Yes, you did." Margaret felt crushed by the intolerable weight of her disappointment. "But what can we do?"

"Do? There's only one thing to do. Get on to the police at once!"

"And have Emma murdered!"

"My dear Margaret, please be a little sensible. Naturally, I shall ask the police to be discreet. It's always done in kidnaping cases."

"What do you mean it's always done? How do you know?"

"Everybody knows," said Stephen, annoyed. "You only have to read the papers."

"That's exactly what I mean! The kidnapers can read the papers, too, can't they? They'll simply kill Emma and disappear with ten thousand pounds. And that will be that."

Stephen walked across the room and put his two hands on Margaret's shoulders. "Now, look here, darling," he said, "you seem to have got hold of some idiot idea that I care less about Emma than you do. Believe me, I wouldn't risk a hair of her head. There'll be nothing in the papers, no publicity. All I want is to get her back. But it's foolish to try to do it alone. We need the power of the police behind us."

His hand tightened on her shoulders and Margaret became aware of a strange, dreamlike feeling—an infinitely pleasant sensation of renouncing responsibility, of letting herself fall into the eternal arms beneath her. Stephen, with his strong hands and his strong will, was supporting her, taking control of the situation, and behind him she seemed to see a vista of serried ranks of comforting dark-blue tunics and domed helmets. She saw herself and her defiance as puny and pathetic. Hubris, she thought, that's all it was. What a fool she'd been. She felt very tired.

She heard herself saying, "Yes, Stephen. You're perfectly right."

"That's my girl." Quickly, he stooped and brushed her forehead with his lips. Then he walked over to the writing desk and took a pen out of his pocket. "Now, we'd better marshal our facts before I telephone. What was the exact date when you contacted the Students' Baby-Sitting Bureau for the first time?"

Still feeling dazed, Margaret repeated the whole story. Stephen took notes. At last he said, "Right. I'll call Scotland Yard. You're sure you're quite happy about it?"

"Yes, Stephen."

"Right. Now, go upstairs and put on the bedroom light. I'll turn this one out just in case. And make sure the curtains are securely drawn."

He took a small pencil-shaped flashlight out of his pocket, shone it on the telephone in the darkened room, and very deliberately began to dial.

Chief Inspector Harlow was reassurance personified. As Margaret came back into the dark drawing-room and stood beside Stephen, the deep unemotional voice on the other end of the line seemed to bring the whole nightmare into the focus of everyday life. The Chief Inspector was gently rebuking that Stephen and Margaret had not informed him sooner, but on the other hand he sympathized with their feelings. Of course there was no need for them to worry. The police would do nothing whatsoever to put the kidnapers on their guard. For that reason, he would not suggest coming to Wilberforce Square himself, in case the house was being watched, nor would he advise the Canningtons to visit a police station, as they might be followed. Could they suggest a rendezvous—the house of a trusted friend or relative, perhaps?

At once Stephen said, "Miss Juliette Dean is an intimate friend of both my wife and myself, and she is the only other person who knows about the kidnaping. I'm sure we could meet at her house."

In the darkness, Margaret looked at Stephen in surprise. She had not told him of Juliette's visit. Stephen was still talking. "Yes, a hundred and one, Belgrave Mews. I shall have to call her, of course, to make sure she's back from the theater—she's appearing at the Frivolity. Yes, I'll ring her right away. If I don't get in touch with you again within the next twenty minutes, you can assume all is well." He glanced at the luminous figures on his digital watch. "It's a quarter to eleven now. We'll meet you there at midnight. Thank you, Inspector."

As he rang off, Margaret said, "Did you have to drag Juliette into it?"

"Have you a better suggestion?"

"I'm sure Freddy Barnstable would have—"

"That," interrupted Stephen, "would *not* be a good idea. I'll call Juliette."

"I thought," said Margaret, "that she wasn't very pleased with you right now."

"Oh, that was just a misunderstanding," said Stephen lightly, already dialing. "I contacted her while you were at the theater. She told me she'd been here and that you'd explained everything, so all is now sweetness and light again. Hello, Juliette? Stephen. Just as we expected, I fear . . . Anyhow, Margaret has finally come to her senses and we've informed Scotland Yard. Now, I'm calling to ask if we might . . ."

Big Ben was chiming midnight into the icy air as Stephen rang the doorbell of the pretty little mews house in Belgravia. He had called a radio cab from home, agreeing to meet it a couple of blocks away from Wilberforce Square. The Canningtons had then put off all the lights in the house and left by the back door, walking quickly to their waiting taxi. As far as they could see, they had not been seen or followed.

Juliette answered the door herself. She had dressed carefully for the occasion in demure but provocative black chiffon and had applied a pale and interesting complection. Her voice was low, and vibrant with sympathy.

"Margaret, dear Stephen. Please come in." She closed the door almost furtively. "Your—your friend is waiting for you in the drawing-room. I'll leave you alone with him. Just put your coats down here. If there's anything you want, call me."

Chief Inspector Harlow was sitting on the edge of a fragile, silk-covered chair, looking altogether too burly and masculine for Juliette's white-and-gold drawing-room. He wore civilian clothes of the most unobtrusive sort, but his sturdy frame was so obviously designed for uniform that he gave the impression of being in fancy dress. He stood up as Margaret and Stephen came in.

"Good evening, sir—madam. Mr. and Mrs. Cannington, I presume?"

"Yes," said Stephen. "You must be Chief Inspector Harlow."

"That's right, sir."

"It's very good of you to take all this trouble," said Margaret.

Harlow looked shocked. "Trouble? Not a bit of it, Mrs. Cannington. It's my job. No, you're the people with the trouble, I'm afraid. I do assure you of my deepest sympathy in your predicament." The Chief Inspector had gone rather red. "I don't want to scold you, not at a time like this, but I do wish you'd let us know right away. I really do. The trail has cooled by now, if I may coin a phrase."

"I felt I must give them a chance to play fair," said Margaret.

Harlow shook his head sadly. "Play fair," he repeated. "They don't know the meaning of the words, people like that. The more you give in to them, the greedier they get."

"Exactly what I said," remarked Stephen.

"There's only one thing to do in a case like this," the Inspector went on. "Track 'em down without them knowing they're being tracked."

"How?" asked Margaret bluntly, trying to keep her voice from rising.

"You'll have to leave that to us, Mrs. Cannington." The Chief Inspector sounded as though his mouth were full of warm treacle. "No question of jeopardizing the little girl's safety. Now, if we could just have all the facts . . ."

For what seemed the hundredth time, Margaret went over the story, while Harlow took voluminous notes. When she had finished, he said, "This Mr. Barnstable, could we have a little more on him?"

"More? What do you mean, more?"

"Well—is he an old friend, for instance?"

"I've known him for ten years," said Margaret defensively.

"I see. An old friend of the family."

"Hardly," said Stephen. "I've never met the man."

Harlow looked taken aback. "Really, sir?" There was an uneasy pause.

Margaret said, "He used to be a colleague of mine when I worked on a magazine, before I married. I lost touch with him for a while, but recently I met him again. He arranged for me to do this job, reviewing a play every week. You see, I've been—my husband has been away from home a great deal lately. I was on my own and getting rather bored."

"I understand, Mrs. Cannington," said the Inspector wisely, from the depths of his ignorance. He evidently didn't keep up with London's society gossip. "Well, there it is. Business is business, and we all know about the penalties of success." He looked at Stephen almost roguishly. "I don't suppose there's anyone in Great Britain who hasn't heard of Cannington Electronics."

"You're very flattering, Chief Inspector," said Stephen, actually sounding pleased.

Harlow nodded appreciatively to himself. "Yes," he said, "what you might call a household word. As a matter of fact, we've got a Cannington color telly at home. My wife thinks the world of it. However, that's by the way. What I'm driving at is that these people are no fools. They picked you very carefully. They know you're a rich man, and they also know that you have heavy business responsibilities and are away from home a lot. They've also noticed that Mrs. Cannington goes out every Wednesday evening and employs a baby-sitter."

"I told her it was idiotic to go out on the same evening each week," said Stephen.

"I've said I'm sorry," said Margaret. "For God's sake, what more can I say? Do you think I dreamed Emma would be kidnaped?" She heard her voice soaring toward hysteria.

"Nobody is blaming you, Mrs. Cannington," said Harlow with ponderous tact. "Naturally, you couldn't be expected to foresee this. Nevertheless, it established a pattern—no getting away from it. And a pattern does make things that much easier for criminals. However, what's done can't be undone, so let's not cry over spilt milk." He consulted his notes. "The girl, Grace Bridge, was obviously the operator chosen to gain access to the house. I see that Fisher of the Baby-Sitting Bureau told you she had specifically asked to be sent to you. Very interesting. And now she has conveniently disappeared.

Well, don't worry—we'll lay our hands on Miss Bridge, or whatever her real name turns out to be. But that'll only be the beginning."

"How do you mean?" Stephen asked.

"Well, sir, I don't see the Bridge girl as the brains behind this thing. Not a young girl like that, a student. As I figure it, she was acting under the influence of some man. There may be others involved as well, but you can take it from me there's a man behind it. An older man. Which brings us back to Mr. Barnstable."

"What do you mean by that?" Margaret demanded.

"Well, now, Mrs. Cannington—you say you've known the gentleman for ten years and yet Mr. Cannington has never met him."

"I told you—I knew him before I was married."

"I see," said Harlow woodenly. "And how long ago did you meet him again?"

"A couple of months ago. At a party."

"May I ask what party?"

"As a matter of fact, it was at the Bassetts. Our neighbors in Wilberforce Square."

"Mr. Cannington wasn't with you?"

"No." A little pause. "He was away."

Harlow consulted his notes. "Would that be retired Major-General Bassett, residing at No. 12?"

"Yes."

"Now, that's very interesting, Mrs. Cannington. As Mr. Cannington so cleverly noticed, No. 12 is one of the houses from which it is possible to see into your drawing-room. Tell me—have you ever known Mr. Barnstable to be short of money?"

Margaret stood up. "I won't have you picking on Freddy like this," she said.

"Sit down, Margaret, for heaven's sake," said Stephen.

"I assure you, I didn't intend to upset you in any way, Mrs. Cannington," said Harlow blandly. He sounded like a cross-examining counsel who has just trapped a witness into a damaging admission. "It's just that I have to make a thorough investigation of everybody concerned."

"Then you might start with Miss Dean," said Margaret angrily.

"Margaret, stop being childish and sit down." Stephen sounded dangerous. Margaret sat down.

Stephen favored Harlow with a charming, diffident smile. "My wife is naturally rather wrought-up," he said.

"I quite understand, sir," said Harlow almost conspiratorially.

"Now to get back to Mr. Barnstable. Is he a rich man, did you say, Mrs. Cannington?"

"I didn't say," said Margaret, "but if you must know, he isn't. He's not exactly poor, but—"

"I believe he works for Incorporated Newspapers, as Chief Features Editor for their provincial group. That would be a well-paid job, I should imagine."

"Yes, it is. But Freddy—" Margaret stopped.

"Yes, madam?"

"Well, he's inclined to be a bit extravagant. That's not a crime, is it? Why are you going on and on about him?"

"Well, madam, it just occurred to me that you said you didn't see anybody you recognized at the theater tonight. But that's not quite true, is it?"

"Of course it's true!"

"Not if you think for a moment, madam. You saw Mr. Barnstable."

"But—he arranged my ticket for me!"

"Exactly."

"I mean, I rang him and asked him to!"

"At the suggestion of the voice on the telephone."

"Yes, but—"

"So the kidnapers knew of your friendship with Mr. Barnstable?"

"Apparently. Why shouldn't they? There's no secret about it."

"You know where Mr. Barnstable lives, of course?"

"Of course. Flat 428, Flaxman Court, Chelsea."

"He's a bachelor, I believe."

"You even manage to make *that* sound like a crime," said Margaret angrily.

Harlow went on placidly, "Were you surprised to see him at the theater?"

"I—yes. No. Not really. It was a very kind thought. He felt sorry for me." Harlow looked up for a moment from his notebook. Margaret added defensively, "I've been alone a great deal lately."

"I see. Well . . ." The Chief Inspector took a deep breath and seemed to change gear. "That seems to cover Mr. Barnstable. There's nothing else you can tell me about the Bridge girl?"

"No. I only saw her for ten minutes. I told you that her brother knew my brother."

Harlow smiled sadly. "So she said," he remarked. "A very old trick. Creates a sense of confidence. You didn't stop to think, I suppose, how easily she could have found out that you had a brother in the Foreign Service and where he had recently been stationed."

"No, I'm afraid I didn't."

"People don't." Again a change of tone. "Well, now, I think we can lay our plans for tomorrow."

"Good," said Stephen.

"First of all," said Harlow, "we'll have some enquiries to make—very discreetly, you may be sure, Mrs. Cannington. None of our subjects will have the least idea they are under observation."

"How can you be certain of that?"

Harlow smiled. He did not actually say "We have our methods," but he implied it. "In the evening, we will keep the appointment at the cinema," he told her.

"We?" said Margaret sharply.

"You will keep the appointment, Mrs. Cannington. We will also be there, but you won't be aware of it, I assure you, and neither will the kidnapers. The number of your cloakroom ticket will be noted and whoever claims it will be trailed. I think we can safely say that the little girl will be home before the night is out."

"But supposing they get suspicious?"

"Do leave things to the Inspector, Margaret," said Stephen. "He knows what he's doing."

"Thank you, Mr. Cannington," said Harlow. "Now, as far as the ransom is concerned, you'd better sew the appropriate number of pieces of paper into the coat so that—"

"No!" Margaret stood up again. "They'll kill Emma if—"

"Margaret, don't be ridiculous."

"I'm not being ridiculous! You're proposing to do exactly what they warned us not to do! They'll realize they're being watched, they'll realize the money is fake, and they won't even try to pick up the coat! They'll simply murder Emma and disappear. I won't allow it!"

"Now, now, now, Mrs. Cannington—"

"I'm not interested in anything you have to say," said Margaret. "Emma is my child and I—"

Stephen was standing now, too. "Emma is also *my* child," he said, "and I entirely approve of the Chief Inspector's plan. I would also remind you that the money is *my* money."

Harlow glanced from one to the other appraisingly. Then he said, "Look at it this way, Mrs. Cannington. If you simply take the money along tomorrow evening, you don't imagine that these people will hand your child back, do you?"

"They might," said Margaret. She sounded to her own ears like Emma in one of her stubborn, sulky moods.

"I assure you that they won't," said Harlow. "They didn't the first time, did they? They'll simply step up their demands. And there's a more serious aspect that I didn't want to bring up for fear of distressing you, but you force me to do it." He leaned forward impressively. "Mrs. Cannington, don't you see that the actual physical presence of the child is highly embarrassing to the kidnapers? They want to be rid of her but as long as you cooperate they'll go on demanding money. You may go on paying for weeks or even months, but what makes you think they'll keep the little girl alive all that time? Each time you pay, you put the child in worse danger."

Margaret felt very cold. Obstinately she said, "I think they might send her back."

Harlow shook his head. "If they'd demanded a really large ransom in the first place, I might have advised taking a chance on it. If kidnapers only had a bit of sense," he said more in sorrow than in anger, "they'd take their money and release the victim. And they'd likely get away with it. But they don't have the wit to see that. No, if they're not satisfied with the first payment, they're never satisfied. They go on asking for more and more, and soon they find they can't keep the child hidden any longer, and so . . . " He shrugged eloquently. "Mrs. Cannington, will you please trust Emma to me? I've more experience in these matters than you have, you know."

Margaret said nothing. Stephen went to her and put his arm round her. "The Chief Inspector is perfectly right, my dear," he said. "We all want to get Emma safely home and he knows the best way to do it."

Margaret was standing stiffly, her arms at her sides. At last she said, "Very well."

Harlow exhaled deeply and the tension relaxed. He began to pack his notebooks back into his briefcase. "That's very wise of you, Mrs. Cannington, if I may say so. I'm sure you won't regret it." He glanced at his watch. "One o'clock already. I'll be off then, and I'll contact you by telephone tomorrow. If you have news for me, call Scotland Yard and ask for me. Oh, by the way, Mr. Cannington, you must, of course, visit your bank tomorrow morning, though there's no need to cash any money, of course. Well, goodnight, Mrs. Cannington—Mr.

Cannington. We'll meet again tomorrow. Try not to worry too much. I'll see myself out by the back way, same as I came in."

When he had gone, Margaret and Stephen stood looking at each other in silence, like strangers. There seemed nothing to say. Margaret was relieved when Juliette came in, carrying a tray.

"Has the sleuth gone?" she asked with mock-caution. "All clear now?"

Stephen went over and took the tray from her. "Yes, he's gone. A very nice, sensible, professional fellow. I must say it's a great relief to have the thing in the hands of an expert."

"Oh, Stephen, I *am* glad," said Juliette. "So now you can sit back and leave it all to the police. Now, I've made coffee and I suggest you both have a brandy with it. Margaret, dear?"

"No, thank you," said Margaret.

"You're sure?"

"Perfectly."

Juliette flickered a glance at Stephen, her beautifully groomed eyebrows just slightly raised. Stephen replied with the faintest of shrugs and a rueful grin. Margaret said, "As a matter of fact, Juliette, I won't have any coffee, either. I'm very tired. I'd like to go home."

"Oh, have a heart," said Stephen. "Let me at least drink a cup of coffee before—"

"There's no reason why you should come with me," said Margaret. "Now that the whole matter is in the hands of the police, I imagine you'll want to go back to your flat."

"But—"

"I think," said Margaret, "that it would be much better if you slept at the flat and came round to Wilberforce Square in the morning."

Before Stephen could answer, Juliette said, "Margaret's right, Stephen. It's no use being emotional. That nice Inspector is coping with everything and you can talk it over in the morning. Shall I call a cab for you, Margaret?"

"Yes, please."

Juliette started toward the door, then turned and came over to Margaret. With a faintly theatrical gesture, she took her hand. "Thank you, Margaret," she said, "for being so civilized."

"If you'd just call that cab—"

"Of course. But you're to promise me you'll sleep well and not worry any more."

"Oh, go to hell," said Margaret. "I'll find a cab for myself." She walked out without turning her head.

In Eaton Place, she hailed a cruising taxi.

She was still trembling when she reached Wilberforce Square. "Here we are, lady," said the cabby cheerfully. "Number Sixteen you said?"

"Yes. Thank you." Margaret took three pound notes from her purse, trying to control her shaking fingers. "Here. Keep the change."

"Thank *you*, lady," said the cabby. He added, "No holly wreath this year?"

Margaret looked up, surprised. The cabby chuckled. "You don't remember me but I know this Square well. It's not the first time I've driven you home. And there's been a holly wreath every Christmas that I can remember."

"Not this year," said Margaret.

"Ah, well. Happy Christmas all the same." He slammed the taxi into gear and executed a smart U-turn. As he pulled away, Margaret saw that a small black Ford was parked at the curb. The registration number was AJX 5067 and a man in a dark overcoat was just opening the driver's door. For a moment he and Margaret looked at each other in surprise under the light of the streetlamp. Then Margaret said, "Why, Mr. Fisher—"

"Mrs. Cannington!" Donald Fisher moved away from the car and came toward her. "I'm so sorry I didn't recognize you for a moment. Of course, you live here in Wilberforce Square, don't you?"

"Yes," said Margaret. "I live at No. 16."

"I've just been visiting my aunt," said Donald Fisher. "Her company is somewhat formidable, but she does live in one of the prettiest houses in London."

"Your aunt?"

Donald jerked his head in the direction of the corner. "Number One."

"Oh. Lady Percival."

"That's right. Well, I must be off. I hope your little girl is well?"

"Very well, thank you."

"That's good. Well—goodnight, Mrs. Cannington. I hope we'll be seeing you in the office again soon. You'll give us a second chance, won't you?"

"Yes, of course. Goodnight, Mr. Fisher."

"Happy Christmas!"

The young man waved a light-hearted salutation, climbed into the little car, and moved off noisily in the direction of Kensington High Street. Margaret opened the wrought-iron gate and walked slowly up the path to the house. Inside, she did not switch on the lights at once. Instead, she went into the drawing-room and stood by the window, looking out toward Number One. A light was still burning in Lady Percival's drawing-room, throwing out golden streaks between the dark curtains which had been carelessly drawn. Had the curtains been pulled back, Margaret could have seen clearly into the room.

For perhaps three minutes she stood looking out at the dark Square. Then she switched on the lights, drew the curtains, and looked at her watch. It was half past one. That would mean it was still only half past eight in Washington, D.C. She picked up the telephone and dialed the transatlantic number. A few seconds later, her brother's voice said, "Hello. Thornton here."

"Dick, it's Maggie."

"Maggie! My dear girl, where are you?"

"In London, of course."

"But what on earth—?"

"Listen, Dick— did you ever know a man called Bridge in Nigeria?"

"Yes, of course I did. Harry Bridge. One of my best pals."

"Did he have a sister called Grace?"

"Yes, now you mention it, he did. I never met her, but he had a photograph of her on his desk. A dark girl with a sharpish sort of face. Rather attractive. She was just a school kid then, of course."

"Dick, this is terribly important. Do you know where Harry Bridge is now?"

"I say, why all the drama, old thing? Certainly I know. He's in Paris. We correspond every so often. In fact, if you'll hold on for the shake of a gnat's tail, I can give you his address."

"Bless you. I'll hold on."

"It's somewhere here in my diary ... Yes, here we are. Harry Bridge, 28 Rue Belfort, Paris 8. Telephone Elysée 289754. Now you might tell me what it's all in aid of."

"I can't explain on the phone, Dick. I'll write. It's—I'm trying to trace the sister, you see. I must go now."

"How's my niece?"

"She's—fine."

"Give her my love. What news of the rat Cannington?"

"No news. The divorce is going ahead. It's all in the hands of the lawyers."

"Well, I hope you soak him good and proper for alimony," said Dick Thornton with brotherly solicitude.

"I'll do my best. Goodbye, Dick. Give my love to Martha."

"I'll do that.

" 'Bye, Maggie. Happy Christmas."

Margaret slept little that night. She lay motionless in the dark, plotting and thinking. Now that she had made up her mind and decided on a positive course of action, she found she was quite calm. The trembling had stopped and she was able to think clearly. Also, the success of her phone call to Washington was immensely heartening. At about half past two, she fell into a dreamless sleep—from which she awoke at six, feeling refreshed. She got up, dressed, and made coffee. At eight o'clock, she decided that if Harry Bridge was not up and about yet, he should be. She put through a call to Paris.

" 'Allo. C'est Monsieur Bridge qui parle—"

"Mr. Harry Bridge?"

"Oh, you're English." The sleepy voice sounded relieved. "Yes, Bridge here. Can I help you?"

"I'm afraid you don't know me," said Margaret. "My name is Cannington, Mrs. Stephen Cannington. I'm Dick Thornton's sister."

"Good old Dick! How is he? Still enjoying Washington?"

"I think so. I spoke to him on the phone last night. He gave me your address and number."

"Well, now, Mrs. Cannington—when are you coming to Paris, and what can I do for you?" Bridge sounded resigned. He obviously received many similar calls. "I may as well tell you straight away that I can't get you tickets for the Opera or the Comedie Française or an introduction to the President. Anything else within reason—"

Margaret laughed. "You can relax," she said, "I'm not coming to Paris. I rang you because I need to get in touch with your sister Grace."

"Grace? Oh, you're a day too early."

"What do you mean?"

"She's still in London. She doesn't arrive here until tomorrow morning."

"You mean you're expecting her in Paris?"

"That's right. She's coming over tomorrow, spending Christmas with us, and then going on to Nice in search of some sun."

"I wonder if you could tell me where she's staying in London at the moment? I know she's left the hostel where she was living and I especially want to see her before she leaves."

"She's staying with friends of the family—somewhere in Hampstead, I think. Hang on a moment, I'll see if I have the address."

A couple of minutes later, Harry Bridge was back on the line. "The people are called Minton-Stacey, and they live in Avenue Road, No. 208. I haven't got their phone number, I'm afraid."

"It doesn't matter. That's all I wanted to know, " said Margaret. She hesitated, and then said, "I shall miss Grace—she's been doing some baby-sitting for me."

"Baby-sitting?" Bridge sounded astonished. "Grace? Baby-sitting?"

Margaret laughed. "There's no need to sound so shocked," she said. "It's perfectly respectable. Lots of students do it nowadays to earn extra pocket money."

"Oh, I know that. But, well—Grace usually spends her evenings at theaters or concerts, and besides, to be frank—" He stopped.

"Go on," said Margaret.

"No, no. Nothing."

"Do you mean," said Margaret, "that Grace has a perfectly adequate allowance and has no possible reason to—"

"Adequate? Ridiculous, I call it, for a kid of her age. Still, father stipulated the amount in his will and the trustees have to pay it, whether they like it or not. Personally, I don't approve of students having too much money. To do her justice, I don't think Grace does, either. That's why she insists on living in hostels and going to the gallery with the others when she could easily afford the Royal Box. But she does seem to be carrying things a bit far, baby-sitting for a few pounds."

"Well," said Margaret, "I expect she just did it for fun."

"Or to help somebody out perhaps. She's a good-natured child, as you probably know."

"Yes," said Margaret. "Yes, I think you're right. Well, thank you, Mr. Bridge. I'll get in touch with her today."

"Give her my love. Tell her I'll be at the airport to meet her tomorrow."

"I'll do that. Goodbye, and thank you again."

Margaret rang off and looked at her watch. Half past eight. She went over to the window and pulled back the curtains. The December morning was still dark. Here and there a lighted window showed

that at least some of the inhabitants of Wilberforce Square were up
and about. For example, Lady Percival's establishment was showing
signs of life. A light was burning in the drawing-room, and, as
Margaret watched, a maid in an old-fashioned cap and apron drew
aside the heavy velvet curtains, giving Margaret a clear view into
the room, with its pretty Regency furniture.

Once again, Margaret picked up the telephone. With her eyes on
the drawing-room of No. 1, she dialed Lady Percival's number. The
maid, who was still clearly visible in the drawing-room, did not react
at all when the ringing tone started. Margared nodded to herself.
This confirmed her rather hazy recollection that there was no telephone in that room.

After about half a minute, a thin genteel voice said, "This is Lady
Percival's residence."

All the other front windows were curtained. It was impossible to
tell in which room the telephone had been answered. Margaret said,
"This is Mrs. Cannington. May I speak to Lady Percival, please?"

"Just a moment. I'll see if—"

"All right, Taylor—" the thin voice was supplanted by a rich deep
one "—I will take this call. Good morning, Mrs. Cannington. What
may I do for you?"

"I was just ringing to talk about the Jumble Sale," said Margaret
mendaciously.

"How exceptionally kind of you." Margaret was almost sure she
could detect a note of ironic amusement in the old lady's voice. "Most
people have to be hounded into corners before they will even discuss
such matters. Well, for a start, the principal of the hostel at No. 13
has kindly put a room at our disposal, and all jumble is to be delivered there. The students are away for Christmas, you see. You might
pass that information along to your helpers. I will arrange for everything to be collected and sorted before the sale. I am relying on you
to organize the Jams and Preserves, as you did so well last year . . . "

For several minutes the conversation took a purely technical turn
and Margaret found herself committed not only to Jams and Preserves but to judging the Home-Made Millinery Contest and staying
behind afterward to count the takings. When these matters had been
agreed to Lady Percival's satisfaction, Margaret said, "Oh, by the
way, I met your nephew last night. He was just leaving your house."

"My nephew?"

"Yes. Young Mr. Fisher, who runs the Students' Baby-Sitting
Bureau."

"My dear Mrs. Cannington," said Lady Percival firmly, "I really do not follow you. I have four daughters, two sons, and ten grandchildren, but I am delighted to say that I have no nephews. I have always been given to understand that they are very tiresome young men."

"But—"

"We shall expect you at the Committee Meeting on the fifth, Mrs. Cannington. Please remember me to your husband. *So* nice to see him back from his travels. Don't let him work too hard, will you? I thought he looked a little seedy yesterday. Goodbye, Mrs. Cannington."

Margaret finished her coffee and went to take a bath. She was drying herself when the telephone rang. She put on her dressing-gown and ran downstairs to answer it.

"Maggie? This is Freddy. I say, I hope I didn't put my foot in things by ringing you last night. I'd no idea that Stephen was—well, was with you."

"Don't worry, Freddy. It didn't matter at all. He was only here on business."

"Rather fortunate that you came home early from the theater, wasn't it? Otherwise you'd have missed him."

"Yes, wasn't it lucky," said Margaret blandly, ignoring the curiosity in Freddy's voice.

"I mean, I thought you weren't supposed to see him until the divorce is through."

"Business is business," said Margaret.

"I know it is, my dear," said Freddy. "Which brings me to the reason for this call."

"What do you mean?"

"I hate to harry you, love, because I know you've been laid low with migraine and so forth, but this is Friday and we must have this week's copy from you before the day is out."

"Oh, Freddy! I'm most terribly sorry. I—" Margaret bit back the word "forgot." In fact, she hadn't given a thought to the fact that her weekly column was supposed to be on Freddy's desk by four o'clock.

"You will let me have it by lunchtime, won't you, old thing? I can't stretch the deadline any further, even for you."

"By lunchtime? I. . . Freddy, I can't explain properly, but I can't do the column at all this week. I simply can't."

"You mean you're really ill?"

"No ... Yes ... No, not really. I just can't do it, that's all."

"I see." Freddy sounded far from pleased. Margaret knew that there had been opposition to giving her the job, on the grounds that she was a wealthy amateur who would only play at working. She knew that Freddy had fought and won on her behalf, staking his reputation on the fact that she was still a professional journalist at heart. The last thing she wanted was to let him down—but it wasn't humanly possible for her to write and deliver fifteen hundred words of copy by lunchtime with everything else that she had to do.

"Freddy, please believe me, I've got a very good reason and I'll tell you about it as soon as I can. Will you just take my word that it's impossible for me to do the column this week?"

"It all sounds very mysterious," said Freddy. "However, I seem to have no choice. I suppose I'll have to do it myself. What did you see on Wednesday?"

"*A Case in Point.* At the Lyric."

"Haven't seen it. Never mind. I'll do a piece on *Small Green Apples.* Not that anyone from the provinces has a hope in hell of seeing it for a couple of years."

"Freddy, you're an angel."

"That's all right, old thing. I shall quite enjoy doing it." Barnstable seemed to have recovered his customary good humor. "So long as you're not on the sick list, that's the main thing. You had me really worried last night. Which reminds me—"

"What of?"

"I meant to ask you last night on the phone, but Stephen put me off my stride."

"Ask me what?"

"Whether you got your coat all right."

Margaret tried not to hesitate and failed. She hoped Freddy would not notice. "My coat? What about it?"

"You picked it up from the cloakroom before you left?"

"Of course."

"Well, that's all right then. But it may interest you to know there's a double of it running around London."

"What do you mean?"

"Well, it's a fairly distinctive design, isn't it, with that high-set belt and the ermine collar."

"It's made from a Paris *toile.* It was one of the last presents Stephen gave me."

"Anyhow, after the show last night I stopped in the foyer to have a word with the house manager. There was one hell of a scrum around the cloakroom, as you can imagine. While we were talking, a girl emerged from the milling throng and I could have sworn she was wearing your coat."

"How very odd," said Margaret. "What sort of a girl?"

"Oh, just a girl. Dark-haired. Rather good-looking. Anyhow, it must just have been a coincidence."

"That's right," said Margaret. "Just a coincidence. I believe Harrods sold quite a few of those coats."

There was a pause, then Freddy said, "Well, I'd better get cracking on that piece."

"It's so kind of you, Freddy."

"That's all right, old thing." Barnstable hesitated, and then went on, "You'll take care of yourself, won't you? Don't do anything foolish. It could be dangerous."

"What do you mean dangerous?"

"Migraine can be very nasty. You don't want to take any chances."

"Don't worry. I won't."

"And if there's anything I can do, just call me. Promise?"

"I promise."

"Goodbye, then, Maggie."

"Goodbye, Freddy."

Nine o'clock. Margaret dressed quickly and came downstairs. There was no sign of Stephen. She dialed the number of his apartment but there was no reply. She considered ringing Juliette's house and decided against it. Luckily, she had given Stephen the spare set of keys to No. 16, so that he could come and go freely. She scribbled a note: "Stephen, I've gone out to make some enquiries. Will be back before noon. M." Leaving it conspicuously on the hall table, she went out.

It was a cold, dark day, with lowering clouds that threatened snow. The Square was deserted, there was no sign of the black Ford, and even the Students' Hostel was quiet. As Margaret reached the corner, she saw the tall trim figure of Major-General Bassett coming down the garden path of No. 12. He held a leash in each hand, and to each leash was attached an extremely lively black poodle. He saw Margaret and made the mistake of trying to raise his hat—during which process he lost his grip first on one leash, then on the other, and finally on the hat itself. The poodles and the bowler departed at speed in three separate directions, thereby posing a nice problem in strategy and tactics which was clearly going to exercise the Gen-

eral's skill for some little time. Feeling rather mean, Margaret left
him to it. A few minutes later, she was in a taxi, speeding northward
across the park toward the opulent tranquility of Avenue Road.

Margaret paid off the taxi some hundred yards down the road
from No. 208. It wheeled around in a U-turn and made off toward
Regents Park, leaving Margaret feeling a little desolate. There was
no traffic on the side residential street. The big houses stood self-
consciously isolated, each behind its protective wall, each enclosed
by its large garden, but it was December and the trees were bare,
exposing the houses to view, revealing their fish ponds and sun dials,
their verandas and frilled white curtains.

Some of Margaret's confidence began to ebb away. How could she
be sure that it might not be dangerous—to Emma as well as to
herself—to approach this house, with its well kept secrets? It would
be a perfect place to hide a kidnaped child—too large and aristocratic
to have prying neighbors, too respectable to excite suspicion. Outside
No. 208, Margaret stood hesitantly on the pavement, wishing she
had mentioned her destination in her note to Stephen. She longed
to run away, to abandon the whole rash enterprise, but tearing at
her heart came the ever-present image of Emma's small, scared face.
If there was the faintest chance of helping Emma, she must go
through with it, whatever the cost. She took a step toward the house.

It was a massive cube of neo-Georgian red brick, dating from the
early 'thirties and built as a family house in the days when money
was still money. Eight or ten bedrooms, three bathrooms, four re-
ception rooms, large garden. Margaret wondered whether the Minton-Staceys owned the whole house or whether, like so many of these
modern mansions, it had been converted into apartments. In either
case, it seemed a ludicrous background for a mean kidnaping and
a twenty-thousand-pound ransom. Through the open door of a built-
in garage, Margaret could see the sleek hindquarters of a Rolls
Royce which must have cost at least twice that amount. But then,
of course, this was not Grace Bridge's home—and there was always
Inspector Harlow's mysterious "older man," the presumed Svengali
behind the scenes. Margaret tried to make up her mind what to do
next.

As it turned out, the decision was taken out of her hands. The
sound of a horse's hooves clattering on the tarmac road behind her
made her turn sharply—and there was Grace Bridge, dressed in

immaculate breeches, riding jacket, and bowler hat, mounted on a gleaming chestnut mare.

"Why, Mrs. Cannington!" Grace reined the horse to a stop beside the gate. "Fancy meeting you here!"

"I—I came to see you, Grace," said Margaret. She felt in a most literally one-down position as she craned her neck upward to speak to the girl on horseback. The transformation of Grace Bridge from a student in blue jeans to a glossy debutante was breathtaking.

"I've been riding in the park," said Grace. "It was wonderful. Do come in."

She leaned forward expertly and pushed open the wrought-iron gate leading to the sweep of drive in front of the house. Once inside, she said, "Do you mind waiting for a moment? I'll just take Tessa round to the stables and then I'll be with you."

She gave Margaret a friendly smile and walked the mare round the corner of the house and out of sight. A few minutes later, the front door opened from the inside, and she said, "I'm sorry to have kept you waiting, Mrs. Cannington. Do come in. I'm afraid nobody else is up yet."

Margaret followed her into a big parquet-floored hall that smelled of furniture polish and chrysanthemums and from there into a light, chintzy sitting-room, where a wood fire crackled in the hearth —fulfilling a purely decorative purpose in view of the competent central heating.

"Do sit down, Mrs. Cannington," said Grace. "I've ordered coffee, but if you'd rather have something else—"

"No, coffee will be fine, thank you." Margaret sat down in a large armchair.

Grace threw herself onto the sofa with the loose coltish elegance of the young. She had taken off her bowler, revealing her black hair twisted into a neat chignon at the nape of her neck. Her pale-beige breeches and shiny black boots showed off her long legs to great advantage. Her fine, sharp features looked more patrician than ever and might have been formidable had they not been illuminated by her genuinely sweet smile.

"I hear you're off to Paris tomorrow," said Margaret.

"Yes, that's right—but how on earth did you know?"

"I telephoned your brother."

"Harry? In Paris?" Grace sat up straight. "This is all very mysterious."

"Not really," said Margaret. "I got his number from my brother Dick. You remember, you told me they were friends."

"Yes, but—" Grace frowned. "What's it all about? Why did you want to see me?" She hesitated, and then said, "It was all right about the other night, wasn't it?"

"I don't know what you mean by all right," said Margaret. "You promised me you'd stay until half past eleven."

"Yes, but—"

"I got home at eleven. You had already gone."

"I know, but—"

The door opened and an elderly woman in an apron came in, carrying a tray with coffee and cups. Conversation stopped while the small ceremony was conducted. Margaret accepted milk and sugar, refused a biscuit, and felt thoroughly put out. As the door closed behind the maid she made an effort to recapture the initiative.

"Why did you leave early?" she demanded.

Grace Bridge opened her green eyes very wide. "But surely Sheila told you—"

"Sheila?"

"Sheila Durrant. The red-headed girl. Surely you remember her?"

"Certainly I do," said Margaret. "She was supposed to come to me on Wednesday but her mother got ill and so you came instead. As far as I know, she went to Dorset on Wednesday and is still there."

Grace looked astonished. "You mean Sheila wasn't there when you got back?"

"Of course she wasn't."

"Oh, *gosh!*" said Grace. There was a pause. "I can see why you're so angry."

"I'm not angry," said Margaret. To her surprise it was the truth. "I just wanted to know what happened."

"Well, I had met Sheila quite a few times at the hostel, and I liked her. I was sorry for her, too. She had this sick mother, and very little money. Baby-sitting meant a lot to her—the difference between eating and not eating, as far as I could make out. So when she told me she couldn't go to your place on Wednesday, I offered to stand-in for her. We fixed it through the Bureau so it would be official."

"Yes," said Margaret, "I know."

"Well, I came along to Wilberforce Square, as you know. And you left your little girl with me and went out. And then, soon after nine, Sheila turned up."

"What?"

"Yes. She said that her mother was better so she'd taken the last train back to London and come along to finish the baby-sitting stint."

"And you simply changed places with her?"

Grace reacted at once to the censure in Margaret's voice. "It was terribly awkward," she said. "When she asked me to take her place, I told her I'd give her whatever you paid me, but she flatly refused. She said whoever did the work should get the pay. But then when she turned up at nine she told me she needed the cash desperately—the railway fare had just about cleaned her out. She said I was to take the money for the two hours I'd done and she'd take the rest. What could I do, Mrs. Cannington? Anyhow, I knew that you'd originally asked for her—"

"Grace," said Margaret, "how well do you know Sheila Durrant?"

"I told you, I met her at the hostel."

"You didn't meet through your studies?"

"No, she's at an acting school, not University."

"Did you meet her through friends?"

"No. No, I don't think I did. It was in the canteen one evening. We sort of chummed up."

Margaret made up her mind. "Grace," she said, "after you left on Wednesday, my little girl was kidnaped."

"Was—?" Grace Bridge seemed to be robbed of the power of speech. At last she said, "I don't understand."

"It's not very complicated," said Margaret. "She wasn't there when I got home. Nobody was. There was a note."

"A note?"

"Later, I got a ransom demand. That was paid, but Emma wasn't returned. Now there's been another demand."

Grace put her coffee cup down on the table. Her hand was shaking so that the silver spoon rattled on the porcelain saucer. "It's all my fault," she said.

"Of course it isn't, my dear," said Margaret. "You were taken in by this Sheila creature, just as I was."

"Can't the police do anything?"

"You don't understand, Grace. We dared not contact the police because of what might happen to Emma. The kidnapers threatened—"

Grace nodded. "I see. How absolutely bloody. Can I help you?"

"I hope you can," said Margaret.

Suddenly Grace said, "You must have thought it was me. When you got home and there was nobody there and the child was gone—"

"Yes," said Margaret. "I did think it was you."

Grace stood up. "Why should you decide to trust me now? How do you know I'm innocent?"

Margaret smiled. "There's no need for melodrama," she said. "I remembered that you'd told me your brother knew Dick—"

"I'm leaving the country tomorrow. Don't you find that suspicious? Hadn't you better notify the police at once?"

"Don't be silly, Grace. I know you're going to Paris. I spoke to your brother this morning. That's why I had to find you today, to ask you to help me." She didn't add that if Grace Bridge did attempt to fly to France the following day, using her own passport, Chief Inspector Harlow's net would surely catch her and she would be arrested.

Grace sat down again. "I'm sorry," she said. "It's a little unnerving having this sort of thing sprung on one before breakfast. What do you want me to do?"

"Just answer a few questions, if you will."

"Fire away."

"Sheila Durrant. Will you describe her for me?"

"But you know her, Mrs. Cannington!"

"I know a girl who calls herself Sheila Durrant."

"Oh. I see. Well, the first thing you notice about her is her hair. Short and curly and the most wonderful auburn-red color. Otherwise she's nothing sensational. Figure good but ordinary. Complection fair. Voice pleasant—a bit of a soft west-country accent. The only other things I know about her is that she says her home is in Dorset, that she's a drama student, that her mother isn't well, and that she's chronically broke." She studied Margaret. "Does that tally with your information?"

"Almost exactly," said Margaret. "How much contact did you have with the Baby-Sitting Bureau?"

"Me?" Grace looked surprised. "None at all."

"You've never worked for them before?"

"Good Lord, no."

"You didn't tell them that you particularly wanted to work for me?"

"Look, Mrs. Cannington," said Grace, "I don't know who has been telling you these extraordinary stories, but I can assure you that I never went near the beastly Bureau. Sheila rang me at the hostel with her tale of woe. I said I'd take her place to help her out and she said she'd ring the Bureau and get them to notify you so that it would all be in order."

"When was this?"

"On Wednesday morning. When did they ring you?"

"At lunchtime," said Margaret. "That seems to tally all right."

"Well—that's all there is to it," said Grace. "Have some more coffee?" Margaret passed her cup. "Yes, I came along to your house, as you know, and then at about ten past nine, it must have been, Sheila turned up and took over and I went back to the hostel. That's all I know."

"You don't know where Sheila lived? In London, I mean."

"Not the faintest. She just used to use the hostel canteen sometimes."

"I'm wondering," Margaret said, "why Sheila specifically called you. The Bureau could have found somebody else easily enough. Didn't you think it was a bit odd?"

Grace looked down and went a little pink. "Well," she said, "I should have told you sooner. Sheila told me that if she could get back on the last train—it's only a couple of hours by express—she'd try to get around to do the last couple of hours. She said the money meant so much to her. I told her she could have the lot— but, as I explained, she wouldn't agree to take it."

"So you weren't entirely surprised when she turned up."

"No—that is, yes I was, because I never thought she'd get back that evening."

Margaret put down her cup and looked at her watch. It was a few minutes after ten o'clock. She stood up. "Thank you, Grace," she said. "You've been very helpful."

"I haven't. I haven't told you anything."

"But you have—"

"No—don't try to make me feel better about it. It was all my fault. I was a damn fool. Surely there's something I can do?"

"You can telephone me," said Margaret, "if you think of anything else useful. And particularly if you hear from Sheila Durrant again—but I don't think you will. Here's my card. If I'm not home and somebody else answers, ask when I'll be in and call back. Don't say a word to anybody else—not anybody at all."

Outside in the hall, there was a tapping of feminine footsteps on the wooden floor and a braying voice called, "Grace? Are you back?"

"And don't tell anybody who I am or why I came here," added Margaret quickly.

Before Grace could answer, the door opened and a thin middle-aged woman with blue-rinsed hair came in. She wore a quilted housecoat and high-heeled slippers with little sprouts of ostrich feathers on their vamps. "Ah, there you are, Grace. I—" She stopped dead when she saw Margaret.

Grace said easily, "Hello, Elvira. Up already? Amanda, this is Mrs. Minton-Stacey."

"How do you do?" said Margaret.

"How do you do, Mrs.—er?"

"Amanda came to say goodbye to me," said Grace. "She's off to the country for Christmas. By the ten-thirty train from Waterloo."

"Which I shall miss if I don't go at once," said Margaret. "Goodbye, Mrs. Minton-Stacey. It was so nice to meet you."

"Goodbye, Mrs.—er . . . I didn't catch your friend's name, Grace."

"Oh, don't bother, Elvira. I'll show Amanda out."

Grace opened the door and ushered Margaret into the hall. On the doorstep, Margaret whispered, "Thank you. You managed that beautifully."

"The woman's a fool," said Grace casually. "But an inquisitive fool. Goodbye, Mrs. Cannington."

"So you see," Margaret said with a certain amount of self-satisfaction, "it's all perfectly simple."

She smiled at Chief Inspector Harlow, stirred her coffee, and sat back, waiting to be complimented. She had telephoned the Chief Inspector from a booth at Baker Street Station a few minutes after leaving Avenue Road and they were now both ensconced in a nearby coffee-bar, the only two customers in the place.

Margaret had told her story crisply and, she felt, creditably. She didn't understand why Harlow didn't reply at once. Then it occurred to her that his professional pride had probably been wounded by the fact that she, an amateur and a mere woman, had stolen a march on the police. "Of course," she said kindly, "I had a lot of luck, remembering what Grace had said about her brother and mine. It really wasn't difficult for me to trace her."

Harlow shook his head sadly. "No," he said. "It wasn't, was it?"

"I mean," said Margaret, "I don't want you to feel that—"

"Mrs. Cannington," said the Chief Inspector, "you've just said that it's all perfectly simple. Would you like to explain just what you mean by that?"

"But of course." Margaret was surprised that he should be so slow on the uptake. "Grace Bridge is obviously in the clear. She was simply used as a red herring by these people. They knew that she lived in the hostel in Wilberforce Square, and that she was leaving there on Thursday and going to Paris on Saturday. She made a splendid suspect."

"And who do you think 'these people' are?"

"Donald Fisher and Sheila Durrant," Margaret replied promptly. "They're obviously in league. Sheila Durrant came twice to my house to spy out the land and then pulled that trick on Grace. And now she's disappeared."

"And how does Fisher come into it?"

"Well, you yourself said that there must be a man involved. And I've caught him out in two definite lies."

"What lies?"

"First, he told me that he'd employed Grace before, and had a complaint about her. Actually, she'd never worked for him nor even been to his office."

"And yet he had her address in his files?"

"Of course he did. He got it from Sheila Durrant. He wanted to give the impression she'd worked for him before. And then there was the second lie—telling me that he was Lady Percival's nephew when she says she has no nephews at all. He was just trying to explain away the fact that he was hanging round Wilberforce Square in that awful old car of his. I told you how he followed us the other day."

Harlow stirred his coffee thoughtfully. Then he said, "I'm sorry to disappoint you, Mrs. Cannington, but given the set of facts that you've just told me I'd come to a very different conclusion."

"What!"

"It's perfectly natural," Harlow went on, "that you should be impressed by the Bridge girl, with her smooth talk and her fancy friends and so on—"

"That has nothing to do with it! Her brother knows my brother!"

"I dare say. Which may well have given her the idea of the snatch in the first place."

"But she's rich!"

"How do you know that? By what her brother told you—went out of his way to tell you, in fact, on the telephone. You, a perfect stranger. A bit odd, I'd say."

"Not odd at all. It came up in conversation."

"I see. Well, be that as it may, Fisher's story is just as likely to be true as Bridge's. It's just a question of one person's word against another's."

"The Minton-Staceys—"

"Are only friends, as I understand, putting the girl up for a couple of nights. They may be quite innocent, of course. On the other hand, if they are in on the conspiracy, that house you've described would be a perfect hiding-place for the little girl. Had that occurred to you, Mrs. Cannington?"

Margaret ignored the question. The fact that it had occurred to her did nothing to improve her temper. "You've just said it's only a question of one person's word against another's," she said. "You're simply choosing to believe Fisher and disbelieve Grace, for no reason. And you can't get away from the fact that Fisher said he was Lady Percival's nephew, and he isn't."

Harlow sighed. "There's rather more to it than that," he said.

"What do you mean?"

"Several things. First of all, I was interested to hear about your call from Mr. Barnstable."

"What about it?"

"That mention of the coat. Very interesting. Very singular. I take it your coat is of distinctive design."

"Yes—but there may be others like it."

"At the same theater, the same evening? No, Mrs. Cannington. Either Mr. Barnstable really did see a girl leaving the theater in your coat or else he had some other reason for making up the story. Do you agree?"

"I suppose so. But I wish you'd stop accusing Freddy of—"

"I'm not accusing him of anything, madam. No, indeed, I was about to suggest that his story was almost certainly true."

"What of it?"

"The girl he saw was dark-haired." Harlow paused, impressively. "And Miss Bridge is dark-haired."

"But—"

"Whereas Miss Durrant is a redhead."

"That's no proof of anything!"

"It helps, Mrs. Cannington, taken in conjunction with other facts."

"What other facts?"

Harlow took a long drink of coffee and crumbled a sweet biscuit in his stubby fingers. "We haven't been idle since last night, you know."

"What have you done, then?"

"For a start, we've traced Miss Sheila Durrant."

Margaret said nothing. The Chief Inspector reached into his raincoat pocket and pulled out a typewritten sheet. He adjusted his glasses and scanned the paper.

"This is the report from the Dorsetshire police," he said. "I won't bother with it all. What it boils down to is that Miss Sheila Durrant is with her parents at Red Acre Farm, Hampton Parva, and has been since Wednesday. Her mother isn't well, it seems. Miss Durrant is well known in the village— a very popular young lady, it seems. Description, five feet six inches tall, slim build, fair complection, striking auburn hair.

"It so happens that on Wednesday evening when she was supposed to be at your home, taking over from Grace Bridge, she was in fact attending a Whist Drive in the village hall in aid of the Church Organ Restoration Fund. This is confirmed by the local constable, who was also participating. He interviewed Miss Durrant today and she told him she had received a telegram on Wednesday morning, purporting to come from her father, telling her that her mother was worse and she should come home at once. Funnily enough, her mother turned out to be no worse and her father never sent a telegram. Miss Durrant couldn't understand it—but since she was planning to go home for Christmas anyhow, she simply decided to stay on. So, you see, Mrs. Cannington—"

"There must be some explanation," said Margaret.

"There is. Indeed there is. Miss Grace Bridge has taken you for a proper ride, madam, if you'll forgive my saying so. However, I think I may say that it has all worked out for the best."

"What do you mean?"

The Chief Inspector beamed at Margaret. "You've been very helpful, Mrs. Cannington—perhaps without quite meaning to be. First of all, you traced Grace Bridge more quickly than we were able to, thanks to your brother. Your proper course would have been to notify us, and I ought to be very cross with you for going along there by yourself. However, as things have worked out, all you've done is give the girl the idea that you don't suspect her at all—and that just suits our book. Give her all the rope she wants. I daresay she's feeling pretty good just now, imagining that she's fooled you. Did she ask you what we—the police— were doing?"

"Yes, as a matter of fact, she did."

"Ah, yes. She would, of course."

"It was a perfectly natural question."

"In the circumstances—yes. What did you say?"

"I said we hadn't dared contact you, because of Emma."

Harlow nodded approvingly. "Very good. Excellent. Well, now, Mrs. Cannington, I ought to be getting back. I'll have a strict watch put on the Avenue Road house, and naturally Bridge won't be allowed to leave the country tomorrow—if she's still at liberty, which I doubt. I suggest that you go home and wait for this evening."

"You mean to say," said Margaret slowly, "that you're not going to go after Fisher, or—"

"We shall go ahead with our original scheme, Mrs. Cannington—greatly helped by your contribution. Now, go home and try not to worry."

Harlow stood up and picked up the bill. As far as he was concerned, the interview was over, and he was a busy man . . .

In the taxi home, Margaret came near to tears of frustration, anguish, and anger. It seemed to her that nobody else cared a rap about what happened to Emma. Harlow, she told herself, was only concerned with catching the criminals and gaining himself credit for a successful prosecution. Margaret knew in her heart that this was unfair, even as the thought came to her, but the Chief Inspector was so stubborn, so *stupid.* She must convince Stephen that she was right and Harlow wrong, and yet Stephen seemed to believe implicitly in the Inspector—and Juliette didn't help, with her easily complacent comfort. And all the time, Emma was in terrible danger, which grew deadlier every hour.

Margaret's mood was not improved by the sight of the pale-blue Alfa Romeo standing outside No. 16. As she put her key into the front door, she could see through the drawing-room window that Juliette was sitting on the sofa, langorously plying a needle and thread as she sewed bundles of newspaper into the lining of Margaret's favorite winter coat, which had been ripped open for the purpose. Stephen was sitting by the fireplace, looking bad-tempered. The fire had not been remade and last night's dirty ashes still lay in the hearth.

Margaret walked in and addressed herself to Juliette. "What are you doing?"

"Oh, *there* you are, Margaret." Juliette smiled, like a cat. "I'm doing your work for you."

"You're very kind," said Margaret, "but it isn't necessary."

"What do you mean?"

"I'm sorry, Juliette, I must speak to Stephen privately. Will you please go now?"

"Go?" Juliette's eyebrows went up.

She turned mutely to Stephen with an injured expression.

He stood up. "You'd better go, Juliette."

"Well, really—"

"This is something that concerns only Margaret and myself," Stephen told her gently.

For a moment it seemed that Juliette might launch into a histrionic tirade, but something in Stephen's face stopped her. She jabbed her needle viciously into the arm of the sofa. "I shall be delighted to go," she said. "You can do your own bloody sewing!"

"Juliette—" Stephen began, but Juliette snatched up her pale beaver coat, swung it round her shoulders, and almost ran out of the room. The front door slammed and a few moments later the engine of the Alfa revved up savagely and the car roared out of the Square.

Stephen said, "You didn't have to be so rude to her."

"She was rude to me," said Margaret.

Stephen sighed. "You're behaving like a child," he said, "but I suppose it's understandable."

"Don't patronize me!"

"You'd better tell me where you've been. I got a very nasty shock when I found you weren't here this morning."

"How terrible for you. I suppose you immediately rang Juliette to come and hold your hand. Or did you bring her with you in the first place?"

Stephen flushed angrily. "I rang Juliette because I was worried about you."

"How very curious," said Margaret. "I'm afraid I don't follow your mental processes."

"Oh, for God's sake, stop it," said Stephen. He sounded beaten.

Margaret was aware of a quick, warm flush of reprehensible pleasure—like a child who knows it is behaving badly and getting away with it. At once, she became contrite. Having won her little victory, she was ashamed of it. "I'm sorry," she said. "I know I'm behaving horribly. But I had to talk to you, Stephen. I've just seen Inspector Harlow."

Quickly, she outlined the events of the morning. "And so you see," she ended, "the wretched man has got it all wrong and he won't budge an inch. He's concentrating all his forces on poor Grace Bridge, who is completely innocent. If we're going to save Emma, we're going to have to do it ourselves."

"You don't seriously mean that you're going to try to find the child yourself?"

"It's the only thing to do. Surely you see that?"

"I think you're out of your mind," said Stephen. "Look here—sit down and think sensibly. First of all, the police know what they're doing. Second, you're on the warpath against Sheila Durrant, who is apparently living a blameless life in Dorset. You may have something in the case of Fisher, but how on earth do you propose to follow it up? Far better to leave it to the Chief Inspector."

"There's an explanation about the Durrant girl, I know there is. If only I could think of it."

Stephen walked over to the sofa and sat down beside her. "Margaret, darling," he said. Margaret was intensely aware of his arm stretched along the back of the sofa behind her head. The temptation to abandon responsibility and relax against that comforting arm was almost irresistible.

She sat up even straighter.

Stephen went on. "You've been under a tremendous strain, and you've been wonderful. The Inspector thinks so, and so do I. But this thing is out of our hands now. The police are dealing with it. All we can do is cooperate with them."

"So you won't help me."

"Of course, I'll do anything that—"

"Will you or won't you?"

"If you insist on putting it like that, no. I think it's insane."

"I see," said Margaret. Stephen moved his arm so that his hand was touching her shoulder. She stood up.

"There's some cold meat and salad in the fridge," she said.

"What do you mean by that?"

"Just that you can get yourself some lunch if you want to. I'm going out."

"Where to?"

"I think," said Margaret, "that you had better get on with the sewing. What will the Inspector say if it's not done by this evening?" And before he could answer, she walked out of the house.

As a matter of fact, she had no clear idea of where she intended to go. Feeling herself let down by both Harlow and Stephen, she hadn't thought out her next move with any great coherence. All she knew was that it must start at the Students' Baby-Sitting Bureau.

As she walked toward Kensington High Street, Margaret considered how she could get into the office of the Bureau without being recognized.

Dark glasses and a black beard, she thought to herself ruefully. Not my line at all.

The window of a small hairdressing salon caught her eye. In the center of it a severed wax head displayed a bouffant blonde wig and a card announced that similar models in any color would gladly be made to order for clients. For a moment it crossed her mind that here was a form of disguise . . . but, no, it was ridiculous. She would simply look like Margaret Cannington in a blonde wig. She walked on, her problem still unsolved. As far as she knew, Fisher worked alone at the office. If she could be sure that he was out of the way— She went into a phonebooth and dialed the number of the Bureau.

Fisher's voice answered at once. "Students' Baby-Sitting Bureau, can I help you?"

False beards and wigs might be impractical, but Margaret could disguise her voice. Adopting a super-refined accent, she said, "I wonder if you could tell me your charges per hour?"

"Certainly, madam." Quickly and efficiently, Donald Fisher outlined his prices.

"I see," said Margaret loftily. "Would it be possible to engage a girl for next Thursday evening, the twenty-third?"

"I'm terribly sorry, madam. We're closed next week. In fact, we're officially closed now, but I just happened to be in the office when you called. It's Christmas, you see. All our girls are on holiday."

"Oh, what a pity. Well, thank you all the same."

"A pleasure, madam. I hope you'll call us again in the New Year."

Margaret rang off. Then she took a taxi to the corner of the street where the Bureau had its office and went into the small ladylike tearoom she remembered having noticed just across the road.

She was in luck. The window table was free. From it, she had a good view of the Bureau's front door, outside which the black Ford was parked. She suddenly realized that she hadn't eaten all day and was extremely hungry. She ordered poached eggs and orange juice and sat down to wait.

She had finished the eggs and ordered another glass of orange juice before anything interesting happened. Then the door of the Bureau's house opened and Donald Fisher came out. He was not alone. With him was a girl—an attractive little thing with mouse-brown hair and a tip-tilted nose. His girl friend, Margaret presumed.

It could hardly be a baby-sitter or a client, since the office was closed. In fact, Margaret was not very interested in the identity of the girl. The important thing was that Donald Fisher had at last decided to go out to lunch, leaving the coast clear.

Margaret paid her bill and walked to the doorway of the restaurant. Fisher was still standing on the pavement, talking to the girl. Margaret lingered in the shelter of the doorway, out of sight. At last the couple over the road decided to part. Fisher got into his car and drove away. The girl turned in the opposite direction and began to walk toward Kensington High Street. Margaret came out of the tearoom doorway, crossed the street, and began walking up the hill toward the Bureau.

Then she saw to her annoyance that the girl had stopped. She was standing looking earnestly into the window of a shop displaying Christmas decorations. The shop was only a few doors from the Bureau and Margaret would have to pass it in order to reach her goal.

Well, it couldn't be helped. She and the girl were strangers to each other. There were other enterprises in the same house as the Bureau, any of which Margaret might be visiting. She hoped the girl wouldn't notice her going into the house, but even if she did it shouldn't matter. She was abreast of the girl now, walking quickly and trying to appear unobtrusive. Suddenly, with no warning, there was a sharp report, like a gunshot. Instinctively, Margaret stopped and both she and the girl turned to locate the source of the noise.

It was nothing—only a motorcycle backfiring. The girl readjusted the big scarf that she wore round her neck, and began walking slowly down the road. Margaret, however, stood transfixed. For in that brief moment when the girl had turned round and the scarf had slipped, she had had an excellent opportunity to study the girl's profile and she had recognized it. The girl was Paddy, the Irish medical student, the first of her baby-sitters. And yet, she wasn't. Something was different. Another couple of seconds and she had the answer—Paddy had been a platinum blonde.

Suddenly the pieces of the jigsaw clicked together. Paddy, Sheila, Grace . . . Donald Fisher and Freddy Barnstable . . . Lady Percival and the Bassetts and the Students' Hostel . . . Sheila Durrant in Dorset and Grace Bridge in Hampstead and a dark girl at the Majestic Theater in a Persian-lamb coat. It all fitted. Margaret felt a surge of panic. What was she to do now? There was no time to contact Stephen or Inspector Harlow. Paddy had reached the corner and in another moment she would be engulfed in the crowds of Christmas shoppers in the High Street. Margaret hurried down the road after her.

She had no idea how difficult it would be to shadow somebody. Her impression of sleuthing had always been of the tracker taking pains to avoid being detected by his quarry. She very soon realized that in Kensington High Street, in midafternoon a week before Christmas, the problem was to keep her prey in sight. The pavements around the big stores were crammed to suffocation point with shoppers. Harassed women, many shepherding broods of children, purposeful men who had slipped out of the office for ten stolen minutes and were determined not to waste a second of them, idling teenagers drawn magnetically by the crowds and the lights, bewildered foreigners questioning passers-by, street traders with hot chestnuts, balloons, jumping beans, and mechanical toys. Every other minute a leviathan of a double-decker bus would draw up and disgorge a milling mass of more shoppers, while absorbing a struggling and exhausted throng of humanity and parcels.

Through the maelstrom, Paddy walked quickly and purposefully. She was carrying a small square case made of red leather—the kind women models use for their makeup and accessories— and the splash of red more than once helped Margaret locate her where the crowds were especially dense. Then, without warning, Paddy stopped and Margaret had no option but to walk on past the girl, who was gazing, apparently fascinated, at a window-display of Christmas decorations and animated toys.

A few yards farther on, Margaret stopped and bought an unwanted evening paper while Paddy still studied the Teddy Bears' Band, the Orbiting Space Rocket, and the Kute Kittens Ballet, all of which were performing energetically, to the delight of the children on the pavement outside the window.

Then Paddy seemed to make a sudden decision. She walked briskly into the store.

Following her up the escalator to the Toy Fair on the second floor, Margaret felt a pang of doubt. Suppose she was all wrong about Paddy? Suppose she was just a nice innocent Irish student who did a bit of baby-sitting to make pin-money and had spent some of it on a blonde wig, just for fun? Well, it was too late to turn back now. Margaret stopped and pretended to examine a complicated computerized toy while Paddy made her way to the counter displaying

Christmas decorations. With no hesitation, she made her purchase. It was a small holly wreath made of shiny plastic. She slipped the parcel into her model-box and walked back to the escalator.

It was at this point that Margaret nearly lost her, for somehow it never occurred to her that Paddy would choose to go up rather than down. Just in time, Margaret squeezed onto the mounting staircase. Up and up the Irish girl went, through Model Gowns, Coats and Rainwear, Millinery, Underwear and Corsets, Furniture and Carpets. At each floor the crowd thinned out more and more. There isn't a very brisk trade in Furniture and Carpets the week before Christmas, nevertheless a good many women remained faithful to the escalator as it mounted to its final stage, and the reason soon became obvious. For the seventh floor, as well as Accounts, Enquiries, and Telephones, housed the Ladies' Powder Room.

Margaret arrived at the head of the moving stairway just in time to see Paddy's red box disappear through the pink swing-doors.

Margaret looked around quickly, seeking cover. She dared not follow Paddy into the cloakroom, and the arrowed sign to Enquiries and Accounts directed customers through a solid wooden door. If she was to keep the Ladies' Powder Room in sight, she must stay here in the foyer. But how could she keep out of sight? Then, with huge relief, she spotted the row of telephone booths along the wall, each discreetly screened in soundproof material. From one of them, she could not only keep watch but she could ring Inspector Harlow. It was the perfect solution. Delighted, she hurried over—and then stopped in dismay. She had overlooked one small snag. Every booth was occupied.

Even under ordinary circumstances, there are few more frustrating experiences than waiting for a public telephone to become free: watching the fortunate occupants as, with maddening slowness, they hunt for numbers in the wrong telephone book, seeing in dumb-show the utterly futile small talk and chatter of teenagers with all day to spare, observing with sinking heart the deliberate lighting of a cigarette, the comfortable settling of shoulders against the wall which are the preliminaries of a long leisurely gossip. All this Margaret had to endure, together with a sense of utter vulnerability. She was trapped in the bare, circular foyer, where at any moment Paddy might emerge and recognize her. No amount of hiding behind her newspaper gave her the remotest feeling of security. And, to crown it all, the chance of contacting Scotland Yard was growing slimmer and slimmer . . .

After what seemed a lifetime, an ample lady in a tweed coat gathered up an armful of parcels and came slowly out of one of the booths. Margaret made a dash for it and estblished herself inside only a fraction of a second ahead of a woman who had only just come up on the escalator. The money was ready in her hand. Feverishly, she dialed Scotland Yard. "Inspector Harlow, please. Quickly. It's very important. Tell him it's Mrs. Cannington."

There was an endless pause. Then the voice said, "I'm afraid he's just gone out to lunch. If you'd like to—"

And at that moment, Paddy came out of the Powder Room. Or rather, the red leather model-box came out of it, for it was this which Margaret recognized. A girl with mouse-colored hair, a navy-blue raincoat, and a scarf had gone in but out came a brunette with long straight hair, wearing a sand-colored coat and no scarf. Only the red box remained constant.

Of course, it was perfectly simple. A reversible raincoat, of the kind that could be bought almost anywhere, a black wig carried in the box, now replaced by the scarf. Yet the transformation was so complete that Margaret was horrified to realize how nearly she had let the girl slip by unrecognized. She slammed down the receiver and resumed the chase.

From then on it was quite straightforward. Paddy took the escalator to the ground floor, went out into the street, and hailed a taxi from the rank in the middle of the road. Margaret, close behind her, took the next one—and heard herself uttering the immortal and unlikely words, "Driver, follow that cab!"

The driver, a little man with a face like a walnut-shell, grinned broadly. "Wot's in it, then, lady? The Crown jools?"

Margaret forced herself to laugh. "No, just a friend of mine. I've a date with her, but I don't know her address. So mind you don't lose her."

The driver shot her a swift, shrewd look in his mirror, but said nothing. The cab in front pulled away from the rank and headed for Hyde Park Corner.

It wasn't a long drive. The leading taxi negotiated the complicated arrangements at Hyde Park Corner and turned up Park Lane, then cut across to the far side of Oxford Street, took a couple of right and left turns, and pulled up outside the main doors of an enormous modern block of service apartments. Margaret's driver began to slow up behind it. She leaned forward and spoke urgently through the partition. "No, driver. Don't stop. Pull up round the corner."

The driver did as he was told, making no comment. As Margaret jumped out and pressed the fare, plus a generous tip, into his hand he remarked, "Another friend of yours, eh?"—but he said it to himself, for she had already gone. The driver sighed. He had been about to draw her attention to the fact that another car had, in his opinion, been following him. But it was none of his business and he drove off.

There were quite a number of people in the hallway of the building, most of them returning Christmas shoppers laden with gaily wrapped parcels. In the small crowd waiting for the two elevators Margaret could see Paddy's dark head. She made a quick decision. She knew that she would lose her quarry at once in this rabbit-warren of furnished apartments if she didn't at least establish which floor the girl was bound for. The risk was considerable, but she had to take it.

Thanking her stars for the evening paper, which she still clutched, she boarded the same crowded elevator as Paddy, hiding herself in the farthest corner, behind a man who was carrying a small Christmas tree. Then she opened her paper and buried her nose in it, peeping round the edge at every stop. First floor, second, third, fourth, fifth—the elevator was emptying fast, but still Paddy rode upward. Sixth, seventh, eighth—by the ninth floor, there were only the two of them left. The automatic doors slid open, and Paddy stood back, with a polite gesture, waving Margaret to leave the elevator first. She showed no sign of recognition. There was nothing for it but to obey, keeping her face as well shielded as she could. In the corridor, Margaret started to walk to the left. After a few steps, she risked a quick look behind her, but Paddy was nowhere to be seen. The elevator doors had closed again, and Paddy had started on the downward ride, having neatly ditched her pursuer.

Furious, Margaret ran back to the elevator. The illuminated indicator showed that it was traveling down non-stop. The colored lights flickered on and off. Eight, seven, six, five, four—then, at three, it stopped just long enough to take somebody on or let somebody off. There was no telling which, but it was the only indication Margaret had. Urgently, she pressed the button for the second elevator, which arrived a few seconds later with a passenger. Within a minute, Margaret was standing on the third floor, wondering which way to turn. She didn't have long to wait. While she stood there, undecided, the other elevator arrived, traveling upward. The door opened and Donald Fisher came out.

He looked at her without surprise. Then he said, "May I direct you, Mrs. Cannington? You're looking for No. 340."

Margaret said nothing. The numbness had come back, and she felt like a zombie. Fisher said, "To the left, Mrs. Cannington. Quickly, please, I don't like hanging about." His hand was in his coat pocket and Margaret could see the outline of something hard grasped between his fingers. She turned left along the corridor.

At once, Fisher came up beside her. She could feel the gun in her ribs now, propelling her to walk faster. A turn to the left, another to the right—Margaret tried to remember the way back through this green-carpeted maze. At last Fisher stopped outside a door marked 340. He pulled a key from his pocket, opened the door, and pushed Margaret in ahead of him.

It was a furnished studio apartment, a replica of the hundreds of others in the block. Yellowing, cube-shaped furniture grown shabby from continual use by strangers; two divans made up to impersonate sofas in red-hessian covers; an alcove for a kitchen; a shower.

Margaret saw all this, and yet did not see it. All she registered was that the girl called Paddy was sitting on one of the divans, unwrapping the holly wreath—and that on the same divan Emma was lying sprawled in a deep, unnatural sleep.

She managed to say, "Emma," and then she was on her knees beside her daughter, holding her, kissing her, begging her to wake. But Emma did not wake.

Paddy stood up. "She followed me from Kensington," she said. "I thought I'd shaken her off."

"Well, you hadn't." Fisher's voice was light and very cold. Margaret recognized it. She had heard him use it several times. "What in hell made you go buying Christmas decorations, for heaven's sake?"

"She keeps asking for a holly wreath, whenever she's awake." Paddy was defensive. "I thought it would keep her quiet. People will start asking questions if she cries any more."

"There's a perfectly good way to stop her from crying," said Fisher.

"Not if you want to keep her alive," said Paddy. "You can't give her much more of that stuff. It's too strong for a kid."

"That's my business." Fisher transferred his attention to Margaret. "You're wasting your breath trying to wake her. She's had a good dose. She'll be out for some time, thank God." He looked at Margaret again. Then he shook his head. "You must be crazy."

Clutching Emma, Margaret said nothing.

"On your own, aren't you? You thought you'd be cleverer than Cannington. And now we've got you. We've got the child, and we've got you." He paused and lit a cigarette. When he spoke again, it was in the attractive, wry-mouthed way that had made such a favorable impression on Margaret when she first visited the Baby-Sitting Bureau. Now it didn't sound so appealing.

"We've got you," he said again. "The question is—what are we going to do with you?"

There was a long silence. Then Fisher said, "This creates a new situation, which we must appraise very carefully. In one way you're an asset to us. In another, you're a liability. I hope I'm not boring you." Margaret shook her head, dumbly. "Let me explain. To have both you and the child puts me in a very strong position vis-à-vis your husband. On the other hand, you are now in a position to identify both my wife—" he nodded toward Paddy "—and myself, and to set the police on us. You must see that it is virtually impossible for me to let you go alive."

Margaret found her voice. "I swear," she said, "I swear I won't tell the police. Just let me take Emma home and you'll hear no more about it. Not a word. Ever. I swear it."

"My dear Mrs. Cannington, you must think me very gullible. Even if you didn't go to the police, your husband would."

"The police couldn't force me to—"

"I think, Mrs. Cannington, that your attitude might be rather different once you were safely home again and under police protection. They would point out the danger to other innocent mothers and children. Your duty to the community, your obligation to society, and all the rest of the claptrap."

"I promise you—"

"And if by chance the police didn't convince you, your husband would. D'you think he'd allow you to keep your mouth shut? Of course he wouldn't." Fisher laughed. "I have made quite a study of Mr. Stephen Cannington."

"Stephen and I are—" Margaret began, then stopped.

"Oh, I know all about that. You have separated and you will shortly divorce him so that he can marry Juliette Dean. Or will you? I don't think you have quite made up your mind." Fisher was speaking almost to himself. "Yes. Yes, that's a very interesting thought. Stephen Cannington doesn't care about you any more. I'd put it even more strongly. It would be very convenient for him to have you out of the way. You do agree, don't you?"

"Stephen would never—"

"Oh, he'd never risk the child's life. He would do anything to save her—and to have her to himself. Anything at all, Mrs. Cannington. And I'd have no objection to sending Emma back to him if the terms were right. Emma has never seen me, and she's only seen Paddy in a black wig. I think it suits her rather better than either the blonde or the red one, don't you? However, that's neither here nor there. The point is that a four-year-old who has been doped for several days isn't going to help the police much. No, I think I could do a deal with Mr. Stephen Cannington. It's a nuisance, mind you. I have no desire to kill you. It's dangerous and messy. But you do see that I've no alternative, don't you?"

"You're not serious, Donald!" Paddy said. "You wouldn't!"

"Nothing for it, I'm afraid, love," said Fisher. "Unpleasant but unavoidable."

Paddy had gone very pale. She began to cry. "You promised nobody would get hurt," she sobbed. "You swore to me, Donald. You—"

Margaret said, "He's bluffing. He'd never be so crazy as to kill me. He doesn't want to face a murder charge."

"Certainly I don't want to," said Fisher equably. "Nor a kidnaping charge. Nor do I want to lose the ten thousand pounds which will be waiting at the Superdrome Cinema this evening. I presume that is all organized?"

Margaret's throat felt dry.

"Of course it is."

"No double-crossing?"

"We didn't double-cross you the first time, did we?"

Fisher appeared to be meditating. At last he said, "Naturally, with this new situation, different arrangements will have to be made. Which reminds me—Cannington may be getting worried about you. I think we should telephone him. I also think we should give him the opportunity of making the final choice."

"What do you mean?" Margaret asked.

Fisher was smiling, with secret and frightening enjoyment. "You'll soon know," he said.

On the divan, Emma still slept, breathing deeply. Fisher dragged her small, unconscious body unceremoniously to one side, sat down beside her and picked up the telephone. Fascinated, Margaret watched him dial her number. "Cannington." She could hear Stephen's voice on the other end of the line.

Fisher switched on his mock American accent. "Ah, Mr. Cannington. How are you keeping? Everything organized for tonight?"

Margaret couldn't hear Stephen's reply. Fisher went on. "It occurred to me that you might be wondering where your wife had got to. There's no need to worry. She's here with me."

Margaret heard a sharp exclamation from the telephone.

Fisher grimaced. "There's no need to be abusive, Mr. Cannington. Your wife has behaved rather foolishly, I agree, but you'll be able to discuss that with her when you see her—I hope. After we have collected the money tonight, and after three clear days have elapsed—and on the understanding that the police are not informed, naturally—neither now nor later— Please don't shout, Mr. Cannington. Yes, the little girl is—not exactly *well*, perhaps, the sedatives don't seem to be suiting her, but it's nothing serious. I hope very much that she'll stand up to the next three days, but—"

Margaret heard herself shouting, "Don't listen to him, Stephen! Don't—"

Fisher took no notice, but Paddy was on her feet in a flash. Before Margaret knew what was happening one of Paddy's wool-clad arms was across her nose and mouth, stifling her. One of her arms, pinioned behind her back, screamed in silent agony and as it was twisted Margaret felt sure that it must break. In her ear, Paddy said, "Quiet now, or I *will* break it." Margaret managed to nod, and the unbearable pressure relaxed.

Fisher was saying, "Yes, I'd very much like to send Emma home tonight. Frankly, she needs some medical attention that we can't give her, for obvious reasons. It would be rather more expensive, of course. Say fifteen thousand. Surely you can raise another five? What about the night safe at your office? . . . There's just one snag, though. It may be a little more difficult to return Mrs. Cannington to you. . . No, no, I meant tonight or any other night . . . Now, please don't take that attitude, it won't get you anywhere . . .

"Well, I wouldn't have put it quite like that myself, but if you insist, you might call it a choice between them. If you were already divorced, it would be rather different, wouldn't it? But if she contested the divorce, after all, and decided to hang onto Emma, your money would have been wasted in a way, wouldn't it? Whereas for just fifteen thousand pounds, you can have Emma back tonight and no further worry about— Good, I'm glad you've grasped what I mean.

Now, let me see, what's the time? Half past four already. Quite dark outside. I can give you ten minutes to make your decision, Mr. Cannington . . . Oh, dear me, no, *I'll* call *you*—in exactly ten minutes."

He replaced the receiver very quietly and turned to Margaret, who was nursing her bruised arm. He did not refer to her attempted outburst, but merely said, "Poor Mr. Cannington. Quite a dilemma for him, I'm afraid. Still, he wouldn't have got where he is without making a few unpleasant dicisions, would he? I feel sure he will be able to make up his mind quite quickly."

Margaret said, "May I sit beside Emma, please?"

"But of course." Fisher stood up, leaving her his place on the divan. Margaret gathered her daughter in her arms and buried her face in her brown hair. Fisher said, "I'm really very sorry, Mrs. Cannington, but it was your own fault. You must admit that."

Margaret lifted her head. "I don't believe you ever intended to give her back to us," she said. "You were going to kill her."

"That's not true!" said Paddy.

Fisher said nothing for several moments. Then he took a deep breath and said, "That's a hypothetical question, isn't it, Mrs. Cannington? One which I am not prepared to answer. You'll never know, I'm afraid, just what I planned to do. However, if you really believe that I was going to kill the child, it may be some consolation to think that by dying yourself you are saving her life." After a moment, he added, "In all probability."

"Won't you even promise me that much?"

"I never make promises, Mrs. Cannington." Fisher looked at his watch. "Five minutes to go. I don't suppose Mr. Cannington is finding it easy to make up his mind. Or perhaps he's merely concerned with raising the extra money."

Margaret stood up. "Please, Mr. Fisher," she said, "shoot me now. Quickly. I'm not very brave, and I don't want to make a fuss, but if you can tell Stephen that I'm dead already, then he won't have to make that decision, which is a decision no man should ever be asked to make. At least I can spare him that."

Fisher looked surprised. "You don't want to wait—" he consulted his watch—"just another three minutes, until I phone him? After all, he may have decided that you are more important to him than Emma is."

"No," said Margaret. "I don't want to wait."

Fisher smiled, and Margaret thought that she had never seen anything so evil. "I think," he said, "that you're afraid."

"Of course I'm afraid."

"I mean," he said, "you're afraid that he won't choose you. You dare not wait for his decision. You'd rather die not knowing, believing that perhaps he might still care enough for you—"

Margaret said nothing. She could not, for there was a grain of truth in his words. He went on, "Eight minutes. That's long enough. I'll ring him."

It was very quiet in the little apartment, and very warm. From outside the windows came the distant roar of traffic and, as it grew darker, a soft white curtain muffled the sky. It had begun to snow. As Fisher dialed, each tiny click and whirr of the apparatus sounded unnaturally loud—but when the telephone was answered, the voice at the other end was so subdued that Margaret couldn't hear a word. She could only follow Fisher's side of the conversation.

"Mr. Cannington? I think you will find that the ten minutes are up . . . Well, let's say nine, I'm in rather a hurry . . . No, nothing has changed, my position is still the same, and I trust that you have made up your—You can't? . . . No, I'm afraid I can't give you any more time . . . Surely the night safe and the petty cash between them— No? Well, that's too bad, isn't it? Still, twelve thousand five hundred is not too bad, I suppose—it shows you've really tried and we shall have to be satisfied with it . . .

"So you've definitely decided. That's very sensible. You don't want to take any chances with Emma's health, and it would kill two birds with one stone, as it were . . . Yes, perhaps that was an unfortunate simile, I apologize . . . No, I don't think she will. I think she was expecting it . . . Well, that's settled then.

"Now, we must make plans. The cinema scheme is canceled, of course . . . Why should you be surprised? My dear Cannington, you've certainly informed the police by now. You didn't think I'd be fool enough to repeat the same trick twice, did you? Now, listen carefully. The Students' Hostel in Wilberforce Square is making a collection of second-hand clothes for the Church Jumble Sale— Never mind how I know. You will wrap up your wife's coat with some other clothes and take them over to No. 13. Mark the parcel on the outside with the one word 'Jumble' in red ink. You have a red pen? . . . Good. Do that at once. Have no fear, we shall get the coat, and the money with it. Oh, and by the way, your movements are under close observation, so don't try to— Good . . . Good. I thought you'd be sensible. Well, now, Mr. Cannington, I think that's all you need to know. Provided that the money is there, Emma will be home before the night is out. I can't give you any more details, just stay at home—in Wilberforce Square, I mean—and wait. Goodbye, Mr. Cannington, and may I congratulate you on a very sensible decision."

He put down the receiver and turned to Margaret. His handsome face was grave, but there was a sort of unholy enjoyment in his grey eyes. "I fear," he said, "that the decision went against you, Mrs. Cannington." Slowly and gently, he took the revolver out of his pocket. "It was he who decided. Not I. Not I."

Margaret couldn't take her eyes off the revolver. The lamplight glinted on the chilly metal as Fisher checked over the mechanism—it was wickedly hypnotic and Margaret had to wrench her attention from it with an effort. She said, "Promise me you'll take Emma back tonight."

He did not look up from the gun. "You heard what I said."

"Yes, but—"

"But what?"

"Supposing—" Margaret thought of Juliette sewing bundles of cut-up newspaper into the blue coat. "Supposing the money isn't—"

Fisher did look up at that. "Isn't what?"

The girl called Paddy suddenly said, "We'll take the child back anyhow. We've got to be rid of her. She won't last much longer under these drugs, poor little rat."

"It was kind of you to buy her the holly wreath," said Margaret.

Fisher stood up. "Well," he said, "there's no sense prolonging the agony. Fortunately, these apartments are well sound-proofed." The gun came up and there was a deafening explosion of sound. Instinctively, Margaret flung herself onto the floor on her face and lay there, waiting for the *coup de grace*. And then she became aware of a curious fact. The noise was continuing, and it was not gunfire. There was a tremendous splintering crash, and then another—and Margaret lifted her head to see the door of the apartment flying open under the blows of a pick-axe.

All at once the room was swarming with blue uniforms. Men were shouting and Paddy was screaming. Only Donald Fisher seemed quite still and silent, like the eye of a hurricane. With only one thought in her mind, Margaret crawled to the divan. She managed to get her arms around Emma before the child stirred, writhed uneasily, and at last opened her eyes.

"It's all right, darling," said Margaret. "Mummy's here."

"Mummy," said Emma, very feebly. Then she fell asleep again.

Suddenly a door slammed and the bedlam stopped. Margaret felt a hand on her shoulder and looked up to see the room empty except for Chief Inspector Harlow, who was looking down on her paternally.

"Well, now, Mrs. Cannington," he said, "that all ended very satisfactorily, I must say, although we had a few awkward moments, and I daresay you did, too."

Margaret nodded, and swallowed.

"So this is the little girl," Harlow went on. "Pretty as a picture, if I may say so. The doctors at the Children's Hospital are waiting to take a look at her. We've a car at the back door, so I suggest we get along there right away. I'll take the young lady." He helped Margaret to her feet and then stooped to pick Emma up in his solid arms. As he walked with her to the door, his large feet trampled the plastic holly wreath into the cheap, worn carpet.

Outside, it was still snowing. Several young constables were waiting at the back door of the building to escort Margaret and Harlow through the flashing ranks of reporters and photographers to the black police car. As soon as the door had closed behind the Inspector, the limousine moved off down the dark wet street through the curtain of snow.

The hospital, with its dazzling cleanliness and brisk, kind efficiency, seemed quite unreal to Margaret. Inspector Harlow vanished after handing Margaret and Emma over to the care of the nursing staff. Then Emma was whisked away, while Margaret herself was given a quick check-over, some sedatives, and a friendly chat—not one word of which she could recall afterward—by a pleasant young doctor. She was then given a cup of tea and asked if she would like to lie down while she waited to hear the verdict on Emma. She supposed that she must have slept, for though it didn't seem very long before the nurse came back when she looked at her watch she saw it was already nine o'clock, so that she and Emma must have been in the hospital for four hours. She felt much better.

"I've good news for you, Mrs. Cannington," announced the nurse "Your little girl can go home with you this evening. You'll need to keep her in bed for a couple of days, but after that she'll be as right as rain. We've contacted your local doctor, and he'll be waiting at your house to see Emma to bed. How do you feel yourself?"

"I feel fine," said Margaret.

"Splendid. Then I expect you'd like to get your coat on and be off home with your little girl."

"Could you be very kind and call me a taxi?"

The nurse beamed. "A taxi? Dear me, that won't be necessary. We were going to send you in an ambulance, but your friend the Chief Inspector has insisted on the privilege of driving you home himself in a police car. You'll be going in style, don't worry."

Harlow was waiting in the corridor and once again insisted on carrying Emma—who was still sleeping— to the car. Once inside, he handed her gently into Margaret's waiting embrace. Then, as the car moved off, he said, "I thought you'd like a full explanation of all that happened, Mrs. Cannington. As far as we've been able to reconstruct it, that is."

"Yes," said Margaret. "Yes, I would."

"Well," said Harlow, "for a start, you owe a big thank you to your friend, Mr. Barnstable. He almost certainly saved your life."

"Freddy did? But how?"

"Well, it seems he was on his way to visit you this afternoon when he caught sight of you in Kensington High Street. And the next thing he saw was the dark-haired girl he'd seen wearing your coat at the theater. She got into a cab, and you jumped into the next one and set off in pursuit. This intrigued Mr. Barnstable. He was very worried about you and suspected you were in some sort of trouble that you hadn't told him about. So he turned his car around and followed you. He tracked you as far as the block of apartments and then we took over."

"You did?" Slowly, reality was beginning to come back to Margaret and with it, curiosity. "How did you manage that?"

Harlow looked a little abashed. "I admit we had the wrong end of the stick, Mrs. Cannington," he said. "You see, my men were tracking two suspects. Two wrong suspects."

"Who?" Margaret asked, her sense of reality slipping again.

"Grace Bridge and Freddy Barnstable. So it was quite a procession that came up from Kensington—you following the Fisher woman, Mr. Barnstable following you, and my man following him. Naturally, young Burnaby—that's my detective—recognized you as well. At the apartment block, Barnstable seemed undecided what to do next—he didn't get there in time to see which apartment you'd gone to. Burnaby reported back to me at once, and I told him to pull Barnstable in for questioning right away, to find why he'd followed you. He reminded us about the dark-haired girl he'd seen at the theater—and that convinced us he was innocent and that we were close behind the kidnapers.

"Then Mr. Cannington reported from Wilberforce Square that he'd had a call from the kidnapers, claiming they'd got you as well as the child, and that they were going to ring back in ten minutes. That was our real break. You see, you can't trace dialed automatic calls, as Fisher well knew, but once we knew the call came from that building, it was merely a question of finding from which apartment it came—and by the grace of God, the building has a switchboard through which outgoing calls pass. The flats don't have individual telephone lines, you see. When you lift the receiver, there's a tiny pause before the dial tone while the operator in the basement connects you to one of the building's outside lines. In that ten-minute respite we managed to get our chaps in control of the switchboard so we were easily able to trace the second call to No. 340. After that, it was just a question of getting Mr. Cannington to keep Fisher talking until we could get to the door of the apartment and break it down."

"Who is he? Fisher, I mean?"

"Who? Hard to say, really. An ambitious young man, quite brilliant in some ways, but antisocial. He's been in trouble before, stealing cars. The sort of Clever Charlie who thinks society owes him a living," added Harlow. "The girl is a medical student. Or was. He married her last year and they set up this Baby-Sitting Bureau. Seems they've been making a very good thing out of it."

"Baby-sitting, you mean?"

"No, no. That was just chicken-feed. Blackmail was their line. All very discreet, but a baby-sitter can get to know a lot of things. The actual baby-sitting business was very efficiently run, of course, and the blackmail victims were few and far between, and carefully selected. However, they'd been after a big kidnaping job right from the start, building up a reputation among the smart set, waiting to be asked to sit with the right baby. Your little girl happened to be the one. It was all very carefully planned."

"Those wigs," said Margaret.

"That's right. They picked Grace Bridge as the perfect suspect, the ideal red herring—living in a hostel on the same Square as your house, leaving the hostel a week before Christmas to go abroad. It seemed perfect. Of course, they didn't realize that Miss Bridge was a very wealthy young lady or they wouldn't have used her. Nor did they imagine that her brother and yours would be friends. Bit of bad luck, that—for them.

"But you see how cleverly it was done. The first Wednesday the Fisher girl came to your house herself, wearing her blonde wig, to spy out the lie of the land. The next two weeks Fisher sent you Sheila Durrant of the striking red hair. Meanwhile, Mrs. Fisher—in her red wig—introduced herself to Grace Bridge at the hostel as Sheila Durrant. Throwing suspicion yet another step away from herself, as it were. And when a girl has really remarkable red hair, as I gather Miss Durrant has, well, it's the first thing people mention when describing her. You and Grace Bridge discussed Sheila Durrant, didn't you? And it never occurred to you that you weren't talking about the same person."

"Actually, it did occur to me," said Margaret. "Grace said that Sheila had a lilting voice, but I knew she had a very precise way of speaking. Probably as a drama student—"

Harlow was not listening. He was in full spate. "On the actual day of the kidnaping, the real Durrant was lured off to the country by a faked telegram and the red-wigged Paddy—whom Grace Bridge knew as Durrant—played her little scheme and got into your house. And then we come to the second reason why your child was such a perfect victim for Fisher. He could actually see into your house from his aunt's front room."

Margaret sat forward. "That's not true. Lady Percival told me she wasn't his aunt, and she wouldn't—"

"Lady Percival? Dear me, no." Harlow chuckled at the very idea.

"Then—Mrs. Bassett—?"

"No, no, no. Fisher's aunt is Miss Taylor, Lady Percival's companion. Lady Percival is a cripple, as you know, and lives entirely on the ground floor. Miss Taylor has her own sitting-room on the first floor above the drawing-room in the front of the house, with a telephone extension in it. That's where Fisher phoned from the first time, and where he kept watch. When he couldn't be there himself, he set poor Miss Taylor to watching No. 16 and reporting your movements. She didn't know what it was all about, of course. She idolizes Fisher—she never married and he's her only nephew. Sad in a way," the Chief Inspector conceded with a sigh. "I'm afraid she'll take it very hard when she learns the truth. Very hard indeed. Still, she's not as deeply involved as she might have been, which is a blessing."

"How do you mean?"

"Well, this latest scheme of Fisher's for including the coat and money in a bundle for Lady Percival's Jumble Sale. Miss Taylor would have been sent to the hostel and ordered to pick up that parcel and bring it to Fisher. That would have put her in a very awkward position." Harlow took his eyes off the road for a moment and looked at Margaret. "Why are you smiling, Mrs. Cannington?"

"It's just," said Margaret, "that it's ironic that all my suspicions of Fisher were founded on the only true thing he ever said to me."

"The only true thing?"

"That he'd been visiting his aunt. It was the solemn truth. But I thought it was a lie and it sent me off on a wild-goose chase—"

"Not wild-goose at all, Mrs. Cannington. We might never have caught them without you, and we're very grateful. Ah—here we are."

The big dark car pulled up noiselessly on the white carpet that covered Wilberforce Square. The snow was falling under the yellow lamplight in big fluffy flakes, like cotton wool. There was one car outside the house—a modest saloon Margaret recognized as belonging to her local doctor. So Stephen had gone.

The front door of the house opened at once and the doctor came out to meet them. He took Emma from Harlow's arms and said, "I'll take her upstairs to bed. If you'd like to come along, Mrs. Cannington . . ."

Chief Inspector Harlow said, with a touch of awkwardness, "Well, I'll be off now, madam. Of course, we'll be in touch in the morning, but for the moment—well, you and your husband will want—that is, you won't want—well, goodnight then." He backed out of the hall into the darkness.

Margaret followed the doctor upstairs. Soon Emma was safely tucked into her own bed. The doctor pronounced her fit and well, prescribed rest and quiet and a mild diet, shook Margaret warmly by the hand, and congratulated her on the happy outcome of such a dreadful affair. Then he took his leave.

Margaret listened to his footsteps clattering cheerfully down the stairs and the click of the front door as it closed behind him. Then there was silence—the silence she had been dreading. Somewhere in the distance outside, children's voices began to sing "Silent Night," accentuating the stillness inside the house. Margaret sat down on the stairs and wept.

The children were still singing when the key turned in the latch and the front door opened. Margaret lifted her tear-stained face and saw that Stephen was standing there. He looked strangely tentative, almost shy. He was holding a bulky parcel in both his hands. He said, "Margaret . . . "

Margaret pulled herself together.

"She's all right, Stephen. Emma's all right. I expect you want to see her. The doctor said—"

Stephen said, "Of course I want to see her. But I want to see you first."

"Oh, Stephen, not tonight. I can't face a row tonight. I'm too tired. You can say all you like in the morning. Or get your lawyers to say it. Just leave me in peace tonight."

"You don't think—you don't imagine I'm angry with you?"

"Of course you are. You must be. And quite right, too. But just for tonight—"

"Margaret Cannington," said Stephen, "you are a goose."

Margaret looked at him, wondering. It was a year since he had used that affectionately insulting epithet.

He said, "I've brought you something. Been all over London to get it. That's why I wasn't here when you got back."

He thrust the clumsily wrapped parcel into her hands "Well, go on. Open it."

"What is it?"

"Open it and see."

Margaret pulled away the paper. It was a holly wreath. A real one, with dark shining leaves and big red berries.

"It wouldn't be Christmas if we didn't have a holly wreath on the front door," said Stephen. "Tomorrow I'll get the paper chains and the mistletoe for the hall. And a Christmas tree."

"Stephen," said Margaret, a little uncertainly, "it's all over now. There's no need to—"

Stephen smiled, and it was the old Stephen. Then, with a touch of the new Stephen, he said, "For God's sake, don't hound me into a corner and make me apologize on my hands and knees, because I'm damned if I will. And I still say that you can be a pretty awkward person to live with. But can't you take a hint, woman?

"Or," he added, very seriously, "are you really trying to throw me out?"

Ten minutes later, the carol singers were belting out "Good King Wenceslas" just outside the front door of No. 16, but to their disgust nobody came out. Instead, the lights in the house went out, one by one, until only the little lantern over the door remained lit.